SHADOW PLAY

Other Books by
Katherine Sutcliffe

A FIRE IN THE HEART
RENEGADE LOVE
WINDSTORM

Katherine Sutcliffe

Shadow Play

AVON BOOKS ◆ NEW YORK

AVON BOOKS
A division of
The Hearst Corporation
105 Madison Avenue
New York, New York 10016

Copyright © 1991 by Katherine Sutcliffe
Jacket art by Victor Gadino
Published by arrangement with the author

Printed in the U.S.A.

Quality Printing and Binding by:
ARCATA GRAPHICS/KINGSPORT
Press and Roller Streets
Kingsport, TN 37662 U.S.A.

Shadow Play is dedicated to my editor,
Ellen Edwards,
with appreciation for all she has done for me.

A special thanks to those who have done
what they can to help:

Ron Hickman, FEC News, West Palm Beach, FL

Cessalee Hensley, Bookstop Book Stores,
Austin, TX

Gerald Ratcliff and John Cowley
of Bookrak and Cowley Distributing,
Jefferson City, MO

Vernon Clemans, Austin Periodical Services,
Paducah, KY

Jack Hunter, Publishers News Company,
Fort Wayne, IN

Angela Butterworth, Char Daniels,
Susan Heimann, and Denise Little,
B. Dalton Books

John Nelson, Ed Wilson,
Dan Whitt, Handlemans,
Troy, MI, and Little Rock, AR

Everett Ferris, Jemco, Tuscaloosa, AL

James Hollis, Jefferson News, Birmingham, AL

Jon Butler, Mr. Paperback, IN

All those wonderful ladies
in Avon's Dresden, TN, warehouse
who do such a wonderful job for us all.

And also . . .

Debbie Pickle Smith, Sarah Gahagan,
Christine Dunham, Phil Rosenberg,
Bill House, and Jim Whitener:
Sales Reps who took the time to care

Jenny Jones, The Book Shelf,
Jo Bell, Bell's Books,
and Carole Williams, The Book Rack
Just a few *Bookstores That Care*
who provide authors with such wonderful
support.

As always to:
Kathryn Falk, Kathe Robin, Carol Stacy,
Melinda Helfer of *Romantic Times*

And to all you wonderful booksellers
and book buyers I haven't met yet,
but hope to meet soon.

To that high capital, where kingly Death
Keeps his pale court in beauty and decay,
He came.
Lost Angel of a ruined Paradise!

—PERCY BYSSHE SHELLEY

Prologue

1875, Somewhere on the Amazon

THE DRIFTWOOD PLUNGED INTO THE SWELL OF THE BORE TIDE, writhing and flailing like an animal snared in an unescapable trap.

Morgan Kane clutched at the tree limb in desperation as water filled his nose and mouth and eyes, choking the breath from his lungs and rushing to his brain like fire. He was beyond caring that his life was about to end. He would die here and now, be murdered by a bullet from Rodolfo King's expert gunmen, or perhaps skewered by an arrow from the fierce Xavante Indians who had been chasing him for the past hour.

The bore wave rose to Goliath heights, hurling man and tree back up the river he had tried so frantically to escape. Then it crashed downward, sucking everything in its path into the undertow, plunging Kane into a rushing, thundering world of blackness and sound. A shadow shot before his eyes, then another and another, until there seemed to be a thousand shapes and forms swarming around him.

Piranhas!

With a kick he surged away, clawing at the wall of water. As his head broke the surface his lungs drank in the heavenly air. Then the splintered trunk of a kapok tree dragged him under again. He grabbed for the gnarled branch that clawed at his face. Even a minute portion of blood would send those piranhas into a feeding frenzy.

He heaved himself upon the tree, which spun round and round beneath him like a leaf caught in a whirlpool. Animals floated by, many struggling to hang on to whatever flotsam drifted within their grasp. Others were thrashing as helplessly as he had been moments before, some disappearing completely into the storm of water and mud.

He never heard the gunshot, only felt the blow of the bullet as it glanced off his brow. He grabbed his head as the tree slid from beneath him, and he tumbled back into the water. The river swallowed him, sucked him deep until the world was a gentle, quiet place of suspended emptiness. Images of his past flashed before him, childhood memories he had long since buried, recollections of pain and heartache, a child's disappointments and shattered innocence—oh, God, so much grief. Then nothing . . .

A woman's laughter echoed in his mind like bells and he imagined she was wrapping her arms around him, floating him toward the beacon of light in the sky. Her skin was smooth and iridescent, but then the image vanished, and he wondered who she had been.

No one would miss him when he was gone . . . no one . . .

THE BLOW ON HIS CHEST DROVE WATER UP HIS THROAT IN A BITTER rush. He groaned, gasped, and choked as each rebelling muscle contracted violently. Perhaps he'd died and gone to hell. This agony was punishment for all the lies he'd told throughout the years, all the anger he'd unleashed upon the world . . .

"Easy," came a congenial voice. "I say, old man, but I thought you were a goner for certain. Could you possibly open your eyes?"

Morgan vomited on the ground.

"Jolly good! One more heave for good measure."

He complied with little effort, rolled, and clutched his ribs, then his head.

"Careful," came the voice. "You've a nasty cut on your forehead."

"Bullet." The word burned his raw throat, and he groaned.

"I beg your pardon?"

"Son . . . of . . . a . . . bitch . . . shot . . . me . . ."

"You don't say! Who shot you, sir?"

"King . . ." He heard the lapping of water and chattering of monkeys from somewhere nearby. Morgan did his best to relax, but his body hurt too much. He tried to open his eyes. Impossible. They were full of river water and dirt. He rolled his head, disoriented by the quiet. "Who's there?" he demanded.

"A friend," the man said kindly.

"I ain't got any friends. Especially any English friends, and especially none out here." He thought he might throw up again, and turned on his side.

A hand touched his shoulder. "You should rest. You've had a horrifying experience."

The earth felt cool against his cheek, the moss soft. He was glad no sunlight could pierce the canopy of trees. Only quiet and darkness could alleviate the crucifying pain in his head. "How did you find me?" he managed.

The other man laughed gently. "You wouldn't believe me if I told you."

"Try me." He winced.

"I was standing just yonder. Having witnessed that nasty bore tide tear up the river, I was about to return to my camp when, by chance, I noticed a movement in the water. At that precise moment a pink dolphin rose to the surface. When I stepped closer it disappeared. The next moment I was gazing down on your face as you floated up from the very depths of the *River Sea.*"

"Are you telling me I was rescued by a pink dolphin?"

The man chuckled again. "One might come to that conclusion. The Indians talk about such things. Usually children are rescued by the dolphin, but there are stories of adults being saved. Were I inclined to believe myths—which I am upon occasion—I would vow that what I saw first was actually the *boto*—the dolphin—which, transformed into a woman or man, brings great luck, and love, to its worshippers."

Morgan managed to pry open one eyelid. The world looked green and blurry.

"Are you the *boto?"* came the pleasant, amused query.

"Do I look like a goddamn fish?" Rolling onto his hands and knees, he did his best to steady himself. The wound on his head had begun to bleed again. Blood ran down his face and formed tears on his lashes. He was sick and hurt, all right. But he was no longer so stunned that he didn't realize the danger of remaining here. The men who were after him wouldn't give up and return to King's Japurá plantation until they could offer Morgan's body as proof that they'd killed him.

Strong hands steadied him from behind as he swayed to his feet. He forced open his bleary, burning eyes and gazed at the tangled overgrowth surrounding him. A sloth crept along a tree limb overhead. On another a bird drew itself up on its perch, spread the umbrella-shaped crest on its head, and vented its piping call. The sound crashed against Morgan's temples like the bullet that had almost killed him. He collapsed to his knees. Then there was blackness.

WITHOUT OPENING HIS EYES HE KNEW IT WAS DAWN. THE AIR WAS cool and clean. The whirring of night creatures had been replaced by the symphony of morning birds, the raucous cry of monkeys, and the occasional *clang clang clang* of the *curupira*—the wild spirit of the forest which produces all the noises man is unable to explain.

Where the blazes was he?

The smell of coffee teased his nostrils, and little by little his memory returned. He had escaped Rodolfo King and run for the past two days from the rubber baron's hired killers. Then somewhere near the Rio das Mortes he'd plowed smack into Xavante savages. Just when it looked as if they would end his life with a poisoned arrow, the bore tide had swept him up river. He'd been rescued by a pink dolphin and cared for by an Englishman.

"Ah, you're finally awake," came the Englishman's voice.

Morgan eased open his eyes. He touched the cloth strips binding his head. Then he realized that the bandage was all that was left of his shirt.

"The clothing was ripped to shreds anyway, and your head needed attention. I hope you don't mind."

Morgan did his best to focus, but couldn't. There was nothing so black as the rain forest before the sun filtered through the trees. Finally, the pale yellow glow of firelight materialized somewhere in the near distance, and he began to relax.

"Feel free to tell me that this is none of my business, old man, but I couldn't help noticing the lacerations on your back. Did you, perchance, get them from King?"

Morgan closed his eyes. His head was beginning to throb.

"What were you doing in Japurá?" the man asked. "How did you manage to get caught up with a devil like that?"

Growing annoyed with the stranger's persistence, Morgan replied, "I hired on with King a year ago in Belém. He told me I'd get a share of the rubber profits. That after one season I could return to Belém and live like a lord on the proceeds."

"But no one leaves King's Japurá compound alive. Tell me, how did you manage to escape him? The only way in or out is by river, and it is heavily guarded."

Morgan thought a moment. "I struck out on foot."

Silence.

He opened one eye, then the other, waiting for some response. There was no sound or movement other than the dancing light of the fire upon the trees. Finally his companion spoke from somewhere behind him.

"That makes you quite the hero, sir. No white man has ever ventured into the heart of Japurá on foot and come out alive. Are you certain you didn't sneak out on a supply boat?"

Morgan frowned, disconcerted that the man had guessed the truth so easily.

"Tell me," the Englishman continued, "why is King so determined to kill you?"

"He doesn't want the world to know what a murdering bastard he is."

"But the world is already aware of that. King is not the only cruel *patrao* in Brazil. The beating and killing of slaves is hardly a rarity in Amazonia. No, there must be some other reason."

"Why are you so interested?" Morgan demanded.

"Because I have a score to settle with King myself and I do not wish to join up with someone who might get me killed."

"Who the hell said anything about our 'joining up'? Anyway, what sort of ties could you have with Rodolfo King?"

"Upon my return to Brazil from England, I learned he enslaved and murdered my family some years ago. I intend to go to Japurá and end King's tyranny of terror once and for all."

Morgan tried to sit up, but the world began a slow undulation around him, driving him to shut his eyes and force down the sickness in his stomach. Perhaps he was hallucinating. Surely he hadn't heard the man right. "And how do you intend to get into Japurá without King butchering you first?"

"You'll help me, of course."

Morgan almost choked.

"I did save your life," the Englishman said.

"I'll be certain to write a proper thank-you when I get back to Belém. As for returning to Japurá—"

"Oh, but you have every intention of returning to Japurá, Mr. Kane of New Orleans."

Morgan groaned but still didn't look up.

"By Jove, you needn't look so perplexed. Fear not, old chap, I don't read minds. I simply listen to the ramblings of feverish men."

There was a pause. Somehow Morgan knew what would come next. He waited in dread, unable to breath.

"You mentioned something about King finding gold on his plantation. He hasn't reported the fact to the Brazilian officials, which is understandable. The government has the nasty habit of seizing control of mining properties and allowing the landowner only a pittance of the ore's worth. Naturally, if the officials were to get wind of such a discovery, the King empire would cease to exist. You, of course, know about the gold; therefore, he is out to silence you."

Holding his head, Morgan pressed the heels of his palms into his eyes in hopes of alleviating the pressure pounding in his brain. He tried to focus on his surroundings while his thoughts scrambled for some way out of his predicament.

Dim rays of sun had broken through the mists and trees high overhead, setting the dew that clung to the leaves aglitter. The intense colors of the forest—greens, browns, reds, and orchids—made him shield his eyes for a moment. When he looked again, it was toward the fire. What he saw made his heart freeze.

A savage stooped there, with dark, piercing eyes. His black hair had been shaved close to his skull, except at the crown, where it grew in a half-moon from his left ear to his right. There was a tattoo of an anaconda running down the entirety of his torso, disappearing into a loincloth of jaguar hide. He wore bones in his nose and held a gleaming machete.

Morgan leapt to his feet, stumbling while doing his best to back away. His eyes searched everywhere for the Englishman who had saved him. Then it occurred to him that the heathen had killed his companion and intended to decapitate him as well, before shrinking his head to the size of a pomegranate. But that wasn't possible. He'd just spoken to the Englishman and—

The savage moved toward him and Morgan realized that the man hadn't been stooping after all. He was short. Very short. In fact, he was a frigging pygmy!

Extending his hand and smiling, the pygmy said, "How do you do, Mr. Kane. The name is Henry, my good man. Henry Sebastian Longfellow . . . Esquire, of course. I am so very pleased to make your acquaintance."

Chapter One

1876, Georgetown, British Guiana

THE MOURNERS MOVED BY THE COFFIN WHERE THE LATE GOVERNOR of British Guiana lay in state. The catafalque was dressed in fine black cloth and illuminated by eight candles in gold-plated sconces. Servants—Indians of the Caribbee tribe—dressed in black livery, stood guard at each corner of the coffin.

As the procession of mourners passed by the bier, their eyes turned toward the delicate figure of Chester St. James's only daughter. How small she seemed. How alone and heartbroken and desperately trying to control her emotions. Just then the grief welled up in her throat and she cried aloud.

"Not dead. Please, please don't die and leave me, Papa."

Onlookers gasped as she ran to the bier and fell to her knees. The veil which hung from her bonnet's brim to her feet obscured her features, yet there was not a soul in attendance who would not have recognized the Governor's daughter, Sarah. She had been a breathtaking beauty before going to London to attend school four years ago, and though few people had seen her since her return to Georgetown two days before, when she had been greeted with the tragic news of her father's death, word of her extraordinary loveliness had already spread throughout Guiana.

Still, there were those among the mourners in the church that day who trained for a closer look, hoping for a glimpse of the tantalizing blue-green eyes that had fired rumors across the Atlantic. It was said that her resplendent gold hair had caught the attention of someone of great importance in Her Majesty's court, not to mention an Arabian prince who had promised her the wealth of his kingdom—had even vowed to divorce his eight wives—if she would join his harem. Gossip had it that she had turned him down in order to accept the proposal of one of her father's dearest and most trusted friends, Norman Sheffield, the heir to one of the largest steel industries in the north of England.

The bells of the Episcopalian church pealed mournfully as the coffin was carried out of the chapel and the funeral procession moved slowly through the heart of Georgetown. The people crowded the narrow streets —English, Dutch, Indian, and Negro—openly sobbing, tossing orchids into the path of the hearse drawn by high-prancing, black Arabian stallions. They pressed closer as Sarah walked by. She was as close to royalty as they would ever come. They had revered her as a child, and many knew her only as "Princess." The young women of British Guiana, no matter what race, had looked to Sarah St. James as someone to emulate, and though many had viewed her with envy, no one had ever spoken an unkind word about her.

Despite the threat of rain, all of Georgetown turned out at the graveyard. By the time the last mourner had left the cemetery, daylight had turned to dusk. Only then did Sarah approach her father's crypt. Pressing her cheek against the coffin, she closed her eyes.

The servant Kanimapoo moved up behind her. Despite his fearsome history—as the chief of a once hostile tribe of Caribbee Indians—he had been not only a trusted employee of Chester St. James, but also his friend. As he placed his hand on Sarah's shoulder, she whirled, buried her face in his chest, and let the tears flow in earnest.

"Oh, Kan. Whatever shall I do without him?"

The Indian wrapped his arms around her. "Hush, Missy Sarah, everything will work out."

"But it won't. Nothing will ever be right again."

"Kan will help you."

"There is nothing you can do. There's nothing anyone can do."

"Kan will help you," he repeated more forcefully.

She pulled away and shook her head. "You don't understand—"

"I understand," he interrupted, silencing her.

She stood very still as the heat of the evening pressed in on them. In a low voice, the Indian said, "There is someone who may help you, Missy Sarah."

"No one can help, Kan. My father is dead and I shall never see him again!"

"There is a man who lives near the river. He has great magic and bravery. He will keep you safe from the *Kanima,* the spirit of evil. He has been to the green hell and returned." Kan bent nearer and his voice was urgent as he spoke again. "He is the *boto!*"

She gasped and stepped back. As the heel of her shoe sank into the dirt of the grave, the smell of earth rose. "How can you speak of myths now, Kan? Fables of dolphins revered for their magic—"

"Your father speak to him before he die. Governor offer him much money to go to Japurá—"

"Hush!" Sarah glanced around. The vicar stood some distance away, his surplice and cassock billowing in the wind as he spoke to the cemetery attendant. "Never speak of the matter aloud, Kan. Should anyone learn of my father's involvement in such a scheme, it would bring ruin to his name and all he worked for." Turning away, she looked beyond the burial-ground gates to the ocean. "I don't wish to discuss it further. Not now. Not ever. Promise me, Kan!"

He did not respond, but took her arm and led her toward the waiting carriage. At the last moment before boarding, he pressed a paper into her hand, helped her into the seat, then climbed onto the driver's bench and took up the reins. As Kan steered the conveyance back toward town, Sarah slowly unfolded the paper and read the words aloud:

10 Tobacco Row
THE AMERICAN

THE SUN HAD NOT YET RISEN AS SARAH GAZED OVER THE COLORLESS sea. Both hands lay in her lap; in one she gripped a letter from her father. She was frightened, exhausted, angry, and so very alone for the first time in her nineteen years.

She closed her tear-swollen eyes and turned up her face, allowing the punkah to cool her cheeks. Already the stagnant heat was growing intense. Soon the rush screens would be lowered around the veranda, but for now the room was open to the sweet smell of hibiscus and bromeliads. For years she had found pleasure in sitting in this very place, watching Georgetown come to life. Her father would often gently scold her for rising so early. Then he would gather her in his lap, brush her hair from her face, and kiss her forehead.

Her father . . .

She had arrived in Georgetown only three days before, expecting to be greeted joyously by her parent. She had news she was certain would please him, for she had recently become engaged to Lord Norman Sheffield of Sheffield Steel Industries. She had hoped her papa would accompany her to England to give her away. Instead, she had been met by grim-faced officials who had relayed the news of his death.

At first she had refused to believe it. Her father dead? There must be some mistake. Even when those severe strangers had escorted her back to the house and briefly opened the closed coffin to allow her a glimpse at his face, she had refused to accept it. It wasn't until she sat alone in her room that reality had finally hit her. She had returned to the coffin and demanded it be opened again. She had touched her father's hand and kissed his fingers.

Only after her shock had subsided somewhat was she forced to face more awful realities. Her father's associates had first informed her that he had been killed accidentally by his own gun. But when the problem arose of his being allowed a Christian burial, they reluctantly admitted that the fatal injury might have been *intentionally* self-inflicted.

Dear God, she couldn't believe it. She *wouldn't* believe it. She had stood before the vicar and denounced his suspicions of suicide as absurd! Her father cherished life too dearly, and he would never have hurt her in that heinous fashion. The gun *must* have gone off accidentally, she had argued fiercely, and the uncomfortable priest had finally accepted her word and allowed Chester St. James to be buried in consecrated ground.

Desperate to believe that her father had not committed suicide, she returned time after time to the letter that had precipitated her journey back to Guiana, looking for some hint that he might be considering such a drastic act. He had invested too much and too often in the many get-rich-quick schemes abounding in this land of plenty. Anxious to make the money back, he had approached Sir Clements Markham, a well-known South American historian and personal friend, with his problem. Markham had suggested a plan. They would devise a way to take seeds from the *Hevea brasiliensis* species of rubber tree out of the country and back to England. Brazil held the word monopoly on fine rubber, forcing all other countries to pay exorbitant prices. Sir Joseph Hooker of Kew Gardens in London would propagate the seedlings and transplant them to Malaya or Ceylon, in time breaking Brazil's hold on the supply of latex. Numerous British investors, including her fiancé, had paid a great deal of money into the venture, a very risky undertaking since there was an unwritten law against removing the *Hevea* seeds from Brazil. But her father had guaranteed their investments with his own capital, though it was money he didn't actually have.

He had approached a rubber planter in the Japurá section of Amazonia, deep in the very heart of Brazil where the *Hevea* flourished. He offered the planter, Rodolfo King, a sizable fortune for some seventy thousand seeds. King, renowned for his questionable business practices, had agreed, but when couriers delivered the money they received not seeds, but bullets in their backs. Their bodies had been found some days later floating far down the Japurá River.

Her father had considered going to the authorities. To do so, however, would have meant admitting his role in the affair, an end to his governorship, and personal ruin.

Sarah drew in a long breath and left her chair, crushing the letter in her hand. She yearned to hurl it over the wall, but dared not. It was all she had left of him. Soon even the house where she had grown up and her dear mama had died would be relinquished to some unknown diplomat who would arrive from England with his family and move into these cherished walls, as if Chester St. James and his daughter had never existed, had never laughed and played on this very veranda, had never gazed into the night sky and traced the fiery fall of shooting stars across the horizon.

Fresh tears stung her eyes. She struggled to fight them back, knowing how close she was to hysteria.

She spent the rest of the day wandering the house, reminiscing about the happy years she had spent here enjoying her father's success. Few other men in Guiana or England had done as much as he to better the plight of the Indians and free blacks, for Chester St. James had considered men of all colors equal in the eyes of God, law, and mankind. He had done much to nurture the growth of education and religion. Recently there had been talk of his being knighted. Now, because of an error in judgment, his reputation would be destroyed.

And she would be left with . . . nothing.

The thought stopped her. She had been too stunned by grief in the past days to realize the consequences of her father's indebtedness. The sum of his liabilities mentioned in his letter had been staggering. In addition to his own obligations, the amount he owed to the *Hevea* investors was enough to wipe out not only their Georgetown properties but their home back in England and small shipping business as well. She would be left with little more than the dress she was wearing.

How could her father have done this to himself, and to her?

Dinner was served on the veranda, but she had no appetite. It had been so long since she'd last eaten or slept properly that her clothes were loose, and the very idea of food made her stomach queasy. Instead, she again queried the servants.

She learned that on the night of her father's death he'd returned home from a late meeting, ordered dinner in his office, and closed the door behind him. At ten o'clock he had released the servants from their duties. Just after midnight Kan had heard a single shot and found him dead on the floor, the gun clutched in one hand, a paperweight bearing the royal crest gripped in the other.

Suddenly she rose from the table and went to the hall outside her father's office. The door was closed. She had not yet allowed herself to enter. The room, with its leather-bound books lining the shelves and Turkish carpet on the floor, was so much a reflection of Chester St. James that she wasn't certain she could cope with it all. Yet she had to for perhaps she would find something there that would help her come to terms with her father's tragic demise.

The room was casual, yet elegant. Its walls of native letterwood wrapped warmly around her and made her, for a moment, feel as if her father were smiling up at her from behind his desk. The carpet had been removed. Then the realization of why it was missing hit her with a force; she began to tremble as the hysteria she had struggled against threatened to surface.

She did her best to push those thoughts from her mind, to concentrate on more lighthearted memories. Yet she couldn't. The hours she'd spent reading in a chair or peering out the French doors toward the gardens while her father worked had been obliterated by a bullet. Death loomed at her from every corner, as black and suffocating as the ground in which they'd buried Chester St. James.

She avoided the area where the servants had found him and stepped behind the desk, gripping the leather chair almost desperately, doing her best to visualize her father's twinkling blue-green eyes so like her own, the cheerful ring of his laughter, the way he'd nicknamed her "Sunshine" because he vowed the room glowed when she entered it. How could the man who had taught her that nothing was so bad that it couldn't get better with a little work and a lot of faith have reached a point of such hopelessness that he was compelled to take his own life?

She eased herself into the chair. The emptiness inside her was swiftly filling with both anger and a refusal to accept the manner of his death— no matter what the authorities and servants told her. She was certain the gun had accidentally discharged. Yet why would her father have had his gun out in the first place?

He had been holding the gun . . . and a paperweight when his body was discovered.

She scanned the desktop. There were stacks of correspondence, ledgers, papers with notes jotted in his nearly illegible scrawl, a pen thrown upon a partially written reminder he'd made to himself, and finally . . .

She lifted the paperweight, balanced it in the palm of her hand. The half sphere was heavy, the crystal magnifying the royal crest of Her Majesty's court. She placed it back on the desk and reached in her pocket for her father's letter. She read it again, then laid her head on the desk and rested.

She saw the grim faces of the men who had met her at the dock.

She saw the coffin and mourners, heard the vicar eulogize "a great man whose ideals have enriched the lives of so many . . ."

She recalled Kan moving up behind her and whispering: *"There is someone who may help you, Missy Sarah."*

No one can help, she thought. Her only chance to save herself and her father's reputation was to go to Japurá and take those seeds her father had paid a fortune for, only to be swindled out of them by that cold-blooded murderer . . . King.

But she was only a woman. How could she possibly hope to travel to the heart of Amazonia and confront a man as notorious as Rodolfo King?

"There is a man who lives near the river. He has great magic and bravery . . . He has been to the green hell and returned . . . Your father speak to him before he die. Governor offer him much money to go to Japurá—"

Suddenly she could see her father lying dead on the floor, a gun in one hand and the royal crest in the other.

The royal crest.

King. Rodolfo King. He was a known murderer. Could it be that King had somehow murdered her father as well? Is that why her father had been found clutching the royal crest?

She heard Kan walk to the door. The servant waited in the silent hall.

"Kan?" she asked without looking up.

"Yes, Missy Sarah."

"Perhaps we should discuss this American once the others have been dismissed for the night."

"Yes, Missy Sarah," was his only response. The sound of his footsteps died in the darkness.

Chapter Two

IT ALL SEEMED SO ABSURD, THIS MYTH OF A MAN WHO HAD VEN-
tured into Japurá and returned, who had single-handedly fought off cannibals, man-eating jaguars, and snakes, with only his machete as a
weapon. To consider him a hero was one thing, but to think he was the
boto was carrying superstition too far. Imagine pink dolphins that left the
water at sundown and took the form of handsome men who dressed in
white suits and walked the dark wharves seducing virgins. Really . . .

Still, her father had been desperate enough to ask for this American's
help, and if her own father thought this stranger capable of heroism, it
must be true. According to Kan, after learning the man had actually
worked for Rodolfo King, her father had offered him a great deal of
money to return to Japurá and steal the *Hevea* seeds. Yet the American
had turned him down. "Not interested, Governor. I fancy my bloody
neck too much," is what Kan had overheard the man say.

Some legend. Some hero.

Typical American.

If he'd agreed to help, perhaps her father wouldn't have died. Whether
he was a hero or not, she had a thing or two to say to him.

The narrow streets that wound through the city were bordered by
shuttered houses with balconies and steep tiled roofs that glistened in the
moonlight. Sarah hurried along her way, keeping to the night shadows,
avoiding the occasional gas lamp that did little to illuminate the road.
Now and again a stranger approached from a distance; she turned her
head or ducked down a side street, taking no chances that she might be
recognized.

Her excursions beyond Water Street had been infrequent in the past.
Rarely had she strayed from the business district with its rows of dress,

glass, and paper shops. The lower wharf was an alien world from which her father had carefully protected her. Along with the scents of garlic and pungent tobaccos, the tang of spices—chilies, turmeric, ginger—and the acrid smoke of burning hemp, the canals carried a faint, sickly smell from the stagnant water caught within the rotting timbers of old pilings. On the docks, the stench of fruits and vegetables decaying in their crates drew swarms of flies and gnats that hummed in a cloud over the water.

The decision to confront the American and plead her case in person had been made on impulse as she paced her bedroom floor, fighting sleep and thinking about all that Kan had told her just hours before. The sight of the elaborately scrolled iron bedstead and its shroud of mosquito netting had not been particularly inviting, no matter how weary she felt. The heat and moonlight had filled her with a frustration she couldn't explain —and an urgency that she understood regrettably well.

With no more than a moment's thought, she had dressed quickly but sparingly, choosing to leave her corsets and bustles at home. She'd grabbed up a lace shawl from her wardrobe and thrown it over her shoulders, donned a hat with a veil to hide her face. Then, because the Governor's carriage would have brought unwelcome attention, she'd tiptoed out into the night, careful to avoid waking the servants.

Arriving at Tobacco Row, Sarah paused. The music of some distant carimbo drifted to her on the wind, then was gone, replaced by the yapping of a dog. Shanties fronted by weed-infested gardens huddled close to the canal all the way to the bank of the Demerara River. Even as she watched, the lights in the hovels were being doused, and through the quiet Sarah could hear the soft sound of a mother singing her child to sleep. Spellbound by the lullaby's haunting lyrics, Sarah felt stirred by a feeling she had not experienced since she'd set sail for London four years ago. She suddenly understood why her father had fallen so completely in love with South America.

There was magic in the hot tropics, in the flower-scented air, in the pleasant faces of the people who spoke and smiled and waved when meeting a stranger on the street. She had been too young before to fully appreciate the climate and lush beauty of the countryside. But recalling the past years of cold rain and frigid winters, and the wretched poverty of the beggar children who wandered the London streets, she was shaken with an appreciation for her present surroundings . . . and a sense of regret. Very soon she would leave Georgetown forever for a staid existence in England, teatime walks in the garden and an occasional jaunt to the countryside to watch her husband net butterflies. Her fiancé traveled the world to snare the most elusive butterflies, which he fixed to boards with pins and mounted under glass. Just before her departure from London he had spent enough for a crimson-winged *Cymothoe coccinata* from Cameroon to feed a family of five Caribbees in Guiana for a year.

She forced the thought of leaving Georgetown aside, telling herself that she wasn't simply returning to London, but to Norman Sheffield and a life that was safe and secure. Then she reminded herself that if she didn't find a way to meet her father's debts, there would be no marriage to Norman Sheffield or *anyone* of her class.

Desperation flooded her, and for one last time she checked the address Kan had scribbled on paper: *10 Tobacco Row.* She moved out of the shadows and into the moonlight, her heels clicking in the silence, the skirts of her mourning dress rustling like wind through dry leaves.

The American resided in the last house on Tobacco Row. Its garden, if one could call the scrap of weed-infested ground a garden, sloped to the riverbank, where mangrove and curida bushes grew. A fishing vessel was anchored at the end of the dock. Sarah could hear the lapping of waves upon its bow, and could just make out its shape glowing dimly white in the darkness. She was surprised and disconcerted to learn that a man with such a reputation would live in this area of Georgetown, and in such apparent poverty. Perhaps he simply wanted to be near the people who adored and revered him.

She moved toward the house, then paused. The sound of footsteps advancing down the street warned her to take refuge in the foliage growing along a rock wall surrounding the neighbor's garden. She didn't breathe as the footsteps came to a halt no more than two yards from her, so close she could detect the jangle of what sounded like keys or coins in a pocket. Shifting aside the tangle of oleander, she peered at the pair of men who regarded the American's house from the shadows near the street. One wore a wide-brimmed hat and a long, loose-fitting coat that hung unbuttoned to his knees. The other wore a blowsy white shirt tucked into a pair of white broadcloth breeches, with huaraches on his feet. He moved nervously, glancing up and down the street.

Finally they spoke, murmuring the words in undertones, so she was unable to catch everything. The conversation alternated between English and Portuguese.

"Are you certain this is the place?" the taller man asked. "Have you seen the American come here?"

"Only this afternoon. I was at the dock when I noticed him. It was chance, my friend. Pure luck. But very good luck, *sí?*"

"We must be careful. We must do nothing to arouse suspicions. He is thought of very highly in Guiana."

"So I've heard. These imbecilic savages believe he is the *boto.*"

Laughter sounded, then the taller of the men struck a match and held it to a cigar in his mouth. The flame danced upon his swarthy features and the heavy black mustache above his lip. Across his cheek was a twisted and puckered red scar.

He blew out the match and tossed it to the street. "I look forward to seeing our good friend again. Don't you, Diego?"

"*Sí.* I'm certain the Americano will be very pleased to see us too. When do you propose we drop by to give him our regards?"

"In time. But for a while we will let him enjoy this lavish success he has attained." He removed the cigar from his mouth, allowing his fingertips to trace the wound on his cheek. Then the men turned up the street and merged with the shadows.

Sarah remained in the bushes until she was certain they were gone. Only then did she venture into the American's garden, deciding to put the unusual conversation from her mind. It had nothing to do with her, after all.

Yellow light glowed from the shanty's unshuttered window. A hint of cigar smoke drifted across the garden to tease her nostrils. A woman's throaty laughter startled her, and she froze.

The door opened. Sarah shrank back into the shelter of a drooping fig tree and stood very still, holding her breath. A cascade of scented creepers brushed her face and shoulders, yet she hardly noticed. Her eyes were fixed on the couple poised in the doorway.

The dark-skinned woman might have been a *caboclo*—a person of Portuguese and Indian blood—or she might have been a mulatto. Whatever she was, she was strikingly beautiful. Her ink-black hair tumbled to her hips in glossy waves. Her dark skin shone. Her mouth was full, her eyes as wide and brown as Brazil nuts.

But it was the man who captured and held Sarah's attention. He stood half a head taller than his companion and was powerfully built. His shirt was open down his chest and hung loosely from his shoulders to his narrow hips. The flesh of his torso was damp. The thick raven-black hair on his head and chest glistened in the lamplight.

The breath left Sarah in a rush as the realization hit her: *this* was the American. *This* was Morgan Kane!

He caught the woman's face in his hand and tipped back her head. His arm slid around her and pulled her close, his free hand firmly cupping her buttock through the worn material of her cotton dress. He pressed her intimately against his hips as he kissed her, his mouth moving hungrily on hers, his tongue sliding over her lips and driving into her again and again until the woman was raking his back with her fingernails and running her hand down the front of his breeches, stroking, caressing as guttural sounds came from his throat.

The man pulled away, took hold of her arm, and dragged her back into the house, slamming the door. Frozen, her heart pounding, Sarah heard their laughter followed by unintelligible murmurings that made her face burn with the knowledge of what was taking place beyond those thin walls. She had not been so sheltered all her life that she didn't know. What did shock her, however, was the fact that simply watching the amorous display had awakened something inside her, stirring and warming her—and frightening her too. She thought she might faint. Snatches of the Indians' conversations about the *boto,* the mythological seducer, came to mind, but she dismissed them, refusing to acknowledge such silly superstitions.

What now? If she fled for home she would never get up the courage to return.

The door opened again and the woman walked out, easing the hem of her dress down over her thighs, which were long and sleek and the color of cafe au lait. The American filled the doorway; his dark fingers were buttoning his trousers.

"Good night," came the woman's husky voice.

The American didn't answer. He leaned indolently against the doorframe as the woman melted into the shadows with the grace of a specter.

Sarah shivered.

Riveted, her arms clutching the twisted trunk of the fig tree, she watched him. He was not what she had expected—neither middle-aged nor distinguished. Obviously she was accustomed to comparing every man with her father or Norman. This American was dark and pagan and frightening. His skin was a golden bronze, only slightly lighter than that of the Indians who resided in Georgetown. His face was lean, possessing a barbaric handsomeness. His thick black eyebrows curved in a slant over his deep-set eyes—and those eyes!

Even from a distance she could make out their color, silver, as cold as the machete he was reputed to have wielded through Japurá. Those quicksilver eyes looked like they could cut through steel, and that body was hard and lithe like an animal's. Yes . . . She could believe these stories. This man was as wild as the rain forest creatures—and just as dangerous. She could imagine him glibly turning down her father's offer. Dear Lord, she could imagine women like the one who had just left his arms finding in him an excuse to believe in mythical lovers. If she were smart she would forget this silly notion and go home. But she wasn't feeling smart right now. She was desperate and growing more so by the moment.

She waited until he had gone back into the house and closed the door. Only then did she approach and rap on the weathered wood.

"It's open," came the deep, sharp voice.

Her pulse quickened and her stomach turned over. The impulse to flee became fearfully strong.

At that moment the door was flung open. Aghast, Sarah stumbled back.

MORGAN KANE STARED DOWN AT THE BLACK-DRAPED CREATURE IN surprise. He had been expecting Henry.

He said nothing for a moment. Obviously his abrupt response had set the woman aback. For an instant he wondered who the hell she was to be banging on his door in the early hours of morning. Then he noted the mourning garb, and the realization struck him: the governor's daughter.

The day before, he'd stood in the back of the church and watched her weep over her father's coffin. In truth, she had been his reason for attending Chester St. James's funeral. He'd heard rumors about the lady ever since his arrival in Georgetown a year ago, how she was cherished by British aristocrats and peasants alike. A child-woman of extremes, Sarah St. James had won over an entire nation by frolicking barefoot with the natives in the morning, then appearing in the evening on her father's arm as resplendent as royalty.

When he'd been invited to the Governor's residence a week ago, Chester St. James had pointed out a portrait of his daughter on the wall. It depicted an extraordinarily lovely young girl in a pale green crinoline and a yellow sash, with eyes full of mischief and fiery gold ringlets falling onto fragile white shoulders. One delicate hand held a bouquet of vibrant daffodils. The painting was titled "Sunshine."

He'd found himself mesmerized by the haunting image of childish innocence and loveliness reflected in the bluish-green eyes and rosebud mouth. That image had driven him to stand throughout the ceremony yesterday, his eyes on the sobbing figure in the front of the church, hoping for a glimpse of her mature features, suspecting that, in the process of growing up, she must certainly have lost that look of naïveté that had lingered with him after leaving the Governor's mansion. He'd followed her all the way to the cemetery in hopes that the wind would lift her veil, but it hadn't.

Now she was trembling in his doorway, peering up at him through the black lace barrier of mourning. For an instant he was stunned. Then confused. Then the realization of why she was there hit him like a hammer and he stiffened.

She brushed past him before he asked her to enter. Even in her mourning attire she seemed oddly out of place, the understated magnificence of her dress, her regal deportment, serving to exaggerate the shabbiness of her surroundings. The fact piqued him.

"Won't you come in," he drawled, then slammed the door.

A moment passed before she faced him, her black-gloved hands gripped together. She reminded him of a kitten on the verge of bolting. She began, "My name is—"

"I know who you are."

"Then I suppose you know why I've come to see you," came her timorous voice.

He took a step toward her; she backed away and continued. "I understand you spoke to my father shortly before he died."

"So?" he replied. "What about it?"

"He asked for your help with certain . . . matters."

"And I told him in no uncertain terms that I wasn't interested."

She dropped her clenched hands to her sides. That, as well as the set of her small shoulders, was evidence of her growing anger.

He walked to a chair near the open window and dropped into it, tipped back against the wall, and took up a dead cigar from the windowsill. He relit it before looking at her again. "Not interested," he repeated.

"Surely for the right price—"

"Not for any price. I like living too much, Miss St. James."

"But you went to Japurá before and returned unscathed."

"That's a matter of opinion, *chere.*"

"But your bravery has become legend. You are a hero, sir."

Gripping the cheroot between his teeth, he laughed and narrowed his eyes. In the glow of the nearby lantern the veil could not entirely hide the fiery glint of his visitor's curls. He saw the portrait again in his mind's eye and experienced a stirring of frustration, just as he had at the church, as he tried to see beyond that frilly black gauze.

Withdrawing the cigar from his mouth, he exhaled a stream of smoke through his nose before saying, "Tell you what, Princess. Take off that hat so I can see who I'm talking to, and I might reconsider."

"Don't be absurd. I'm in mourning."

"I'm not and I don't like talkin' to a friggin' shadow."

She gasped. A silent battle was waged between them as she stubbornly refused to move and he obdurately continued to stare. Unexpectedly, with a flourish of taffeta skirts, she whirled back toward the door as if she meant to storm from his presence in fury. She'd taken no more than two steps, however, when she stopped. Hands clenched at her sides, she appeared to totter in indecision. Finally, she grabbed the bonnet from her head and flung it to the floor.

She spun around, and the caustic grin slid from his lips.

Despite the rigidity of her slight figure in its cumbersome mourning attire, Sarah St. James painted a poignant portrait of grief and despair. This was no woman, but a child. Her small face was the color of warm ivory. Her enormous turquoise eyes were red-rimmed, their magnificent shape and color exaggerated by the slant of her light brown eyebrows. Her lionlike mane of gold hair spilled over her shoulders and back. Her face did not fit the accepted standards of Victorian beauty, for her cheek-bones were too pronounced; giving her face hollows and angles. And perhaps her mouth was a touch too full and red to suit most men's idea of perfection. But to a man such as he, it was a mouth that conjured up images of passion and pulse-pounding desire. In a flash Morgan believed the rumor of a smitten Arab sheikh, willing to forgo his entire harem of wives in order to own her.

He dropped his chair to the floor and tossed the cigar aside. Standing, he moved to the window and turned his back to Sarah to stare out over the Demerara River. He took a breath before speaking. "What your father asked me to do is against Brazilian law. More importantly, it's against Rodolfo King's law. While one may escape Brazilian officials, one does not escape King . . . at least not for long."

"But you worked for him—"

"It's common knowledge that signing on with King is like selling yourself to the devil, Miss St. James. No one simply works for Rodolfo King. He owns you, body and soul, for as long as he needs you. When he tires of you, or grows angry, you die a very unpleasant death." He leaned against the windowsill, allowing the night air to cool his brow and clear his head of memories. "I escaped, for the time being, by leaving Brazil and coming here." He turned to face her. "Your father knew the kind of man he was dealing with, yet he risked everything he owned, and most of what his friends owned, on a gamble that was doomed from the start. I'll tell you what I told His Excellency, the Governor, to his face: He was a goddamn fool."

She flew across the room and slapped his cheek. He grabbed her wrist, twisting it behind her so that she fell against him, her breasts pressed against the sweating wall of his chest.

"Just who the hell do you think you are?" he demanded. "Let's get something straight, beautiful. You may control men across five continents with a bat of those long, pretty lashes, but I'm not so easily impressed."

"Barbarian!" she hissed through her teeth. "Take your hands off me."

He shoved her away.

Her cheeks burning with color and her eyes flashing with green fire, she swept her bonnet from the floor and planted it back on her head. She stormed to the door before facing him. There was a cold determination in her voice that sounded nothing like the frail, frightened girl who had first addressed him only moments before.

"I intend to get to Rodolfo King somehow, with or without your help. And when I do, he will sadly regret the day he was born. Good evening, Mr. Kane, and thank you so much for your generous show of compassion over the death of my father."

Then she was gone, leaving in her wake a rush of wind that smelled of jasmine and night air.

He was still staring at the door and rubbing his cheek when Henry entered. The pygmy, dressed in a gray flannel suit with a diamond stick-pin twinkling in the folds of his pristine cravat, shook his head and frowned.

"I say, Morgan, I really must teach you the finer art of wooing beautiful women."

Morgan snorted, grabbed a bottle of whiskey from the table, and uncorked it.

"My, my, Miss St. James has left you rather frazzled and . . . ah . . . red-faced. She's quite lovely, don't you think? Of course you do. I must say I'd heard stories of her somewhat fiery nature while I lived in London, but you know how rumors are. Once a sheikh imported a camel because she said she'd like to ride one. She rode the dromedary through Hyde Park on a bet—wearing a stableman's breeches, if I recall. Seems she wasn't impressed. She climbed off the woolly bugger, handed the sheikh the reins, and said, 'Sorry, your Highness, I cannot marry you.' When he asked why, she replied, 'Your mounts are uncomfortable . . . and they smell.' "

"Ah. Well, no doubt she's a spoiled bitch, no matter how beautiful she is. As my dear mother used to say, 'Pretty is as pretty does.' " He laughed in his throat and added, "What she was trying to tell me, of course, was that I was as likable as a wood-rattler with a hangover." He drank the liquor, then wrist-wiped his mouth—tried to ignore the smarting of his slapped face and the rat that was nibbling a piece of hard bread on the floor. He swigged the whiskey again before speaking. "Someone needs to bring her down a peg or two."

"Someone has. King."

Morgan looked at his companion. "That's *her* problem, my friend. Understand? I told you—I told St. James *and* his daughter—I ain't goin' back into that hellhole for any reason—not even King. That's courting death, Henry, and I've decided the last few months that I kinda like breathing."

"Come, come, Morgan, let's be rational. Think with your brain for the moment and not your bruised ego. You want King as badly as I do. You want revenge, and you want his gold. The opportunity to get both has just been placed at your feet."

"You aren't serious, are you? You got any idea what he'll do to me if he catches me inside Brazil again?"

"Tsk, tsk, Morgan, that yellow stripe down your back is showing."

Morgan dragged the chair to the window and straddled it. He grabbed up the cigar he had earlier tossed aside and slid it into his mouth, rolling it between his lips as Henry moved up behind him. Insects hummed in the silence as he waited for his companion to speak—to take his mind off the memory of Sarah St. James's moist red mouth and the smell of her night-warm skin.

"Have you ever wondered, just for a moment, how the other half lives, Morgan?"

"Nah." He shook his head and tilted up his whiskey flask. He almost laughed at the lie. He'd fantasized about being rich all his life.

"Think of it for a moment," Henry continued. "Imagine a dining room sixty feet long and ceilings soaring twenty feet high. Think of Carrara marble, crystal chandeliers, brocade drapes, and velvet-covered walls."

"Sounds like a whore's boudoir."

Henry raised one eyebrow and scowled. "Very well. Think of women. Beautiful, wealthy women . . . like Sarah St. James. There will be dozens of them. Hundreds! All clean and smelling like lavender. With sweet breath and shining hair and impeccable manners."

Morgan closed his eyes, trying not to imagine the enticing picture. "They're all a lot of lushes and whores, no doubt."

Henry's smile was kind. "Morgan, you can't compare all women to the floozies you find skulking around Georgetown's back alleys."

"Or N'Orleans."

"Or New Orleans. You could work the rest of your life down in that mosquito-infested wharf and bazaar and never save enough money to claw out of this poverty."

Morgan stared out at the river, feeling his cheek throb. He rubbed it with his knuckles and recalled how the St. James girl had looked while tearing off her hat, hair flying and eyes flashing at him in contempt. Who would have guessed that beneath that porcelain veneer and angelic facade hid the heart of a young tigress?

He laughed to himself, then blotted the sweat from his forehead with his wrist. He cursed the stifling heat. Ordinarily it wouldn't have bothered him; he'd grown used to the sultry South American nights long ago. But for the past week he'd been disquieted by a lot of things—ever since he'd visited the Governor's house, but he hadn't been able to place the reason for his restlessness until tonight.

"At least think about her offer," Henry said. "Just for tonight, imagine what kind of comfort and pleasure King's treasure could buy you. You could live in a palace. You could have any woman you ever dreamed of possessing . . . and perhaps you could at last put the demons inside you to rest. At last you could sleep at night without the fear of King finding you."

"I'll think about it," Morgan told him.

In a quieter voice, Henry said, "Think hard, my friend, because I've heard from reliable sources that you've had visitors lately."

"I always have visitors. People just don't know when the hell to leave me alone." He pinned the pygmy with his eyes as if to make his point.

"I'm not referring to the bevy of lovelies who are constantly lined up outside your door, Morgan. I've heard from a few of your neighbors that two men have come here several times, asking if this is the residence of 'the Americano.'"

Morgan didn't blink as he stared at his friend. "That's a cheap trick, trying to scare me into accepting Sarah's offer."

"My intention is not to scare you. My purpose is to warn you."

"It might have been anyone."

"Perhaps. Or it could have been King's men. Tell me, Morgan, do you intend to run again? You have said yourself that King will stop at nothing to destroy you."

"So what's your point?"

"Would it not be better to meet him face-to-face, as we have often discussed, and end this cat-and-mouse game once and for all?"

"Easy for you to say. He's not after your little brown butt."

"Ah, but I'm well aware of the atrocities he is capable of inflicting on innocent people. Don't forget, thanks to him, I no longer have a family. Thanks to him, the few remaining Putumayo pygmies of Japurá have been wiped from the very face of the earth. Do you know what it is like to be the last living specimen of a race, Morgan? It is a little like being

Gulliver stranded for eternity in Brobdingnag, land of the giants. There is never a hope of going home again. Ever."

Morgan stared down at his whiskey flask. "You don't have to be the last of your race to be lost, Henry."

A dog barked and a boat whistle boomed out in the stillness.

"King has to be stopped." Henry walked to the door, paused, and looked back, the frustration on his face easing into the softer lines of fondness. "Morgan," he said, "you know I wouldn't let anything happen to you out there. I have faith that we can win this confrontation. I haven't let you down before, have I? I saved you from the *Pororoca,* the bore tide. I brought you to Georgetown and found you those jobs at the dock and market. I made you a hero to everyone in Guiana. I've supported you in everything you've done, haven't I?"

Morgan said nothing, recalling the past months that he had sweated the nightmarish memories of Japurá from his system, or tried to. Henry had always been there as friend and supporter.

"Please think about it. For me."

"All right."

"Good-bye then," Henry said.

Morgan drank his whiskey and cursed his ability to hold his liquor. He'd been roaring drunk only two times in his life. Both times he'd been attempting to kill thoughts of his past, only to find, upon sobering, that there was no solution in a bottle to the ugly realities of life. One coped or one didn't. Burying one's head in the sand might delay trouble for the time being, but eventually it had to be faced. Henry was right about that.

But there was such a thing as pushing one's luck too far, which was exactly what he'd be doing if he confronted King again. He'd witnessed the *patrao* 's vengeance too many times to naively believe he could walk away from another meeting with the man unscathed. He knew from personal experience: the man was a monster. Flogging was the mildest form of punishment King inflicted on his workers, but it was often fatal. The whips he used were made of tapir hide, five strands twisted into one whip. It wasn't as deadly as the infamous hippo hide used in the Congo, but in the hands of a man who knew what he was doing, and whose blood was as cold as King's, it could cut deeply. Ninety percent of King's workers—women and children as well as men—bore the scars of the lash. Hell, he bore them himself. Now and again the stocks were used along with the lash, sometimes to facilitate rape. At other times the slave was locked in and left to starve.

Morgan closed his eyes against the memory and drank again, feeling the scars on his back throb as if they'd been opened for the first time.

Of course, there were times when King was in the mood for a bit of sport. Then he'd choose his victims on a whim and have them tied up. They would be beaten with the flat sides of machetes, then butchered. Occasionally they were burned alive. Once King had been awakened from his nap by a child. He'd walked into the yard, grabbed up the small boy by his hair, and cut off his head with a machete.

Morgan gazed out the window. Before him the river stretched wide and looked as black as obsidian. Soon a blood-red sun would creep up over the horizon and turn the air into steam. He'd spend the next ten hours working the docks until his back was breaking, and for what?

He flung the cigar into the dark, crossed his sweat-slick arms along the back of his chair, and rested his chin upon them. He tried to put King out of his mind.

There was little use in going to bed. The sex he'd had with Miranda had left him tense and on edge. He wanted more. He needed more. He felt as if something were alive inside him, in fact had been feeling that way since Sarah St. James had stumbled into his house.

He moistened his lips with his tongue and tried to swallow.

Forget it, he thought.

If he needed a woman who was rich and clean, there were plenty where she came from. All it took was a walk down the dock and he could find all the companionship he could ever want—for the remainder of the night, anyway.

He left the chair, stomped his foot at the rat, and watched it scurry through a crack in the wall. He glanced about. The whitewashed room was almost bare of furniture. There was dusty matting on the floor, and soldier ants had left a long trail of bread crumbs along the base of the wall. The stringed cot was low to the ground but was capable of providing a comfortable night's sleep when not infested by bugs—which wasn't often.

He thought of King's gold and what it could buy him.

He didn't feel like sleeping. Not that he usually did. Mostly his nights were spent in paralyzed half wakefulness, with dreams roaring out of his past with the force of the bore tide. One night leeches from the inner swamps of Japurá came to him in a nightmare, their flaccid bodies covering his body, gorging themselves on his blood. He was awakened by his own screams to find his chest and arms and throat ribboned with bloody streaks he'd inflicted with his own fingernails.

Henry's words kept aggravating that old emptiness inside him. Money could make up for a lot of things—no doubt about it. But to attain it, he would have to face King. There was no getting around it. He could deny his hunger for revenge to Henry from now until doomsday, but it ate at him every day, visiting him in the dead of night in flashing images of burning children and screaming babies still gripping their decapitated parents. And there were the other memories that were becoming harder and harder to ignore, of those last days in Japurá, memories that made him burn with such loathing for King he wanted to strike out.

Grabbing his whiskey flask, he threw back his head and drank until the liquor spilled from the corners of his mouth and his chest burned. Then he shivered, with drunkenness, fear, and hate—such immeasurable hate. He wanted King, all right, but the memories of pain and humiliation he'd experienced in Japurá were sometimes stronger than the hate.

He was a coward.

No doubt about it.

He felt sick with the realization, sick at looking at himself in the mirror every day, tasting the foulness of his hate and need for revenge in the back of his throat. Slowly but surely he was choking on the self-loathing that came with the horror of returning to Japurá—hell, from walking down the street every day. King or his men were out there somewhere; they might already have found him. It was only a matter of time before one of them stepped out of an alley and put a gun to his head.

Returning to Japurá had been impossible until now. He'd needed men, ammunition, and supplies in order to venture into the Amazon. Despite his jobs, both at the docks and at the bazaar where he worked on the weekends, he'd never managed to save much, and Henry's salary as a guide was minimal at best. Then along came Chester St. James with his asinine scheme which Morgan had turned down, due to his damnable cowardice.

Now there was Sarah. The sunshine girl. The embodiment of all the good, purity, and innocence that he had failed to attain during his lifetime. She was offering him the chance to go to Japurá and end this nightmare . . . one way or another.

Falling into bed, he stared at the ceiling and concentrated hard until all thoughts of King and Japurá were blotted out by visions of flashing turquoise eyes, tumbling silken hair, and lips a man could lose himself in. . . . if he let himself.

Chapter Three

Night was coming, presaged by a blinding orange sun piercing a fragmented wall of clouds to the west. There would be rain by midnight.

Sarah stood on the veranda, watching the sea turn from blue to violet to gold in the space of minutes. She listened for the sound of Kan's footsteps, her every muscle tense with anticipation.

Where was the American? He was half an hour late.

She paced.

She must have been insane to believe he'd accept her invitation to dinner. She must have been crazy to extend such an offer after the fiasco of last evening. But Morgan Kane was her only hope. Somehow she had to convince him to go to Jarupá. Her future depended on it.

While in London she had fine-tuned her coquetry to an art, plying it just enough to titillate the imagination with perhaps a flick of her skirts to expose a flash of ankle, or a tip of her chin so that she peered at her admirer through the fringe of her lashes. But only so much charm could be expended on a man like Kane. One had to tread carefully where ne'er-do-wells were concerned; the game could become dangerous. Americans were not noted for their *savoir vivre*.

Kane was a hero to the natives of this country. Even now her own servants were scurrying about as if in preparation for royalty. Kan had dressed resplendently in the uniform he wore for state dinners, a green coat with scarlet facings and lapels. A crimson sash fit snugly about his flat stomach. The effect was somewhat diminished by the heavy black hair spilling over his shoulders and the large hoop ring dangling from his left ear. But all in all, he looked rather dignified. The women, on the other hand, could be heard giggling and whispering in the hallways. Even they had taken pains with their appearance, donning their finest uniforms and adding beads and flowers to their hair. However, much to their displeasure, the menservants vowed to banish the maids to the kitchen the moment Kane arrived.

He was, after all, the *boto*.

Upon first learning from Kan of the American's infamous reputation as the mythical lover, Sarah had scoffed. Surely these people, who had lived under Great Britain's influence for a hundred years, had grown beyond such superstition. Yet she'd discovered that customs died hard among the people she had grown to love and respect. They believed in the *boto*. They revered it in every way imaginable, down to selling its potent powders in the marketplace. For a very high price one could purchase the left eye of the pink dolphin. Dried and grated into a woman's food, it was believed to make her mad with desire. The left eye socket of the *boto* could be shaped into a ring which, when a man viewed a woman he desired through it, made her immediately attracted to him.

Only once in a century did the *boto* actually leave the sanctuary of the Amazon River and take on human form. When he did, no maiden was safe on the streets at night. One look in his eyes and her body and soul were his.

Frowning and thinking of Morgan Kane, Sarah couldn't imagine him seducing anyone of rational sensibility. Then she recalled her own quick-ened pulse when she'd watched him make love to the beautiful, exotic woman the night before. Surely her body had responded as it had because of the forbidden thrill of secretly witnessing such a private, passionate act, and not because she found him remotely appealing.

Not in the least.

She didn't care for sweat and unshaven faces, or brooding lips and eyes. His body was too hard, his skin too brown, his hair too black. She preferred fair men like her fiancé . . . blond hair, blue eyes . . .

"Missy Sarah."

Startled, she spun around. Kan stood at the veranda door, his eyes intense as he watched her.

"He has come," he said quietly.

She didn't speak. Her heart was racing too fast.

"Shall I show him here?" Kan asked.

She nodded, unable to release her breath until Kan had disappeared. Only then did she notice how quiet her surroundings had become. The maids had stopped their tittering. The night creatures had ceased their whirring. There wasn't a hint of a breeze. Even the air seemed to crackle with anticipation as she awaited the American's arrival.

Taking a deep breath, she leaned against the low wall surrounding the veranda and steeled herself for their confrontation. The sky had grown dark. She wondered if the light streaming from the house was adequate enough to display her gown. She had prayed for her father's forgiveness when she'd replaced her mourning garb with a lavish creation she had purchased in London for a dinner honoring her engagement to Norman. In it, her ice-blue satin bodice, tiny waist, and soft, slender, flower-wreathed shoulders rose up out of a crinoline skirt of ivory gros de Naples with an overskirt of gauze trimmed in white and swagged at the back in a bustle adorned with bouquets of pink primroses. Her gold curls were adorned with more primroses, and behind her right ear she had fixed a miniature orchid. Everything had to be perfect if she was to succeed at her plan.

Briefly she closed her eyes, until she heard a noise. She turned toward the house.

He moved into the doorway and stopped. The outline of his body was as detailed as a silhouette, the light from behind splashing over his broad shoulders and momentarily blinding her. She threw up her hand and blinked. When she looked again he had not moved, but stood as still as the banyan tree at her back. One knee was bent in an arrogant show of masculinity, throwing his hip slightly off center.

"Mr. Kane?" For a moment her question hung in the air.

He did not respond, but stepped onto the porch, disappearing and then materializing from the light as if by magic. She shrank toward the wall as he stopped before her.

"Mr. Kane?" she repeated, stunned by his heart-stopping image.

He smiled. It wasn't an altogether pleasant smile, but his voice remained level. The drawl that she had detected the night before was now more pronounced.

"Miss St. James."

"You came."

"So I did."

"You're also late."

"So I am." He smiled again and shrugged. He handed her an orchid whose silken petals were beaded with moisture. "A peace offering," he told her.

Her cheeks warmed. Accepting the flower, she twirled it in her fingers while she moved away and did her best to collect her thoughts. This could hardly be the same man who had so rudely and indecently accosted her the evening before. Gone was the stubbled beard; the stench of whiskey, cigar smoke, and sweat. The man was immaculate in white linen.

The only thing slightly out of place about his appearance was the fringe of black hair spilling over his brow.

"I'm happy you could join me," she said.

"So am I."

"I wanted to apologize for my behavior last night. It was inexcusable."

He leaned against the wall and his suit coat spilled open, exposing a white silk shirt. He gazed out past the banyan leaves to the ocean beyond. The hard smile on his mouth told her that he didn't, not for a moment, accept her apology. "This invitation to dine wouldn't have anything to do with your trying one last time to convince me to go to Japurá, would it, Miss St. James?"

A gust of wind blew in from the sea and drove a swirling cloud of dust across the veranda. It ruffled Sarah's hair, and she shivered. The shiver, however, had more to do with the mesmerizing vision the American made standing half in and half out of the dark than with the breeze. She could not seem to take her eyes off him, and the silly idea occurred to her that she was acting like a woman bewitched. Her mind cried out its shame over her response—what decent woman would feel this way in a man's presence?—but her body was suddenly a stranger to her, frighteningly eager to believe in the tales of this legendary lover, to experience—

"I must confess, sir, that I had hoped to discuss the matter rationally. I fear that, in the throes of my grief, I acted hastily and unduly harshly during the course of our conversation."

"Conversation? Was that what it was?" His lips formed a lazy smile. "I've seen two scorpions go at each other with less vehemence, Miss St. James."

"Yes . . . well . . ." She cleared her throat and forced herself to look away. "If you'll excuse me, I'll check on dinner. In the meantime, shall I have Kan bring you a drink?"

"Whiskey would be fine."

Nodding, she quit the veranda, putting the American at a safe distance behind her. She was standing in the hallway staring at the flower in her hand when Kan joined her.

"Dinner is served," came his voice, dragging her thoughts back to reality.

"Very well. Please see Mr. Kane to the dining room. I'll join him in a moment."

"Is something wrong, Missy?" he asked.

"No." She shook her head, laughing silently at the lie. When Kan didn't move she faced him again. His eyes were black as jet, his mouth a stern line. "I'm fine—just a little shaky, is all," she assured him with a smile and placed a hand on his arm. Only then did he leave her to get her guest.

She fled to her father's office.

Why had she run and closeted herself with her memories when her last hope for survival stood waiting for her on the veranda? Because—dared she admit it?—she felt afraid.

She was not accustomed to dealing with men like Kane. One look at that dark face and she felt overwhelmed. She was skilled at banter and innocent flirtations with gentlemen of her class, but this American knew nothing of etiquette. He wasn't even gracious enough to pretend he didn't know her reason for inviting him her.

There must be some other way.

Again she imagined herself writing her fiancé and explaining the circumstances of her father's indebtedness, then again dismissed the idea. It simply wouldn't work. The letter would take weeks to reach Norman, and besides, even a hint of scandal would send the Sheffields into a panic.

Twisting her hands together, she walked the length of the room. Around her, crates were piled toward the ceiling, each packed with her father's belongings—all she had left of his life and achievements. Already plans were in motion to place the furnishings in a warehouse where they would await shipment back to England. And for what? Even these meager articles would be gone as soon as the investors learned of her father's bankruptcy.

She had no choice.

She must convince the American . . . somehow.

THE NIGHT WAS HOT AND STILL, THE SILENCE INTERRUPTED ONLY by an occasional rumble of thunder that tinkled the crystal prisms of the chandelier overhead. They ate without conversation. Sarah could not find the courage to bring up the subject of Japurá, and the American seemed content to drink his whiskey, pick at his food, and study his surroundings at length.

He appeared most interested in the portrait of Sarah that hung on the wall behind her. He would stare at it for minutes, then watch her for such an excruciating long time that it made her uneasy.

When it became apparent that neither of them was particularly hungry, she suggested that he might prefer to finish his drink on the veranda, where it was cooler. He agreed, asked Kan for another whiskey, and escorted her from the room.

Even out of doors there was little relief to be found from the pressing heat and humidity—or the tension that was mounting between them. The

American still refused to speak, just stood at the veranda wall and watched a spot of light from a ship on the horizon. He reached into his coat and withdrew a cigarette, slid it between his lips, then dug for a match in his pocket; he struck it on the wall. Sarah watched the yellow light dance upon his features as he cupped his hands around it and touched it to the cigarette. His brows drew together as he threw back his head with a heavy exhalation; then he tossed the matchstick into the darkness, looked at her, and grinned.

"Isn't it about time we get down to business, Miss St. James?"

She sat on the edge of her chair, as stiff as marble.

The American laughed and leaned one hip upon the wall ledge, allowing his leg to swing back and forth. His hand rested on his thigh, cigarette apparently forgotten for the moment. "You want me to risk my neck to go back into Japurá and confront King."

She remained motionless, her body tense, her eyes captured by the hand on his leg. It was brown and long-fingered, a hand capable of strength and gentleness. Suddenly she recalled him caressing the woman the night before, first roughly, then tenderly.

"Miss St. James."

She turned her gaze to his.

"I believe you were about to make me a sizable offer to go to Japurá," he said.

"Sizable?"

He flicked the butt of his cigarette with his thumb, spilling ashes to the floor. "A journey involving such risks would demand a sizable prize."

"Such as?"

A shaft of dread sliced through her as one corner of his mouth tipped up in something just short of a smile. His eyes grew darker, shadowed by his lowered lashes.

"That would depend," came his quiet reply.

"On?" She wet her lips and wondered if Kan was close by.

"Some rewards are richer than money for a man, Miss St. James."

"Just what are you asking?" she said.

"What's it worth to you?"

She looked at him without flinching. "Everything I own."

"Everything?" The smile flashed again. She yearned to slap it from his face; then, recalling the sting of her palm against his cheek the night before, she felt hot. She glanced at the punkah overhead and longed for a hankie to blot the dampness from her brow. She wished she'd never set eyes on Morgan Kane kissing that woman with his tongue. It made her flustered and confused and angry every time she thought about it. The very idea was indecent. Imagine a woman allowing such a thing.

Hands gripped in her lap, she took a deep breath and released it slowly. In a voice that sounded level and determined, she said, "Name the price, Mr. Kane. But I must warn you, I haven't much money. There is little left beyond the furnishings you see here. Perhaps I can sell some of the silver pieces—they are quite old, I think—but most of the furniture belongs to the government. We have a town house in London. Those furnishings will bring a nice sum, but that would take a great deal of time . . ."

She took another breath, gazed out at the sea, and began again. "There is some money, but not much. Perhaps enough to finance the journey, but beyond that . . . of course, you'll expect to be paid generously for your trouble. Perhaps some arrangements could be made."

"Perhaps."

Silence fell again while she gathered her courage to face him. She found him watching her intently under hooded eyes. A ribbon of pale gray smoke streamed up from his cigarette and disappeared in the dark above his blacker-than-night hair.

He took up his whiskey glass and slid away from the wall, tucked the cigarette between his lips, and walked past her to the doorway where he stood for a long moment, one hand in his pants pocket, the other swirling his liquor as he perused the room's interior. As he entered, Sarah hurried to follow, watching him guardedly. He moved through the house occasionally reaching for a silver candlestick, an ornamental vase, a porcelain figurine, replacing each carefully on its pedestal before returning to the dining room, where he paused in front of her portrait. He removed the cigarette from his mouth before looking at her over his shoulder.

"How much money do you have?"

She glanced about the room.

"Those silver candlesticks won't fetch a farthing," he told her, his eyes on the painting again. "And while the vases may have a great deal of sentimental value, they're worth nothing on the docks. How much cash do you have, Miss St. James?"

"Five hundred pounds," she snapped.

"I'll do it for a thousand."

"But—"

She bit off her words as he turned his back on her and returned to the veranda. She stalked after him, anger and frustration coloring her cheeks. She stopped abruptly as she came face-to-face with him at the door, and the sudden memory of her body pressing against his the night before flooded through her. Yet she could not look away even for a moment. She could not move. Even as a large moth fluttered in the air between them, battering its wings around the glass of the glowing oil lamp over the American's shoulder, she could think of nothing but the brooding slant of his mouth as it closed around the moist end of his cigarette one last time.

He inhaled deeply, then flicked the butt away without looking from her face. At last he smiled. "You're a very savvy young woman, Miss St. James, but not quite savvy enough to outfox a fox. You see, I was here a week ago, as you recall." He leaned against the doorframe. "You've replaced the more expensive pieces with a lot of cheap reproductions, no doubt thinking that I might accept a few of these worthless trinkets instead of money. I'm quite certain that even those diamonds twinkling on your lovely little ears are paste."

She blinked and grew angrier.

The American laughed, a throaty rumble that vibrated to her toes. He touched her cheek with his fingers. "I might have been born on the wrong side of the river, *ma chere,* but I'm wise enough to know that the aristocracy doesn't flaunt its wealth to anyone who might have a tow sack tucked down the back of his pants. So tell me, *chere,* what exactly are you willing to sacrifice to save your father's reputation?"

He slid his hard fingers around her nape and pulled her closer, so close his whiskey-warm breath brushed her mouth as he looked into her eyes. Instinctively, she braced her hands against his chest and felt his heart hammering against her fingertips. As his shirt turned warm and moist against her palms, the idea occurred to her that he might be drunk. His eyes were very bright, his thick hair lightly ruffled by the breeze. She did not move, but watched his mouth and eyes turn as dark and moody as they had been the night before. Something turned over inside her that was neither anger nor fear. She shuddered in anticipation, vaguely aware that she had leaned closer to him, could feel the heat of his body warming her even through her clothes. For a shocking instant she imagined his big hand sliding down the small of her back and cupping her buttock, pressing her close . . .

Her eyes drifted shut and she wondered if she had imbibed too much wine with her meal. She felt entranced, like one on the verge of sleep, foreseeing the recurrence of some agreeable dream. She became dizzy, her body limp. Her shape molded to his as his hand slid down her spine, all five fingers splaying wide over the exposed portion of her back where her dress swooped down between her shoulder blades. Her skin burned where he touched her. Her heart pounded.

With all her effort she forced open her eyes. His head was bent low over hers, his lips parted and poised above her mouth as tenuously as a hummingbird above nectar. In the periphery of her mind a voice cried out to flee; he was dangerous, and she was an engaged woman, after all. She shouldn't be within a mile of a man like Morgan Kane . . .

Yet she could do nothing but clutch at the lapels of his coat in an endeavor to stay on her feet while his dark hand came up to wrap around her throat and tip up her chin with his thumb.

He kissed her.

First with his mouth.

Then with his tongue.

Just as he'd kissed the woman the night before, sliding between her lips and into her mouth, making lazy, swirling motions inside her so that she felt delirious and furious and shocked all at once. She managed a small, strangled sound of protest and tried to squirm away. He paused only long enough to say, "You said this venture was worth everything you own. Does that also include you, *chere?*"

He kissed her again, harder this time, burying his free hand in her hair, his fingers gripping her skull to keep her in place. She clutched at his shoulders, then, doubling her hands into fists, drove them into his chest with all her strength, fighting her body's own scandalous response as much as his use of blatant, brutal force. Then with stunning quickness he spun her toward the wall, pressed her against it, his knee shoved between her legs in an effort to pin her there. His hand closed over her breast and squeezed.

For an eternal moment she couldn't think or move. The shock of what his tongue was doing to her mouth was so strong that at first she failed to realize that his fingers had worked her nipple into a hard, throbbing core that jutted up like a pebble between his thumb and forefinger. Then her entire body came alive under his hand, growing and straining and burning in a hot stream of fire that reached all the way to that sensitive place that was becoming hotter and wetter where his thigh pressed against her and rubbed. Not until he had raised his head and regarded her with feverish, hungry eyes did the consequences of her actions hit her with sickening force.

In an instant the spell was broken, dissolved by the cold onrush of reality. All at once she felt terrified—of him and herself. They were both breathing hard and unevenly. Kane's face carried a dark flush and a sheen of perspiration, the passion she had aroused in him as vivid as lightning against a night sky.

Dear God, what had happened to her?

She turned her face away, shielding her raw, wet mouth with the back of her hand. "Stand away!" she ordered, her voice low and breathless, edged with desperation and fear. "Get away from me. Now! How dare you touch me! Stand away before I scream."

He did not move and she remained quite still, refusing to look at him again, somehow knowing the outcome if she did. She wiped her mouth with the back of her wrist and said, "You are a filthy blackguard to think I would consider giving myself to you for any reason!"

He laughed, and with a gasp of horror she pushed herself away from him, lifted her skirt with one hand, and dashed across the room. Not until she had put some distance between them did she face him once more, her breasts rising and falling in indignation. He was leaning against the door again, his hands in his pockets, his infuriating mouth curled up in that mocking half smile.

"So, *chere*. Did we decide on a thousand?"

"I don't have a thousand!"

"No?" He shrugged and moved away from the wall. "Very well, then, our business is finished. I will bid you *adieu.*"

Panic rose in her as he started to leave. "Wait!"

He stopped and looked around, regarding her with a long, penetrating stare. She moistened her lips and forced herself to speak with less vehemence.

"I don't have a thousand, Mr. Kane. I can prove it if you care to see my father's records." She met his look directly. "I—am willing to meet whatever other requirements you have in mind . . ."

The American's lips curved in a cynical smile that made her cheeks burn with shame. She backed away as he approached her, yet set her shoulders with grim determination, refusing to allow the cold fear and numbness settling throughout her body to show on her face.

He stopped in front of her, towering nearly a head taller than she, his white-suited shoulders blocking out the world beyond. His eyes were dark now, like building storm clouds on the verge of dusk.

She jerked her chin up a notch before speaking. "I am well aware of your reputation, sir. You are a base seducer of the worst kind. You are a crude, arrogant boor, Mr. Kane, and I cannot imagine why the gentle people of this country respect you so. There are names for people like you back in England."

"*Chere,* there are names for people like me everywhere. Back in N'Orleans we're known as poor white trash. But we learn to get by the best way we can, finding our pleasures wherever and however we can. We make things happen, Miss St. James, or we die."

"And I suppose that includes blackmailing respectable women into your bed?" she demanded sharply.

For a moment he looked as if he might strike her, so deadly still did he become. Only the bunching of his left hand into a fist and the slight twitch bothering one corner of his lips hinted at his fury. Then the moment passed. His shoulders relaxed again into their habitual insouciant set.

"Mademoiselle St. James, I have never had the need to blackmail a woman into my bed. However . . ." He slid his hand around the back of her neck and she thought she might swoon. Odd how her dread and fear over this moment seemed inconsequential compared with the shocking thrill his nearness evoked. He twisted his fingers slowly yet determinedly in her hair and pulled her close. "There is always a first time," he finished.

She couldn't have moved if she wanted to, spellbound as she was by his closeness. His grip on her hair was angry, yet there was something going on behind those eyes that was even more disquieting than his fury. There was desire, yes. He wanted her, and by the look on his features and the hardness of his body, she would not have been surprised if he had dragged her to the bedroom that moment, or taken her right there on the floor. But there was something else, an emotion less obvious than desire and anger, but just as unnerving. It crossed his face like a shadow, turning the fury into a look so haunted and confused that it left her breathlessly aching to hold him.

He dropped his hand as if she'd burned him, then turned and walked to the door before stopping. He considered her frozen features for a long moment, then continued, his voice deep and unsteady. "For five hundred pounds and that portrait entitled 'Sunshine,' I might consider going to Japurá."

"The portrait? But why—"

"Damned if I know, Princess. I guess there's a little part of us all that never outgrows the need to believe in fairy tales, no matter how cruel and ugly reality always becomes."

He left the room, dissolving into the dimly lit corridor. Seconds ticked by before Sarah could grapple her way out of shock and follow. She ran to the entry just as he was sauntering down the front steps, his gait loose-limbed and graceful. He was digging in his coat pocket for a cigarette by the time she called out:

"Kane, are you agreeing to my request or not?"

"I said I'd consider it, Miss St. James. I'll let you know." Then he disappeared into the night.

* * *

LATE THAT NIGHT MORGAN STOOD WITHIN THE VAGUE FLARE OF A
gas lamp, his body propped against the pole, his back to the rain-threat-
ening wind. The ocean waves slapped at the docks while on the horizon,
where the black sky met an even blacker sea, lightning danced in spears
and sparks. He smoked a cigarette, stared into nothingness, and thought
of Sarah.

He had known a great many beautiful and sophisticated women, but
few as desperate as the late Governor's daughter. Or as naive when it
came to dealing with bastards such as he. To a man jaded by experience,
her unawakened passion held an excitement that was new. No doubt
about it, he could have taken her tonight, just as he'd imagined doing
throughout the day. She'd virtually offered herself to him if he would
escort her to Japurá. She was that desperate. It certainly wouldn't have
been the first time he'd taken advantage of a situation, or a woman, but
something had happened when he'd stared down into her wide eyes. The
very innocence he'd seen reflected in the eyes of that portrait had gazed
back at him, and he knew in an instant that no matter how badly he
wanted to drive his body into hers, both in anger and in passion, to do so
would be a mistake.

He could have seduced her; he had no doubt about that. Sarah St.
James was ripe for the plucking. All that pent-up passion no decent
woman would admit to feeling was just itching to be released. By the time
he had finished with her, she would have been applauding the sacrifice of
her virginity.

He was the *boto,* after all.

He knew all the tricks it took to turn any frigid woman into a writhing,
clawing slut begging him for one more go. More often than not it was in
her husband's bed, or coach, or a time or two across his office desk when
he was out at a meeting. Yet he, who had seduced some of the grandest
bitches on the continent of South America, had chosen not to debauch
Sarah.

When did he get such scruples?

Flicking the fiery stub of his cigarette toward the water, he swore
under his breath, reached for another in his pocket, and slid it into his
mouth. He struck the match against the rough surface of the lamppost
and cursed as the wind blew it out. He tried again, breathing deeply of
the pungent, sulfuric smell as the fire danced vividly against the cigarette.

So why hadn't he taken her?

Because, bastard though he might be, he'd never taken a virgin in his
life.

It was the innocence of that portrait that had befuddled him the first moment he saw it. It had haunted his dreams and driven him from his bed. He had never known naïveté.

His first memories had been of his mother, a dark-haired French-woman, turning tricks in a tar-paper shanty to earn enough money to purchase food for the only meal he would eat that day. Sometimes the finely dressed planters with diamonds on their fingers would pay her for her time and body, and sometimes they wouldn't. Sometimes they would beat her instead. And occasionally they would make her go to her knees and beg for her pennies—and perhaps make her do things while she was on her knees that made her throw up after they'd gone. Now and again more than one would show up, stinking of whiskey and flashing fists full of money to get her to accommodate them all at once.

He hadn't understood what was going on, but he hadn't liked it. He'd begged her not to do it. It hadn't ended until some drunken, ham-handed overseer of a cotton farm blundered in one evening when his mother was out, and found him alone . . .

Having forgotten the cigarette between his fingers, Morgan jumped and grimaced before flinging what was left of it to the ground. He lifted a hand and rubbed it across his forehead. Weakened and sweating, he swayed back against the cold, hard lamppost and closed his eyes.

"Mr. Kane?"

The feminine voice was caught by the wind and lost in an instant.

"Mr. Kane?" it called again, more urgently this time.

He opened his eyes. A drop of rain spattered the lapel of his fluttering coat as he turned to see a coach. A pale face appeared in the dark, glassless window. Lady Gastrop. He could smell the scent of violet water from where he stood.

"Thank God I found you," she said. "I've waited for nights . . ."

The coach door swung open as the lady's visage disappeared from sight. He gazed at the yawning entry before approaching and swinging aboard. The coach lurched into motion before he was settled into the velvet-covered seat across from his hostess.

They rode in silence down Water Street.

Finally he said, "I take it your husband is out of the country again, Lady Gastrop." He saw her head dip a little. Her hands clutched together in her lap.

"I've missed you these past weeks. I've thought of you often, Morgan."

"Really?" His mouth curled and he relaxed, his spine conforming to the plush contour of the seat, his body swaying in rhythm with the coach.

He eased one leg between her knees before meeting her eyes directly. "You didn't seem eager to bid me hello two days ago when we bumped into each other on the dock, m'lady."

Her mouth pursed. "You aren't angry with me . . . you know it would be disastrous if we were seen together . . ."

"Because you're married? Or because of what and who I am?" When she didn't respond, he flipped his hand in dismissal and said, "Never mind."

"Don't be cruel to me tonight, dear Morgan. I've missed you too badly. I sent messages to your house—"

"I can't get away during the day. Some of us have to work for a living."

Cautiously, she touched his knee with her fingertips; they trailed teasingly up his thigh. "I hoped you would come to the house after dark." She leaned toward him and her perfume washed over him in a sickening cloud. Her hand cupped the bulge in his pants and she lost her breath.

"Oh, God," she panted. "Morgan, we'll go back to the house—"

He closed his hand around her wrist and twisted, making her slump and gasp. "The children—" he whispered.

"Will be in bed asleep."

He tightened his grip, and she whimpered, slid off her seat so she lay half on and half off Morgan's lap, her face turned away from him in misery. He dragged up her skirt as he said in a low growl, "I don't screw women when there's children in the house, m'lady. Just what do you think discovering their mother in bed with someone who wasn't their father would do to them? Did you stop to think about that? How would it make them feel to learn that their mother is a slut and a whore? You don't do that to children, Lady Gastrop. Seeing that sort of ugliness does something to a child. It makes 'em feel dirty, and then you'll come to resent them for reminding you that you're a failure as a mother."

"I'm sorry." Her eyes closed, and as he pressed her back onto the seat and shoved open her legs with his knees, he said,

"Look at me."

Reluctantly, she did so. "You're cruel. So cruel."

"And you're a slut. Now open your legs. Wide. Wider."

He released himself from his breeches, and she groaned.

"Please. Please—"

"Please what?" he asked softly.

"Come inside me. Now. Please, now!"

He did, slowly, sliding and withdrawing little by little until she was twisting and whimpering and begging for surcease.

Morgan reached for the drape on the window, hesitating as the lights of the Governor's mansion shone out in the darkness. Then he eased the curtain down and got on with his business.

Chapter Four

SARAH PEERED THROUGH HER VEIL AT THE STALLS RUNNING THE length of the wharf. At half past ten in the morning the docks were congested with people, natives and British alike, searching the contents of the crates newly arrived from ports throughout the world. The stall-keepers sold an extraordinary assortment of goods, from dried fish to Bibles to ice skates, which made Sarah smile. Ice skates in British Guiana made as much sense as the wool clothing some of the shoppers were purchasing in abundance. There was also furniture, like the oval-backed sofas and gilded mirrors designed to grace stately European drawing rooms. In the heart of the bazaar was Little China, where Chinese merchants sold silks, carved ivory, and painted porcelains. It was whispered that there was an opium den there as well.

Although the market was cheerful during the morning and afternoon, no sane person would venture there after nightfall. Robbery and throat-cutting were rampant. Even during the heat of midday pickpockets were as numerous as flies preying upon the unwary shoppers who were at their most lethargic. Therefore, Sarah, with Kan at her side, clutched her reticule in her hands and moved cautiously through the market in search of the American.

The decision to confront Morgan Kane one last time had not been an easy one. Desperation was new to her. Somehow she had to convince him to go to Japurá, even if it meant giving him more money. She would find the resources somewhere, even sell the extravagant emerald engagement ring Norman had given her if she must. It was a trifle on the gaudy side anyway, although she would never have hurt Norman's feelings by telling him so. She simply wore the ornament in his presence and tucked it away at all other times.

The air felt heavy and hot to her. It reeked with the odor of unwashed bodies and burning tobacco, and the pungent smell of essence of turtle perfume. The shoppers pressed close to the stalls, haggling over less-than-perfect merchandise, their voices rising and falling and occasionally bursting out in ribald laughter. Gradually, as Sarah moved further into the hub where the stalls were packed closer together, allowing little sun to enter, the wares were displayed in eerie dimness. The dried boa skins and tapir skulls draping the stalls were ghostly in the smoky air. Here and there bedraggled men or women without stalls had spread blankets over the ground and strewn trinkets upon them, mostly jewelry which had been carved from many of the native trees. Others displayed more elaborate pieces, no doubt stolen from the wealthy residents of the city. Sarah pressed closer to Kan as he shoved the loitering Indians aside. Finding the American in these surroundings might be impossible. There were so many merchants and shoppers and—

She stopped.

The tobacco smoke drifted just above her head in a fog, burning her eyes and nose, so that she was forced to blink and gasp for breath. Removing her hat, she strained to see through the acrid cloud, every nerve alert as the American's image appeared and then vanished behind masses of people. Forgetting Kan, she barreled her way around and through the crowd, stumbling on bits of splintered crates and slipping on the remains of a disemboweled fish before stopping in front of his stall.

His head was down, spilling damp black hair to the bridge of his nose as he counted his money. His once white shirt, unbuttoned completely, showed stains of dirt and sweat, and the sleeves had been rolled back, exposing his forearms nearly to his elbows. He clamped a burning cigarette between his teeth.

She cleared her throat.

Without moving his head, he looked up through his fringe of hair. She felt herself blanch and become light-headed. As he contemplated her, neither moving nor blinking, something came into his face, a strange, unexpected vulnerability that left her disarmed and, for a moment, hopeful that he would at least hear her out. But in a flicker of an instant the old arrogance returned. She saw it in the pressed line of his mouth, the narrowing of his eyes.

As silence stretched out between them, she struggled with the overwhelming need to turn and flee. Riveted, she steadied her breathing and said, "I must speak with you, Mr. Kane."

A long moment passed.

"Don't tell me you're in the market for a little snake oil."

She shook her head, and his grin became indolent.

"The snout of a white-lipped peccary, perhaps?"

"Mr. Kane."

"The beak of a toucan, or maybe a bottle of essence of hoatzin for that special someone you hate . . . hmm?"

A group of hagglers approached, and fearing she would lose him to the customers, she frantically searched the ramshackle booth for something to buy. Spying a finely webbed butterfly net, she pointed to it and said, "I'll take that."

He laughed.

"I'm serious," she said. "Give me that net."

"To catch what?"

"Butterflies, of course. Norman, my fiancé owns an extensive collection of butterflies from around the world. I promised I would bring him several when I return home."

"Your fiancé likes to pull wings off butterflies, does he?"

"No, he only—"

"Drives pins through their guts."

Frowning, Sarah lowered her voice as the crowd moved to the next stall. "Mr. Kane, I didn't come here to haggle over butterfly nets. I came to ask you one last time to help me. Have you given my proposition more thought?"

He nodded.

She waited, but got no further response. "Well?" she prompted.

"No chance," he replied with a finality that made her cringe.

Tossing her hat aside and placing her gloved hands on the stall counter, she leaned nearer, so that the ash of his cigarette was only inches from her nose. She noted the tiny lines of dissipation around his eyes and the faint scar cutting slightly into his lower lip. "Please," she said in a whisper. "Can we not discuss this like rational adults?"

He raised one eyebrow and a bead of sweat trickled down his unshaven cheek. He blew a stream of smoke through his lips, shook his head, and lifted a pair of hairy withered sacs of skin before her eyes. *"Chere,* do you see these?"

She glanced at them and shuddered.

"They're jaguar testicles. Mine will look just like that if King catches me in Japurá again."

"If it's more money you want, I'll get it somehow."

He looked at her mouth.

"A thousand? Is that what you want?" She dug inside her reticule and pulled out the ring. She slammed it onto the counter. "It must be worth five hundred. Take it. It's yours, along with the five hundred I've already offered, as well as the portrait." He started to swing away; she reached for his arm in desperation, her fingers sinking into his granitelike muscle. It stopped him in his tracks.

"Damn you," she hissed. "I refuse to beg. If you'll not help me, I'll find someone who will. I'll go without a guide if I must. I'll boat up that river to King's front door and demand what he stole from my father!"

He yanked his arm away, the motion spilling ashes to the ground. "Who the devil said anything about *you* going to Japurá?"

"Surely you didn't think I would meekly hand over my money and wait patiently in Georgetown. That is what got my father into this predicament in the first place."

"You? In Japurá?" He threw his head back and laughed. "I can just imagine your reaction the first time you find a bat in your bedding. Or better yet, a Xavante headhunter."

"How dare you," she whispered in a voice tight with emotion. "How dare you laugh at me. I am just as capable of surviving the journey as you are, Mr. Kane."

His eyes mocked her. "Yeah. Right."

"Then I'll simply go without you." She turned away.

"Hey!" he shouted. When she looked at him again, he shook his head. "You little idiot. You don't know what the hell you're saying."

"I am desperate, sir."

"And soon to be dead if you think you can deal with King on your own."

"What choice do you leave me?"

Kane raked one hand through his hair. His face looked whiter; his voice sounded deeper and more hoarse. "Darlin', you're dealin' with a madman. King's a devil. Worse'n a devil. You got no idea what he'd do to a woman like you—to any woman, but especially to one as beautiful as you."

"But you'll be there to protect me, Mr. Kane."

"You gotta be jokin'. Even if we survived the journey into Japurá, we'd never survive King."

"Rubbish. If we are adequately armed and prepared, I see no reason why we cannot succeed."

Closing his eyes, praying for patience, he replied as if reasoning with a belligerent child. "If we survived the jungle. *If.* Lady, you got any idea what's waitin' for you out there?" He jerked a strand of tiny fish teeth from a peg on the wall and threw them on the counter. "Piranhas. They eat the flesh off people in a matter of seconds." He grabbed a snake skin and tossed it at her, so she was forced to jump aside. "That one was only six feet long. Wait till one of those sons-a-bitches measuring thirty feet comes sailing at you out of a tree, intent on swallowing you whole. First he'll slam you in the head and knock you unconscious. Then he'll crush every bone in your body."

Feeling the blood drain from her face, she backed away as the American came out from behind the counter, sweeping up the anaconda skin and wrapping it around his hand until all that was left was the broad flat edge where the head had once been. He waved it beneath her nose as he said, "Once you're crushed to a pulp, he spits a lot of slime and saliva over your head before swallowing. Hopefully by that point you're already dead. If not, the last thing you're gonna see is several rows of teeth . . ."

She gasped.

"And that's a lot nicer than what King would do to you. He'd have you on your knees praying for death by the time he'd finished—he and his two dozen *matteiros* and *seringueros,* who are more accustomed to screwing monkeys and one another than they are women."

She slapped him, yet he hardly flinched. His eyes were hot and piercing and slightly wild. He grabbed her, fingers digging into her arms as he lifted her to her toes. From the corner of her eye she saw Kan step forward, then hesitate, and not for the first time she cursed the power the American wielded over all the Indians of British Guiana. She cursed, too, the effect he had on her own senses. She felt weakened by his presence. His hands felt oddly caressing, even as he gripped her in anger.

"You little fool," he said softly. "You're gonna get yourself killed."

"That is a chance I'll have to take, Mr. Kane. Please understand. Without your help I'll lose everything: my home, what little money my father left me . . . my fiancé."

She stopped, blushing painfully, and bit her lip, ashamed she had stooped so low as to plead, frustrated even more by the confusing desire to throw herself into his arms. She suddenly ached so badly for compassion she felt as if she would collapse.

She turned her head in an attempt to hide the tears spilling from her eyes. Gradually he released her and cupped one hand against her cheek, gently turning her face back to his. His mouth, no longer surly or angry, carried a hint of a smile. The effect was staggering—like an unexpected punch that left her breathless. She felt herself falling unwillingly under his spell, forgetting her father, even her fiancé, whose presence had never, ever affected her in this way. The cacophony of noises around them dimmed as she waited for his next move. God help her, but even if he kissed her here, before a bazaar full of people, she wouldn't care.

"*Chere.*" He brushed a tear from her cheek with his thumb. "Are you telling me that this fiancé—this Norman—would love you less if you were poor?"

"Yes," she replied, her voice breaking the tiniest bit.

Kane's dark brows drew together. "What the hell kind of love is that, Princess?"

She didn't respond and finally he released her.

As Sarah waited in anticipation for the American's reply, she was shoved from behind by an overzealous marketer of squirrel monkeys. The bamboo cage balanced on the man's stooped back came perilously close to spilling as the animals inside scattered in alarm. The old man rattled unintelligibly at Sarah, and when he shoved his way around her, Kan hurried to usher him away, berating the old Indian for his lack of manners. Only after the two had merged with the crowd did she turn back to Kane, intent on demanding his answer. She'd had enough of his indecision. She was sorry she had come here, and as the raucous cries of the shoppers rose to an earsplitting pitch, her aggravation intensified.

Due to the swarms of people around them, Sarah was momentarily separated from the American, and it was all she could do to elbow her way toward him again. That was when her eye caught on the features of a man in the distance. Standing several yards behind Morgan, he appeared and disappeared in the flood of people between them. Only when he turned his head to speak to his shorter companion, revealing the jagged scar on his cheek, did she realize who he was.

The American grabbed her arm and attempted to move her out of the stream of traffic. "Look," he said, "I'm sorry about your fiancé." He raised his voice and spoke louder. "But the Amazon is no place for a man, let alone a woman. Now, why don't you run along home and write your fiancé a nice long letter explaining—"

"Mr. Kane."

The men began moving through the crowd, their eyes fixed on the American. There was something sinister about the taller man's sharp features, and the thin smile showing beneath his shaggy mustache sent a chill up Sarah's spine.

"Mr. Kane," she repeated more urgently.

Taking her hand, he slapped her ring into her palm and closed her fingers around it. His smile was unexpectedly tender as he said, "*Chere,* asking me to take you to Japurá is a little like—"

"Mr. Kane! Please! There are two men approaching you, and if you will only shut up long enough to hear me out, I will tell you that I saw them outside your house the night I came to visit you."

His every muscle froze. Very slowly he straightened and, staring over her shoulder, said, "How many of them are there, did you say?"

"Two."

"What do they look like?"

Doing her best to keep her eyes on his face and not allow them to drift toward the pair who were now no more than twenty feet away and closing fast, she replied, "One is tall and gaunt with a mustache and a scar."

Morgan caught her arm and, turning her up the crowded alleyway, gave her a nudge that almost toppled her. "Get lost," he ordered, "and don't come back. Ever. Understand me? Go home to your fiancé and his pretty butterflies and—"

Someone screamed.

Morgan ducked, grabbing Sarah as a volley of gunfire ripped through the fetid air, the staccato bursts reverberating among the myriad sounds of the bazaar. Cheers erupted from oblivious shoppers who believed that someone had set off fireworks. Others who'd witnessed the attack shrieked and scattered in all directions.

Sarah hit the ground first, then Morgan, diving and rolling, grabbing her wrist and dragging her behind him even as he leapt back to his feet and began pushing his way through the crowd in search of a route of escape from King's assassins. By the time he banged against the first stack of wooden crates with his shoulder, he had removed his hunting knife from its scabbard.

"What are you doing?" Sarah cried. "Kane, what in God's name is happening?"

The stack of crates tumbled over, spilling chickens and roosters to the ground with high-pitched, frantic cackles and a flurry of white feathers. Someone began screaming obscenities over the melee as Morgan kicked several of the shattered boxes aside. Dragging Sarah with him, he began zigzagging down an alleyway despite the shoppers and vendors who were pressing in curiously.

"Stop him!" the man with the gun cried to the onlookers.

Morgan wove through the crowd using his elbows, cursing the idiots who had attempted to kill him during the peak shopping hour, when three quarters of Georgetown's residents were at the bazaar.

Ducking around a corner, he dragged Sarah up against him, shoved her back against a wall of reeking hemp and chopped cane, and slapped his hand over her mouth as she attempted to speak. He peered cautiously back the way they had come. "Shit," he said, and without bothering to say another word, spun on his heels and struck out once more, ignoring Sarah's cry of dismay as he forced her down one corridor after another.

Like a maze, each row of stalls melded into another. The faces of the vendors all looked alike, with features worn by sun and heat and hunger, no more interested in why they were running for their lives than if they were beggars pleading for handouts.

The alleyways had grown foul with human and animal refuse, the fumes rising with those of rotting fruit to draw flies, rats, and dogs that bared their teeth and raised their hackles if approached too closely.

But it was in the Oriental heart of the bazaar that the air grew the thickest. Here run-down tenements and stalls, stacked one on top of the other and reached only by bamboo ladders blocked out the sunlight completely. Added to the putrid dampness were the cloying odor of burning hashish and the sweet, acrid bite of vaporized opium. The merchandise in Little China was expensive. Men and women sold their bodies for high prices and their narcotics for a fortune.

Of course, Morgan had seen it all before, had been known to wander Little China's dimly lit streets on occasion.

Now, finding a deserted shanty, he cast a watchful glimpse over his companion's head, then shoved Sarah inside. He knew from experience that you did not dally along Pleasure Alley, at least not if you valued your life.

Only then did he look at Sarah.

Her neat chignon had long since collapsed. Her hair, honey-gold in the gloominess, tumbled over her shoulders, several loose strands clinging to her moist cheeks and neck. Her eyes, wide with fear, were fixed on the stall directly across from them. A man stood there, totally nude, his dark eyes mere slits in his face, his waist-length black hair braided in a rope that hung over one shoulder. His hand curved around his erection as he waved, laughed, and said, "You come here, yes?"

Morgan took Sarah's face in one hand and turned it away, pressed her head against his shoulder, and whispered, "I'm sorry."

"You!" the Chinaman called. "You want come see me?"

"No," Morgan called. "The lady is mine."

"Not lady I want. You! You come see me, yes? I give you much pleasure, mister. You wait and see."

A woman's catcall joined the voice of the Chinaman, then another and another, until the entire alleyway was alive with men and women crying out their wares.

"This—this is disgusting!" Sarah finally managed, her voice quavering between horror and fury.

"You can thank your own countrymen for it," Morgan told her. "Seems the Orientals were brought over by a lot of rich Brits who weren't

finding their wives entertaining enough and thought the Indians too ignorant in the ways of pleasure."

Her head came up and she glared at him with blazing eyes. "My father
would never have allowed such heinous behavior!"

"Chere, your father was probably one of their best patrons."

She might have clawed his face had he not caught her hands and
shoved her back against the wall of the ill-lit shanty. The structure trembled with their impact. "You filthy animal!" she cried. "How dare you
slur my father with your nasty, false innuendos!"

He smiled at her coldly. "What's so nasty about it? Hmm? Ever think
that it might be those small-minded sentiments that are driving your
men, and occasionally women, to wander these alleys in search of companionship?"

"It's degenerate!"

"How do you know unless you've tried it?"

"Never! Now I demand that you get me out of this wretched place
before your friends murder us both."

"Saucy little thing, aren't you, love?"

She shook her head in disbelief. "There are men out there trying to kill
us and you don't seem to give a damn. I think you're crazy. You are!
You're—"

He slammed his hand over her mouth again as voices rose in the distance.

"Kane! We know you're here! Come out and we'll let the woman go.
She has nothing to do with us . . . Kane, we'll search every shanty until
we find you. If you don't come with us peaceably, we'll be forced to deal
with the young lady more . . . shall we say . . . thoroughly when we
find you."

"Gilberto de Queiros," Morgan said under his breath. "I should have
killed him when I had the chance."

He glanced up and down the shadowed alleyway. The hawkers and
prostitutes had vanished like smoke in the wind, wanting no part of the
coming trouble. Then he looked back at Sarah. If he made a run for it
now, leaving her behind, he just might make it. But if they found her
. . . she'd never leave Little China alive. King's assassins weren't about
to allow any witnesses to testify that he'd been hunted down like a rabid
dog and slaughtered.

Still, if he led them far enough away . . .

She must have sensed his train of thought, for as he measured the
distance of the alley with his eyes, she grabbed him and shoved the hand

from her mouth. "Don't you dare, Kane. You are not leaving me in this
. . . this festering bordello."

"The alternative might be worse," he warned her.

"You've confronted and escaped worse danger than this. Think of your
journey over Japurá, of the cannibals, the animals—"

"I didn't have a woman hanging on my shirttails."

"I won't get you killed, if that's what you're implying."

"Promise?" He drawled it, smiling sarcastically down at her mouth,
which was partially open and panting short, warm breaths against his
chest. When she didn't respond with more than a lift of her white chin
and an arch of one eyebrow, he grunted in amusement. Taking a deep
breath, he nodded and said, "You asked for it."

He struck out running, dragging Sarah behind him, knowing for certain she would hold him back, trip, stumble, or do something that would
get him killed. Within four strides, however, she was keeping up respectably well, lithely dodging in and out of the shadows and around the stalls.
For a moment, just a moment, he considered that they might make one
hell of a team in Japurá after all. They might even get out of Little China
if their luck held. Then their shoes hit a puddle of something slimy, and
their feet flew out from under them; they hit the ground hard, scattering
what at first looked like kittens from the rotting carcass of a dog. Only
they weren't kittens. They were rats.

Sarah screamed.

"Ah, Christ," he groaned.

The sound of running feet and shouting voices echoed in the alleyway
as Morgan yanked Sarah up and ran again, knocking vendors' carts
askew and toppling merchants' tables. A sudden hail of bullets split the
air as King's men rounded a corner behind them. One of the voices cried
out, "Diego, that way! Pronto!"

The gunfire came again, and this time a bullet missed Morgan's head
by inches, splintering the garish green lantern an old merchant had hung
over his table littered with jade ornaments and tiny animal bones. Finally
there was daylight ahead. They burst out of the darkness, gulping air that
was still rank with rot but somewhat fresher. The harsh sunlight was an
assault on their eyes, and they stumbled along blindly, bumping a child's
pram and spilling a beggar's tin can of coins at his feet.

Dissonant music rent the air as dancers whirled and leapt around
them, spinning yards and yards of bright paper streamers in their faces,
forcing Morgan to shove them away or rip the pennants from their hands.
Others, covered from head to toe in dragon costumes, undulated between
the stalls like startling monsters flushed from their caves, their fire-

breathing masks muting the almost maniacal-sounding laughter from within.

Sarah and Morgan rounded a corner and skidded to a stop. For a heart-stopping instant there appeared to be no way out. A wall rose up ten feet ahead of them, and in front of it sat a withered old man, his yellow skin seamed and his straight gray hair plaited all the way to his knees. In one hand he held an iguana as long as his arm. In the other, a knife. With a lift of the bloodied blade, his knotted hands slit the reptile's belly, spilling entrails to the ground by his feet where numerous snakes lay coiled, asleep in the sun, or already skinned. Nearby, several burlap sacks convulsed with doomed reptiles whose hisses of outrage could be heard even over the distant music.

Sarah gasped and turned away, terrified.

Morgan, however, stared down at the ancient one's lap, where a *surucucu* lay as docilely as a cat. Its beadlike black eyes stared up at Morgan with a cold malevolence that almost succeeded in turning his blood to ice.

Behind them, footsteps drew nearer, and Sarah whispered with strained urgency, "Morgan . . . Morgan, oh God, Morgan, do something. *Please . . .*"

The Chinaman's eyes rolled up at Morgan, their pupils cloudy white with cataracts. As he smiled, revealing nubs for teeth and a tongue which had been split like a snake's, the hide of the reptile he'd been skinning rolled smoothly from the limp carcass and fell to his robed lap.

"Yes?" he seemed to hiss.

"Morgan, he's coming!" Sarah cried.

"The snake," Morgan said quietly. "Give me . . . give me that snake. There." He pointed to the cobra coiled within the folds of the old man's lap.

"We've got to get out of here!" Sarah looked around, her features freezing as Morgan walked to the old man. As if sensing his presence, the snakes in the burlap bags began a thrashing that strained the string-bound enclosures to their limits.

The Chinaman only smiled and stroked the serpent's head, closing his gnarled hands behind the snake's hood as Morgan drew nearer.

As he reached for the cobra, the creature raised its head and hissed its vehemence. He froze. Sweat beaded his brow as he realized that if the old man decided to release his hold on the snake, he was a dead man.

"How much?" he sneered at the Chinaman. "How much, you slant-eyed bastard? How much!"

"What is it worth, your life?"

His mouth curving in a smile, Morgan again withdrew his knife from its scabbard and, holding its glinting blade up for the Chinaman to see, said, "How much is *your* life worth, old man? Before I die from the *surucucu* 's venom, I will have cut your throat a dozen times and skinned you like that iguana."

Their eyes met in understanding.

Slowly, very slowly, hearing King's men closing in on him Morgan reached again for the *surucucu,* eased his fingers around the cobra's body, and gripped it just behind its massive jaws.

"Sarah," he ordered quietly, "get behind the old man." As she did so, shying away from the snakes as much as possible, he said to the China-man, "There has to be another way out of here. Where is it?"

"Beyond those crates." He motioned toward a stack of bamboo cages, then, smiling, added, "Be very careful. Many snakes hide in alleyway."

"Thanks for the warning, you old—"

"Kane! Drop your knife!" came a harsh voice from just behind him.

Morgan spun and threw the writhing snake in his pursuer's face, and as Sarah screamed, he bent over and cut the cord of one of the burlap bags, spilling the reptiles in a squirming flood over the ground and onto the terrified assassin. In another lithe move, he grabbed Sarah and shoved her out of the way.

Without hesitating, Sarah ran through the shadowed corridor made up of hundreds upon hundreds of snake cages piled one atop the other, forming an eerie, wavering mountain above them. They broke into the open, gasping in much-needed air. But as Sarah spun around to grab Morgan in relief, Gilberto de Queiros appeared out of nowhere and moved up behind her so quickly that Morgan had no time to react. De Queiros closed his arm about her throat, pulled her back against him, and slammed the barrel of his pistol into her temple. As Morgan froze, his eyes pinned on Sarah's stunned face, de Queiros said, "At last we meet again, Senhor Kane. It is about time, *sí?*"

Morgan closed his eyes in frustration.

"Drop the knife, senhor. And kick it over to me, *por favor.*"

Morgan did as de Queiros said. Blotting the sweat from his face with his sleeve, he tried to breathe through the stifling heat. Another moment passed as he allowed his frantically pounding heart to slow. Yet each time he looked into Sarah's white face trepidation washed over him again.

"Let her go, de Queiros. She has nothing to do with me."

"No? She's not another of your many *putas?*"

"No." He shook his head. "She's nothing to me. Let her go and you can do what you want with me."

De Queiros tightened his grip around Sarah's throat. "You're a liar, Kane. You always have been. Senhorita, you must know that when this man says something is white, it must be black. Therefore, you must be of great importance to him, *querida.*"

Morgan took a step toward him, but was brought up short as de Queiros pulled back the hammer on the gun.

De Queiros smiled and shrugged. "You would not do anything foolish, senhor. You know by experience that such stupidity is met with grave consequences where we come from. You have already committed the unforgivable—"

"Then kill me, but leave her out of this."

"That's not our friend's way, is it? It's a shame, however. She's very young and beautiful. But she made the grave mistake of becoming involved with a condemned man. Now she must die."

Sarah whimpered, her eyes wide and bright with tears as she looked at Morgan. She bit her lip to keep from crying aloud, and a drop of blood oozed from the corner of her mouth. Then, with no warning, her eyes rolled back in her head, and with a sigh, she sank in a faint against de Queiros. Taken by surprise, he stumbled back, her weight too much to control as her body slid toward the ground in a heap of tattered taffeta and silk.

Morgan ran, sprinting up the cobblestone passageway between two buildings.

"Stop!" The gun exploded and a bullet splintered a brick to the right of Morgan's head. "I'll not miss next time, senhor!"

Morgan slowed, then stopped, turning his face up to the yellow light overhead, waiting for a bullet to blow out his brains. He counted the seconds, hoping his attempted escape would give Sarah time enough to recover and escape before de Queiros went back to finish her off.

De Queiros walked to him. "So we are face-to-face at last, and this time I have the knife." He turned the weapon so the sunlight glinted off the blade like a streak of lightning. "Perhaps we shall see how brave you are without the knife, *sí?* First, though we'll see how manly you are without your dick. What you say, big man? *Mucho hombre.* Think the senhoritas will like you so much then?"

Pressed back against a wall, Morgan winced as the blade sliced through his trousers and bit into the skin of his scrotum. "What difference does it make if I'm dead?" he said with a tight smile.

"You're right. Why waste time? I'll have more fun carving up your face and disemboweling you while you watch." De Queiros raised the knife and pressed it into the underside of Morgan's chin. If he swallowed he would cut his own throat. Then he realized there wasn't enough spit left in his entire body to make him swallow.

"So, amigo, have you any regrets that you would like me to relate to our mutual friend?"

"You mean that bastard King?"

"I see your disposition hasn't improved. It's a shame after all he did for you."

"Did *to* me, you mean."

"I'm sorry, but I could never understand your attitude. Randi showed great benevolence toward you during your stay."

"Imprisonment."

"Had you only shown some gratitude. But you were always so belligerent, so rebellious. You could have become as powerful as Randi himself; there's nothing he would not have given you had you only . . . cooperated a little more. Now, I regret to say, I must kill you. It's nothing personal, you understand. Were it up to me, I might simply cut open your face, as you did mine, and leave you with a remembrance of our friendship. But Randi is King, after all. And his word is law. Regrettably, you never understood that. *Via con Dios,* my friend."

The edge of the wood plank hit de Queiros solidly at the base of his skull, driving him into Morgan, who grabbed his hand before the knife could cut into his throat. The killer sank slowly to his knees, his eyes vacant pools. Then Sarah brought the board down over his head a second time, and he toppled to the ground, facedown in a puddle of sewage.

Morgan and Sarah stared down at de Queiros's body as if anticipating his immediate resurrection. Finally, covering her mouth with her fingertips, she looked up at Morgan, her small face almost lost in her wild spray of gold hair.

"Oh, my," she said. "Have I killed him?"

Morgan bent, grabbed a handful of hair, and jerked back de Queiros's head, then released it and frowned. "Nah, he's still breathin'." Morgan pried the knife from the man's hand and slid it back into the scabbard. "You should've got the blazes out of here when you had the chance," he told her.

"Probably, but then he would've killed you."

Morgan shrugged and turned up the alleyway, anxious to put distance between himself and de Queiros.

"I should have let him kill you for all the thanks I get for saving your bastardly life!" she cried out after him. "Especially after you said those horrible things about my father!"

"So why didn't you?"

"Because I need you," came her small voice.

Stopping, he turned. She reminded him of a brightly colored rooster come up on the short end of a cockfight. But there was something, too, in the willful set of her chin, and in the eyes that, though shining with tears, refused to cry.

He shook his head. "You see what you're up against. You can multiply this sort of danger by a thousand and not begin to equal the perils that are waitin' for you in Amazonia. Sweetheart, faintin' just ain't gonna cut it when you're face-to-face with Xavante headhunters."

Raising her skirts, she stepped over de Queiros's unconscious form, her eyes locked on his. In a firm voice, she informed him, "I didn't."

"Didn't what?"

"Faint. I only pretended to, knowing he would be forced to drop me. I counted on you running so I'd have the chance to find a weapon and sneak up behind him." She beamed him a proud smile. "It worked."

"Yeah." He grinned. "I guess it did."

"So will you do it? Take me to Japurá?"

Sarah waited, the minutes dragging by like an eternity as the American considered her request. When he smiled again, the rigid lines of his face relaxed into an odd sort of acceptance that fluttered her already pounding heart.

"Yeah," came his soft drawl, "I'll do it."

Her reaction was immediate, surprising even herself. She ran to him and threw her arms around him, burying her face against his chest. Laughing and crying at once, she breathed in the musky scent of his skin. For an instant the past horrible minutes might never have happened.

"Thank you!" She wept and held him tighter, only vaguely aware of how stiff he had become in her arms. When she looked at him again, her head falling back so that she peered through tears of relief, she saw a strange light in his silver eyes. With a stunned amazement, she was conscious of an overwhelming impulse to take his stubbled face in her hands and kiss him.

But she didn't. She wouldn't dare. The very idea of such a thing shocked her. Instead, she fled up the alleyway in search of Kan.

BY THE TIME HENRY ARRIVED AT TOBACCO ROW, MORGAN HAD finished his evening meal of whiskey and *feijoada,* a mixture of meat scraps and black beans that had cooked all day. He had bathed and changed into his fine linen suit. He was positioning his white, wide-brimmed Panama hat low over his brow when his friend knocked on the door.

"Yeah," he said.

Henry stepped in, his brown face unusually somber as he regarded Morgan. "I say, old man, I spoke to Kan. He told me what happened at the market today."

"Well, ain't it always the way? Where the hell are your friends when you need them?"

"You seem to have handled yourself respectably well."

"We're alive, by the skin of our teeth." He cocked the Panama rakishly.

"Kan told me about the snakes."

"Christ, I hate snakes." He shuddered.

"I'm proud of you, Morgan, not only for the way you handled yourself but also for deciding to go to Japurá."

He swept several coins from the crumb-littered tabletop into his pocket. "Don't go getting the idea that I'm being valiant. It's just that until now we haven't had the resources to go into Japurá. Now we do. We'll get King, and his gold."

"Along with a few thousand rubber seeds."

Angrily, Morgan faced him. "I ain't goin' into Japurá for rubber seeds."

"But—"

"But nothin'." He flipped open the top two buttons of his shirt, exposing a dark vee of hair on the upper portion of his chest. "You were right," he told Henry. "The only way to deal with King is to confront him face-to-face. I can't keep running, Henry. I can't look over my shoulder for the rest of my life. Eventually one of his henchmen is going to kill me, and believe it or not, I'd rather know it was coming than to get it in the back. So I figure, why not take the bastard with me when I go?"

"You make this sound like some sort of suicide mission."

"That's exactly what it is, and if you think otherwise, my little man, you're a fool."

"But Sarah—"

"We use the lady's money to buy enough supplies to get us to Japurá. We let her ride along as far as Santarém or Manáos. One night while she's sleeping, we leave without her. By the time she discovers we've gone, it'll be too late."

Henry stared at him in shock. "Good Lord, are you meaning to dump her, Morgan?"

"Right."

"In Santarém or Manáos?"

"Right again."

"Good gosh."

He grabbed a handkerchief from the windowsill and tucked it into his breast pocket. Henry padded across the floor and peered up at him in concern, his eyes dark, the white bones in his nose gleaming dully in the twilight.

"But, Morgan what does she do then?"

He jerked out the cloth and refolded it, refusing to look at his friend again. More carefully, he eased it into his pocket until the triangular point lay smoothly against the jacket.

"Morgan?" Henry said.

Morgan swept up the whiskey flask and dropped it into his pocket. Then, on second thought, he withdrew it and uncorked it. He drank deeply before returning it to his coat. "What?" he finally replied.

"What does she do then?"

"That's her problem."

"By Jove, have you no compassion, man? No conscience at all?"

He laughed in response.

"I cannot possibly allow you to do this," Henry protested.

"No?" Morgan started for the door. "Then how do you intend to get to Japurá, old boy?"

A dozen chickens scattered from his path as he swung up the road. By the time he reached Water Street and the docks, he had finished one cigarette and started a second. He kept close to the shuttered bazaar stalls, venturing onto the wharf only after darkness had fallen completely. Then he took his place by the flickering gas lamp and waited.

Four years ago he had come to South America in search of get-rich-quick schemes that had ruined far better men than he. He'd sold his soul to the devil in hopes of grabbing the brass ring, escaped hell by the skin of his teeth . . . Now he was being lured back to the very pits of Hades by an angel.

But oh, what an angel!

Gazing out at the black sea, he recalled the joyous sound of her laughter, her courage . . . the feel of her arms around him, and the fire of appreciation in her eyes before she left him burning for her on the street.

He must be very, very careful. He could fall for her if he let himself. He might begin to hope that those beautiful eyes would shine at him with some emotion other than fear and awe, and occasionally anger. As if he cared if she smiled at him or looked at him as something other than white trash—or a means to an end.

He laughed and flicked the burning stub of his cigarette into the dark.

Chapter Five

Two weeks later, Belém, Brazil

SARAH SAT SIPPING TEA BENEATH A PUNKAH IN THE BELÉM HOTEL, surrounded by men—British botanists mostly, who were as eager to undertake their rigorous voyages into the Amazon as she. She was up and about earlier than usual, but she was determined to see Morgan. For the past three days, since their arrival in Belém, he had avoided her, leaving the hotel long before sunrise and returning well after dark, if at all. Since Kan had been busy helping the American prepare for the next stage of their journey, Henry had made a pleasant companion as she whiled away the long hours in the hotel lobby. But spending her days chatting with scientists who spoke as if the world's survival hinged on the propagation of orchids had quickly become monotonous, as tedious as Norman's discourses on butterflies.

Henry had informed her that he was to meet Morgan at eight o'clock in a supply store near the dock. Well, she would be there, too. It was time Kane stopped excluding her. She should have some say in their arrangements; she was financing this expedition, after all.

As her napkin slid from her lap to the floor, a suited gentleman leapt to retrieve it, offering it to her with an affected flourish that reminded her of Norman. She frowned, then wondered why. Then she realized that, while such manners were de rigueur in London, they seemed pretentious here, surrounded by bamboo furnishings, half-naked Indians, and monkeys that ran freely throughout the hotel. She smiled her thanks and had just put her teacup aside when Kane's voice came to her from the restaurant. She would have recognized it anywhere. It tolled through the room with the resonance of a bell, and was followed by the sound of giggling females.

She jumped to her feet; so did the half-dozen men surrounding her, one scrambling to pull back her chair while another grabbed her parasol and gently offered it to her, handle first. "Gentlemen, it has been a great pleasure," she told them, her gaze still on the door, her heart racing.

"Oh, no," they responded almost in unison. "The pleasure was ours, Miss St. James."

She hurried toward the restaurant, pausing long enough to attempt to steady her breathing. The fact that her body responded in such a way every time she came face-to-face with the American was most disconcerting. That he knew it further frustrated her. He used her nervousness to his advantage, sending her into a flutter with the narrowing of his eyes or a sardonic curl of his lips. Blast the man and his reputation. Be he *boto* or not, it was time to get a few things straight between them!

He was sitting at a table on the far side of the room, partially hidden by potted palms. He wasn't alone. Then again, he rarely was. A woman was with him, a tall, slender, dark-skinned beauty dressed in little more than strategically placed straps of brightly colored cotton. A flicker of displeasure, and confusion, sluiced through Sarah at the sight of her. How relaxed other women appeared to be in his presence. Even as she watched, the woman laughed and touched his face . . . and he smiled.

A stunning smile.

An unabashedly handsome smile.

He had never smiled at *her* like that.

"Would the senhorita care for a table?"

She blinked and looked at the waiter. "I'm joining Mr. Kane."

The man's eyes lit in approval. The realization of what he must be thinking turned her cheeks hot. She said, "I can find my own way over, thank you."

The waiter bowed and departed; and gathering her wits about her, Sarah moved to Kane's table as gracefully as her knocking knees would allow. He caught sight of her right away, one side of his mouth curving as if to challenge her to confront him.

"Mr. Kane," she greeted him as she stopped at the table.

"Miss St. James."

Sarah glanced toward the woman, who had yet to take her hands off Morgan. "May I speak with you privately?"

He shrugged and went back to eating his breakfast, a plate of eggs and ham and biscuits. Finally Sarah turned her attention to his companion and smiled. "I do beg your pardon, but do you think I might have a moment of Mr. Kane's time?"

The woman raised one eyebrow and, very slowly, rose from her chair until she was towering over Sarah by at least six inches. With only a single pointed glance at Morgan, she turned and walked out the door. Sarah tried to relax. The effort was futile. Moving to the vacated chair, she sank into it.

"Hungry?" Kane asked as he continued to cut his ham.

"I didn't come here to eat," she replied. "I came here to talk."

He shoved his plate away, then wiped his mouth with a napkin. Sitting back in his chair, he fished inside his shirt pocket, withdrew a toothpick, and slid it between his lips. "So talk."

The way he was looking at her made it difficult for Sarah to breathe. He no longer wore the white suit she'd seen so often in the past days, but had reverted to the garb of a dock worker. She found her eyes drawn to the vee of his shirt that plunged open to the middle of his chest.

"Well?" he prompted, making her gaze fly back to his face.

"I—I feel we should discuss our plans for the journey." She swallowed hard.

He slid the toothpick from one corner of his mouth to the other with his tongue. A moment's silence ensued, then, "The arrangements have been taken care of."

"By whom?"

"By me."

"Didn't you forget something?"

He shook his head, spilling a fringe of hair over his brow. "I don't think so."

"You forgot to consult me."

Kane smiled. "I didn't forget, Miss St. James. I just didn't do it."

Her mouth dropped open as he reached for his hat, then shoved his chair back from the table. She sprang from her seat as he moved toward the lobby.

The Brits remaining in the spacious foyer leapt to their feet at her entrance, but she rushed on to keep up with Kane's longer strides. They were halfway across the street by the time Sarah lost her patience completely and grabbed his arm, stopping him in his tracks. Jerking him around, she glared up into his face. "Don't you dare walk away from me when I'm talking to you. I have a few things to say to you, and you are going to listen!"

"Yeah?"

"Yeah." She mocked him.

He pivoted on his heels and continued toward the docks. Sarah watched him go, her anger escalating beyond control. Never had she met a man so arrogant, so rude, so lacking in morals or etiquette or respect for propriety. It took all her willpower to recall that a lady should never show anger in public. Clenching her teeth, she opened her parasol with a snap, planted it none too gently against her shoulder, and struck off after him.

By the time she reached the supply store, the boardwalk was crowded with children, their small, dark, mostly nude bodies pressing toward the doorway. Their eyes were alight with an anticipation that nearly crackled the air, their faces beaming with pleasure.

Then Sarah saw Kane step from the store. Suddenly the children were swarming around him, jumping and grabbing for the candy sticks he had piled high in his hat.

Sarah stared. She felt weak-kneed and dizzy, as if something had melted inside her. Gone was the hateful twist to Morgan's mouth, the iciness in his eyes. There was a warmth in his smile, an easiness in his manner, a kindness in his laughter as the children crawled over him in quest of the treats. The sight brought the myth, the legend of his special magic with people, surging up to remind her that there was goodness buried deep inside this man—no matter how callously he behaved toward her.

At last, candy in hand, the children scattered up and down the street. All, that is, but one. A tiny girl, hardly taller than Morgan's knee, clung to his leg with one arm while she sucked on her lolly and gazed adoringly up at him. He grinned, stooped beside her, slid his arm around her middle, and pulled her up against him. She held out her candy for him to lick, then kissed him on the cheek and sped off down the street as fast as her little legs would carry her, black braids flying behind her. Morgan watched her go, the smile never leaving his mouth.

Then he saw Sarah.

She expected that wall of belligerence to come slamming down between them again, yet it didn't—at any rate, not right away. For a heart-stopping moment it seemed to Sarah as if he had been left vulnerable and exposed, his emotions clearly revealed on his face. There was an ache there that turned Sarah's insides to jelly. For a moment she wondered whether his infamous facade was only a mask he presented to the world to conceal emptiness and loneliness.

Ridiculous. Morgan Kane was never lonely, not with women and awe-struck Indians falling to their knees in either worship or lust each time he snapped his fingers.

As he re-entered the store, Sarah remained rooted to the walk, twirling her parasol on her shoulder and trying her best to retrieve a small portion of the anger that had driven her to storm after him in the first place. Finally she forced herself to move through the doorway, where she tried to focus in on the room's darker interior. Kane stood in the back, running his finger down a lengthy list of supplies. Henry was perched on a counter, swinging his bare feet and nodding each time Morgan read aloud from the series of items.

Sarah cleared her throat.

"Miss St. James!" Henry declared. "Please, come in."

Morgan looked up, "Here comes trouble."

Sarah yanked her parasol closed and stepped inside.

Henry leapt to the floor and hurried to her. "My dear, what brings you out so early?"

She smiled, finding pleasure in Henry's company. Kane had mentioned during their brief conferences after the market incident that he had a partner who would see to the hiring of the men who would attend them on their journey. Of course, she had been extremely shocked upon first meeting him. But they had become fast friends since leaving Georgetown. His story of how he'd been raised and educated in England had brought her hours of pleasure.

"I've decided to become more involved in the arrangements you and Mr. Kane have been making." She swept the cluttered shop with a glance. There were crates of supplies stacked near the door. Two were labeled "Whiskey."

"I told you," came Kane's voice. "Everything's been taken care of."

"So I see. I do hope, Mr. Kane, that you have provided us with something more substantial to drink than whiskey."

"Don't worry, you'll get your tea, lady. I believe Henry's even provided you with a china pot to brew it in."

"Do I detect some sarcasm in your tone, Mr. Kane?"

He tossed the supply list onto the counter. "So what?"

"So what?" She slammed the tip of her parasol against the floor so hard that it stirred up a little cloud of dust. "I will tell you what, Mr. Kane. It is my money that is financing this journey *and* paying your salary. You would do well to remember that I am your employer, and therefore have some say about the outfitting of this expedition."

"Yeah?"

He walked toward her, his height exaggerated by the low ceiling, his footsteps heavy on the wooden floor. Henry, who had been watching Sarah carefully, placed himself between her and Morgan and said, "By Jove, but we're getting along smashingly, aren't we?"

Morgan nudged him aside as Sarah quelled the urge to flee. Instead, she gripped the parasol in both hands as if it were a weapon and met the American's stare without blinking. An eternity ticked by as he stood towering above her, the heat of the musty room bearing down on her, the smell of Kane's skin burning her nostrils. His was the scent of bay rum and sweat; it made her chest constrict so tightly she could hardly breathe.

"All right," he finally said, making her jump. "It's your move, boss lady. I'm open to suggestions. What have you got to say?"

Unnerved by the gleam in his eyes, Sarah backed away, but only slightly. Twisting the parasol in her hand, she moved about the room, chewing her lip and studying the collection of gadgets hanging on the walls and piled high on tables and counters.

She cleared her throat. "Of course you've supplied us with the necessary foodstuffs."

No reply.

"And guns—" She stubbed her toe on a crate labeled "Ammunition" and frowned. Only then did she spy the proprietor of the store where he leaned on the counter at the back of the room, watching her through the smoke of his burning cigar. "We'll need a compass," she told him politely.

"Got it already," he replied condescendingly.

"Maps?"

The man smiled and shook his head.

"No maps?" She lifted her eyebrows and looked back at Kane. "No maps? Why, surely, Mr. Kane, you didn't overlook something so crucial as maps?"

"There are none," he said.

"Then, by all means, get some, sir."

"There are none," he repeated in the same blunt tone.

"Such an oversight is—"

"I said . . ." He moved toward her again, and as inconspicuously as possible Sarah backed away, until she was pressed against the counter and unable to move. She snapped open her parasol and positioned it like a shield between them, pointing the tip like a dagger toward his chest, and peering at him over the upper edge of lacy frill and ribbons.

"I said," he continued, "there are no maps. Not where we're going. They don't exist, Miss St. James, because no one has ever ventured into Japurá by land and returned."

"*Au contraire,*" she replied, lifting one delicate eyebrow. "*You* have, sir."

Silence prevailed as Morgan looked from her to Henry, who pursed his lips in a soundless whistle and turned for the door.

"I have every faith that you'll manage to retrace your journey," Sarah said, inching away from the counter and Morgan until she could walk without further threat about the room. She pointed to such articles as ropes, winches, machetes, and axes, only to be told time and again that they had already been purchased and were being loaded on the steamer, *Santos,* in preparation for their departure tomorrow afternoon.

At last she stood staring out the door, her face burning in frustration and anger. As usual, Morgan Kane had succeeded in making her appear the fool.

"Hey, boss lady," he called. "You forgot something."

She looked back just as he tossed a pile of clothing at her. She'd barely caught the items when a helmet came sailing through the air, which she had to scramble to catch. She regarded the coarse, drab-colored material of the breeches and shirt in her arms for a long moment before asking, "What, pray tell, are these?"

"Your clothes, of course. The proper attire for trudging through the Japurá jungle." Smiling, Morgan plunked a pair of knee-high leather boots atop the clothing. "I'm certain you'll look smashing in them." Then he dropped a large bottle into the pith helmet she gripped to her chest. "One dose every night before you go to bed or you'll die of malaria. You do know what malaria is, don't you?"

"Yes," she said through her teeth.

He winked. "Just checking, *chere.*"

She spun on her heels and, with her parasol dragging, stormed from the shop in a flurry of petticoats and bouncing hair. Standing in the doorway and holding a match to the cigarette in his lips, Morgan watched Sarah go while Henry stood at his side and shook his head.

"You really should try harder to get along," he said.

Morgan exhaled smoke through his nose. "Right."

"I shudder to think what will happen when she learns that the story of your escaping through Japurá is all a fabrication."

"We'll be long separated before that happens, my friend."

"I feel terrible about ditching her somewhere along the way, Morgan. I like her, you know. She's been very nice to me. I think, if you tried harder to get along, she would be a very pleasant companion for you."

"For me?" Morgan laughed softly. "Not for me, Henry. I'm not clean enough to wipe the lady's shoes."

Henry regarded him with sad eyes.

More quietly, and to himself, Morgan said, "She wouldn't want me within a mile of her if she knew . . ." His voice faded, then he crushed out his cigarette with his boot heel and walked away.

* * *

THE HOUR WAS LATE AS SARAH SAT IN BED, WRITING A LETTER TO Norman. Spread out before her were the breeches and shirt and helmet Morgan had thrust upon her at the supply store. So far she still hadn't put them on. She supposed that, in a sense, this small act of rebellion was a last attempt to hold on to the few shreds of civilization that remained available to her. When she'd arrived in Belém, she had quickly discovered how different and chaotic things were in the Amazon. The Indians wandered as free as the wind, with their bodies barely clothed. There was no order among the townsfolk, who opened and closed their businesses on a whim and set no time for meals or sleeping. During the hottest part of the day they curled up in odd places to take a siesta. At night people sang and caroused drunkenly in the streets.

She signed her name to Norman's letter. By the time he received it, he would have already heard the news of her father's death. What version of the story he would get, God only knew. Her father's associates had assured her that all suspicion of suicide would be snuffed, but she found that highly unlikely. The British did so love to gossip. By the time the news reached London, it would undoubtedly include every last horrible detail of her father's demise. Somehow she had to prove that her father had been murdered, and get those seeds to pay off his debts, or her future was doomed.

Wearily, she fell back on the bed and stared at the ceiling. As always, the night was stiflingly hot. She longed to immerse herself up to her chin in a tub of cold water.

She closed her eyes and dozed, dreaming of Morgan Kane surrounded by gleeful children, looking almost like a child himself. Then there were women, long-legged, beautiful, and dark-skinned. They were worshipping him with their eyes and hands, and suddenly she was among them, reaching but never quite touching, afraid her body would experience those shameful sensations that flurried in her stomach each time he was near— but still wanting to feel them. She'd never felt that way with Norman. Norman, who was so staid, so in control. She felt safe with Norman, and ordinary, and satisfied with her life.

Morgan Kane made her feel restless and hungry for . . . what?

She heard a noise in the hall . . .

She opened her eyes and blinked sleepily, then jolted to awareness as she heard Kane's voice in the corridor. The blood rushed like fire through her body, humming in her brain, tingling in her fingertips. Rolling out of bed, she dropped lightly to the floor, her bare feet making little noise as she moved to the door and opened it a fraction of an inch.

A draft of cooler wind sluiced up the hallway, stirring the potted palms along the way. Near the end of the corridor at the top of the stairs, sleeping parrots in a cage roused, fluttered their green and red wings, and squawked before falling silent as Kane appeared. His broad shoulders and wide-brimmed hat were outlined by a faint nimbus of gold from the light below.

He moved up the narrow hall toward his room across from hers, his stride slow and fluid, his head down slightly and the red ember of the cigarette in his mouth glowing in the shadows, only vaguely illuminating his features. The breath left her as her mind and body acknowledged the dark, savage image he made amid the backdrop of shadows and foliage. He was everything forbidden to decent women; he was the fantasy that made them imagine what it would be like to be held by a man who was driven by primitive desire instead of polite convention.

Of course, she knew already. Since the night he'd kissed her on her father's veranda she had thought of little else when left alone to muse.

He stopped at his room and slid the key into the lock; the door swung open with a creak . . . then he turned and looked directly into her eyes.

He knew what she was thinking. Oh, God, he knew. She saw it in the narrowing of his eyes and the curving of his lips around his cigarette. She felt his gaze slide down her, from the crest of her tumbling blond hair to the tips of her naked toes. Its intensity was that hot and damning, and though some voice screamed inside her head that she was barely dressed, that the dampness of her body had no doubt turned her lawn chemise into a filmy transparency, she couldn't move. Suddenly she was a temptress, and she liked it. Such excitement surged through her that she felt winded and giddy and trembly all over. What would she do if he crossed that hallway and asked to come in? Then again, he wouldn't ask. He would just do it.

He entered his room, closing the door between them. Sarah shut her eyes and pressed her face hard against the wall, feeling her body burn.

THE SUN WAS A BLAZING ORANGE BALL SHIMMERING OVER THE CARA-mel-colored Amazon River. It dazzled Sarah where she stood by the railing of the *Santos.* As the fiery sphere sank into the horizon, the streaked sky cast a purple-and-lavender tint over the boats that crowded the mouth of the river. The ship on which Morgan Kane had booked them passage to Santarém was white and tall like a wedding cake, with filigree and railings of shiny brass, resembling a Mississippi side-wheeler.

The decks around Sarah were crowded with passengers and cargo piled high about the railings; hammocks swayed under sparsely placed awnings. Though dusk was nearing, the air was still hot and thick with anticipation as the *Santos* let out a long blasting whistle from its smoke-stack high above. With a sense of resignation, Sarah realized that life as she had known it would soon cease to exist.

Dear Henry had attempted to divert her from worrying about entering the Amazon. And while in the American's presence she had done her best to act as if venturing down the river were no more bothersome to her than a stroll through Hyde Park. In truth, the idea of the Amazon didn't bother her nearly so much as the prospect of confronting King. How did one face a man and accuse him of murder—especially one as cold-blooded and ruthless as Rodolfo King? Well, she would deal with that problem weeks, or months, from now. There were other, more pressing concerns, such as surviving the journey and keeping an eye out for Gil-berto de Queiros, who by now must have learned of the American's departure from Georgetown. It was Morgan and Henry's hope that de Queiros would suspect Morgan of leaving South America completely. Surely he would not be so imaginative as to realize Morgan was running *to* King, not from him.

And then there was the problem of the American himself.

Gripping the ship's rail, Sarah stared blankly at the distant shore, vaguely hearing the churning steam engines and the rhythmic slap of the paddle wheel on the water. She couldn't get him out of her mind. Her eyes searched for him constantly, and she leapt for any excuse whatsoever to confront him. Much to her chagrin, she realized she was close to becoming one of those bewitched women who so shamelessly sought his attentions, and that would never do. She was a lady, after all, and he was . . . fascinating. Mesmerizing. Notoriously wicked. Everything Norman wasn't.

SARAH SPENT THE REMAINDER OF THE EVENING RESTING IN A DECK chair beneath a bright-colored awning, updating her diary, describing the passing countryside and the river, which seemed to stretch like a sea in the distance. At some point, she dozed.

The throbbing of the engines woke her. Night engulfed her, as heavy and black as the oily water rippling in the wake of the steam-powered ship. She was startled by the brilliance of the stars overhead. Never had she witnessed such a display of celestial splendor. They took her breath away, disoriented her until she was forced to sit up and grasp the chair arms for fear of somehow falling.

"Better enjoy it while you can, Princess. This time tomorrow the night sky will be nothin' but a memory."

She turned to find the American nearby, one hip casually balanced on the ship's rail. As Kane eased from his perch and approached, her gaze shifted to the razor-sharp knife he carried on the wide leather belt that hung on his hips, then back to his face. Despite her resolve to remain unmoved, her heart did a familiar discomfiting somersault and her lungs constricted. Too easily she recalled the feel of those powerful arms sliding around her, those hands moving through her hair—making her forget that she was engaged to another man who didn't have powerful arms and whose chaste kisses left her feeling dissatisfied, though she could never really understand why. Until now . . .

His features masked by shadows, his thumbs hooked over the waistband of his breeches, Kane studied her without speaking. She wasn't certain she had ever known a man as remote and wary as this American.

"You'd better get inside," came his deep voice. "In another hour the mosquitoes will eat you alive."

She said nothing, just swung her feet off the chair and sat up, spilling the book in her lap to the floor. Before she could move he bent and retrieved it. He studied it the best he could in the faint light. "A diary? Fanciful, loving thoughts about your fiancé, perhaps?"

She watched nervously as he flipped open the needlepoint cover and thumbed the pages as if he had every intention of reading her very private thoughts—most of which had little to do with Norman and a lot to do with Morgan Kane.

She grabbed the diary from his hands. He grinned. "What's wrong, *chere?* Surely you've not written something you'd be ashamed of?"

"What I've written is no business of yours, Mr. Kane."

"You're a saucy little thing when you get your back up."

"Perhaps you should try harder not to get my back up."

"Now why would I do that, sweetheart?"

"So we could pass the time with less turmoil between us? I've never known anyone who so enjoyed making mischief with people's sensibilities."

"Is that what I do to you, *chere,* play mischief with your sensibilities?" His laughter was soft. "How very flattering."

"I had not meant it to be flattering."

"No?" He flashed that unnerving smile and Sarah felt her body, from her scalp to the tips of her toes, vibrate like a plucked bowstring.

"No!" she replied, perhaps too vehemently. Tucking her diary against her fluttering stomach, she added less emotionally, "If you'll excuse me, I'll be off to my room."

"I'll see you to your cabin."

"That won't be necessary."

"But I insist." He caught her arm, making her hesitate in her attempt to flee. At his touch those new and shocking sensations burst through her again, and she did her best to tug her elbow out of his gentle but insistent grasp.

"I'm perfectly capable of finding my way to my cabin," she argued.

"Miss St. James, I don't doubt that you're capable of walking on water, but you're paying me to see you safely down the Amazon and that's what I intend to do."

"How very chivalrous of you, considering you didn't seem overly bothered about my welfare in Belém. Every time I saw you, you were cavorting about town with loose-moraled women."

"A slight exaggeration, I think. Besides, cavorting is hardly my style. I tend more toward a low-keyed seduction. I find women are usually more intrigued by the understated."

"Not *this* woman, Mr. Kane, and you'd do well to remember that." She jerked her arm away and hurried across the deck.

"You like the more aggressive sort, huh?" came his infuriating words behind her.

If her emotions had not been in such a quandary, she might have retained her tenuous grip on her temper; as it was, she turned with a furious snap and walked back to him. "Mr. Kane, I have employed you to escort me safely to and from Japurá. I have not—I repeat, have *not*—hired you to seduce me."

A suggestive smile curved his mouth. "Is that what I'm doing, *chere?* Seducing you?"

It was difficult not to acknowledge the sensual promise of those lips. Struggling for breath, she managed, "Mr. Kane, I am not so naive as to believe in the ridiculous notion that you are some magical lover who casts spells over hapless females."

"No?"

"Positively not. I've grown too old and cynical for such nonsense."

"Chere," he said, and his rich voice was tinged with amusement, "you haven't a cynical bone in your sumptuous body. Now, unless you want me to disprove your bravado by doing something totally in character, you'd better get your little bustle below."

"I am also not paying you to give me orders. From here on out we travel as a team. We discuss whatever course we intend to take and make decisions together."

"Ah. Very well. In that case, I have to take a leak into the river. Do you think it best to do so up bow or stern?"

Stiffening her spine, she turned toward the door, cheeks burning, vaguely aware that he was following as she made her way down the narrow flight of stairs, into the dimly lit corridor, finally arriving at her cabin after what felt like an eternity of doing her best to ignore the American.

She had dreaded this moment since first boarding the *Santos* that afternoon, when Morgan and Henry had shown her the quarters and she had been forced to pretend indifference to her shabby surroundings. The cabin —or royal suite, as Kane had so glibly referred to it earlier—was a tiny room with a porthole that would not open due to rust and corrosion. That was just as well, Kane pointed out. No one in his right mind would sleep with the porthole open anyway, not if he didn't wish to be drained of blood by mosquitoes or vampire bats during the night. She had hidden her shudder by pretending to laugh. Only he hadn't laughed back, just stared at her with eyes the color of quicksilver.

The bed was a fishnet hammock that hung from the ceiling and was lined with a mattress covered with a tattered yellow sheet. The lantern on the table near the wall cast dancing light over the cabin and reflected from the cracked mirror on the wall. Sarah did her best to view it all with a modicum of pleasure, as she had everything since leaving Georgetown. It wasn't easy. For the first time in her nineteen years she would be forced to dress without the help of a servant, thanks to the American. He had refused to allow her any personal servants, so she had been forced to wave her lady's maid good-bye in Georgetown. And although Henry and Kan constantly vied to take care of her, they couldn't do everything. She would have to manage to undress somehow . . . even if she was forced to rip every last seam of her frock from her body.

Remaining in the hallway, Morgan watched Sarah cross the room and place the diary on the table next to the lamp. He did not miss the look of dread she made toward the hammock, nor the grim line of her mouth as she surveyed the less-than-spotless floor. She made a poor job of smiling as she turned back to face him.

"How nice," she said. "I'm certain to sleep very well."

She was a sorry liar. No doubt about it. But she was showing more stamina than he'd given her credit for. He'd expected a tantrum when he'd shown her the room earlier. He'd anticipated a bad case of the vapors when she realized she was the only white female bound up the Amazon on the steamer. Her only response had been a shudder. Now she was poised like some china figurine or forlorn child, completely different from the sophisticated, yet desperate young woman who had accosted him on two occasions and then ably saved his life as de Queiros attempted to end it. Neither was she the seductress, the memory of whose scantily dressed body had driven him to pace his room throughout the previous night. As it was, the need to take her in his arms rocked him. Ironic that he had kissed her that night on her father's veranda out of spite, to shock her, to prove to her that he wasn't a man who could be impressed by beauty, sophistication, or the flash of a delicate ankle—he'd seen it all a thousand times. What he'd walked away with, however, was the sweet memory of her responsive lips, the erotic scent of her body warmed by the hot tropical night, and the feel of her firm young breasts pressed indelibly upon his chest. With that in mind, he turned from the door and left her staring after him.

MIDNIGHT. THE AIR IN THE CARGO HOLD WAS THICK WITH SMOKE and rank with the smell of unwashed bodies. The boisterous noise of the gamblers had grown to an unbearable level as Morgan made a drunken swipe at the dice, missed, then tried again. The grinning faces surrounding him were bleary as he blinked his burning eyes and did his best to count the dwindling stack of bills before him.

"Morgan!" came Henry's voice. "Morgan, what's going on here? Morgan!"

On his knees and swaying a little, Morgan glanced around to see Henry pushing his way toward him through the crowd.

"Morgan! Don't you dare throw those dice again!"

He threw them anyway. Snake eyes.

Sitting back on his heels, Morgan watched the last of his money disappear into the pocket of a toothless, grinning Brazilian with most of his nose missing. Henry moved up beside his friend, shaking his head. "Morgan, Morgan. I told you to stay away from here. You're a wretched gambler, especially when you're foxed. Come along before you ruin us completely."

"Let the stupid bastard alone, ya squatty pissant," a gravelly voice called out to Henry.

Frowning, Morgan shouted back, "Who are you callin' squatty?"

Henry rolled his eyes.

"That pissant with the bones in his nose!"

Morgan stumbled to his feet, fists clenched as he shoved Henry aside to face the antagonist. "No one calls my friend squatty."

"Says who?"

"Says me, you mother—"

Someone grabbed him from behind, spun him around, and planted a fist across his jaw; Morgan tumbled backward, bouncing against a stack of crates and sliding toward the floor. Suddenly a high-pitched shriek resounded above the racket of whooping men. Henry, dressed only in a loincloth, leapt atop the boxes of cargo, Morgan's knife in his hand. As the stunned, drunken spectators gaped at him in surprise, he shouted something unintelligible and sliced the air with his weapon.

They gasped and stumbled backward.

Henry climbed down slowly from his perch, his features uncharacteristically menacing, the wavering light of the oil lamps making the anaconda tattoo on his bare chest appear to be gyrating. He grabbed Morgan by the shirt collar and dragged him to his knees.

"My good man," he said as quietly as possible, "I suggest that we remove ourselves from the premises before I am forced to revert to my more primitive self, whatever that might be. I really haven't an inkling any longer, so I wouldn't chance it. Just get the devil out of here before they realize I'm a lot of hot wind."

By the time they reached the deck, Morgan's jaw was throbbing and his stomach roiling. He leaned over the rail and vomited into the river. Then Henry gave him back his knife.

"What brought this on?" the pygmy asked.

Morgan shook his head; he wiped his mouth with his shirtsleeve and vomited again.

"You needn't tell me," Henry said. "You've been thinking about King again. You always get this way when you dwell on him. Best put him from your mind for now. There will be enough time to ruminate over the bastard once we reach Japurá."

Bent at the waist, his forehead resting against the railing, Morgan closed his eyes and prayed for the ship to stop pitching.

Henry placed a hand on his shoulder. "It's all right to be afraid, Morgan. You're only human."

"Since when did I become human? I thought I was the *boto* who dared to go where no man has gone before, and lived to tell about it. Myths aren't supposed to be human, Henry. They're supposed to be invincible." He heaved again toward the water.

A long silence ensued, punctuated by the throb of the engines. Finally Henry sighed and slapped him on the back. "Would you like me to help you to your hammock?"

He shook his head.

"Very well. Good night, Morgan."

"Good night."

Henry watched him for a moment longer, then turned and walked off into the dark.

Little by little the world steadied; at last Morgan could stand upright by gripping the rail with both hands and focusing on some invisible point over the black water. He didn't care to return to bed. That, after all, was what had led to this bout of gambling and inebriation. For hours he'd lain in his hammock, vacillating between thoughts of King and Sarah. He'd needed something—anything—to get his mind off them. He'd learned to deal with his thoughts of King, but those of Sarah were something else.

Disturbing feelings were awakening inside him, and he didn't like them. He'd first acknowledged them when he'd turned down several offers of sexual dalliance the night before in preference of a decent night's sleep. At least that was what he'd told himself until he found himself alone, with only the narrow corridor separating him from Sarah. He'd paced like a caged horny cat, fighting a conscience that he was shocked to discover he still had. A taunting voice in his mind had urged him to knock on her door, make up some excuse to see her, turn on the charm, seduce the hell out of her, and spend the remainder of the night working his magic on her. To hell with her virginity. She was gonna lose it sometime; why not save good old Norman the bother?

He'd come close. Damn close. So why hadn't he done it?

Taking a deep breath, Morgan reached for the whiskey bottle in his pocket and turned it up to his mouth. He didn't swallow, but swished the liquor around in his mouth, then spit it in the river. A few turns around the deck to sober himself up, and then he'd go below to his hammock. Perhaps by that time he'd be tired enough to fall asleep . . .

He rounded a corner and stopped. There stood Sarah in a puddle of light from an oil lamp, and she wasn't alone.

"Perhaps you would care to share a drink with me in my cabin?" the tall, swarthy man said to her.

"You're most kind," she replied, "but I think not. I've quite enjoyed our conversation, but I should return to my cabin now."

"Then you will allow me to accompany you?"

She shook her head and backed away as he stepped nearer.

"But I was under the impression that you found my company stimulating."

"The lady said no."

Sarah jumped at the sound of Morgan's voice. The man spun around to face him. Stepping from the shadows, Morgan grasped his shirt and shoved him away. Sarah gasped, and for a moment the stranger looked as if he might challenge Morgan's right to act as her protector. The heat pressed in on them, as did the night and the heavy smell of humus from the nearby riverbank.

Morgan wondered briefly if he was too drunk to stand his ground, then dismissed the idea. The rush of anger, and jealousy, that had gripped him when he'd seen her with another man had left him stone-cold sober.

At last the man straightened his clothing, spun on his heels, and departed. Only then did Morgan look at Sarah.

"What the hell were you doing out here with him?" he demanded.

Her face had turned as pale as the blouse she was wearing. Her eyes were round. "I—I only came up for a breath of fresh air," she told him. "I couldn't sleep."

"In case you haven't noticed, this isn't England, Sarah. A woman like you doesn't parade herself around a ship like this, in the dark, without an escort."

Her look of fright turned to irritation as she glared back at him. "It's not exactly as if I'm alone on this ship, Mr. Kane. Had I been forced to cry out—"

"It's after midnight, damn it."

"I am perfectly capable of taking care of myself!"

"Perhaps back in England among your hoity-toity friends, but not here. Not where any ne'er-do-well could be lurking in the dark just waitin' to get his hands on you."

"Don't be ridiculous." She spun away and started off down the deck. Morgan stared after her, struggling to control the emotions running riot in him. Jesus, she was beautiful, with her hair full of moonlight and her face flushed with anger. She was too damn innocent to realize the effect she had on men like him, who normally didn't take no for an answer.

He followed her. "Sarah."

"Good night, Mr. Kane."

"I'm not finished."

"I am."

He caught her arm and pulled her around so forcefully her hair spilled from its pins, tumbled down between them as he lifted her off her feet, turned, and pressed her to the wall before she could do little more than gasp.

Then he was kissing her, brutally, forcing her mouth open with his tongue until he could slide it between her wet, silken lips. She struggled, whimpering in her throat, doing her best to turn her face away, to no avail. He kept on kissing her even while his hand jerked up her blouse and plunged beneath it to search frantically for the nipples he knew would be taut and high, and they were—oh, Jesus, they were . . .

This is what happens when you dally in the dark with bastards like me, he thought as his tongue danced against hers and his hips moved upon hers, his knees thwarting her legs' feeble attempts to kick him away.

Just when she stopped fighting, he couldn't be certain, but suddenly he realized that her arms had fallen almost limply over his shoulders, her fingers weakly twining into his hair. Her mouth had become supple, malleable, molding to his lips' demands with a novice's eagerness to learn. He could feel her heart beating like a bird's beneath his own.

He slid his tongue down her neck and felt her skin quiver. She rolled her head from side to side, spilling her hair like golden moonbeams over her shoulders.

This had to stop. Of course it had to stop, he told himself. They could be discovered at any moment. He'd only meant to scare her. Show her what could happen if she found herself in the dark with a man with no scruples. He would teach her the consequences of trifling with bad boys who'd learned about sex on the dark and seedy side of New Orleans, and taken their first woman at the age of twelve, a whore who was especially talented in accommodating little boys.

He slid his hand down her thigh, his fingers inching up her skirt while he buried his face against her breast and smelled the scent of her skin through the thin material of her blouse. Just to taste her, to take that rosy, high-pointed tip in his mouth and savor the flavor of a woman who wasn't still stinking from the last man she'd slept with, or reeking with the alcohol that had given her the courage to search him out.

His fingers slid through the slit in her pantaloons and touched her flesh. She gasped and her eyelids flickered open; her eyes appeared glazed and dreamy; her lips were dark and swollen from his kiss. No doubt she would come to her senses now and slap him, remind him that he was only the hired help, white trash who had no right to touch a real lady in such a way.

"Wha-what are you doing?" she asked in a whisper.

"Touching you," he whispered back. "Don't you like it?"

She made a soft purring in her throat that made him grow bolder, working the magic on her body that he'd accomplished with so many others, only with them he had gone through the motions, a ritual as predictable as the sun coming up in the morning. Ah, but there was nothing remotely predictable about Sarah. For the first time in his life he was witnessing the true awakening of womanhood, the wonder of Sarah discovering the pleasures of her own body. This was naïveté in its purest sense; it was unfolding before him like the bursting open of a new flower beneath a spring sun. Oh, God, to share it with her, then perhaps . . .

Perhaps some of her goodness, her innocence, would rub off on him. Make him feel, just for a moment, like he was clean again.

He closed his eyes, then withdrew his hand, forced himself to look away, to stare up at the black sky and listen to the throb of the engines. As Sarah stirred beside him, his eyes were drawn back to hers, despite his resolve. Reluctantly, he smoothed her hair from her flushed face and straightened her clothes. She seemed benumbed, like one only half risen from sleep. He'd seen that look before, when desire became a force that obliterated the mind's better judgment. Soon she would come to her senses and hate him for what he'd done, then hate herself for allowing it. She was in love with another man, after all. No doubt she was fantasizing that it was Norman holding her . . . loving her . . .

He forced the thought from his mind with a shake of his head, turned away, and dug for a cigarette in his pocket while Sarah stood behind him, her eyes large and confused. He struck a match. "Go to bed," he told her. "And don't let me catch you out at night again without Henry or Kan."

Her soft mouth turned under.

"I could have raped you just then, right there on deck, and who the devil would have known? I could have snapped your beautiful neck and tossed you overboard to the piranhas, and no one would have been the wiser."

"Is that why you did this?" she demanded in a restrained but furious voice. "To teach me a lesson? To humiliate me? To prove that I'm no better at ignoring that idiotic myth about your being the *boto* than every other woman you meet? Which is it, Mr. Kane?"

"All of the above, *chere*," he lied.

She looked staggered, then she slapped him so hard the cigarette in his mouth was knocked into the river. Without another word she fled into the dark, leaving him standing in the shadows, alone.

Chapter Six

MORGAN CURSED THE HUMIDITY THAT PRESSED DOWN ON HIM LIKE a steamy blanket. The discomfort would get worse once they entered the forest. The air would turn so hot and thick and damp that breathing would be an effort. Then he reminded himself that breathing would be the least of their worries once they reached the heart of the Amazon. If the forest didn't kill them, the Indians would. If they were fortunate enough to survive the savages . . .

Sarah's laughter sounded over the mumble of conversation and the *chug chug* of the engines. As Morgan turned his back to the rail to watch her, he pulled his flask of whiskey from his pocket and uncorked it. She sat, just as she had for the past two days, at a linen-covered table on the bow of the ship shaded by a makeshift awning. Henry sat at her side, pouring tea, while Kan paced nearby like a guard dog on a tight leash. As if that wasn't enough, every man aboard the *Santos* was trailing about her skirts like a pack of hungry jackals.

When Henry glanced his way, Morgan lifted his flask in salute, then turned it up to his mouth. Henry excused himself from his companions and started toward him, carefully weaving his way among the brightly colored hammocks whose occupants resembled larvae in cocoons.

"You look like hell, old man," Henry said.

Morgan drank again.

"Won't you join us for tea?"

"You gotta be jokin'. Who drinks tea when it's hot enough to fry eggs in the shade?" He watched the ship's captain, Lloyd Chambers, take Henry's chair and exchange words with Sarah. The captain was a man of about forty, clean-shaven, with short red hair and sleepy eyes set in a pleasant chubby face that turned the color of claret each time he found himself in Sarah's company, which was becoming ever more frequent as their journey progressed—leaving Morgan to wonder who the blazes was steering the floating crate up the river.

He turned back to the rail, leaned his elbows on it, and gazed out at the shoreline dotted with small palm-thatched houses on stilts. Henry sidled up to him and, standing on his toes, peered out over the river. They watched in silence as families emerged from their hovels and waved in response to the boat whistle blaring across the water.

Finally Henry said, "You've certainly made yourself scarce since we set off from Belém."

"So have you." Morgan took a long drink of his whiskey, then recorked the bottle and slid it into his pocket. He fished for a cigarette in another, then dug for a match. He looked over Henry's head at Sarah. The hot sun radiated off the deck in shimmering waves, yet beneath the awning the girl looked as cool as an orchid kissed by dew. Her voice was lilting as she laughed and spoke with the captain and a few of his crew, who gaped at her beautiful face like love-addled pups. She didn't even have the decency to look uncomfortable in the ungodly heat. Aside from that day in Little China, he'd never seen her sweat, never heard her complain.

"She's quite extraordinary," came Henry's voice.

"Yeah," he replied, more to himself than to Henry.

He forced himself to turn away, to get the image of her passion-drowsy eyes out of his mind. The memory of her smell, her taste, the exquisite feel of her tight, wet flesh quivering in response to his touch had driven him mad the past days and nights. For his own good, and hers, he'd kept as much distance between them as possible.

He watched the shoreline slide by, a wide stretch of iridescent sand crowned by towering green trees. Finally Henry gazed again at Sarah and said, "Sometimes I wish I were white and taller, Morgan. What do you wish?"

He drew on his cigarette and considered the question for a long while before responding, then grinned. "That I was short and brown and had bones in my nose."

Henry chuckled and looked pleased.

SARAH COLLAPSED INTO THE CHAIR IN HER CABIN AND BURIED HER face in her hands. Tears stung her eyes. Exhaustion and heat made her nauseous. Three days into her journey down the Amazon and she wanted to go home. Not just to Georgetown, but to London. She yearned to throw herself on Norman's mercy and forget Japurá and rubber seeds and a murderer called King. Pretending indifference to the heat and insects was becoming increasingly difficult. One could sip tea and make pleasant conversation and be charming for only so long without sweating or swooning or wanting to scream.

Standing, she struggled to pull the bodice of her dress up over her shoulders. It clung to her skin and snagged on her chemise. She had swept her hair up off her neck in a braid, but the tendrils curling around her temples and nape were now plastered to her flesh as straight as hat pins. Fastening the buttons up her back was impossible. Her shoulders and fingers were aching from the effort.

She wanted to curse, and the heat, mosquitoes, and monotony of the damnable voyage had little to do with it.

Burying her face in her hands, she tried desperately to rid her mind of Morgan Kane. One moment she was appalled by what had happened between them two nights ago, and the next she was reliving each startling, tantalizing touch in glorious detail. Even now the mere thought of his kissing her, holding her, did shocking things to her body, things she'd never experienced before. Her breasts ached. Her heart raced. She burned, not just at skin level, but deep inside in that place he'd stroked so tenderly between her legs, turning it as hot and thick as sun-melted honey. Even now it was taking hold of her again . . .

A rap on the door brought an exhalation of relief from her. She flung it open, Kan's name dying in her throat as she stared up at the American's face. "Oh," she said, a catch in her voice. "I thought you were Kan."

His eyes moved from her face to her shoulder where her dress drooped like a flag in dead air.

"I was having trouble with my dress," she pressed on, feeling a telltale blush stain her cheeks crimson. "I had hoped Kan could help me."

"Kan was detained and asked if I would see you to supper."

Silence fell as Kane remained in the companionway, his hands in his pockets, the murky lamplight shadowing the hollows in his cheeks and deepening the color of his eyes. At last he said, "Perhaps I can be of assistance."

In normal circumstances Sarah would have refused his help; no decent woman would allow such familiarity, especially with a man of Kane's reputation—*especially* in light of what had happened between them two nights ago. They hadn't even spoken to each other since she'd slapped him and considering the way she'd been feeling only moments before, to allow him in the same room with her would be folly . . .

She stepped back and opened the door, her eyes lowered as she waited for him to enter. As always, the familiar thrill that came with his presence returned. He stepped inside, and with her back to him, Sarah smiled as the delicious intoxication of desire swept through her. It made her tingle. It made her breathless. It made her feel . . . *alive.*

She closed the door and faced him. His eyes were wary. She swept up her braid with one hand, slowly turned, and offered Kane her back, allowing her head to fall slightly forward. A moment passed before he touched her, hesitantly at first, his fingers fumbling with her dress as he closed it. His warm male scent, tinged with a faint hint of whiskey, made her senses reel. If he took her in his arms this very moment, what would she do? How would she react?

"Done," came his voice.

Sarah dropped her hair and turned to face him, her head falling back as she searched his closed face for his thoughts. Dear Lord, what was happening to her sense of decency when all she could think of was how wonderful it would be if he kissed her again?

Please, she thought. *Please kiss me again.*

He gazed for a long moment into her eyes; his lashes lowered a little as he studied her lips, his own curving up at one end. Then he walked to the door. "I'll see you to supper. I believe you're dining with the captain tonight . . . aren't you, love?"

The steamer rocked and the throb of the engines seemed to hesitate. She grabbed the hammock as it swayed, never once taking her eyes from his. She felt furious and chagrined and disappointed all at once. He hadn't lied when he'd told her that his reasons for holding her, kissing her, touching her were simply to frighten her, to teach her not to tarry in the dark with scoundrels. He didn't want her, and she felt let down. Why? Dear God, what sort of woman was she becoming?

MORGAN WATCHED SARAH THROUGHOUT DINNER FROM HIS TABLE near the door. He had pushed his plate away, concentrating instead on the bottle of warm wine that left a sour taste in his mouth and made him sleepy. Henry sat across from him, ruminating about Santarém as he last remembered it, when it was mostly under floodwater. Morgan wasn't daft or drunk enough not to realize what his friend was doing. Henry was trying his best to change Morgan's mind about dumping Sarah, but it wouldn't work. The sooner they got rid of her the better—for both their sakes. She was occupying too much of his thoughts. He should be preparing himself for the confrontation with King. So far he hadn't given that a great deal of attention, didn't want to, really, because to do so he would have to face the sobering reality that his days on this earth were probably numbered. And while once, when he lay sweating and racked with nightmares and self-loathing in that rat-infested hovel on Tobacco Row, he might have thought that he didn't give a damn about dying, now he found himself looking forward to each day, actually envisioning what life might be like were he to settle down and marry. What *if* he made it out of Japurá alive? What *if* he could steal enough gold to make him a presentable marriage possibility to . . . someone?

Who the hell was he kidding? He didn't know the first thing about being a husband. Or a father. Nonetheless, in his fantasies he had a home, children, and a woman who loved him despite his past . . .

Gradually, the *Santos*'s passengers departed the dining room, leaving Sarah and the captain, and Morgan and Henry. The hour had grown late, and although Morgan could sense that Sarah's usual bravado was waning, the captain had not. Finally, with a sigh Henry rose from his chair and said, "I'll leave you the pleasant task of seeing the lady back to her cabin, if the good captain ever sees fit to give her up." He took one last look at Sarah before quitting the room. Then Morgan settled back to wait.

He smoked. He poured another glass of wine and sank deeper in his chair. He closed his eyes, hearing Sarah's soft voice rise and fall but unable to understand the words. Now and again the portly captain's laughter boomed out, and Morgan opened his eyes to find Sarah poised within the candle's halo, her chin delicately balanced upon the palm of one hand as she appeared fascinated by her host's conversation. Yet . . .

Sometimes her gaze shifted toward his, and though the captain droned on and on, she continued to regard Morgan from behind her gold-tipped lashes. Perhaps he should have taken her in his arms while in her cabin and kissed her; she was miffed because he hadn't, he could tell. So why hadn't he? He wanted her. He wanted her like hell. But he'd seen that look of desire on women's faces a thousand times, and he knew it was the fantasy they wanted, not the man. They didn't give a damn about Morgan Kane. They only ached for the legend he represented.

Damn, cursed *boto.*

Sarah St. James wasn't immune to his magic any more than other women. He must remember that. It was the allure of the forbidden that had enticed her to spread her legs for him two nights ago; it wasn't because she cared for him even remotely. She was engaged to another man, after all. If he allowed himself to believe that something other than lust made her eyes turn smoky when she looked at him . . .

He finished his wine and reached into his pocket for his whiskey and a smoke. At that instant the ship came to an abrupt and unexpected stop. The jolt sent the captain's chair hurling backward, end over end, so that he lay stunned and motionless on the floor for several seconds. Sarah was spilled facedown over the table, her skirt draped in waves of golden fawn organdy and silk across the linen tablecloth. Morgan, having been thrown against the wall, responded with the litheness of one who is accustomed to surprises. By the time the engines had shuddered and quit completely, he was back on his feet and running for Sarah.

She had no more than raised her head when the American's arm closed around her, lifting her up as if she were weightless. She came to her senses when she saw the blade of his knife flash in his hand, and for an endless agonizing instant she actually believed he was about to cut her throat.

Then all hell broke loose on the deck above them.

The pilot of the boat appeared at the door. He had a dark, oval face, beaked nose, and straight black hair. He was built like a barrel, an image accentuated by the broad red-and-white-striped sailor's shirt he wore. *"Capitaine!"* he cried. "Come quickly, *Capitaine.* We have run aground!"

The outcry of the passengers could be heard above. While Kane set Sarah on her feet, the captain struggled to stand, then ran for the door. Morgan was hot on the officer's heels, gripping Sarah's hand and forcing her to follow at such a speed she tripped repeatedly on her skirts and might have fallen had he not caught her.

Pandemonium besieged the dark deck as the terrified passengers, having been tumbled from their hammocks by the impact, stumbled over one another in an attempt to escape whatever evil, real or imaginary, had struck the vessel. Sarah gripped Morgan's arm in an effort to keep from being swept up in the flood of bodies pushing and shoving their way to the stern of the ship. Occasionally the captain's and pilot's voices could be heard crying out for calm, to no avail. The panic only intensified as a wild, earsplitting shriek rose from the melee. The horrible sound froze Sarah in fear. Then Morgan moved against her, shielding her body with his as the first rush swept over them.

They came from everywhere at once, the small manlike shapes and shadows, pouring over the ship's railings from the tangle of debris scattered over the bow. A great howl of terror rang out as the monkeys skittered over the awnings and leapt onto the heads and shoulders of the cowering humans. The dim lamplight contorted the animals' faces into heathenish masks with sharp pointed teeth and wide eyes that danced with fiery light. Somehow Sarah managed not to scream as an Indian boy stumbled into her, shoulders stooped as he fought furiously to drag the clawing animal from his back before it could bite his neck again. She saw Morgan reach out in one swift motion, grab the creature off the boy, sink the blade of his knife into the flailing monkey's throat, and toss it to the deck.

When the snakes began dropping from the branches, the chaos crescended. Suddenly the floor was writhing with them, the light and shadows elongating their sleek black bodies as they slithered in every direction. In that moment Sarah's mind seemed to collapse in total confusion and fear. Her only thought was to escape, yet there was no place to go. Between her and the stairs leading belowdeck were a hundred hysterical humans with the same thought. The only alternative was to jump overboard, which was out of the question. As calmly as possible, she looked to Morgan.

He had partially turned toward her, yet his gaze was locked upon some distant horizon that was invisible beyond the wall of steam rising from the river. He looked pale as he rolled the grip of his knife in his palm. Then he glanced over the deck and, without speaking, bent at the waist and tossed her over his shoulder.

The breath left her in a rush as the world tipped upside down. She clutched at his shirt as he leapt upon a stack of crates; the precarious perch swayed like a pile of top-heavy dominoes, making Sarah scream and squirm and beat his back and yell, "Put me down, I can do it myself!" to which he responded by flinging back her skirt and swatting her pantalooned derriere. Then, much to her horror, he was jumping for the ornate gingerbread affixed to the pilothouse overhead, swinging his body as lithely as an acrobat in an attempt to catch his boot upon the jutting configuration of cutout swirls and ornamental designs. She might have screamed again. She couldn't be certain. Her head was pounding too loudly and painfully, the blood rushing through her ears.

He heaved them up and through the glassless windows of the pilothouse wall where they spilled over the floor in a cloud of skirts and petticoats.

A half-dozen monkeys scattered, screeching and chattering, to all four corners of the room, scampering out the windows and through the open doorway. Just as Sarah started to rise, Kane's breathless voice said softly, "Don't move, love. Not an inch."

She froze. A sudden, painful ache of terror washed over her as, from the corner of her eye, she saw the *jararaca* lift its coiled black body from the floor and stare at her with eyes that were ebony pits. Its mouth was a barely discernible ridge where a forked tongue slid in and out with a hiss.

So stealthily did Morgan move from her side that she didn't notice.

Her eyes were locked on the snake, which, should it decide to lunge, would hit her directly on the face.

The arrow-shaped head wavered back and forth, then stilled.

Dear God.

It was going to strike!

Chapter Seven

A BRIGHT LIGHT BEAT AGAINST HER CLOSED EYELIDS, AND THE FOG
of confusion peeled away from her mind like mists burned off by a hot
sun. She had been dreaming of murky shadows and swirling waters from
which a dolphin, and then a man, had emerged. White-suited and breath-
takingly handsome, he had walked over the water until stopping an arm's
length from her. *"Chere,"* he had whispered before he gradually disappeared.

She lay very still, refusing to move, wondering if she were dead or
alive. But for the throbbing pain in her face she felt numb, removed from
her body and reality by a gray nothingness.

She tried opening her eyes and focused on the familiar ceiling of her
cabin. Faint and few at first, the murmurings of voices came to her from
beyond the door. A movement caught her eye and the American came
into view. He walked to her bedside. Dressed in a soft-textured shirt open
at the throat, he looked very tall and young. His unshaven face appeared
haggard and tired. She did not break down and weep, though the realization that she was alive came with a storm of relief. Instead, she began to
pant and shiver as the memory of the serpent reaching out for her with
bared fangs tumbled through her mind.

She grasped the front of the American's shirt in her trembling fingers,
and with as much bravado as she could manage, said, "Am I dying, Mr.
Kane? I am. Dear God, I am! I can see it in your eyes. That vile reptile
has snuffed out my life. Take up a pen and paper, sir, so that I can bid my
fiancé good-bye. Quickly! Use the diary, if you must. Tell him that—that
he is sweet and kind and much too good for me. Tell him that I insist he
find someone else to marry as soon as possible so he can get on with his

life. Tell him that I cared for him very much and—oh, Mr. Kane, I feel weak. I must surely be going now. My head is spinning . . ."

She closed her eyes and allowed her hand to fall to her side. She waited for death to take her, yet the only change in her body was a slight escalation of her heartbeat as she imagined herself expiring in the American's arms.

Yet he did not take her in his arms.

And she didn't die.

Gradually, she opened her eyes again and found Morgan peeling a papaya with his knife. He cut a long pink sliver of the juicy meat and, raising it on the blade of the weapon, slid it into his mouth.

"What are you doing?" she asked.

"Eating."

"While I'm dying?"

"You're not dying." He laughed softly and the sound made Sarah's throat constrict.

"Are you certain?" she asked.

"Positive."

"But the snake—"

"Didn't bite you."

"Oh." She carefully touched her throbbing cheek with unsteady fingers. "But—"

"I kicked you."

"You—"

"I kicked you," he repeated. His gray eyes were brimming with humor as he grinned and shrugged. "Sorry, but it was the only way to get you out of the snake's range. It bit my boot instead."

She should thank him, she supposed. He'd saved her life, after all. But the feeling that gripped her in that moment was not gratitude, but fury. She shook with it. With each throb of pain ricocheting through her temple the anger mounted. Once again they had come very close to dying. His blasé attitude was infuriating.

Morgan sliced the fruit again and, bringing the knife to Sarah's lips, offered her a taste of the succulent meat. She refused it, turning her face away so the juice that dripped from the blade ran down her cheek to her chin. He caught it with his thumb, but instead of wiping it away, his finger hesitated, brushing the aching, swollen skin of her cheek with a motion so gentle that Sarah blinked in surprise. He had never struck her as a tender man. Yet there was something so stirringly kind in his touch, in his eyes that looked a little like rain clouds with silver linings, that she sensed he was apologizing for her pain in the only way he knew.

Just then the door was flung open. Henry entered, allowing the sickly-sweet stink of stale blood to fill the room. At the same instant Sarah noted the skinned carcasses of monkeys hanging side by side up and down the hallway. Nausea reeled through her, and she dropped back on the bed. "Dear God," she whispered. "What next?"

Morgan moved away and assumed an indolent stance near the port-hole. The humor that had crinkled the outer corners of his eyes just moments before was now replaced by his usual hard and brooding mien as he continued to peel and eat the fruit with no apparent regret for having caused her such misery.

Henry stood only inches taller than Sarah's hammock, so he could easily look into her eyes. He took her hand and wrapped his short fingers around it. "My dear, you have no idea how worried we've been. Haven't we, Morgan?"

His shoulders rose and fell in a gesture of unconcern as he peered out the porthole. "I suppose," he answered, and her irritation mounted.

Henry squeezed her hand. "Of course we were. By gosh, Morgan hasn't left your side in the last twelve hours. He feels just terrible over this ordeal. Don't you, Morgan?"

He ignored the query.

Sinking in the hammock, Sarah allowed herself to relax. A smile tipped up the corners of her mouth as she looked at Henry. "What happened? The pilot said we'd run aground. Did we hit an island or something?"

"The island hit us," he replied. At her look of confusion he explained. "The river is always changing, its current felling trees and shifting great portions of earth. The fallen trees are swept downriver. Gradually, more and more collect and eventually are so massed together they make a sort of floating island. The creatures that were trapped on the trees when they fell are therefore captive on the island until it runs aground at some point. Certainly the trees offer sanctuary to any water snakes along the way. We were highly unfortunate to have run upon the island at night, but such an accident is only a small example of the dangers awaiting us on the Amazon. Are you quite certain you wish to continue this journey, Sarah? Morgan and I are capable of carrying out this purpose on our own."

"I wouldn't dream of asking you," she stressed, though her gaze had shifted to Morgan, who continued to ignore her and eat his fruit. "I take it that the ship is sound enough to get us to our destination?"

"Certainly," Henry answered. "We've been under way for hours now. The threat of danger is over for the time being. However—" He cleared his throat. "There is a problem with snakes. We've done our best to flush them out, but that's no guarantee that we won't find a few coiled up among the cargo now and again. I urge extreme caution, my dear. Shake out your garments before putting them on. And take care when you move around the deck. Were one to slither into your skirts, we would be hard pressed to locate it before some damage was done. You might consider wearing the breeches you bought in Belém. At least—"

"I'll wear the clothing once we begin our journey through the floresta," she interrupted wearily. "When it's absolutely necessary."

She did not miss the look Henry shot the American. Had her head not been pounding so brutally, she might have queried them both further. As it was, she was forced to lie back and close her eyes until the world ceased spinning. She must have dozed, for when she opened them again she was alone.

THEY ARRIVED IN SANTARÉM ON THE MORNING OF THE FIFTH DAY OF their journey up the Amazon. Sarah smelled the village before she saw it. She awoke to the odor of fish so heavy in the air she could hardly breathe. Oddly enough, it seemed a pleasant change from the stench of rotting monkey carcasses the passengers and crew had hung from every available corner of the steamer. What animals had not been stewed, fried, or baked for food would be sold for pennies in the market as soon as they docked.

Henry and the American made short work of rounding up Kan and the few Indians they had hired to join them on their journey. Within a half hour they had all disembarked and stood on the banks, somewhat befuddled by the concentration of people and activities around them.

Since Santarém was as far as the *Santos* traveled, Morgan ordered them all to stay put, then disappeared into the crowd of natives to arrange for passage to Manáos, another two hundred miles upriver. An hour passed, then another as Sarah and her entourage waited impatiently for his return. The sun climbed higher and the air became hazy with steam, the sky washed by a dingy yellow light.

Henry came and went, fetching a great flat palm branch which he held over her head in place of a parasol. Soon she was forced to remove her hat and use it to fan away the insects buzzing about them. As always, Kan stood close by, his usual silent, cautious self. Yet there was a change. Gone was the starched servant's uniform he'd worn while in her father's employ. His straight black hair, once tied or braided at the nape, was allowed to spill over his shoulders. Unlike Henry, who continued to wear only a loincloth, Kan wore a pair of khaki breeches and no shirt. Several strands of bright beads and one of piranha teeth hung from his neck, and his earrings tinkled like chimes as he paced.

Eventually Morgan returned. Sarah saw him walking up the footpath running next to the docks. Towering a head taller than the dark-skinned natives of the village, he wore his sweat-stained hat pulled low over his eyes. His shirt was moist too, and stuck to his chest and back and armpits in damp splotches. The ever-present cigarette hung from his sensual lips. His strides were long, graceful, and confident. Despite her aggravation over being left to swelter in the ungodly heat for hours, she felt a jump in her heartbeat at the sight of him. Then she notice he wasn't alone. A white man followed him.

Sarah forgot her irritation with him when she discovered his companion was English. His name was Sir Henry Wickham, and he recognized Sarah's name immediately.

SIR HENRY WICKHAM HAD BUILT HIS HOME ALONGSIDE THE RUINS OF a Jesuit seminary near Santarém. Its deteriorating walls were barely visible behind the gargantuan creepers that had grown over and around the building since the priests had deserted it more than a hundred years ago.

Late that afternoon, as Sarah sat near a window of Wickham's adobe dwelling enjoying the breeze and a cup of *cafezinho*— strong black coffee sweetened with cane sugar—she did her best to keep down her panic. Upon finding her in this Amazonia hellhole, as he termed it, and learning of her father's tragic death, Wickham had immediately suspected her reasons for being there. She had been stunned to learn that Wickham had been involved in her father's scheme, and worried that he'd join the American in warning her not to venture to Japurá herself.

"My dear," said the Englishman, "men have attempted to smuggle seeds from Japurá before. In fact, it was I who convinced your father's friend, Sir Clements Markham, of the necessity of cultivating rubber in the east. In '73 a gentleman managed to make his way out of Brazil with some two thousand seedlings. There have been another couple of tries, one being your father's. As you well know, it was a disaster."

"But surely you can understand my reasons for trying," she argued. "I'm ruined if I cannot repay those investors. Besides, I'll be safe enough. Mr. Kane not only worked for Rodolfo King, he also escaped from Japurá overland. I couldn't be in better hands."

Wickham appeared shocked. "Indeed," he said to Morgan. "Is this true?"

Slouched in a chair, one leg hooked over the other by an ankle, he looked up at the Englishman from beneath his hat and said, "Yeah."

"Good heavens, man! However did you manage it? King is a madman."

Morgan's gaze shifted to Henry, who was enjoying a cup of oolong tea. Finally he said, "Lucky, I guess."

"Lucky? I would say that is an understatement. Tales of King's barbarism are always filtering down the Amazon. Why, not long ago rumor had it that he annihilated an entire village because one of its inhabitants had infected his *matteiro* with venereal disease. You cannot think to subject this young lady to a monster like that. And this nonsense of your escaping through the forest—"

"But it's true," Sarah cut in. She paced the floor, refusing to look at Wickham or Morgan, or even Henry, unwilling to acknowledge—even to herself—the nagging fears that plagued her about this journey, and the American's effect on her sensibilities. "Mr. Kane is well known in Georgetown for his heroism. The Indians revere him as a god. Why, my own servants believe him capable of anything. Besides . . ." She faced her host and steadied her voice. "What recourse do I have, sir? This mission must be accomplished. My father's reputation—"

"Your father is dead, my dear."

"But I am not, Sir Henry! I'll be forced to live the rest of my life in shame and destitution if this matter is not put to a satisfactory end."

"But even if you thought you could survive a confrontation with King, a young lady such as yourself could never come through such a hellish expedition unscathed. My dear, has Mr. Kane and his friend described in detail just what sort of nightmarish dangers await you in the forest?"

Morgan, who had withdrawn a cigarette from his jacket, proceeded to light it with a sulfur match, his eyes still fixed on her face as the flame danced in the cup of his upraised palm. It seemed a hundred images flashed before her mind's eye in that moment, pictures of a white-suited lover luring her with a kiss, a mad race through the eerie underworld of Little China, coiled black snakes with fangs full of venom. Without thinking, she touched her cheek where it was still sore from the American's kick, then her side that still ached from when she'd been thrown over his shoulder like a sack as he vaulted to the steamer's pilothouse. It was becoming so easy to believe the heroic stories . . . because she wanted to? Or simply because she must?

Forcing herself to turn away from his arousing, hypnotic gaze, she said, "I may be a lady, sir, but I'm stronger than I look, and I'm well aware of the dangers. Of course I'll take every care to assure my safety. Even now I take quinine to ward off the fever."

"Fever?" He looked amused. "My dear, fever will be the least of your worries. Quinine cannot save you from the floresta itself. It is a teeming organism whose sole objective is to destroy any man who trespasses within its boundaries. Look about you." He walked to the open window and pointed to the seminary. "See how it has swallowed up all trace of earlier habitation."

"I shan't stay in one place long enough to be swallowed up," Sarah replied with a laugh that was not echoed by Wickham, Morgan, or Henry, who was pouring himself a second cup of tea and lacing it with brandy their host had supplied. Morgan, on the other hand, was drinking the liquor straight and still watching her with that unwavering intensity that made the fine hairs on her nape stand on end. Those eyes appeared to laugh at her, then undress her, and finally drive through her like ice picks.

Wickham perched on the windowsill and regarded her without blinking. "I have seen the flesh eaten from a man within minutes by ants the size of my thumb. There are spiders here large enough to capture birds for food. The bite from a fer-de-lance can kill in a matter of minutes." He held up one hand that was missing a finger. "I was fishing and speared a piranha. I thought it was dead. But when I reached for it, the damned fish sliced off my finger with a single snap. Can you imagine what an entire school of the creatures could do?"

"I'm well aware of all that," she said, all the more determined as she stared at his hand, repressing a shudder of revulsion. "While living in Georgetown I read William Edwards's *Voyage up the River Amazon,* as well as Humboldt's *Personal Narrative.* I've also read the account of Madame Isabella Godin, who was the last remaining survivor of an expedition that set out to locate her husband, who had disappeared in the Amazon. After weeks of wandering naked, starving, and ill through the forest, she was saved by a Jesuit priest and eventually reunited with her husband. If she, a lady of middle age, could survive the Amazon, then, sir, so can I."

"And she suffered for it the rest of her life, I can almost assure you," Wickham replied. "Besides, this effort to propagate rubber outside Brazil is futile. Of the two thousand or so seeds that were smuggled out years ago, only a dozen or so germinated. One can hardly monopolize the industry with so few trees. Aside from that, I have to wonder if the damnable trees are subject to cultivation. While living here I have done my best to propagate the *Hevea—*"

"You don't say." It was Henry, speaking up at last.

"Yes," Wickham replied. "Experimentally I have planted seedlings on the Tapajós plateau not far from here. Most have died, I confess. Not long ago I heard a passing *serinquero* say, 'If God had intended rubber trees to grow in rows, He would have made them like that.' By Jove, but I have almost come to believe it."

The American left his chair and, taking up the bottle of brandy, walked out the door into the sunbaked garden. Within moments he was surrounded by a dozen naked, brown-skinned children offering him carvings and baskets for any treasure he had on his person.

"Odd chap," the Englishman said; then, noting the frown of concern and fatigue on Sarah's face, he stood. "You should rest. I'm certain conditions on the steamer were far from comfortable."

The thought of sleeping in a real bed lit Sarah's face with a swift and appreciative smile. Excusing herself from Henry and glancing one last time out the window, she followed her host from the room.

She did not sleep immediately. She was too hot and restless and fearful that Wickham would convince her companions to return her to Belém. She stripped off her clothes, leaving on only her chemise and drawers, and paced the sparsely furnished chamber before settling in a chair by the open window and turning her face into the warm but pleasant breeze. Swatches of light and shadow sliced through the shifting foliage and the air hummed with the constant drone of whirring insects and calling birds. Propping her elbow on the windowsill, she cupped her chin in her palm and watched a dozen or so children kick a coconut in the dust, their squeals of laughter seeming oddly relaxing. Soon she found herself chuckling too, imagining joining them, as she might have years ago, before womanhood had robbed her of the right to such freedom that only the young were allowed. Somehow it didn't seem fair, such fun. Someday they, too, would grow up and find themselves encumbered with the tedious responsibilities of adult life. The sobering idea made her sigh, and leaning her head upon the window frame, she closed her eyes, allowing their musical laughter to send her almost, but not quite, to sleep.

Then the breeze died, and the air became warm and stagnant. The children's laughter dwindled as they hurried away, and all that was left was the rustling voice of the living forest.

Forcing open her heavy-lidded eyes, Sarah drowsily raised her head and discovered Morgan leaning against a nearby kapok tree. His shirt was open to the waist, his hair falling over his forehead in a rich black wave that stirred with some wisp of air. Spellbound, she could not move; the ability to breathe normally seemed to have left her. Like that night in Belém, she was aware that he could easily see her state of partial undress from where he stood, and was just as cognizant that she didn't care, though she should—oh, she definitely should. Such behavior would be deemed scandalous back in England. But this was Brazil, six thousand miles away from the strict moral code of London society.

And it was hot, so very hot. Perspiration coated her face and throat and shoulders, making the fine cotton of her chemise cling damply to her breasts, which felt sensitive and full. She was filled with the shocking urge to release her hair and shake her head so the gold waves spilled over her breasts and around her face. But somehow she sensed that the act would cause her more restiveness than it would Morgan. He was used to loose women throwing themselves at his feet, but no decent woman would allow herself to remain in the same room with him for more than five minutes—not if she valued her innocence. Yet she had allowed him to kiss her, to touch her . . .

Here she was, and there he was, and while she had begun to tremble with the memory of their passionate meeting on the *Santos,* he had not so much as blinked. What was he thinking? That she would fail miserably at this mission, no doubt. She really shouldn't care what Morgan Kane thought of her or her body. But she did. God help her, she did. Suddenly she wanted to prove to him that she wasn't just a pretty face with flighty ideas. She wanted to show him that she could be strong. Then perhaps he would come to respect her and . . . what?

Why should it matter whether or not he cared for her?

She lowered her lashes to cover her eyes, wondering how the air had so suddenly managed to turn to steam. Her skin burned unbearably. Even the trickle of perspiration down the back of her neck felt annoyingly uncomfortable.

At last, when she was able to control her confused senses, she lifted her gaze to the kapok tree with the intent of putting Morgan in his place, of showing him that his presence meant no more to her than the irritating hum of a persistent insect; that no woman of her quality could be the least bit moved by his subtly arousing gaze or the sensual promise of his experienced mouth—a mouth that had given her not one moment's peace since it had kissed her that night on her father's veranda.

But he was gone.

THE RIVER WAS NARROWING. FROM WHERE MORGAN SAT ON THE end of the pier he could just make out the image of trees on the distant shore. Awash in sunset, the lofty branches appeared ablaze against the violet sky. The cooling air hummed with sounds, each noise magnified by the falling shroud of night. At dusk the jungle was a symphony of distant hisses, crackles, peals, and whistles. If he listened closely he could recognize the breaking of tree limbs or the rustle of branches as a rare breeze sighed through them. And like the forest, which never really slept, the water kept flowing, as smoothly as liquid glass on the surface, but always dark and deep, as mysterious as any ocean and twice as dangerous. As Morgan gazed out over the seemingly tranquil surface, the water would suddenly boil in places, disturbed by schools of fish, snakes, or perhaps the monstrous piraiba, the three-hundred-pound Amazon catfish that scoured the shallow waters just offshore in search of food—which, if one could believe rumors, included small children who happened to be swimming or bathing too far from their parents. When the river churned just below his feet, Morgan shivered and drew back onto the pier. Only then did he realize that Wickham had joined him.

"Pleasant evening," the Englishman said.

Morgan continued to smoke and said nothing.

"We missed your company at dinner."

Silence.

"Very well," Wickham said. "I take it you're not a chap for small talk. Then I shall get to the point. I cannot believe you would undertake such a futile task as venturing overland into Japurá, Mr. Kane, especially with a woman—a lady—such as Sarah St. James. Why, the trip on the *Santos* has brought her to exhaustion's door. Oh, yes, yes, I realize she tries to hide her fatigue, but it is most obvious if you only take a moment to notice. She will die out there and you know it. You all will. I beg you: reconsider this madness before it's too late."

Morgan studied the glowing tip of his cigarette, wondering why he didn't assuage the man's concern with the truth. For the last hour he'd sat on the pier staring out at the devil's paradise—hell's green door—thinking the same thought. Before arriving in Santarém he'd had every intention of dumping Sarah, if not here, then in Manáos. But Henry was right. Manáos was far too remote; few whites ventured as far as that isolated village. Except for the rubber growers, who were mostly of Portuguese descent, the Indians rarely met outsiders. No telling how long she would be forced to live among the natives until she found her way back down the Amazon. On the other hand, it seemed fate had played right into their hands. Here in Santarém was an Englishman who would see to her welfare were he and Henry to disappear into the night.

Wickham came to the edge of the pier and squatted beside him, resting on his heels as he gazed out over the river. Without looking at Morgan, he said, "Henry and I have come up with an alternative plan. Are you willing to listen?" At Morgan's brief nod, he continued. "Leave the girl here. I'll see to her comfort, you can be sure. You, on the other hand, continue on your quest. I will supply you with men who are capable of dealing with the dangers of the floresta, and I'll arrange for enough small boats to see you to your destination. You'll need supplies—food, medication . . . guns. What you've brought won't last you a week in that hell. If you had truly survived an escape overland through Japurá, you would know that." Looking at Morgan directly, he added, "Personally, I think the story is a lot of poppycock. The last reported expedition that ventured into Japurá was never heard from again. They were a lot of botanists on some hunt for orchids or some such rot. But that is beside the point. Quite obviously you have succeeded in convincing Sarah and those Indians that you are capable of such a feat. I'm not certain she truly believes you, but she is desperate enough to try anything, I think."

Morgan exhaled smoke through his lips before saying, "And just what do you get out of this—I mean besides Sarah, should we decide to leave her here?"

"I assure you, my intentions toward the young woman are strictly honorable, Mr. Kane. I care only for her welfare. You see, I don't think for a moment that you will survive this journey. In fact, I don't quite believe your reasons for making it. She has told me how much—or how little—she paid you to bring her here. A few hundred pounds seems far too slight a reward for such an arduous task. Therefore, I suspect you have some ulterior motive for wishing to breach King's compound. I won't press you for the details. It's really none of my business as long as it's your own neck, and not Sarah's, that you are sacrificing. As for what I get out of it . . ." He shrugged. "It is only what I've wished to achieve by remaining here. I want to collect enough of the *Hevea* and smuggle them out of the country so the world rubber market is no longer under the domination of men like King."

"That won't happen overnight," Morgan replied.

"Quite right. Once the seeds are planted, it will take some twenty or thirty years before the trees are mature enough to produce enough sap to be profitable. By then the Amazon as we know it will no longer exist. Peaceful villages like Santarém, Manáos, and Coari will be awash with a decadence that we are unlikely to see anywhere else in the world. And all will be controlled by people like King. They will rape this country for all it is worth. America's barbaric slavery of the Negroes will dim in comparison to what the *patraos* will do to the natives of Amazonia. I tell you, it will be a bloodbath."

Standing, Wickham arched his back to alleviate the strain of stooping for so long. Morgan remained sitting, his legs outstretched upon the weathered dock and crossed at his booted ankles. His cigarette had burned low. Its smoke filled his nostrils and made his head swim. Or perhaps the sensation had been brought on by too much whiskey and sun. Or simply because he knew the time had come to walk away from Sarah St. James and never look back.

Removing his hat, he wiped his brow with the sleeve of his shirt and looked up at the Englishman. "What do you want?"

"Make certain Miss St. James gets her rubber seeds. A hundred thousand at least. After I've seen to Miss St. James I'll await you in Coari, since chances are better there of hiring a freighter large enough to accommodate our load. I'll do what I can on this end to make arrangements for passage down the Amazon, through customs, all the way to England. Do we have a deal, Mr. Kane?"

Morgan replaced the hat on his head, cocked it at an angle over his right eye, then tossed the smoldering cigarette butt into the water. He regarded Wickham's extended hand for a long moment before shaking it. "Yeah," he said. "We have a deal."

WICKHAM WAS TRUE TO HIS WORD. WHILE MORGAN RELAXED IN Santarém and Henry accompanied Sarah on excursions to catch butterflies, the Englishman arranged for their journey to Japurá. By day three all was ready: men, boats, supplies, guns, and ammunition. There were enough Winchester Model '66 rifles, capable of firing fifteen rounds before reloading, to outfit a small army. Then Morgan realized that they *would* be waging a war . . . against nature, and the devil. He wondered which would prove the deadliest foe.

They were to set out an hour before dawn—without Sarah. By the time she awoke to discover them gone, they would be several hours upriver. The decision to leave her behind had not been easy. He'd been tempted to change his plans and allow her to come along just for the sake of bolstering their spirits. So far she'd handled herself respectably. But it was one thing to brave the heat and discomfort of the steamer without complaining, and another to face the perils of the Amazon, where death could come at you out of nowhere and snuff out your life in a second. She couldn't stand up to the rigors of the journey. Resilient and obstinate though she might be, she was still only a woman. A beautiful, gentle creature more suited to a manor house than the Amazon.

The sky was dark as the Indians boarded their canoes. Morgan and Henry stood at the end of the pier watching Wickham relay his orders to Kan, who aside from Wickham, was the only man among them who could speak the Indians' language fluently.

"I feel terrible about this," Henry said. "Sarah trusted us."

"Yeah, well, this was your idea. Just swagger on down to Japurá, you said. Prove your manhood and filch a bunch of rubber seeds for the little lady."

Henry huffed and turned away so quickly the bones in his nose clattered together. He paced the length of the pier before rejoining Morgan. "We could at least give her her money back, since you've bamboozled Wickham into this deal."

"Me?"

"All right. So I might have convinced him to supply us with more Indians and guns. Regardless, we don't need Sarah's money any longer." He held out his hand. "Let's have it. I'll leave it with Wickham. At least on that point my conscience will be clear."

A moment passed before Morgan said, "I don't have it."

Henry frowned and looked suspicious.

"I lost it on board the *Santos.*"

"Doing what?"

"Gambling."

Henry groaned and with a muttered expletive stalked away, leaving Morgan to look toward the village. He started walking and Henry called out, "Where are you going? We're about to leave."

"I forgot something."

As he made his way down the footpath, an eerie squeal arose beyond the trees surrounding the village. The shroud of fronds, lianas, tree trunks, and pockets of impenetrable darkness loomed around him, so that the sound of his footsteps crashed like cymbals in his ears. The first hint of dawn's light crept into the darkness when Morgan entered Wickham's house. There he stopped abruptly.

Sarah stood in the doorway of the bedroom, her petite figure draped in a white gown with ruffled cuffs and hem. Her glorious hair tumbled over her shoulders and brushed her hips. Her toes peeked from beneath her skirt, shining like tiny pale stones in the twilight. She was rubbing her eyes with her balled-up fists, reminding Morgan of a sleepy child. The image took his breath away.

He said her name once—*Sarah*— acutely conscious for the first time of the wealth of emotion the sound of it stirred in him. All the feelings he had denied unraveled in his chest at the sight of her. She swayed and he quickly moved toward her, then reached for her and was flooded with the sweet smell of her being. *"Chere,"* he whispered. "What are you doing out of bed? It's early yet. You shouldn't be up."

She released a sigh and, closing her eyes, leaned against him. He looked down on her small head and felt his throat close. The warmth and softness of her body, the fast beating of her heart against him, were like a well-driven lance.

"Dreams . . ." she said.

"Dreams?" Smiling, he wrapped his arms around her and turned her back toward bed. "I fear you're still dreaming," he told her. He flung back the mosquito netting, pulled aside the sheet to expose the hollow of her form in the mattress. He urged her down on the bed, caught the sheet, and let it drift over her.

Her head lay in a tumble of coiling, shimmering hair, her face a translucent oval of innocence that stopped his breath. Asleep again, her wispy lashes a pair of crescent shadows upon her ivory skin, she looked like an angel. If he only could, he would sit here the remainder of the morning and drink in her beauty like a thirsting man. For the past weeks she had been a calm in the eye of his internal hurricane, forcing his mind from dark memories and regrets. She'd allowed him to believe that he was worth something. She had evoked a spark of true heroism from him that day in Little China, and then again the night on the *Santos*. Briefly, he had harbored the image of his battling through Japurá in search of the elusive *Hevea brasiliensis,* which he would claim in her name to the rubber hungry world. She would gaze upon him with adoring eyes, turn her back on everything she held dear, and walk with him hand in hand into the sunset.

But he was no hero. His dread of dying was as monstrous as his fear of living. He could face neither with any modicum of dignity. That had become obvious to him while living in Japurá. King had understood about the goblins that drove men to do things against their will. He understood fear. He understood pain. He understood the self-loathing that could turn a man into a mindless animal that cared for nothing but ending its own mental torment. Morgan had been like the fox that found its foot caught in the jaws of a trap. The only escape had been to chew off its own leg in an effort to end the pain—only to cause itself such immeasurable agony that it inevitably lay down and died.

Dreams? Sweet God, he would gladly trade her dreams for a few of his. No. He wouldn't want her to experience even a small portion of the dark and dirty little secrets of his past. She would turn from him in disgust. And who would blame her? No, it was best this way. He wouldn't leave Japurá alive. He knew that as surely as he knew that he had fallen under Sarah's spell the moment he'd turned his eyes up to her portrait. He had cheated death too many times to escape it again. He was just too damn tired of running anymore. Besides, by his knowing Sarah, the realization of what he wanted and needed and could never have was too staggering. He could be happy with nothing less, so why continue?

He eased down on the bed beside her and stroked her hair. Her lips parted. In her sleep she turned her face to nuzzle his palm, and he smiled. "Have a good life, Sunshine." It was an act of aching hunger that made him bend his head to hers. As he tipped her face up to his, he paused, his breath falling upon her lips. He kissed her brow instead, stood, and left the room.

He was halfway back to the pier before realizing that Henry had joined him. He slowed, knowing his friend was forced to take two steps to his every one. They walked in silence until his companion said, "What do you think will happen to her, Morgan?"

"I don't know."

"If she returns to England without those seeds, she'll lose everything, even her fiancé. Can you imagine that?"

"No, I can't. But what are we supposed to do about it?"

"We could get those seeds—"

"Forget it."

"So what will it cost us, Morgan? We'll be there already—"

Morgan swung around to face him. "Why the hell should I help her sail off to Norman's arms?" Henry looked shocked, then puzzled. Realization dawned in his eyes. "Besides," Morgan continued, "by the sound of it, she'd be better off without him."

"Perhaps," Henry replied more cautiously. "But I've lived among those people, Morgan. I've dealt with their prejudices and lofty airs. Sarah is too fragile to survive their scorn. It'll be catastrophic to her. Do you want that on your conscience?"

"I don't have a conscience."

They walked again. Just before they reached the pier, Henry put a hand on Morgan's arm. They stopped and stood in silence, Morgan looking one way down the path, Henry gazing up the other. Finally Henry asked, "Do you want to turn back? I know what an ordeal it is for you."

He shook his head. "You don't know the half of it, Henry."

"Perhaps I do."

Morgan met his friend's eyes, sensing the old panic rising, the self-disgust. "You don't know," he said, and his voice was a rasp of desperation he couldn't control.

Henry caught his arm as he started to leave. "Remember the day I pulled you from that bore tide, Morgan? You were wounded and delirious with fever. You rambled all night about the atrocities—"

"I don't want to hear this." He yanked his arm away and started down the track. Henry stopped him so roughly their feet skidded on the path.

"Morgan, I honestly believed that by facing King, perhaps destroying him, you could put the nightmare to rest and get on with your life. I was wrong. Take Sarah; go back to Georgetown."

"Forget it."

"Your killing King won't stop the memories. It won't undo what he did to you. Nothing will. You must put it behind you or—"

"Shut up." Fists clenched, Morgan towered over the smaller man like a Goliath. "I'm gonna kill that son of a bitch," he stated. "But first I'm gonna castrate him for every man, woman, and child he's raped. He's gonna be on his knees before me, Henry; I swear it."

He hurried on to the pier, his pulse so deafening he couldn't hear the directives Wickham was giving the Indians. He was vaguely aware of someone taking his arm again and turning him. He raised his fist with the intent of striking out, as he had so many times before, and froze.

"You were going to leave me. How could you? I trusted you . . ."

Sarah's face came into focus. It looked very white, washed out even more by the lusterless light of morning creeping through the breaks in the trees. Her hair was loose and wild, as if windblown. But there had been no wind, no storm except the maelstrom raging inside him. Her eyes were wide and wet, the color of the aqua-green waters of the Tapajós. Her lips were parted, her hands raised for protection, should he strike her.

It was then he noticed the silence. Every eye was trained on them, from the Indians who sat two-by-two in rocking canoes, their oars resting upon their knees, to the Englishman and Henry, who stood at the edge of the pier as if frozen. Lowering his fist, Morgan took a step toward her, noting that she made a move backward even though her face wore an expression of severe aggravation, a look too incongruent with her cherubic features to be convincing.

"Sarah." His throat was dry as dust. "Sarah," he repeated, "come here."

She did not come to him willingly. He closed his arms around her and pulled her against his chest, gritting his teeth as she beat his shoulders with her fists and cursed him for being a swindler, liar, and cheat. Finally, with tears rolling down her cheeks, she allowed him to hold her. As his hand rested upon her head and his fingers wove into her hair, his previous anger settled inside him like sand in an hourglass. He was amazed how she could bring that, the peace, when no one else ever could. "Will you let me explain?" he asked. She didn't respond, just stood as stiff as a stump in his arms. "It's too dangerous, Sarah. There are a thousand reasons why you should stay here. If something happens to us, Wickham will be able to see to it that you return to England, and your fiancé."

"If you don't return, my going home to England is a moot point," she stated in a voice meant for his ears alone. "He won't have me."

"Sarah, I can't believe—"

"You don't understand!" Her fists twisted into his shirt as she attempted to control her emotions. "I'm not one of them. I don't have a long line of pedigrees. My grandfather worked for everything he attained, as did my father. They were merchants, Morgan, not blue bloods. The aristocracy accepted me because of what he'd become, not because my birthright obliged them to do so." She stared off over the river, remote and sad.

He had the overpowering need to wrap her in his arms, but there was no security there, not in his embrace. There she would only find nightmares more horrible than any she could conjure in her naive dreams.

She turned to him again. "Please. Let me go. I'll stay out of your way. You won't even know I'm there."

"That'll be the day. Wherever have you floated, fairy mine, that all of creation didn't stop to bask in your sunshine?" He brushed a tendril of hair from her cheek. "God help us, but I'm almost tempted to say yes, black-hearted bastard that I am."

Realizing that his fingers were tracing the creamy plane of her cheek, he turned and walked to the edge of the dock, where he stared down into the murky water at his reflection. In a moment her white-clad image joined his; each wavered dreamlike in the ripple and dance of the water and light below their feet.

"We could die out there," he stated.

"But we won't. You'll be leading us, and you can do anything. Everyone knows that. You're their hero." She pointed to the Indians. "My father must have believed in you too."

He thought, *Your father believed Rodolfo King's word was good, and look where he is today.*

It occurred to him then that if he allowed Sarah to accompany him into that hell, he was as big a murderer as King. But perhaps she could accompany them to Manáos, and no further. Besides, she was onto them. Skulking away was obviously out of the question, for the moment. "How quickly can you dress?"

"Ten minutes. Five, if I have help with the buttons."

"Be back here in five or we're leaving without you."

He watched her run down the dock, the dirtied hem of her gown flapping about her dusty feet. He directed several Indians to help her with her trunks, then looked to Henry, whose own faltering resolution was as obvious as the Amazonia forest was dense.

"This is preposterous!" came Wickham's voice. "You cannot think to allow that young woman to accompany you on this journey."

"That's the young woman's decision to make," Morgan returned.

"It's too dangerous, not to mention unseemly. Her reputation will suffer."

"Only if you intend to besmirch it, in which case you'll find a hundred thousand rubber seeds sprouting from every orifice of your body." Morgan landed with a wobbling flourish in the bottom of a canoe. "I hope you're still planning on meeting us in Coari. We do have a deal."

"Yes, of course." Wickham sighed. "But I tell you again, what you're doing is insane."

Morgan smiled grimly. To Henry, he said, "Coming, Longfellow?"

Henry scurried to join him, their eyes meeting as Morgan thrust an oar into his hands. Morgan gazed out over the bright, broken pattern of the river and mentally chided himself for allowing Sarah to manipulate him with her tears, telling himself that he always had been a sucker for weeping, desperate women, and that his decision had nothing to do with the fact that the act of telling her good-bye had been more distressful than the possibility of dying in Japurá.

He raised one eyebrow as Henry's face broke into a compassionate and knowing smile. With an edge to his voice, he said, "Don't grin at me. Until we reach Manáos, she's your responsibility. Keep her away from me, or I might do or say something nasty."

"Such as?"

"I don't know. I'll have to think about it."

"That's your problem, Morgan. You have to work too hard at being a bastard for anyone to take you seriously."

Sarah joined them in a flurry of silk bustles and bare feet, stockings in one hand, shoes in the other. Morgan groaned inwardly at her attire, wondering whether she'd ever forget her silly inhibitions and wear the trousers he'd provided. The boat rocked as Henry helped her from the pier.

"Oh, yes," came her hesitant voice behind Morgan. "There is something you should know, Mr. Kane."

Her knees pressed into his back as he gazed up the river. Why did he get the feeling he wasn't going to like what she had to tell him? "Yeah?" he replied. "What is it?"

"I can't swim."

He closed his eyes, and with a sense of resignation, shook his head. Then he dipped the paddle in the water and began their journey to the green hell.

Chapter Eight

THE CANOES CUT QUIETLY THROUGH THE RIVER, THE SILENCE DIS-
turbed only by the murmur of the oars driving through the water. As the
river narrowed, the trees overhead became a canopy of foliage that might
have been spectacular had it not seemed so forbidding. Rising hundreds
of feet toward the sky, the limbs were laden with creepers and vines that
climbed to the tops of the highest boughs in their quest for sunlight.

High and higher the sandbanks grew, like massive but inadequate
dikes. Along those tenuous boundaries grew an array of trees that could
supply the entirety of London with fine wood for a lifetime. There were
palms, laurels, rosewoods, and mahoganies. There were cedars, steel-
woods, figs, and acacias, all of which boasted giant bouquets of flame-
colored orchids that drooped sixty feet toward the ground. As Sarah
regarded it all with wonder, a spray of parakeets exploded out of the
foliage and fluttered noisily across the river. Butterflies, disturbed by the
birds' belligerent chattering, poured forth from the trees in such profu-
sion that she cried aloud in surprise.

At any other time the splendor of it all would have thrilled Sarah, but
she was still fuming over the fact that Morgan and Henry had attempted
to desert her in Santarém. Had she not been awakened by an odd dream
of Morgan kissing her, she would surely be stranded there now. She
glared at Morgan's back throughout the day, speaking only when spoken
to, doing her best to focus on her irritation and not on the alluring width
of his shoulders or the black hair that curled lazily around his nape and
behind his ears.

Yet time after time her thoughts drifted and she discovered herself
comparing Morgan with Norman—as if there could be a comparison.
The idea seemed almost laughable. Norman was so staid, so predictable,

so . . . safe. The moments spent in his company were never charged with tension. Her stomach didn't flutter each time he turned his pale blue eyes on her.

She tried concentrating on the floresta, taking mental notes and wishing for her diary so she might jot down the vivid images before they escaped her. Norman would adore her descriptions of the butterflies and birds. He might even look at her with some respect as she detailed the terrifying ordeal on the *Santos* . . . and how Morgan Kane had saved her life.

No matter what topic she tried to concentrate on, her thoughts always came back to Morgan. Morgan, the hero, the *boto,* the man who, with one glance of those odd silver eyes, made her feel as if she were the only woman left alive on the face of the earth. For the love of God, she was staring death in the face, marching through Satan's back door, and all she could think about was how wonderful she'd felt when he kissed her, how deliciously wicked the sensations he'd aroused in her had been.

Then he'd tried to desert her.

IT WAS LATE AFTERNOON WHEN THE INDIANS MOVED THEIR CANOES alongside Sarah's. She noted their eyes scanning the water, then she saw the alligator approach. Kan, who sat abow in the boat to her right, warned the creature away by slapping the water with the face of his paddle. With a flourish of its tail the beast sank into the river, only to resurface yards away, where it was joined by others. Soon the water near the marshy banks was swarming with the giant monsters; their grunts and roars drowned out the piercing cries of the birds and monkeys.

Morgan turned and looked at Sarah's face, his own void of emotion. "You all right?" he surprised her by asking.

"Of course," she replied a bit more sharply than she had intended. "Did you expect me to lapse into hysteria at the prospect of being capsized by alligators, Mr. Kane?" Her eyes widened as a bull gator glided toward them and, just at the paddle's end, disappeared beneath the surface, then bumped the bottom of their boat. She grabbed the sides of the canoe as it wobbled. "I—I assure you, I'm aware that you're capable of handling the situation," she added in a higher-pitched voice.

"You are, huh?" Leaning over to look at Henry, he said, "Are we capable of handling this situation, Longfellow?"

"They're only giving us a warning, old man. We're trespassing, you know. They don't usually react aggressively unless they're threatened . . . or hungry. And they don't usually go for anything so large as a man. Monkeys will do in a pinch, or a dog. I once read an account by a man called Bates who said that a gator came into his camp one evening and made off with a poodle that belonged to one of his companions."

Morgan's brows drew together. "Is that supposed to make us feel better, Henry?"

"Would you rather I describe to you how an entire expedition, aside from one terrified Indian who lost a foot and both hands, was once set upon by a lot of hungry alligators and devoured within minutes of—"

"No!" both Sarah and Morgan interrupted.

Henry threw back his head and laughed.

Again and again their boats were bumped, and repeatedly Sarah told herself that everything was going to be all right. She was with Morgan and Henry and Kan, and they could handle themselves in any circumstance. Yet looking toward the bank where more of the reptiles were sliding into the river and approaching their boats, she realized that if only one of the beasts decided to capsize their canoe, the helpless occupants would not stand a chance of surviving.

They drifted, no longer daring to paddle for fear that the commotion would rouse the alligators' ire.

"They're curious," Henry kept assuring them.

"They look damn hungry to me," Morgan snapped.

"We need a diversion," the pygmy said, looking around and overhead, as if by a miracle something might fall from the sky.

"Yeah?" Morgan raised one eyebrow. "Why don't you jump in, Longfellow, and draw their attention while we escape? We'll pick you up on the return trip."

"Morgan, you're such a wit. What would we do without your sense of humor?"

Their boat was hit again, harder this time, making Sarah cry aloud and reach for Morgan, who had thrown his paddle into the bottom of the canoe and was reaching for a rifle.

"No!" Henry and Kan called out in unison.

"What the hell do you mean, *no?*" Morgan shouted.

"The last thing you want to do is threaten them." Henry, whose round face no longer carried any hint of his earlier amusement, gripped his own oar as if it were a bludgeon. "We need a diversion," he repeated.

"Well, in case you failed to notice, we don't have—"

"Wait!"

Everyone stared at Sarah as she pulled up her skirt, frantically tugged on the ties of her petticoats, and began to shimmy them down her hips, legs, and finally her ankles. She looked up to find Morgan's gaze riveted on her calves, which were covered with filmy, white silk stockings. Despite the fear that brought about such a desperate act, she felt a tingling of thrill and satisfaction. She allowed the skirt to slide back down her legs, her mouth curving in a smile as his eyes came back to hers. "Really," he said, "this is neither the time nor the place, *chere.*"

"Give me your paddle," she responded.

"My what?" He grinned.

"Paddle." She reached for it, drawing it across her lap as she forced herself to keep her mind on her task, and not on the way he could make her blush with the sensuous richness of his voice. He was mostly facing her now, one knee pressed against her leg as he regarded her from beneath the brim of his hat.

"You want a diversion, Mr. Kane. Here it is." Having tied the petticoats snugly about the paddle, she thrust it toward him. "Throw it in and see what happens."

He looked at Henry, who nodded. "What do we have to lose?"

Morgan took the oar in both hands, studied the frilly petticoats for a long moment, then cautiously began to stand. As the canoe rocked perilously, Sarah threw her arms around his thighs to steady him, her face pressed to a part of his anatomy that might have made her swoon in any other circumstance.

He flung the oar as hard as he could. It sailed through the air like some huge flapping bird, then landed with a plop and a splash on the river. Seconds ticked by as they watched the petticoats spread and float. Then, with a thrashing of their monstrous tails, the alligators moved toward the disguised oar.

"Quickly!" Henry yelled. "Let's get the blazes away from here!"

Morgan dropped to his seat while Henry plunged his own paddle into the water and propelled them up the river. They looked back in time to see the first alligator strike the object and drag it beneath the surface. A shudder passed through them at the sight, and as Sarah watched the last trace of white sink from view, the realization that that could just as easily have been her struck with horrifying clarity.

They traveled another half hour before choosing a wide, sandy strand on which to camp. As she stood to one side, the men hurried to secure the boats, fetch wood for a fire, and set up a canvas tent in which she was to sleep. In truth, she couldn't imagine enveloping herself in such a claustrophobic contraption. Breathing the air was difficult enough; at times she felt as if she were suffocating in the intense humidity and heat. Every thread of cloth on her body was drenched, and her hair, from roots to ends, was damp and clinging to her neck and shoulders. Repeatedly she glanced toward the canoe with her belongings, waiting for her trunk of clothes to be unloaded so she might change into her cooler nightgown for sleep. Yet the trunk was not unloaded, and she was informed in no uncertain terms by Morgan that this was not a hotel. She would sleep in her clothes unless she wished to be eaten alive by mosquitoes.

"Does this mean I won't be able to bathe?" she asked desperately.

"Bathe?" Teeth clenched around a cigarette, he yelled, "Henry! Get over here and tell the lady why there won't be any servants drawing her bath this evening!"

Henry hurried to explain about piranhas—of which she was already aware—and nasty little creatures called candirus that were two inches long and covered with sweptback quills. The tiny creatures took great delight in invading a person's body through their private parts. He went on to explain other dangers and diseases one could get from the water, but she barely listened. Her eyes were on Morgan, watching how efficiently he saw to the setting up of their camp, never once glancing toward her. The fact piqued her. He hadn't said so much as a word about her ingenuity with the petticoats. She was quite pleased that she had saved their lives, and he couldn't even manage a "Good show." No doubt his pride was bruised because he hadn't thought of it.

Morgan disappeared into the jungle with Kan and several Indians. Within minutes the bark of rifles rang out, and the hunters returned with a few dead monkeys. Sarah shuddered, refusing to watch as the Indians hastened to skin and gut the animals, then skewer them over the fire. Soon the pungent aroma of roasting meat filled the air, and the grease spilling into the flames poured a rancid smoke over the camp that made Sarah queasy. When Henry brought her a plate of meat, she refused it. Looking concerned, he told her, "But you haven't eaten all day."

"I'm not hungry. I'd like to go to bed, please. And I'd like my diary from my belongings. Will you get it for me, Henry?" She stood as he nodded, then dropped to her knees and crawled into the tent. From inside she watched Henry walk over to Morgan, who sat alone on the far side of the encampment. She noted that he looked her way only briefly when Henry spoke, then shrugged before going back to his dinner.

She couldn't place the reason for her growing depression. She had never been one to dwell on the unpleasant aspects of life. She had always thought herself capable of anything, but here she felt insignificant and alien. The farther they traveled into Amazonia, the more she felt like an intruder.

It wasn't long before Henry appeared with her diary, fountain pen, and ink bottle. Squatting before the opening of her tent, he said, "Morgan says you should get to sleep. And don't forget to take your quinine. He wants to know if it was the monkey meat that put you off, or if you're ill."

"Tell him I'm tired. On second thought, don't. No doubt he'll use anything I say as an excuse to send me back to Santarém."

Henry smiled in understanding. "You'd be safer there, Sarah. You've given us quite a responsibility by coming along. Why won't you allow us to go in alone and return the seeds to you? You must try to understand what sort of situation you're confronting."

"I understand completely," she replied irritably.

After wrapping herself in a mosquito net, as Morgan had instructed, she reclined as best she could, finding that the floor of silt beneath her blanket was not as uncomfortable as she had first imagined. It was the heat that pressed in on her and made her restless.

In the glow of the campfire that spilled through the opening of her tent she did her best to fill up the pages of her diary, though the words came harder as she grew more weary. Around her the night sounds intensified, the buzzing, whistling, rasping, and pulsating noises rising to such volume she was forced to throw down her pen and cover her ears in fear that the crescendo might deafen her. Yet a glance out her tent at the others informed her that they appeared to hear nothing at all. Many of the Indians were curled upon the sand fast asleep, while others were grouped together in quiet conversation. Still others, posted around the grounds, gazed out into the night watching for any threatening movement, listening for any suspicious sound that could warn them of impending danger. Sarah wondered how they could hear anything beyond the shrill cacophony; she marveled at their ability to stare out into the pitch-black night and see anything at all.

She attempted to write these thoughts in her diary. Soon, however, the heat and noise drove her to such distraction that she decided to close her eyes. But even her attempt to sleep was unsuccessful. She tossed and turned, becoming so ensnared in the netting that she felt like one of Norman's butterflies, fluttering frantically to escape a finely webbed net. To add to her misery her skin burned with sweat and grime where the high snug collar of her blouse had chafed raw the skin of her neck. Suddenly she thought she would scream if she wasn't allowed to cleanse her face and arms. So she kicked away the netting and eased out of the tent, taking a precautionary glance about the camp. Those on guard were off in the darkness, she supposed, and though she searched for Morgan and Henry, she could not find them.

The campfire had dwindled, and as she hurried into the dark she rushed to unbutton her blouse. By the time she reached the water's edge she had removed it. She fell to her knees and immersed the garment in the tepid water, not bothering to wring it out as she dragged its saturated folds across her face, neck, and shoulders, closing her eyes in pleasure at the cleansing, cooling assuagement it brought to her aggravated skin. She dipped it in again, pressing it to her chest, allowing the water to run beneath her chemise, at last letting her head fall low so the moisture spilled freely from the makeshift sponge, onto the back of her neck. She almost sighed, but the sudden sense that she was being watched from the darkness brought a wave of panic shivering up her spine. She forced herself not to scream, and slowly turned around.

Morgan stood behind her.

She nearly collapsed. Only the surge of fury racing like an intoxicant through her blood kept her from it. Stumbling to her feet, she glared up at his grinning face, her brain flaring between outrage at the apparent pleasure he took in scaring her, and a driving need to throw herself against his chest where his shirt fell open to the low-slung waist of his breeches.

"Something wrong?" he asked.

"That wasn't funny," she declared.

"What?"

"Your sneaking up behind me like that."

"Did I sneak? I don't think so. You were so engrossed in your bath you didn't hear me."

"You sneaked," she snapped.

He dug a cigarette out of his pocket. "What if I did? It wasn't very wise of you to slink out of camp without telling me."

"I was hot."

"Yeah?" As he touched a match to his cigarette, the flame illuminated his sharp features. His lashes were lowered in concentration, then they raised to regard her as he passed the fire downward, revealing her soaked chemise where it clung to her breasts. "How hot?" he asked, then gave the match a quick shake and tossed it toward the water.

Sarah surmised that this might not be the best time to try his patience; he had gone from humor to . . . what? There was an unspoken threat hanging between them that crackled the air, and it was as if the fire of his match had taken light in his eyes. Suddenly her knees felt watery and her heart was jumping in her chest. Her flesh burned one minute, the next she shivered as a gust of wind found its way beneath her sopping chemise. The memory of his kisses scuttled through her mind, and with a betraying blush rushing to her face, she thought, *Oh, God, oh, God, let him kiss me again.*

But he didn't. He just stood there like an indolent statue in the darkness, his towering, broad-shouldered form a black silhouette against the backdrop of the distant fire. She could no longer see his eyes, which was just as well. They were no doubt laughing at her, or scorning her—he was too damned inconsistent for her to tell which.

"I think," he said, "that you should get dressed and get back to your tent."

"And what if I don't?"

"Do you really want to find out, *chere?*"

"Perhaps I do."

The challenge hung in the air.

Finally he said again, "I think you should go."

"Will you torture me if I refuse?" she persisted. "Will you feed me to the piranhas? Cast me to the jaguars? Bind me by my wrists to a mound of man-eating ants? Tell me, Mr. Kane, what will you do if I defy you?"

He said nothing. Nor did he move. At last, in complete exasperation, she attempted to walk around him and return to her tent. She was brought up short as his hand shot out and grabbed her arm, hauling her back so forcefully she stumbled against him and her mostly exposed breasts, gleaming white in the darkness, were pressed to his sweat-moistened chest. His touch shocked her, overwhelmed her. Her earlier bravura evaporated as she blinked up into his face.

"If you weren't a lady," he replied in a voice as smooth and ominous as the river was deep, "I would gladly tell you what I would do to you for defying me."

"Indeed," she replied recklessly, her good sense dissipating as the scent of his skin filled her nostrils and the feel of his hard fingers biting into her arm made her grow weak. All she could do was sink slightly against him as she taunted, "Do you know what I think, Mr. Kane? You enjoy bullying me because you think I am some spineless child. I saved our necks this afternoon and you don't like it, do you?"

Flicking his cigarette to the ground, he lowered his head and whispered in her ear, "I really couldn't give a damn, *chere,* but what I do give a damn about is this. If the men we've hired see a woman continually challenging my authority, it won't be long before they do the same. I'm gonna need complete cooperation from everyone during the next days, and if you usurp my control, someone will wind up getting killed—and it might be you. Now, be a good girl and get back to bed and stay there until daylight, unless you want me to post a guard outside your tent to make certain you do." He released her and turned her around, then gave her a shove. "Good night, Miss St. James."

Sarah walked to her tent, her anger replaced by chagrin. She crawled into her bedding and stared at the roof of her tent, holding her hands to her face, inhaling his pungent scent that permeated her own flesh and made her grow restive with hunger. What, exactly, was happening to her? *Damn him for what he is,* she thought.

THEY GLIDED UPSTREAM AND AROUND THE STILL BENDS IN THE RIVER where blankets of fragrant flowers collected within the shallows. Occasionally they would cease their paddling and allow their vessels to drift along the natural eddies and back currents near the shore. Through the wooden hull of the canoe Sarah could detect the coolness of the water, feel the rush of bubbles vibrating against it as the men accelerated over the surface. The forest had a hypnotic effect on Sarah that left her lethargic and unwilling to talk. Reclining in the bottom of the boat, she studied the green ceiling above, noting the horizontal shafts of sunlight streaming through the upper branches, casting a yellowish haze into the depths of the jungle. She often dozed, and when she awoke she would sit up and write her thoughts in the diary.

Day after day they traveled, the air becoming hotter and damper, until their clothes and hair were continuously soaked with humidity and sweat. Night after night they bedded down on some sandy shoal, Sarah occasionally too drained of strength to stay awake long enough to eat her ration of monkey meat, fish, or, in one case, an anteater that had ventured too close to their camp at dinnertime.

Sarah had once read Charles Waterton's account of his journey up the Amazon. He'd stated that resilience and enthusiasm were more important than professional skill to survive such a trip. Yet remaining enthusiastic was becoming more difficult every day. She was already so drained of energy that the very idea of leaving the relative ease of the river to trudge through the jungle was enough to make her question her own sanity. The mosquitoes, which had come in a black swarm to infest them on their second day out of Santarém, had forced her to hide beneath layers of clothes and hats and veils that touched her elbows. Their constant buzzing made her want to scream.

But even the insects' presence eventually ceased to bother her. At night she no longer noticed the noisiness of the jungle. Lying in the darkness, doing her best to breathe through the smoke from the wet brushfire that smoldered inside her tent to force out the mosquitoes, she mulled over the years she had spent in London and her desperate attempts to fit in with the society her mother thought so important. How silly those aspirations seemed now. One didn't die if the part in one's hair was crooked. The world didn't stop rotating if a man caught a glimpse of a lady's knee. And what did it matter if tea was at two or six o'clock, instead of four? Now she found it hard to imagine a life outside the floresta. Clean clothes and bathwater scented with Rock Dew Water of the Sahara or Royal Arabian Toilet of Beauty seemed a vague memory. Polite conversation between hospitable people might never have existed.

Since they'd met by the dark river on their first night out, the American had kept his distance, always watching but rarely speaking. She was torn between the need to scream in his face and the urge to fall on her knees and thank God he had chosen to ignore her the past days.

More and more, his presence had a disquieting effect on her mind and senses. She found herself searching him out in the hours between setting up camp and turning into bed. Always he would be sitting alone in the dark, a smoldering cigarette between his lips and his bottle of whiskey in one hand. Only twice had she approached him, and both times he had grunted a reply and dismissed her. At first she had attributed his attitude to his belligerent personality. However, she soon discovered that he appeared congenial enough with the Indians, Kan, and Henry.

She wasn't accustomed to dealing with hostility. The ability to make friends had always been one of her greatest assets. Her father had told her that had she been born a man, she might have been destined for a political office.

Deciding to confront the American one evening after dinner, she ventured from her tent to find the campfire roaring as usual, its smoke rising far above the camp to hang suspended along the tree limbs overhead. The acrid cloud, necessary to rid the camp of mosquitoes and sand flies, burned her eyes and made her sneeze, but she'd decided that the discomfort was preferable to the painful, and dangerous, bite of the insects.

Morgan and Henry were stooped in the light of the fire, their heads together as Morgan, stick in hand, proceeded to draw in the sand. Sarah moved up behind them.

"This is the river," came Morgan's voice as he dragged his pointer along a winding groove in the dirt. "We're here."

"I beg to differ," Henry replied. "My estimation is that we're here, and Manáos should be there." He nudged a rock into place with his foot, then made a line in the soft silt with his toe. "This is the Rio Negro, and the Barcelos mission is approximately there. King's plantation should be in that vicinity."

Morgan shook his head. "Not likely. My guess would be here." He poked the ground.

"Let's hope not. It would take us months to hack our way that distance. Our supplies would not hold out that long."

"Three weeks," Morgan said. "From here to here."

"Not through *that* forest, my good man. My guess is . . ."

Henry looked over his shoulder at Sarah. So did Morgan. They glanced at each other before standing and facing her. They resembled two boys caught filching apples from an orchard.

"Is something wrong?" she asked.

They shook their heads.

"Why were you whispering?"

"Were we whispering?" Morgan asked Henry.

"We didn't want to disturb you," Henry explained.

Sarah regarded the drawing in the sand, and Henry leapt forward, took her arm, and directed her to a seat on a piece of driftwood nearer the fire. "You're up late," he commented.

"I couldn't sleep."

"Is something troubling you?" Henry frowned in concern.

She didn't look at Morgan as he stretched out on the ground at the edge of the firelight. Instead, she stared at the toes of her boots—she'd grudgingly begun to wear the heavy things in the hope of saving her legs from mosquitoes and sand flies—and wondered with frustration why she could never look the American in the eye and say what she felt.

Could it be that she didn't know what she felt exactly? Irritation, aggravation, anger—they were all confused inside her with another emotion that was becoming more and more prevalent every day that she found herself in Morgan's presence. She shrugged. "I was feeling a little lonely, I suppose, and started thinking of my parents."

"Ah." Henry nodded understandingly as he prepared her a cup of tea he had been brewing for himself. Morgan, his long legs stretched before him and crossed at the ankles, proceeded to whittle on a piece of wood with his knife, his eyes hidden beneath the brim of his hat. Sarah found herself willing him to look up just so she could see those eyes, no matter how briefly. But he didn't. He rarely even glanced her way these days.

"Did you have a large family?" she asked Henry as he handed her a china cup and saucer. "You've never really gone into detail about how you ended up in England. You said a botanist took you?"

Henry sat down beside her. He appeared thoughtful for a moment. "Yes. I was ten when I happened upon him. He had managed to get himself separated from his colleagues in the floresta. I led him back to the village. He offered to pay me to act as his guide and interpreter for the remainder of his stay. I did so for eight months. In that time he grew fond of me. When he decided to return to London, he invited me to go along. Once there, and with the coaxing of a number of his colleagues, he set upon the course to educate and refine me. The blue bloods were quite amusing, actually. Very entertaining. They thought me curious and I thought them idiots, but that is beside the point. I went on to graduate from Oxford—high honors. When I returned to Brazil, I discovered my family had all . . . died."

"I'm sorry," she said.

Henry sipped his tea and gazed into the dark.

At last Sarah worked up the courage to address Morgan. "And what about you, Mr. Kane?"

The fire snapped as his long fingers turned the carving this way and that; tiny slivers of wood sprinkled his lap.

"What about *your* family?" Sarah prompted.

"What about it?" he replied in a level voice.

"Who were your parents? Do you have any brothers or sisters?"

He pressed his lips together, his concentration fixed on his hands. He still did not look at her as he replied, "My father was an officer in the American Navy. My mother was French."

"Are they still living?"

"No."

"I suppose we all have something in common, then," she said.

He looked at her directly, his eyes reflecting the firelight. "Yeah?" His smile was cold. "What's that, Princess?"

"We're all orphans, so to speak."

"Right." He tossed the wood to the ground and got to his feet. Sarah stared up at his face, then down at the knife gripped in his hand. She didn't care much for the way it shook in his fingers.

As he turned away, Sarah shoved her cup and saucer aside and leapt up. Morgan had crossed the camp before she caught up with him. "I'd like a word with you," she said.

He grabbed his rifle, checked to see if it was loaded. He struck off into the dark, leaving her to glare after him, temper rising. Hands clenched, she followed, jumping debris that had been swept upon the banks by previously swollen waters. The refuse snagged her hem and she was forced to stop and yank the material, so that it gave with a rip. By the time she caught up to Morgan her patience was at its end, her fury too hot to control—though she knew good breeding demanded she do so. But who the hell cared any longer? "Damn you, stop this instant and face me!"

He stopped so suddenly she plowed into him and slipped halfway down his legs before he caught her and dragged her up, plunking her at his feet like some child in the throes of a tantrum. She slapped his hands away and glared at him.

"I've done my best to understand these brooding silences of yours, but I'm at my wit's end. If anyone should be angry it should be me. I'm the injured party here. It's my family King destroyed. It's my future that's at stake. I've gambled all I have left in the world on the off chance that you can get me to Japurá, and what happens? You try to sneak off in the middle of the night and leave me!" She thumped his shoulder with her fist. "And there you stand, as usual, saying nothing. I cannot even carry on a civilized conversation without you stalking off in a huff."

"Are you finished?"

"No, I am not! I demand to know why you've taken such a dislike to me since we left Santarém."

The night and forest pressed in on them, turning the air to steam and the trees into hulking black forms that might have made her shudder had she been able to concentrate on anything other than Morgan's eyes. But she couldn't—dear God, she couldn't. Suddenly all she could think of was the intensity in that gaze—the same intensity that had goaded him that night on the *Santos* to kiss her so passionately she'd lost all reason. Dear Lord, was that why she had followed him into the dark, alone, unchaperoned? Was she hoping to experience the forbidden thrill, to feel her body crushed against his again? "Well?" she demanded, her voice humiliatingly husky.

Her face was a blur in the darkness, and Morgan thought that if she stood there before him another three seconds, looking like a disheveled kitten pretending to be a fierce lioness, he would lay down his gun, drag her to the ground, and say to hell with her virginity, Norman, and his own resolution not to rob her of her innocence. He'd done his best to stay away from her, and it hadn't been easy. She was there when he awoke in the morning; her knees were in his back throughout the day; she was there in the night, wrapped up in her netting with her hair spilling over the ground like rosy moonlight. Now she was challenging his willpower again, intentionally this time, and he wasn't certain he could fight it.

"Sarah, get back to camp."

"Not until you talk to me."

"Oh, yeah, I forgot. You're the boss lady. Well, boss lady, just what is it you want me to say?"

"Must you always sneer?" she demanded.

He rolled his eyes, thumbed back his hat, and stared off into the night. "Why do you avoid me?"

"Why should it matter?"

"It doesn't."

He shifted his eyes back to hers. "Then what the hell are we fighting about?"

"I only want to understand, Mr. Kane. You seem more than eager to fraternize with other women—"

"Whores," he snapped, making her mouth shut. "I *fraternize* with whores, Miss St. James. Women of ill repute. Now, unless I've judged you wrong, I don't think you belong in that category."

"Is there some law that says you cannot associate with a respectable woman?" she cried, going up on her toes, so vehement was her frustration.

"Why the devil would a respectable woman *want* to associate with me?" he shouted back, feeling his control slip as the anger welled up inside him so that he began to shake. Lowering his face to hers, he said, "Lady, I don't know what you call men like me back in London, but over here a woman like you wouldn't acknowledge my existence unless it was after dark and she had an itch between her legs that she wanted me to scratch."

Sarah gasped.

"That's what I am, *chere*. I'm the goddamned *boto*. I'm the man mamas hide their daughters from. I'm the one those same mamas come crawling to when their husbands don't satisfy them in the sack. I'm the one who makes 'em feel pretty and desirable and needed during the long nights, but come sunup, they don't know me."

She backed away as he moved toward her, snapping twigs under his boot heels, his rifle gripped in his hand. "I don't play at lovemaking, Sarah. I don't dally in the dark with flirtatious little girls who want to experiment at being coy."

"Oh!" she cried. "I'm doing no such—"

"You hired me to take you to Japurá and filch a bunch of rubber seeds so you can sail back to Norman and live happily ever after. Well, that's what I'm doing, *boss* lady. Now get the blazes back to camp and leave me the hell alone!"

She fled; Morgan watched her go, wondering if he had ever wanted to hold her as badly as he did in that moment.

Chapter Nine

Despite the rainstorm beating against the ceiling of trees, and the water running in torrents over the leaves to spill on the travelers' heads, the expedition pushed on, arriving in Manáos just before midnight of the following evening. As Morgan struggled to tug the canoe up the embankment, the water surged about his knees until he almost stumbled. Cursing, he did his best to see his companions through the rain, then yelled, "Get the lady indoors! I'll meet you back here in an hour!"

Hurrying to Sarah's canoe, Kan swept her up in his arms and trudged ashore. Hair and clothes plastered to her body, she glared at Morgan and screamed, "And what do *you* intend to do?"

He ignored her and turned to Henry, barely making out his friend's face in the dark and rain. Taking his arm, he propelled him up the slippery bank so Sarah could not overhear their conversation. "All right, what now?"

"What do you mean?" Henry yelled back.

"Get rid of her!"

"Get rid of her?"

"I told you: Manáos is as far as she goes!"

"But it's raining. And it's midnight! This isn't Georgetown. You can't jaunt down to the nearest hotel and rent a room."

"You should've thought about that before you brought her!"

"You're just as much at fault. You could've insisted that she remain in Santarém!"

Removing his hat and wringing it in his hands, Morgan shook his head. "She ain't goin' any further, Longfellow." He slapped the soggy hat back on his head and stared down at Henry through the curtain of rain running off the brim. "Get her settled. As for us, we're leaving here before sunrise."

"But it's raining. The river will be treacherous!"

"We'll survive."

Henry shook his head. "You're crazy."

"I'd be crazy to stay here! King's men are up and down this stretch of the river constantly. If I'm spotted I won't live to get to Japurá. They'll blow my head off. But first they'll torture me. They'll hang me by my feet and cut out my tongue. Do you want that on your conscience, Henry?"

"You know what I think, old man?"

"No, and I don't care!"

"You're in a big hurry to escape something, and it's not King."

Rolling his eyes, Morgan said, "Ah, God. I'm standin' here drownin' and the man wants to turn my head inside out. The deal was, we leave her in Manáos. See that that watchdog chief of hers stays here too. He'll get her back to Santarém. Leave 'em a canoe, a rifle or two, and ammunition, then get your little butt back here, because I'm leavin' before sunup, with or without you!"

He left Henry standing in a puddle of rain and hurried back to the river to help the Indians secure the boats. He had no more than pulled the first canoe out of the river when he was spun around by Sarah. Her face a blur, she shouted, "I'm going nowhere unless you tell me what you intend to do next!"

"I *intend* to get some sleep! Now be a good girl and run along with Henry!"

"No! You've attempted to sneak off and leave me before! I'm going nowhere unless I have your solemn promise that you won't do that again!"

He flung a paddle to the ground and caught her arm, hauled her slipping and stumbling toward the village, ignoring her outraged protests as he searched for shelter, rousing most of Manáos in the process. Eventually Henry, who'd joined the hunt, was directed to a hut on the far side of the village. Morgan and Sarah waited just inside the doorway as Henry fumbled with a box of matches in an attempt to light a tallow candle Kan had produced from a pack of supplies he carried on his back. As the flame leapt to life, barely illuminating the primitive hospice, Morgan said, "Home away from home. What more could you want?"

The group looked around the barren room measuring no more than ten feet in circumference. Rain leaked through the roof, turning most of the dirt floor into mud. Rotting straw and palm leaves had been swept into one corner, filling the enclosure with a damp, disagreeable odor.

"I'll have your trunk brought up," Morgan added. "Get out of those wet clothes and into something dry before you catch your death of cold."

"I'm touched that you care."

He watched her walk toward a small pile of bleached animal bones littering the floor, then she turned back to face him. Her complexion was colorless in the candlelight, and so was her hair. At times, in her fatigue, she seemed almost plain, hardly the ravishing beauty who set continents of men on their aristocratic backsides. Only her eyes, staring at him in hot defiance and suspicion, showed any life at all.

"Where will you be, Morgan?"

The drumming of the rain on the roof grew louder. Standing there in the entryway, the water spraying over his shoulders and back, he stared into her anxious eyes for what seemed an eternity, though in reality it could not have been more than a few seconds. "Sleeping wherever I can find a place dry enough," he replied less emotionally. "I suggest you get your rest as well. The last twelve hours have been hard on us all."

This time as he turned to leave, she grabbed him, one hand clenched about his arm. Beads of rain ran down her cheeks and hesitated at her mouth, and suddenly his need to taste those lips for the last time was as shattering as the thunder above. For the past days, since the night he'd made love to her on the deck of the *Santos,* he'd battled his mind's and body's need to sweep her up in his arms and kiss her, just to assure himself that she hadn't felt as good as he remembered, that she had *not* responded with a hungry urgency that belied her demure appearance. But that was dangerous. He might begin to think that maybe it wasn't his notorious reputation that enthralled her so, or the thrill of the forbidden that turned her beautiful eyes the color of green fire.

He yanked his arm away and strode out into the rain. *Don't look back. It could never work. She's in love with another man. She could never care for you, not with your past.* He'd made his decision to confront King, and falling for Sarah would only drastically complicate matters.

"Morgan!"

Lightning ripped the sky and thunder crashed.

"Morgan!"

Grinding out a curse, he stopped, fists clenched and shaking as the storm roiled above him. Sarah ran toward him, freezing at the sight of him standing spread-legged in the path with torrents of water running off the brim of his hat. The dirty and shredded remnants of her once fine clothing did pitifully little to protect her shivering flesh from the downpour. Her hair clung to her face and neck and shoulders like flax. Her eyes were like fire in the night. "Why?" she cried in a voice drowned by the deluge. "Why do you keep running from me?"

"What the hell do you want from me?" he shouted back. "I won't be another one of your conquests, Sarah, so just turn your drenched little butt around and get back to your hut before it's too late for both of us!"

He turned from her again.

"Coward!" she screamed over the roar of thunder.

He spun around so suddenly he skidded in the mud. Then he was plowing toward her, gasping for air amid the shower of drops driving into his face. She watched him come with a look of horror stamped on her features: fear, shock, regret, and a flash of indecision over whether or not she should turn tail and run as fast as she could to the safety of her hut. She didn't, of course. She was too damned stubborn.

He grabbed her face in one hand, fingers biting into the soft white skin of her jaw, then buried the other in her hair and dragged her head back. Her pale throat was arched and her eyes were unflinching, no longer frightened but glittering with an irony that gave him but a fraction of a second's pause. He kissed her with a passion he had felt few times in his life, grinding his mouth on hers one way, then another, in an attempt to prove to her that he was not a man to tease, or she would regret it. He would *make* her regret it, by God. She wouldn't forget him any time soon. When she was lying with her lovely legs wrapped around Norman on her wedding night, she would close her bewitching eyes and remember when he had raped her mouth with passion and hate and need . . .

He invaded her lips with his tongue as he imagined his sex between her beautiful legs. She tasted like rain. She smelled like a woman whose body knew exactly where his preferred to be in that moment.

She squirmed against him and he held her tighter, kissed her harder until he felt a shudder pass through her like a current. Then he shoved her away and waited for the hail of retribution, perhaps the slap across his cheek. Yet nothing came. All she did was blink her eyes dazedly as the rain ran down her face.

"Are you happy?" he sneered. "Are you? Now get the hell away from me and thank your lucky stars that I didn't rob Norman of his right to your goddamned virginity on his wedding night."

He left her and did not look back again until he had entered the dark line of trees crowding the path. Then he sank against the trunk of an acacia and pressed his face so hard into the gnarled bark that blood ran down his cheek, until the pain in his groin had subsided, as well as the desire to storm back into the rain, throw Sarah to the ground, and show her exactly what it meant to need beyond rational thought, to want her so badly you were willing to give up your last fragment of pride just to hold her, however briefly.

Minutes clipped by before he was able to regain control of his mind and body; then, tilting his hat over his eyes, he hunched his shoulders against the deluge and started toward the river. He looked back only once: a mistake. Sarah's small form, a black silhouette against the firelight, stood watching him from the hut's doorway. He almost hesitated, then gritted his teeth and walked on through the darkness.

Sarah watched Morgan disappear amid the wind-whipped trees and the flashes of lightning, while inside she felt a riot of emotions swirling into a lazy eddy of glowing warmth. She couldn't move. She felt her heart beating in her throat and temples and, strangely enough, on the tip of her tongue. Her fingertips tingled.

How could he walk away when her world had turned upside down? Closing her eyes, she touched her swollen lips and wondered if at any time in her life she had felt so gloriously alive, like a shimmering spirit set free from its mortal bonds. Never. She had never felt this way. She knew now that there was something between them; it had danced around them, flashed like white lightning. Perhaps it had been there all along, since that first night Morgan Kane had swept her up in his arms. No, she hadn't imagined it. And she could no longer dismiss her reactions to his presence as anger or irritation or, as ridiculous as it seemed now, an infatuation brought on by an idiotic belief that he was the mythical *boto*.

An Indian trundled in and dropped her trunk at her feet, spilling the array of feminine attire in a colorful heap on the earth floor. The young man scrambled to scoop the clothing up, but she waved him away with a remote smile and fell to her knees to collect it herself. Her diary was lying open, the script staring back at her to remind her that she had no right to be attracted to another man. She was engaged to Norman.

She slammed the diary closed and squeezed her eyes shut. That wonderful sense of euphoria vanished, leaving her with an aching head. Her lips throbbed, as if reminding her that she had just committed the most grievous of sins.

But she hadn't! It wasn't as if she and Norman were already married. And besides, it would probably never happen again. She would make certain it never happened again. She would stay as far away from Morgan as possible, and . . .

"Who am I kidding?" she asked aloud. "I've been attracted to the man since the night I met him in that hot, horrible little hovel." Attracted was an understatement. Mesmerized. Fascinated. Exhilarated. Intoxicated. Obsessed! Everything she always believed that she should feel about Norman, but hadn't. She'd convinced herself that such emotions existed only deep in the pages of romantic novels—the forbidden sort the girls at school read secretly in the night by candlelight. She'd accepted her feelings of quiet respect for Norman, ignoring her own desires for fireworks and stars and dreamy surrenders, chastising herself for even thinking about them.

A gust of wind whipped through the doorway, spraying her with rain and forcing her thoughts back to a somber reality. What was she thinking? Just because Morgan had kissed her, just because she'd felt the earth move, didn't mean she was in love, any more than it meant that he had somehow fallen for her. Besides, he was used to women swooning in his arms. She'd allowed herself to fall into the same trap as all the others, and now he was no doubt standing out in the rain laughing at her. He must have kissed a thousand women like he'd kissed her. She felt heartsick and foolish and guilty and confused. And she wished he would walk through the door that very minute and kiss her again.

MORGAN AND HENRY AND THE INDIANS STRUCK OUT BEFORE SUN-rise. With rain pounding their shoulders, they steered the canoes up the river at a snail's pace. Occasionally the muted roll of thunder vibrated the air. Now and again the eerie reflection of lightning above the trees shimmered through the drenched sky like static electricity.

The river rose. Where once the shallow bends had been easily navigated, now the shoals were frothing with water. Eating into the tenuous sandbanks, the flood swept trees and bushes into the swirling melee, forming floating islands similar to the one the *Santos* had encountered, forcing the travelers to midstream in order to avoid them. Yet even there they found little respite from the dangers, for whirlpools came close to capsizing their boats on several occasions.

Finally, after battling the impossible tempest, Morgan ordered the expedition ashore, a seemingly impossible maneuver as the water roared against the banks, cutting sharply over jutting tree roots that raked at the hulls of their canoes like knives. He was forced to grab onto a low-lying branch with his bare hands. Briars bit into them, yet gritting his teeth against the pain, he hung tight until Henry could scramble ashore and secure the canoe with a rope. They dragged the vessel up the incline then slipped and slid back down to the water to help the others.

Many of the men had managed to reach safety. Yet farther downriver two overturned canoes attested to the treachery of the rapids. With rain battering his shoulders, Morgan headed back to his own craft, trudging up the razorback ridge, stumbling over fallen trees and buttressed tree roots rising out of the mud.

Damn Sarah St. James! Damn her to hell for turning him into a coward who would rather run than face up to the fact that he was falling for her. At last he had finally accepted his destiny to confront King and die. Then in Sarah had walked, the embodiment of everything gentle and beautiful and innocent that he had ever imagined loving—that he had ever imagined loving him. But she loved another man. "Damn." He beat the ground. "Damn."

THEY MANAGED TO CONSTRUCT A SHELTER OF PALM AND FERN leaves which they crawled beneath before falling into an exhausted sleep. Eventually the storm subsided, yet the rain continued to fall in a slow drizzle throughout the rest of the day and night. Sometime before dawn the spattering of rain ceased and a wave of humid heat washed over them. Little by little the jungle came to life. Steam rose from the floresta floor in clouds of condensation that felt as wet as the rain had earlier.

Perhaps it was the snap of a twig that first brought Morgan around, or maybe it was the heat that made his muddied skin itch and the wounds on his hands burn as if with fever. Gradually he became aware of movement around him, the hum of muted voices. Tired and sleepy, he tried to remember if he had had too much to drink before turning in. Then he tried to recall where he was. He rolled his head and groaned. His entire body ached. His mouth was dry as dust. He needed a drink and a cigarette—badly.

Someone nudged him none too gently in the ribs with a foot. Squinting at the daylight, he opened his eyes and stared up the barrel of a rifle at Sarah.

"Surprise," she stated blandly.

Focusing harder, he looked beyond her to find Kan and Henry at his side. They all regarded Morgan as if he were a leech.

Garbed at last in breeches tucked into high boots, and a shirt that fit her loosely, the sleeves rolled up to expose her narrow wrists, Sarah glared down at him with a look of fury. "You snake," she said. "You swine. Did you think I'd let you get away with it? Did you honestly believe I'd allow you to go to Japurá without me?"

Lowering his aching head to the ground, he closed his eyes. The gladness he felt at seeing her left him weak. But there came as quickly the nagging reality of their circumstances and the responsibility he must assume for her safety. "Look," he managed, "let's be reasonable."

"Reasonable!"

He winced.

"There is nothing reasonable about you. This is my expedition, yet you seem intent on losing me along the way. I'd like to know why."

"My apologies for caring whether you live or die." He opened his eyes. Sarah's face appeared drained of color and drawn by fatigue. She looked very young, and despite the haughtiness of her uplifted chin, extremely frightened and wary, and strangely hurt. Glancing at the rifle barrel still aimed at his nose, he said, "Sarah, Japurá is no place for a woman."

"I've managed nicely up until now."

"I don't know how you made it upriver in that storm, but that'll look like a pleasure outing compared to what comes next. Compared to an overland journey through Japurá, hell is a holiday, and if you don't believe me, ask Henry." Frowning toward the pygmy, he stressed, "Tell her, Longfellow. What are you waiting for?"

"He's right," Henry replied. "We shouldn't have allowed you to come, Sarah. We should have forced you to remain in Santarém—in Georgetown, for that matter. We were selfish swines; there's simply no other excuse—except that we enjoyed your company too much. We wanted you around as long as possible, at a risk to your life. For that we apologize."

She shifted her attention back to Morgan. "I might believe that of you, sir, but not of him." She punctuated *him* with a sharp poke of her rifle at Morgan's nose. "This one cannot abide me. He's made that more than obvious these last weeks. Fine," she told Morgan. "Perhaps once I believed your friendship was important to me; now I don't care whether you like me or not. But I will tell you this: I'm going to Japurá with or without your support. That bastard King destroyed my father, and I'm going to rectify the situation if it's the last thing I do."

"It will be. You'll never leave Japurá alive."

"Yes, I will, because you'll be there beside me. You went in there once. You made it out. You can do it again. I know you can!"

Covering his face with his sore hands, Morgan groaned. Then he sat up. Surrounded by savages whose expressions ran from anger to suspicion to outright adoration, it was all he could do not to laugh at the absurdity of the situation. Finally he climbed to his feet, brushed the foliage from his damp breeches, and stomped the mud from his boots. Only then did he address Sarah again.

Shoving the gun barrel aside, he approached her. She quelled, her bright eyes widening, her lips parting. For an instant he was awash with the need to take her face in his hands and make love to her mouth again until she fought him as she had that night on her father's veranda. Instead, he grabbed her and shook her until she whimpered and stared up at him with a strange sort of pain that made him question the reason for her anger. "What happens to you if I'm killed, Sarah?"

"But you won't be. I have faith that you'll see us through this—"

"Faith! Sarah, I'm not God. I can't work miracles, no matter what you've been told."

"My father believed in you, and so do these men."

He turned away in frustration and walked to the outcrop of rock over the river. He gazed down at the falsely serene surface of water before facing her again. She waited in watchful silence, her features hopeful and desperate.

"Please," she said, her voice ragged with emotion. "We can't do this without you, Morgan."

He shook his head. She wanted a hero, and he wasn't it. God, if she only knew.

Sarah approached him. As she placed her hand upon his arm he noted her fingers were as swollen as his. Turning her palms up, he saw they were covered with blisters. "The oars," she explained. "I helped Kan paddle."

He covered her hand with his, rubbed the raw flesh lightly with the pad of his thumb. "You might have drowned," he told her.

"But I didn't."

Turning back toward the river, he watched a great black bird rise up from the shallows and fly to the tree limbs high overhead. He suddenly ached for the sunshine on his face, for a cool drink of something besides rotgut to quench his thirst, for a world of things that he could never get— chiefly among them, the love of a beautiful woman.

"Will you do it?" came her anxious voice.

"Yeah," he replied wearily. "I will."

Before he could react, she had thrown her arms around him and pressed her face into his back. "How can I ever thank you?" she asked.

Remembering the kiss they'd shared two nights before, he smiled wryly to himself. "Oh, I could think of a few ways," he replied in a whisper.

"You're wonderful." She breathed against his skin.

He closed his eyes and swallowed.

"Wonderful . . ."

Chapter Ten

THE RIVER CONTINUED TO RISE DUE TO HEAVY RAINS ALONG THE slopes of the Serra Tapirapeco mountains, which straddled the Brazil–Venezuela border. Slowly, the land was being swallowed up before the travelers' eyes.

The stillness and gloom had become almost painful. To speak was to shatter the quiet in the most disconcerting way. They found themselves whispering, yet even that seemed to destroy the balance of nature. Eventually they began communicating from boat to boat by hand signals, which was wiser since they had begun noticing signs of Indians along the river. Kan and Henry hotly debated whether the tribes were Txukahameis or Yanoamö.

"The Txukahameis will take us in and treat us like gods. Their women will want to mate with us to show their delight in our visit," Henry explained. "The Yanoamö will boil us alive."

Morgan said, "Then let's hope they're Txukahameis."

Among the patches of green shade and splinters of light, the barrellike trunks of trees rose out of the dark, still water to tower hundreds of feet above them. Their roots were monstrous, rising in an arch to form buttresses as grand and imposing as those of any Gothic cathedral. High overhead, clouds of condensation, trapped against the ceiling of tree limbs and leaves, dripped moisture onto the river, covering the pitch-black surface with ripples that spiraled outward in glistening undulations.

Due to the rising water, campsites that did not need clearing were becoming harder to locate. Each day the hour grew later, the sky darker, before they were able to beach their crafts on one of few remaining sandbars looming up from the black-red water of the Rio Negro, the northern tributary of the Amazon they'd chosen to follow into Japurá.

On the evening of the seventh day of their journey up the Negro, Morgan and Henry had given up all hope of finding a sandbank on which to camp. Dark was descending rapidly, and with it swarms of mosquitoes that made their presence on the river intolerable. Any chance of weaving their way through the marshy undergrowth to solid land was out of the question without daylight to guide them. The tangled vegetation was too dense to hack their way through by boat. The strain of expectation mounted, for they knew if they did not find a campsite soon, they would be forced to travel throughout the night. Tempers grew short with the bombardment of insects and the effects of fatigue. Even Henry, who was always so mild-tempered, had begun to curse.

Early in their journey up the Negro, Morgan had rescued a tiny marmoset that was stranded on a floating tree. It balanced now on the brim of his hat as he turned to Henry and said, "I wish you'd do something about these damn mosquitoes."

"You don't say," Henry replied. "And what do you suggest I do?"

"You're the savage. Rattle some bones or somethin' at 'em."

"I don't have any bones."

"What's wrong with the ones in your nose? They gotta be good for somethin'. They sure as hell don't help your looks any."

"You're an ass, Morgan. Has anyone ever told you that?"

"Every day of my life."

"So why don't you do something about it?"

"Why don't you grow another foot or two so I don't get a backache when I try to talk to you?"

"That's low, Morgan. Real low. At least people like me."

"They think you're funny-lookin'."

"Someday you're going to regret how you talk to me."

"I doubt it."

Morgan flicked his cigarette into the water, where it made a soft hiss and smoldered. He went back to paddling the canoe. Sarah thought, but she couldn't be certain, that she heard him laugh. Then he said, "Henry?"

"What?"

"Know what the cannibal said when he came home one night and found his wife chopping up a python and a pygmy?"

"What?"

"Oh, no, not a snake and pygmy pie again."

Sarah bit her lip as there came a smothered chuckle behind her. "You're disgusting," Henry finally managed in a bland voice.

"Yeah," Morgan replied. "I know."

Soon night was upon them. Maneuvering the canoes closer together, each man strained hard to see through the darkness, alert for signs of impending disaster. Sarah felt her body tense with each dip of the oar in the water. She, too, searched the river for any churning that might signify the approach of night-hunting alligators.

They had just rounded a bend in the river when Kan, who rode in the next canoe, called out and pointed to some object off the bow of the American's boat. What appeared to be a great mound of floating leaves was fast approaching. Lacking time to change course, Morgan rammed his oar into the middle of it in hopes of shoving it aside. For an instant it appeared to disintegrate completely, but as he drew the oar back into the boat and leaned forward to get a better look at what they had hit, the mass exploded in a frenzy of inch-long fire ants that shot up the paddle and swarmed over his hands and arms before he could move.

He appeared stunned at first. Half turning toward Sarah, he opened his mouth to say something, yet as she reached for him, he jumped to his feet and yelled, "No!"

The canoe rocked perilously, causing Sarah to cry out and Henry to react with blinding speed. Shoving her down in the boat, he hit the ant-covered paddle with his own oar, knocking it into the water. Looking up at Morgan, his face void of any emotion, he ordered, "Jump! Jump, damn you, jump!"

In the instant of hesitation that followed, the ants began injecting their venom into the flesh of Morgan's hands, and began pouring in a writhing stream up his neck and over his face. Only then did it become terrifyingly clear to Sarah what was happening. As he reached to claw at the small demons, knocking his hat from his head, she screamed. The next seconds were horrifying as she, too, attempted to leap to her feet and reach for him, her only thought to help him wipe away the furious insects. Yet Henry grabbed her back down, spilling her to the bottom of the canoe, which was hazardously close to overturning. "Jump!" she heard him yell. "For God's sake, man, jump!"

The next fraction of a minute passed like an eternity as Morgan, bending at the waist, groaned and rolled toward the water. He hit it with hardly a splash and sank beneath the surface.

Silence. It was deafening, hovering like a mammoth weight as the canoes gathered about the place Morgan had disappeared, each man ready to grab him the instant he resurfaced. With each second that ticked by, Sarah's panic grew; her eyes ached from the pain of trying to see through the night and dark water, waiting for him to emerge. Henry, on his knees and gripping the edge of the hull in his fists, swore through his teeth in frustration. "Damn you!" he yelled. "Morgan! Where the blazes are you?" He dove into the river, leaving Sarah alone in the canoe. Kan maneuvered his boat near hers and leapt aboard, grabbing up Henry's oar and plunging it into the current to avoid being swept into a partially submerged tree.

Again they waited. Her heart in her throat and her body burning with fear, she searched the watery void, every nightmare she had ever imagined lurking under the surface looming up before her mind's eyes. "Please," she whispered, swallowing back the rise of panic. This wasn't possible. He was there somewhere and—

Henry broke the surface farther downriver, calling out for the others before sliding under again. Time after time he dove until he reached out for Kan, who dragged him into the canoe.

Again the silence descended. Hands pressed between her knees, Sarah huddled in the bottom of the boat, staring sightlessly into the river. The overwhelming emptiness and shock were staggering. Just two minutes before, Morgan had been sitting in front of her, doing his best to antagonize his friend . . . and now he was gone.

She groaned. Not until she looked down and found the little marmoset quivering against her leg did the full impact of the American's disappearance hit her. Agony drove like a fist into her chest. A scream burned up her throat as she covered her mouth with her hands, squeezed closed her eyes, and rocked in such misery she thought she might die. With trembling fingers she retrieved his hat from the bottom of the canoe and, crushing it in her hands, covered her face with it and sobbed, "Oh, my God. Oh, God. No!"

Their boats drifted as the Indians, apparently at a loss without Morgan, seemed confused and as stunned and shaken as Sarah and Henry. With no warning, Henry stumbled to his feet, only slightly rocking the boat. His black hair streaming down his face and into his eyes, he glared down the channel and, doubling his fists in fury, shouted, "Morgan, if this is some sort of joke . . . Morgan! Mooorgaan!" And then he crumbled, buried his face in his wet palms, and cried like a baby.

"It's my fault," Sarah said. "All my fault. Had I never persisted in this ridiculous venture, Morgan would be alive." Wiping her eyes with the back of her hand, she looked over at Henry. He stood on the verge of the campfire light, the yellow glow reflecting off his bronze back as he stared into the dark. The pygmy had not spoken since Morgan's disappearance two nights before. Her own grief had not diminished in the least either. Over and over in her mind she conjured pictures of his heart-stopping image in white, that hauntingly beautiful light in his eyes, and the disturbingly poignant smile that would briefly cross his mouth at the most unexpected moments.

Feeling the grief rise inside her again, she held out her hand to the marmoset curled up in Morgan's hat, which lay close to the fire. The monkey had refused food and water the past two days. It peered up at Sarah with black eyes, yet as her fingers reached to touch it, it shrank away.

Kan brought her a plate of fruit, while another Indian brewed tea. A kettle of rice bubbled on the fire, and a spit of *tucunaré*, fresh from the river, baked over the flames. But the idea of food made Sarah ill. She could not shake free of that moment when Morgan had turned to her with confusion and fear on his handsome features. She had reached out to help him, yet . . .

She understood now why he had jumped up and cried, "No!" Had the insects swept upon her, she would have been inflicted by the stings. He'd saved her the only way possible, by throwing himself into the river.

Sarah had a sudden vision of his face ravaged by the treacherous river creatures, and she shuddered once again. Fresh tears spilled from her eyes, and with little care as to what the others would think, she threw herself to the ground and wept aloud. Then, succumbing to weariness, she drifted to sleep.

SOMETIME DURING THE NIGHT SARAH DECIDED TO FORGET THE RUB-ber seeds and her desire to force a confession from King, and return home. Sleepily, she huddled near the fire and attempted to record her feelings, but the words wouldn't come. Turning back through her diary, she read each entry, beginning with the one she had quickly scribbled the night before her arrival in Georgetown, before she had learned of her father's death. Line after line was devoted to Norman and her dreams of becoming his wife. There were wedding and party plans, long lists of guests she hoped would attend the ceremony. But nowhere was there a mention of love.

Next there were pages filled with grief, desperation, and the ramblings of a young woman, spurred on by a need for revenge.

Then there was Morgan. Little by little, her writings spoke less of Norman and more of the "infuriating, obnoxious, and passably handsome American" who made her blood boil in anger. Gradually the anger changed to respect. Then admiration. And finally . . .

She took a long breath and released it. Somewhere along the way he had worked a sort of magic upon her, as he did upon everyone. She hardly ever thought of Norman anymore. She had managed to put aside her grief over her father. Now that she was being completely truthful with herself, she could admit that her frantic battle up the Amazon in order to catch up with the American after he'd deserted her in Manáos had been due more to fear of losing him forever than to fury over her abandonment. His presence had calmed her these past many weeks. His was the first face she would search out when she arose at dawn. Through the miserable hours of the day her eyes would continually come back to his, searching for reassurance, strength, hope, some subtle sign that he was with her, spiritually as well as physically. And then she recalled his kiss, which was a little like drinking fire, consuming in its burning race through her body, blazing her mind, searing her soul.

Opening her diary to the first blank page, she penned: *"Morgan is gone. And I am heartbroken."*

HENRY DIDN'T APPEAR SURPRISED BY HER DECISION. HE SIMPLY NOD-ded and ordered the natives to prepare to return to Manáos.

The Indians didn't move, forcing Henry to repeat himself.

Kan said, "But we must continue to wait for the American's return."

"The American is dead!" Henry replied angrily.

The Indians spoke among themselves before addressing Sarah. Unable to understand, she looked to Henry. His face was furious. "I have given you orders to break camp," he repeated.

"What are they saying?" Sarah demanded.

Henry stalked to her tent, which he proceeded to take down himself. "Stupid bastards," he grumbled. "They believe Morgan is alive. A *boto* cannot drown, they say. His magic will protect him. Christ." He flung the canvas enclosure to the ground, then swung toward the men again. "Get this through your superstitious heads: my friend is dead. God knows what got him in that water, but he's gone. No ridiculous belief in magical fish is going to bring him back!"

Kan, staring hard at Henry, argued, "But he is *boto!* You told us yourself. You said you saw the pink dolphin walk from water as the man called Kane. You said he is capable of anything, even crossing Japurá on foot."

Standing by the fire, Henry kicked the pot of boiling water, spilling it into the flames. Sarah stared hard at her friend as one minute dragged into another, her own anticipation mounting. Odd how she had come to believe in—in fact, to rely on—the very superstitions she had once scoffed at. But then perhaps it wasn't so strange. Everyone needed something, or someone, to believe in. Morgan had seemed magic, and invincible. Believing in such stories had given her the courage to face danger and hardship on this journey. As long as he was there to lead the way, she could accomplish anything.

Henry turned and, refusing to look at her, said in a quiet, defeated voice, "We've camped in this place for two days, Sarah. If Morgan were alive . . ." Finally he lifted his gaze to hers. He appeared childlike and forlorn, and greatly grieved. "He was special, Sarah, and he didn't even realize it. To most people I am an object of curiosity. Having spent most of my life in England, I returned to Brazil and found that I no longer fit in with my own kind. Yet Morgan accepted me for what I was and never tried to pretend that I was something I'm not. 'So what if you're short and ugly?' he once said. 'I'm tall and not too bad to look at, but where the hell has it gotten me?' "

Henry walked away, leaving her to face Kan and the others alone. Taking a deep breath, she finally said, "We cannot remain here forever hoping for miracles. It's time to go home, Kan. Please follow my orders and let's get out of here."

She walked to the fire and picked up Morgan's hat. She cooed to the marmoset while behind her, Kan carried on a heated discourse with the Indians. Within the hour they were steering their canoes back to Manáos.

A long while passed before Henry spoke. "I wouldn't like to think that you're blaming yourself for Morgan's death. I'm the one who coerced him into bringing us here. He didn't want to do it. He was afraid of King, despite his loathing of the man. Hate for King had become so central in his life that I thought by confronting the bastard he could at last live in peace. But I don't think I would ever have convinced him to go had he not been so frightened of your going alone." He sighed. "He wasn't nearly as disreputable or dislikable as he seemed."

"I know," she replied.

"At first I thought he hated me. He said things that were often unkind. Then I realized it was his way of keeping a wall between himself and the ones he cared for most. That way he didn't have to admit his true feelings, and needs—not to those he loved or even to himself. He was an orphan, you know."

The memory of their conversation concerning their families those many nights ago came back to her in a rush of tears that spilled down her face.

"That poppycock about his father being a naval officer was a lie. He never knew his father. His mother was a prostitute who worked the docks. She was unable to care for him, and when he was six she turned him over to a Catholic orphanage in New Orleans. I don't think he ever saw her again. He was never adopted. He told me in one of those rare moments when he let his guard down that I was the only family he'd ever had. You can't know what that meant to me." He stopped rowing and placed the oar across his knees. Grief washed over him again.

They drifted with the current as the air grew hellishly steamy, condensing in clouds of moisture that hung over the river like fog. Somewhere a bird called out, its high plinking cry sounding like pebbles dropping into a crystal glass. In response there came the donkeylike braying of some animal that made Sarah wish even harder that Morgan were there. She had not realized how safe she had felt with him. Now death and danger seemed to loom at her from every side. How blind and ignorant she had been not to respect—and fear—the jungle.

Ahead of them, Kan's canoe showed intermittently through the mist, appearing, then disappearing as they rounded a bend in the river. Henry and the Indian sharing their boat eased their oars into the water, deftly guiding the craft through the tricky currents, all the while keeping their eyes trained on the vessel ahead for signs of trouble.

It was Kan who first noticed the change in their surroundings. Easing his oar to the bottom of the canoe, he peered back through the fog at Sarah and Henry. It came to them all in that moment: the strange stillness and silence. Through the primeval cloak of swirling steam they watched an iguana ripple through the water and disappear between the vermilion petals of a river flower growing along the marshy banks. Kan, sitting erect and on guard, raised his hand and cupped it around his ear, signaling to Sarah and Henry that he had heard something. Everyone sat forward in rapt attention. A moment passed, then . . .

There came the gasp and splash of a solitary swimmer somewhere behind the submerged trees near the shore. Sarah's heart stopped at the sound. She turned to Henry and grabbed his hand as his dark eyes did their best to pierce the fog rising off the water. Again the sound came, a sigh and gulp of air. It seemed eerily human, yet somehow . . .

The Indian sitting in the bow of Sarah's boat leapt to his feet and, pointing to the water, cried, *"Boto!"*

The water near their vessel roiled, and as Sarah stared in fascination the swimmer surfaced, puffing a spray of air from its blowhole, humping up before plunging underwater, its triangular pink back knifing through the murky surface. Again and again it rose, rolling around the bobbing boats, slapping its tail, and filling the air with noises that sounded uncannily like laughter.

The marmoset in Morgan's hat scuttled up to Sarah's shoulder and chattered as she reached out for the dolphin, missing its glossy hide by inches. But as she began to withdraw her hand it appeared again, sliding its sleek wet body against her palm, from its long bottle nose to the end of its tail, emitting a soft, satisfied sigh that brought a rise to the hairs on her nape. Then, with a flash of its fins, it swirled away, knifing through the water like a silver blade and—before the spectators' amazed eyes—soaring straight out of the river where it danced upright along the surface, in and out of the fog, so that for an instant it looked so startlingly like a man that many of the Indians cried out in fear.

"My God," Sarah whispered. Clutching Henry close to her, she watched as the creature slowly and silently slid back into the water, leaving hardly a ripple in its wake as it sank from view. The minutes hung suspended while each person watched and waited for the *boto* to reappear, to assure them that what had just transpired had been no dream, no fantasy, but reality.

Yet it did not reappear. The stillness moved over them again, the sounds of the floresta returning to swallow them in a cacophony of hums and shrieks and whistles. Overhead a pair of bright red macaws flew, followed by a flock of green and blue parrots. Near the shore the bushes rattled and an alligator slid through the mud and into the river, and there, peered toward the canoes with eyes that were barely visible above the surface of the water.

Relaxing, Sarah released her breath. In that instant, Kan cried out through the fog, "Aaaiyaah! Oooaaaiyaah!" And he motioned toward the opposite sandbank.

"Good God," Henry exclaimed. "Sarah, Sarah—look!" Leaping to his feet, rocking the boat perilously, he screamed out in joy, his laughter reverberating from the floresta walls and ceiling. The Indians, too, began to laugh and cheer, and Sarah broke down and wept.

Morgan Kane stood on a sandbar at the bend of the river. He was alive!

Chapter Eleven

HENRY LEAPT FROM THE CANOE AND SLOGGED HIS WAY THROUGH knee-deep water before reaching the sandbar. Loincloth dripping, he came at Morgan full speed, throwing himself against him like a child would a long-lost parent. They stumbled backward, spilling to the ground.

"Morgan, you're alive. God, I thought we'd lost you!"

His arms and legs thrown wide, Morgan winced as Henry squirmed off him. He had little strength to speak, much less sit up. The effort to stand moments before had been almost more than he could manage. On his knees, Henry gazed down into his face, his look of relief melting into awareness and concern. He placed his small hands on Morgan's cheeks. "Morgan, you look like hell."

"And you're still short and ugly. Tell me something I don't already know." A smile flickered over Henry's lips, making Morgan laugh dryly. "What's wrong? Don't tell me you haven't ever met a man whose face has been ravaged by fire ants."

"Is there much pain, my friend?"

Morgan tried to wet his lips; it wasn't possible. Then Sarah materialized over Henry's shoulder, eyes luminous with tears, knuckles pressed against her mouth in an attempt to hold back her emotions. Morgan blinked to clear his vision, to no avail. He wanted to assure himself that she was not as beautiful as his imagination had pictured her the past nightmarish days. Surely she had to be a hallucination brought on by his pain and fever.

He reached for Henry, who had begun rambling. "We'd given up hope. What happened? Can you tell us? By Jove, but the last days have been torturous for us. I can only imagine what they've been for you."

"Henry."

"The natives never gave up hope. 'The American is the *boto,'* they kept repeating. 'The *boto* cannot drown.' "

"Henry?"

"We made camp about two miles upriver and—"

"Henry!" He grabbed Henry's shoulders and jerked him down to his face. "Be quiet," he said. "There are Yanoamö out there, in those trees."

Henry glanced toward the menacing forest. "You've seen them?"

"Yes."

"Did they see you?"

"Obviously not, or I'd be laid out over someone's dinner plate."

Henry appeared thoughtful. "We could make it halfway to Manáos by nightfall, since the current is with us."

Morgan frowned. "Manáos?"

"Yes. We've decided to forget King and go home. We—"

"No."

"I beg your pardon?"

"I said no."

"But, Morgan—"

"No but Morgans." He gripped Henry more tightly. "Two thoughts have kept me alive these last days. One of them was getting to King. I'm gonna make that son of a bitch pay for what he did to me. He took my dignity. He made me want to die."

Henry nodded.

"The other is . . ." He looked toward Sarah. "Gold," he whispered, his voice slurring as he struggled to remain conscious. "It's gonna make me a rich man, Henry. I'll be able to buy . . . anything I want, includin' a title if that's what it takes to be somebody in *her* world."

"But, Morgan, you need rest. We'll need to do something about your . . . face."

"A real mess, huh?"

Trying to smile, Henry nodded. "You're almost as ugly as me."

"God, how comforting."

"We might make it to the Barcelos mission before dark. The ruins will offer us protection and shelter until you're fit enough to travel. Are you up to the journey?"

"No," he replied. "But we'll do it anyway."

SOON THEY WERE GLIDING BACK UP THE RIVER. MORGAN LAY IN THE bottom of the canoe, his head resting in Sarah's lap. Occasionally she would soothe his hot brow with her cool hands, and although she spoke little, her smile comforted him.

He was aware of voices and noises around him. They swam in and out of his consciousness, as they had for the past two days. The sounds of birds and animals seemed to speak to him in human tongues until, in some corner of his mind, he realized he was hallucinating. Odd echoes of a woman's laughter flitted on the edge of his awareness, yet when he awoke and gazed up at Sarah with his one good eye that was not swollen closed, he found her studying him with a solemnity that belied her young years.

Every so often she spoke to him, and he answered, yet afterward he had trouble recalling the words that had passed between them. He asked for a cigarette once and watched, amused, as Sarah lit it for him, wrinkling her nose at the acrid taste of the smoke and tobacco. Then she slid it between his lips, her fingertips brushing tenderly, and tenuously, against his mouth. "Oh, Morgan," she whispered. "I thought I'd lost you."

He awoke once to find his marmoset perched on his chest, chattering wildly. Sarah forced a piece of fruit into his hand and directed him to feed the upset animal. He did, and the marmoset, with juice running off its elbows, settled into a satisfied silence as it feasted on the succulent treat. Then it curled into a furry ball on his stomach and fell asleep.

When he awoke again the air felt cooler. Twilight had slipped in around them, and with it the fragrance of night flowers filled the air like perfume. The Indians beached their canoes on a stretch of sand that curved like a scythe around a bend in the river. As Sarah and Henry helped Morgan from the boat, he looked up to see a crucifix high above him. Covered with vines of bright flowers, the aged object reflected the last rays of sunlight that spilled through an opening in the foliage canopy. For an awe-inspiring moment everyone paused, taking in the sight. How long had it been since they had seen the sun, since they had seen the sky for that matter?

Sarah left Morgan's side and walked up the crumbling steps to the doorless entry of the deserted mission. As she turned her face up to the sun, light poured over her in a bath of soft yellow, turning her features the color of butter and her hair into a pale fire that might surely have burned him had he buried his hands in it, which was what he longed to do in that moment. Finally she turned to him and smiled. "I thought I would never feel the sun on my face again. Morgan, it's wonderful." Then she entered the mission, leaving her spellbound audience staring after her in silence.

* * *

ONCE, THE REDUCTION OF BARCELOS HAD STOOD FOR ORDER AND permanence in Amazonia. Now, however, the settlement, which had been abandoned a century ago, was in danger of being swallowed completely by the forest. Even from the river one could easily see that the clearing in the *floresta* was not natural, but the remains of what had once been a thriving Portuguese fort situated between the Padauiri and Branco tributaries that fed into the Rio Negro. Its paved alleys were now littered with thorn bushes and serrated jungle grass that had thrust its way up among the stone blocks laid out in the main square.

Henry, having built a fire of rotting wood, perched at the foot of the steps and worked diligently at pulverizing the berries of some plant into a thick mush, to which he added a finely ground powder, the ashes of cecropia, and a liquid steeped with coca leaves, which he had carried with him from Belém. "The cecropia will draw out the infection," he told Sarah and Morgan. "The coca will alleviate the discomfort." His hands stopped their furious grinding as he cocked his head toward Morgan, who reclined in a hammock between two trees. "The effects of this won't be pleasant, Morgan, but it'll be worth it in the end. I take it you're still in a great amount of pain?"

Feeling sweat seep from every pore on his body, he nodded.

Kan moved toward the fire and, bending low, stirred a dark brew that had been cooking for some time. As Henry looked at him curiously, Kan stated, "It is the ayahuasca, the medicine of my shaman. It will give me great power, enough that I may draw the poison from Kane's body and cast it to the dark."

"By Jove," Henry muttered. "That's quite good, old man." Standing, he moved in and out of the firelight, motioning toward Sarah, who had never ventured far from Morgan's side since their arrival at Barcelos. "Help me to get his shirt off. Careful. His arm is badly swollen." Partially turning, he watched Kan drink down the vile-looking tea, then he directed, "Bring me that knife, please . . . that is, if you can manage it, old boy. That's a good chief. You might try calming the others. They seem to believe that if Morgan dies, they will too. Something about their inability to keep him safe from evil spirits. You wouldn't have had anything to do with that rumor, would you, chief?"

Kan retrieved Morgan's knife where it lay by the fire. He delivered it, swaying slightly as if he were drunk. Pressing nearer, his bronze body covered in a film of sweat, he began humming under his breath. Henry, smiling down at Morgan, said, "Try to ignore him and maybe he'll go away."

Morgan could find no humor in the situation. He hurt too damn much. The flesh on the side of his face and neck was swollen to the point of bursting. His right arm and hand, from the tip of his fingers to his shoulder, were distended to twice their normal size. As the sleeve of his shirt was cut away, the sight of his arm told him exactly what he feared most. Infection had set in.

"Morgan, I want you to listen to me very carefully," came Henry's calm words. "Think of something pleasant. Conjure up the most beautiful image you can, and don't deviate from it for a moment. Can you do that?"

Morgan turned his eyes to Sarah. He expected pity, perhaps revulsion at his pus-enlarged features. He anticipated tears or hysteria. No doubt she would swoon, or vomit; at the very least she would stumble away with words of apology pouring from her lovely lips. He did not imagine that she would take up his good hand and hold it pressed against her breast. As she smiled down at him, her face reflecting the glow of the firelight, he was taken by surprise, and awash in an admiration and gratitude he had rarely felt for another human being.

"Morgan, it will be necessary for me to lance your swellings in several places."

Sarah gripped him more tightly. Her smile seemed a little less stolid, more pinched and slightly watery. Still, she clutched him to her as if it were *his* presence giving *her* strength instead of the other way around.

He focused on her face as the first incision was made.

Somewhere beyond the wall of fire and pain he heard Kan singing.

He gritted his teeth, feeling his body jerk involuntarily.

He tried his best not to clench her hand too hard. He might hurt her, God forbid. She was so fragile.

The inferno inside him blazed anew and the pain roared like the *Pororoca* up his throat.

He tried not to thrash his head.

His body twisted and light exploded inside his brain.

Someone called out for Sarah.

Someone was screaming for Sarah.

Then the darkness dragged him down into a pit of nothingness, and deep, deep in the blackness, someone was chanting.

SARAH REFUSED TO LEAVE MORGAN WHILE HE SLEPT. SHE BATHED his feverish skin with water and occasionally took up a fern leaf and fanned him, hoping the cool air would comfort him. The moon was nearing its peak before she gently placed Morgan's hand across his stomach and turned to the others.

The night was an array of jet-black shadows and vivid orange light from the campfire. Kan, who had entered a narcotic trance upon drinking the tea and proceeded to ritualistically suck the infection from Morgan's body and spit it out into the night, now lay in an exhausted heap on the church steps. The others gazed into the flames, dark faces lined with concern.

Henry left his place on the church steps and hurried to meet her. "Are you all right?" he asked.

"I'm very tired."

"I've rigged you up a bed inside. Thought you might appreciate the privacy for a change. I don't know if it'll help the mosquito situation, but . . ."

She turned away and started up the steps. She heard Henry pad up behind her and hesitate at the door before following her in. A hammock hung from the church rafters, the mosquito netting a shroud draped around it. With little effort she rolled into the bed, and Henry hurried to close the netting, gently tucking the ends around her to keep it in place. She gazed at him for a long moment before she could find the will to speak.

"Will he die?" she asked.

"Morgan? Die? He's the *boto,* remember?"

"Will he die?"

"Of course not. I won't let him. He is my only friend in the world. Remember?"

She pressed her open palm against the netting. He placed his hand upon hers. "Promise me," she pleaded.

"The poultice will draw out the poison and the swelling will go down. But that may take a while. If all else fails, we'll let the chief have another go. The old boy seemed to know what he was about." He released a heavy sigh. "Get some sleep. The last days have been hell on us all, Sarah. Good night, my dear."

He turned and walked to the mission's doorway, where he stopped and looked back. His figure was black against the dim light of the distant fire.

"Call me if there's any change," she told him.

"I will. Now go to sleep, Sarah."

He remained where he stood for some time, as if to assure her that all was fine. Then he slipped away without a sound.

The night closed in around her as she rolled onto her side and gazed up at the darkened stained glass, and at the Virgin Mary whose kind face was aglow with moonlight. At some time during the past hours, or days, the seed of doubt and regret had germinated inside her, turning her priorities and resolve upside down. Dear Lord, they were as unprotected and unprepared as infants cast into the harsh world to fend for themselves. They were as weak and vulnerable as newborn lambs against a pack of starving wolves. They had stepped from the very heart of civilization, where man's only enemy was himself, into a world teeming with a danger that was often invisible to the naked eye. Death was real. And waiting, hidden behind every leaf and rock and ripple of water. How swiftly and unexpectedly it had loomed up to strike them. The same thing could happen tomorrow. Or tonight.

Shuddering, she allowed her eyes to search out each dark corner of the church. The mosquito netting fluttered as a breeze blew through the unshuttered windows. There was an unfamiliar rattling somewhere near, and her heart pounded with visions of savages or animals skulking up from the forest to attack them the moment they let down their guard. Then, much to her relief, she realized it was the rustling of leaves in the wind.

Closing her eyes, she attempted to focus her mind on pleasant thoughts of England, her fiancé, and her future as Lady Sheffield. How ironic that now, as she lay sweltering in this godforsaken jungle trying to visualize her fiancé's face, she could not do it. The only images that came to mind were those of steel-gray eyes and intensely sensual lips. Of hands that made her flesh burn as hotly as the equatorial sun when they brushed her. Which wasn't often. Not nearly as often as she would have liked.

Morgan had a way of looking at a woman that made her feel desirable. Not just pretty, but heart-stopping beautiful. As if she were the only woman left alive on the face of the planet. The idea made her smile. She imagined he wouldn't be so standoffish then. More likely, he'd take her in his arms, as he had that night in the rain. Just thinking about it now made the blood move in a molten flow through her veins, her breath catch, and her heart pound in her throat.

In her grief she had promised herself that if she ever saw Morgan again, she would put her feelings for Norman aside long enough to examine the emotions the American evoked in her. She had almost, but not quite, come to the startling conclusion that, with very little effort—and if she weren't very careful—she could love him.

Wearily, she rolled off her bed and walked to the mission door. Henry stood at Morgan's side, one arm slid under his head as he tried to get Morgan to drink from a cup. "Please," Henry begged. "Take just a little.

If not for yourself, then for me, or Sarah. We need you, Morgan. We won't let you die."

Sarah closed her eyes and rested her head against the wall. Oh yes, she could love him, and everything he represented. He stood for freedom from the kind of convention she had secretly found so tedious during her stay in England. His very presence brought a liberation of the human spirit. He made her feel alive—so *very* much alive for the first time in her life.

What, dear God, was she going to do?

MORGAN'S RECOVERY WAS NOTHING SHORT OF MIRACULOUS. WITHIN three days the poultice Henry had concocted had drawn out the ants' poison and his body's infection. The swelling had disappeared completely. There was little to attest to his excruciating and frightening ordeal as he occasionally left his bed to bathe or do odd jobs around camp, gradually building up his strength.

On the morning of the fourth day, Sarah arose and ventured down to the stream behind the mission, eager to sponge the sweat and grit from her body. Henry and Morgan had assured her that there were no piranhas or candirus swarming in its depths, but there were the trees that must be forged before reaching the stream, and God only knew what was lurking in them.

Still, the day was coming when Morgan would be strong enough to travel, and although she and Henry had mentioned that they would be more than happy to forget this perilous venture and return home, Morgan had been adamant about continuing. She would be forced to confront the jungle eventually. Now seemed as good a time as any.

She gathered up her soap, brush, a clean pair of stockings, tucked them all in her shirt, and left the church. Neither Morgan nor Henry nor Kan was about. She went on to the stream, which had a swimming hole, stripped herself of her clothes, and waded into the shoulder-deep water.

It was glorious! Closing her eyes, she turned her face up to the sun and tried to recall when anything had felt so luxurious. She scrubbed her hair and skin with the soap until she felt radiant, and was about to leave the water to dress when the sound of voices stopped her. She looked one way, then the other. Nothing. Perhaps she was imagining things, but to safe she decided to dress quickly and return to camp. She'd dawdled too long as it was and—

There came the sound of furiously rattling bushes—suddenly a tree limb collapsed, spilling Morgan and Henry, yelling, into the water. Sarah screamed and stumbled back, so startled she forgot her nude state until both men surfaced, sputtering and wheezing, their eyes glued on her anatomy as she glared back at them. "My God, you frightened me out of my wits!" she cried.

Water streaming down his face, his black hair in his eyes, Morgan glanced at a rapidly paddling Henry and yanked him up by his arm. "Sorry," they replied in unison.

"What were you doing up there?"

"We heard someone coming," Henry began.

"It seemed the most logical place to hide," Morgan finished.

"Then you've been hiding up there the entire . . ."

They nodded. She realized in that instant just what it was they were gaping at. As nonchalantly as possible, she covered her breasts with her arms and turned her back to them, her cheeks aflame with embarrassment. "If you don't mind, I'd like to get dressed."

"I don't mind," came Morgan's voice. "Do you, Henry?"

"Absolutely not. Go ahead, my dear, we won't interfere."

"Alone!" she stressed.

"Oh!"

"Oh, well, in that case . . ."

She heard mumbled complaints and a great deal of splashing. "I told you that limb wasn't strong enough, but you insisted."

"By Jove, but this is most embarrassing."

After a moment she heard the rustling of bushes, then silence again. Yet she sensed she wasn't alone. She looked back over one white shoulder. There stood Morgan, leaning against a tree, his wet clothes clinging to his body, his arms crossed over his chest as watched her. Her heart danced as she gazed at his ruggedly handsome features. "Well?" she asked. "What are you waiting for? Haven't you humiliated me enough for one day?"

"You don't look very humiliated."

"Oh? How do I look?"

"Wet. And naked. And damned tempting."

She shook her head and her drying hair spilled riotously around her flushed face.

"Like Eve must have looked in the Garden of Eden," Morgan continued.

"Why, Mr. Kane, if I didn't know better, I'd think you were a romantic."

"And if I didn't know you better, I might imagine that you're waiting for me to wade into that water and make love to you."

"I can hardly remove myself when you're watching."

"I'm no threat to you, Sarah. Not as long as you're in love with another man."

She frowned.

"You *are* in love with Norman . . . aren't you?"

A moment of frightening indecision passed as she stared blindly over the rippling water and tried to come to grips with her feelings. She had asked herself the same question these past days. Now the man who had caused all her doubts was demanding an answer.

"Sarah?" came his voice behind her, but now much closer. Her breath caught as he laid his hand on her shoulder. "Sarah, you haven't answered me."

"Please." The word trembled. "I can't."

"Don't you know? You either love the man or you don't."

She spun around with the intent of castigating him, but the words died on her lips. She became breathless as the water lapped at his hips, beaded his lush hair, and glittered on his shoulders. She watched his eyes change from silver fire to steely gray, and she felt mesmerized, shaken by an awakening that was too terrifying to be ignored, yet too dangerous to be acknowledged.

His hands slid along her throat to her face, gliding over and into her coiling hair, and with a moan of despair she knew she could no longer run from the need he aroused in her. She could no longer hide behind her feelings for another when her body burned with a desire she had never felt for Norman. Then one masculine hand was cupping her face tenderly, and she was drifting like a petal on the water into his solid body, unwittingly molding her wet flesh against his as she turned up her face for his kiss.

His warm lips brushed the sensitive corners of her aching mouth, a fleeting touch that burned as sharply as a spark that burst into fire the moment he pulled her nearer, so near her body could detect the shocking hardness of his masculinity within his pants. The blood began to pound in her throat when his thumb drifted over her cheekbone, explored the crescent of her lashes as she closed her eyes. These feelings were new, so new, but everything she had dreamed of feeling—delirious, glorious, burning, aching.

"What will it take," came his lazy voice in her ear, "to make you want me? *Chere,* tell me. You want tenderness?" His fingers swept down her spine with a masseur's caress. "I can be tender."

He placed his broad palm upon her buttock, lifted her so she was floating in his hand, suspended, and vaguely she realized he was coaxing open her legs in a deliciously wicked way and wrapping them around his thighs, which pressed intimately against her. A new swirl of responses flared inside her. Turbulent. Pulsing. Thick and fluid. Fusing deep in the feminine heart of her.

"Do you shiver that way when he touches you here?"

He moved away and the suction of their bodies parting sounded disarming and naughty. Her nervousness made her giddy. She wanted to laugh and cry all at once. She felt as if she were caught in some erotic fairy tale where all her secret fantasies would at last come true.

The moment her nipples made contact with his bare chest, she gasped. The instant his fingers fluttered on the soft white mound of her breast, she whimpered.

"Easy." He kissed her again, a languorous, burning slide of his tongue into her while his head moved round and round, the pressure of his mouth deepened, and her bloodstream turned to fire. When at last he moved his mouth away, his face was a combination of tenderness and pain, and when he caught her chin with his wet fingers and forced her to meet his eyes, his hunger for her was stunning.

"You didn't answer me, Sarah. *Are* you in love with Norman?"

She tried to turn her face away. Her mind was in no fit state to reason, not when her body was fractured into pulsating embers.

"Look at me." Her head snapped back as he shook her. "Is this all you want from me, Sarah? Is it?"

"Please, not now. I can't think. I don't know—"

"The devil you don't. You ought to know when you love a man, Sarah. You sure as hell know when you desire one."

"Oh, Morgan . . ." She dragged her water-heavy arms up over his shoulders, wanting only to bury her face in his chest, to forget the leering obligations of her uncertain future and live, for once, in the present. She yearned to enjoy these wonderful new sensations he aroused inside her. Turning her face up to his, she pleaded, "Kiss me again. I want you to—"

"To what?" His voice was cold as he peeled her arms from around his neck, her legs from around his hips, then shoved her away so hard she spilled back in the water where she fought to right herself. She broke the surface, coughing and gasping, to find Morgan halfway back to shore. He turned on her one last time, and his face was savage.

"I won't be a substitute for your English sweetheart, Sarah. I won't have you opening your legs for me and imagining that it's Norman burying his body inside you. I've had a gut full of being a nobody—always a nobody who was good enough to fulfill a fantasy but not good enough to love." Fists clenched, he stumbled toward her before stopping himself. "I won't take it from you. I can't feel this way for somebody and know she wants me for only one thing. I'd rather die."

He left her there, her eyes riveted to the trees where he had disappeared, her knuckles pressed against her mouth. Shaking, she left the stream and did her best to pull her clothes on over her wet limbs, cursing as they clung to her skin. She gathered her belongings and hurried back to camp, where she found Henry and Kan arguing over the proper way to boil turtle eggs. Morgan was nowhere to be seen.

Henry, noting her dishevelment, hurried to her. "Is something wrong?" he asked.

"Where's Morgan?"

"I thought he was with you."

She shook her head. "We had a misunderstanding and he . . ."

Morgan entered the camp, running scattering all thoughts about their confrontation. "There are Yan out there. Get these men together and let's get out of here!"

The clearing was a mass of silent, hurried movement, each man securing bedding, utensils, heaving up the canoes, and scurrying toward the shore. Within minutes they were paddling up the river, and with a certain sadness Sarah watched the mission vanish in the trees as if it were a mirage.

They drifted through shadows, the rippling of oars in the water the only sound to break the silence. Behind her, Henry whispered, "Morgan, I don't like this. It's too quiet. Did the Yan see you, do you think?"

Morgan looked over his shoulder, his eyes avoiding Sarah as he said to Henry, "We'll know soon enough."

They traveled another hour before Morgan ordered them ashore, directing the Indians to hide their boats as best they could. While the natives hurried to the task, Morgan stood on the shoal with a compass in hand and spoke to Henry as he studied the forest. The men appeared to be debating an issue, and when Sarah approached, she heard Henry say, "I disagree. I feel we should travel one more hour before leaving the river."

"Too dangerous," Morgan replied. "We can be spotted on the river too easily." He stooped, picked up a stick, and proceeded to draw in the sand. "While the river may be a faster route now, it swings east another fifty miles or so north. Cutting diagonally through the floresta from here, we save a great deal of time—"

"How much time?" Sarah asked.

They looked around, their faces solemn.

"Well?" she said. "How long do you estimate before we reach Japurá?"

"Ten days," Morgan replied. Henry looked at him. "You got a problem with that?" Morgan demanded.

"Three weeks," Henry supplied.

"Three—?"

"Three," Henry repeated. "If not longer. You must take into consideration that you don't know—"

Morgan frowned. Henry shut his mouth.

"Know what?" Sarah demanded.

"Nothing." Henry dusted dirt off his hands and gazed up the river.

Morgan removed his hat and mopped sweat from his brow. "What he means is, we don't know what sort of problems we might run up against."

"You must have an idea. You've been this way before. Isn't that so?"

Morgan glanced at the marmoset at his feet before looking at Henry, who refused to return his gaze. "Right," he responded.

"In that case, I agree with you. By all means, let's take the most direct route possible."

Henry groaned and walked away. Morgan, hands on his hips, watched him go.

The strongest of the Indians were instructed to carry trunks and supplies, while the most wiry took up their machetes and prepared to hack their way through the undergrowth. Morgan himself took up a long-bladed knife and, with grim determination, pitted himself against the forest with a vengeance. As the sweltering heat and humidity pressed down on him, the effects of the previous days' ordeal streaked through his body like lightning, until his muscles quivered and his lungs fought for air. Time and again he sagged against the trees as the green world tipped and swayed around him. Occasionally Henry's voice came to him, sounding troubled.

"Morgan, are you all right?"

He nodded, took a breath, and plunged on into the rain forest, swiping and thrashing with the machete, vaguely feeling the bite of thorns and insects that raised bloody welts on his exposed skin. Sometimes he would stop and reach for his whiskey, or a cigarette, finding that his hands were trembling too much to light it. Finally Henry, or Kan, or one of the other Indians would notice and help him, taking the match from his unsteady fingers and touching it to the tip of the cigarette while Morgan inhaled and closed his eyes, savoring the lethargy it brought to his aching body. And always he searched out Sarah. Sarah, who loved another man. Sarah, who would give him her body but not her heart, her soul . . . her love . . .

They chose to camp long before nightfall. A clearing was hollowed out of the forest. Hammocks were suspended from the trees and covered with mosquito netting. Fires were built and the last of the rice ration was boiled. All was done as quietly as possible, for even Sarah realized the silence surrounding them wasn't right.

Sitting upon a neatly stacked pile of tree limbs, she tried her best to keep her attention on the boiling cauldron of rice and not on the intimidating wall of floresta around them. Her skin was hot and sweaty. After the grueling past hours she had little desire to eat. Cupping the bowl in her palms, she stared at the soupy mixture as tears rolled down her cheeks, dropping into her rice soup.

Morgan stooped before her, resting back on his heels as he watched her with concern. In his hands he held a plate of sliced fruit. "Sarah," he asked quietly, "what's wrong?"

She put down her bowl and, leaving her perch, wrapped her arms around his neck. She buried her face into his shoulder and let the tears fall in earnest.

"Chere," he whispered, the sound more like a pained breath in her ear as she wept. A moment passed before he asked in a steadier voice, "Are you ill? Has something bitten you?"

She wiped her nose on his shirt before turning her face into his throat. "It's the soup," she finally managed. "I hate rice soup." It wasn't the truth, of course, but she didn't want to admit that she was already tired of the damnable forest and the threat of Indians and the ungodly heat. She didn't want to admit that she regretted having coerced him into bringing her here. She no longer cared if Norman found her worthy enough to marry. There was a great deal she was loath to admit to Morgan Kane, especially the fact that her feelings were in a quandary over *him.*

He placed the dish of fruit aside. She thought he chuckled. The idea of his finding amusement in her predicament piqued her, but she wouldn't show it. She felt bad enough over her earlier behavior. She hadn't meant to hurt him that morning at the stream. The realization that she had no doubt ruined any chance of his kissing her again brought fresh tears to her eyes.

His hands closed lightly on her arms and set her back on her log. The harsh lines of Morgan's face relaxed until his features showed not a trace of the anger that had frightened her earlier. The awareness, and acceptance, of her feelings for him washed through her in that instant like glowing sunshine. Unable to speak, Sarah threw herself against him again and held him fiercely, her face buried in the curve of his throat, which felt hot and moist and wonderful and real, so real that it made her dizzy. But she was engaged to marry Norman. Wealthy, titled, sophisticated Norman. Maybe if she ignored her feelings for Morgan they would eventually go away.

The world became a blur of colors and sound as she focused on Morgan's face—his exquisite face. She had not noticed before how truly wonderful it was, so dark and lean and hauntingly mysterious. She wanted to know the story behind each flaw, each scar, each tiny line etched into the skin between his eyebrows.

She pulled away and took up her rice soup. She refused to look at him again, and finally he stood, though he remained in front of her for several moments before moving away. Not until he joined the others did she allow herself to watch him, his existence filling her universe.

For the next hour she huddled on her chair of tree limbs, vaguely aware of the Indians taking up their rifles and positioning themselves around the camp as they prepared for nightfall. Gray light turned to black, and with her knees pulled up so she could rest her chin upon them, she gazed into the fire, watching the light and shadows dance upon the ground and trees like seductive nymphs.

Henry sat on a stump on the far side of the camp, talking to Morgan, who reclined in his hammock and peeled fruit for the voracious little marmoset. Kan perched on his heels by the fire, carving on a long thin reed he had plucked from the river days ago. Sarah watched his dark fingers smooth the dry stalk with a thick resin he had collected in a bowl. When the cane was sleek and shiny, he bored out several holes along its length. Finally he lifted the piece in his palm and studied it critically, turning it this way and that in the firelight. Then he placed one end in his mouth and blew gently into it.

The sound was sweet and fluid, filling up the night and silence with music that was stirring and hypnotic. Closing her eyes, Sarah recalled her childhood, when she would dance for her papa because she loved him so. Out of gratitude he would pick her up and hold her close and tell her over and over how much he loved her.

She moved to her feet like one in a trance and began her slow, sensual dance, sliding and swaying with the lyrical sounds, each rise and fall of the flute's music an echo of the rhythm she heard in her head. Rising on her toes and letting her head fall back, she moved her body forward and back, swaying from side to side like a willow in the wind, for that was what the music reminded her of, of gently blowing breezes and singing birds and crashing waves on rocky beaches.

"Sarah."

She opened her eyes and Morgan stood there, on the verge of the dancing shadows, his look watchful and concerned. Only then did she realize that she was crying.

He came to her and put his arms around her.

"Hold me," she whispered against his shirt. "Please hold me."

Chapter Twelve

HE HELD SARAH THROUGHOUT THE NIGHT, WATCHING AS SHE slept and wept in her dreams. Exhaustion had darkened the skin beneath her eyes and hollowed her cheeks more than they had been when she stumbled into his hovel in Georgetown and demanded that he help her in this hellish venture. Lying beside her, her scent filling his nostrils, her warmth like a flame against his skin, he felt himself grow hard with desire. He groaned with it.

Dawn was but an hour away when he eased his arm from beneath her head and rolled off the hammock. He tucked the mosquito netting around her and waved away the insects that rose in a cloud. A flapping of wings brought his head around, and staring through the dark, he made out bats hanging from the trees. Something else moved there as well. Yellow eyes, reflecting the firelight, gazed back at him in the stillness.

Henry lay asleep in his hammock. Kan too, had dozed, the flute placed beside his outstretched legs. Morgan walked to the fire and stooped beside it. He hated the dawn. It was too damned lonely. It gave a man too much time to contemplate his future and dwell on his past. As a child, he would lie in his cot at St. Mary's Charity Home and imagine that today his mother would arrive to take him home. He would forgive her for deserting him. He would forgive her for anything if she would love him again.

But the years had passed.

As a youth, he used to imagine that somewhere in New Orleans there were parents who needed a son, and that today they would venture to St. Mary's and choose him from all the others. Occasionally he would leave his cot and sneak to the church, where he knelt before the altar and the statues of Christ and the saints. He would stare at their lifeless profiles, their unblinking eyes, the white marble hands that were extended and offering salvation. The musty smell of the ancient pews would rise to his nostrils as he clasped his hands and bent his head in a prayer he had stopped believing in long ago. God had never answered *his* prayers. But he continued to come, sometimes hiding behind the side altar of the Virgin Mary, eavesdropping on the men and women who slipped into the confessionals and spilled out their sins for the priests. And when they finally left and silence loomed among the wilting chrysanthemums and melting candles, he would pray for someone—anyone—to find him in this holy hell, and want him.

But the years had passed.

Then there had been the miserable dawns spent aboard pitching ships among snoring sailors. When the wind howled so mightily around the mizzenmast and whined through the foreshrouds, he would fix his eyes upon the bunk above him and weep like the sixteen-year-old fool that he was for running away to sea. Once, when they'd rounded Cape Horn during a storm, he refused to go below when the captain ordered him. Belligerently he stood his ground, feet planted apart, hands clenched at his sides as he prepared himself to be swept overboard by the raging waves. Anything was better than living on rank meat, foul water, and biscuits baked so hard even the weevils couldn't penetrate them.

He hadn't died. When the storm subsided, the captain had ordered him strung from the mainmast by his wrists and whipped for his disobedience. Thirty lashes. The first of many before he sneaked ashore in Kowloon and lost himself among the thousands of people milling along the waterfront of houseboats and squatter shacks. There had been a woman, briefly. Her slanted eyes had fascinated him. Her heavy hair, blacker than his own, had enthralled him. She taught him everything he wanted to know about lovemaking. Then, just when he'd allowed himself to grow fond of her, she disappeared into the night and he never saw her again.

And the years had passed.

He had come to Brazil. The new Eden. Paradise found. He met a young, handsome, richly dressed man who took his hand in friendship, smiled into his eyes, and promised him heaven . . . if he was willing to work for it. One year was all his new friend had asked. He'd flashed Morgan that mesmerizing grin when he'd asked the *patrao* what he would have to do to earn such rewards.

"Why, Morgan, my fabulously handsome young friend, that will be up to you, of course. Trust me."

Morgan closed his eyes at the memory. Standing, he moved toward the darkness, swiping up his rifle as he went. The undergrowth snapped underfoot, splintering the quiet and causing a rustle in the leaves above his head. He cast a cautious glance back at Sarah, then at Henry before carrying on, stopping far enough from the clearing so as to be out of sight should they awaken and discover him gone. Leaning against a tree, he dug in his pocket for a cigarette and thought of his mother.

Upon escaping the orphanage, he'd ventured to the shanties near the Mississippi. He'd stood outside the shack for an hour before he got up the courage to knock. The door had opened to reveal a short woman with black, graying hair and a face wasted by illness, hunger, and fatigue. Her gray eyes had stared up at him as if she had just looked death in the face.

"Margaret Kane?" he'd asked her. Then his eyes had been drawn down to her leg where a boy with a dirty face and runny nose hung on her skirt and gazed up at him with eyes like his own. Behind her a young girl appeared with the same black hair, her age no more than ten years. Angry, Morgan looked at the woman. "Margaret Kane?" he'd demanded in a rising, desperate voice.

"No," she'd said, her eyes belying the words. "You must have the wrong house."

"No, I don't."

"Margaret is dead. Go away and leave us alone."

She'd slammed the door in his face.

He might have forgiven his mother for anything.

Anything but that.

Dawn light filtered through the leaves, and the shadows took on less menacing shapes until they diminished completely. There was movement back at the camp. He could hear Henry and Kan arguing, and to his left, one of the Indians stepped away from the clearing to relieve himself. Morgan pushed away from the tree, glad to put another night behind him. That was when he came face-to-face with the corpse.

The Indian hung upside down from the tree limb, swinging forward and back as a breeze rustled the leaves overhead. His mouth was frozen in a soundless scream. His eyes were bulging in terror. His throat had been cut from ear to ear. All his blood had drained from his body and lay pooled on the ground.

Cold sweat rising to his forehead, Morgan stared into the man's dull eyes and gaping mouth before he whirled away and vomited on the ground. He stumbled back to camp. Sarah was sitting on a tree stump, rubbing her eyes. Henry and Kan were stoking the fire. They glanced up as he approached, their look of expectancy melting into alarm at the sight of his unsettled state.

Henry and Kan joined him. By now many of the others were becoming alarmed as they noted that their comrades were missing.

"Morgan, what's happened?" Henry asked.

"One of the guards has been murdered. There could be more."

Kan spoke sharply to the skittish natives, who rushed for their rifles. A voice called out, first to their right, then to their left. Four Indians had been slaughtered in a similar way.

They buried the men without ceremony. There wasn't time for anything more, and besides, what good would it have done them? There was no Christ, or God, or Virgin Mother in the Amazon. This was hell's paradise, and somewhere close by Satan was waiting, laughing at what fools they were for so blithely knocking on his door and expecting to enter without sacrifice.

Morgan ordered the Indians to break camp as quickly and quietly as possible. Most obliged. Others moved more slowly, their hesitancy obvious as they discussed the matter among themselves.

"Do you think they were murdered by Yanoamö?" Henry asked.

"The Yanoamö are cannibals." Morgan replied so as not to be overhead by the frightened Indians. "They prefer to capture their victims alive."

"Then who do you imagine could have done it?"

Frowning, Morgan stared out into the forest, the image of the murdered man's face looming up in his mind's eye like a grizzly ghost from his past.

"Morgan?" Henry touched his sleeve. "Morgan?" he repeated.

He shook his head. "I don't know," he said, then turned away and left Henry staring after him.

Sarah said nothing. Her face had paled when she heard the horrible news, but she had acted with haste, doing what she could to secure their belongings. She stood by, hands gripped at her sides as Morgan checked the bundles, then nodded toward the Indians, who hurried to hoist them onto their shoulders.

He handed Sarah a rifle. "Stay close to me," he told her, and she nodded with frightened eyes. "Are you all right?" he asked.

"I think so."

"Do you know how to use that gun?"

She turned it in her hands. "I aim it and pull the trigger."

"That's the gist of it. Just make certain you know where you're aiming before you shoot." He smiled, but her expression was serious. "It holds fifteen rounds. Never use more than fourteen. If we're attacked, you'll want to save the last one for yourself."

Her mouth dropped open.

"Believe me, *chere,* you don't want to be taken by the Yanoamö. I'll kill you myself before I let that happen."

They struck out through the forest, the whoosh of machetes and the crack of wood the only sounds to mark their passage through the floresta. Sarah looked back the way they had come, only to discover that for all their chopping they had done little to change the forest. She could understand those stories of people wandering lost in the floresta when civilization lay only a mile away.

Little by little the jungle came alive with shrieks and squawks and whistles, and like the silence that had seemed a precursor of doom before, this cacophony was like a brief amnesty from damnation. Whatever death threat had followed them from the Barcelos mission, it was gone, for the time being.

THREE WEEKS PASSED AND THEY APPEARED TO BE NO CLOSER TO locating King's plantation than they had been when they left the Rio Negro. Neither Morgan's nor Henry's calculations about when they would arrive in Japurá had proved to be correct. Time and again Sarah found them with their heads together, arguing over what course to take next. Tempers grew short. They were hot and so tired they could hardly roll out of their hammocks each morning. Their supply of water had run out, and now they were forced to cut the *cipo de aqua* from the trees in order to get water to drink. Each time Morgan sliced the vine and held it up to Sarah's mouth, she drank thirstily. But too soon he would take it away, warning her of the dangers of drinking too much too fast.

They had used the last of their food rations long ago and were now relying totally on the floresta for sustenance. Repeatedly they were forced to eat the starchy meat of the manioc root. Occasionally there was fruit, but more often than not it grew too high in the trees to be reached.

At night they had little energy left to stand, much less speak. So with the onset of dusk they rolled into their hammocks and did their best to pull their tattered clothes around them before sleeping. Bats came during the night, many of them vampires drawn by the smell of fresh blood and warm flesh. They would find their way under the bedding and feast until bloated on the sleepers' blood. Once, while Sarah slept, Morgan had awakened to discover a bat drinking from a puncture on her neck. He'd grabbed it off her, thrown it to the ground, and shot it with his rifle.

There were ants, of course. One evening Sarah laid out her chemise to dry. The next morning there were only threads left; the sauba ants had chewed the material into tiny scraps and hauled them away. Termites feasted on leather satchels and shoes. And, as always, there were snakes, slithering through the vegetation at their feet, coiling around the limbs overhead, camouflaged by leaves so one was never aware of them until they reared their heads and hissed. One man had died of a bite from a fer-de-lance. Another was weakening due to some parasite that had buried itself under his skin and was slowly rotting it from the inside out.

They had little thought for their ultimate goal. It was enough to endure each moment as it came. Depression pressed in on them, a hopelessness that not one of them would admit aloud. But to themselves, as they sat alone at night, staring into the darkness, they all considered what it would mean to die here and never be heard from again.

Who would care? Who would grieve? For Morgan, there was no one. Nor for Henry. Norman would experience regret for Sarah, and possibly sadness, but no real sorrow. They had no one but each other; the world outside ceased to exist, and dimmed like a dream. They were lost forever in paradise, it seemed.

They came upon a wide turbulent river which there was no way to cross except by boat. They spent the better part of two days hacking down trees and roping them together to make a raft. Kan volunteered to swim across so a rope could be extended from one side to the other, to which they would hook the raft and drag themselves and their supplies across. Sarah watched nervously as the Indian tied the rope round his waist and waded into the foaming water. Morgan, holding the rope, fed Kan its length as he needed it, carefully keeping it taut in case there was trouble. The whirlpools and eddies sucked Kan under, yet he always resurfaced, his powerful arms and legs driving him toward the distant shore.

Sarah stood on the muddy shoal, her hands gripped together as she prayed for Kan. She might have collapsed when he clawed his way out of the water, but the dread of what she must face left her too numb with fear to feel relief. Soon the rope was secured and the raft was rigged to it, loaded with their belongings and shoved into the water. Morgan turned back for her, extended his hand; she took it, refusing to look him in the eye, knowing he would recognize her fear. She'd tried to be brave in the face of every danger, but it seemed that the floresta was throwing every hurdle it could into their path. She followed his orders and, boarding the raft, fell to her hands and knees, holding on as tightly as she could while it heaved like a living being beneath her.

As the roar and spray of water rose around her, the men's shouts came to her like whispers. She could not understand the words. She did not want to understand. Her senses were vibrating with feeling, yet numb with a hypnotic lethargy. Closing her eyes, she lay on her stomach and pressed her face into the raft, vaguely aware of splinters biting into her cheeks. *We're going to make it,* she told herself, wanting desperately to believe it.

The water surged over the raft, lifted it from beneath, and lunged it aside as if it were a piece of driftwood. The ropes snapped taut with the force, and several men lost their footing and were hurled into the river. Supplies tumbled and skidded from their braces. Sarah looked up to see Morgan trying to right the dangerously tipping vessel with a pole, slamming one end of it against a rock as he attempted to maneuver the raft. The pole snapped, sending Morgan diving toward the raft. Henry spun away. Then the world became a rending of sound, and suddenly the raft was disintegrating beneath her.

"Morgan!" She tried scrambling to her feet, only to be thrown to her knees. The waves crashed upon them, spraying daggers of water into their faces. On his hands and knees, Morgan reached for Sarah, only to be hurled to the raft's edge. Only Henry's quick response kept him from being swept away.

Again Morgan reached out with his hand. Sarah could almost touch him, but it would mean letting go of her hold on the raft—and oh, God, if she let go she would be swept into the water and she couldn't swim and—

"Sarah!" Morgan shouted.

She reached. Their fingertips touched. Then she was spiraling backward and Morgan was stumbling to his feet and becoming more and more distant, and she thought, *Oh God, I'm going to die! I've slipped away! He'll never catch me now!*

How keenly she saw their faces, the emotion, the fear as they watched the fragmented raft split asunder, hurling her down the river. And she experienced it all with a sense of detachment, a calmness that she might never have thought possible in the face of her own death.

As Morgan stood and prepared to dive, her only thought was to stop him. She cried out, yet he dove anyway, disappearing under the surface that was thrashing and whirling. Suddenly she, too, was going under, flying like a bullet, the force dragging her along the bottom as helplessly as a child's rag doll, whipping her up again and propelling her out of the water where she gasped for air. Despite her acceptance of death, in that instant she struggled for one last breath before being driven down again.

Then there were hands in her hair, pulling her up. She burst from the water with a scream, pummeling the arms that tried to subdue her, clawing at Morgan's face as he attempted to cry out her name. The river rushed on, tumbling them down until there was nothing but speed and thunder, and as their heads broke the surface one last time, it was to witness the arc of a rainbow amid the purple mists, and all around them the inverted blue bowl of the sky, larger than they had ever seen it. Then the realization hit them at once. The thunder. The sky. The great vastness of space.

"Sarah!" Morgan cried in panic.

Then she was gone, as was he, over the falls with the pounding water, flying, drifting—when would they hit? *What* would they hit?

The wind roared in their ears and the sun kissed their faces. Then they were plunged into a stillness that was bracingly cold and black. Next there was . . . nothing.

MORGAN HELD SARAH IN HIS ARMS AND WATCHED HER FACE FOR some sign of life. "Sarah. Oh, my God. Please, don't die. Sarah."

He smoothed her hair back, wincing with pain. The little finger of his right hand was twisted grotesquely, the bone protruding through his flesh just below the knuckle. His nose was dripping blood on Sarah's chest. "Sarah." He shook her, anger overriding his fear as he acknowledged the deathly pallor of her face. Dragging her farther from the water, he flipped her onto her stomach and drove his hand between her shoulderblades. He cried out with the pain, but gritting his teeth, he did it again and again, until he was frightened of hurting her. Then he rolled her over, and out of desperation and not knowing what else to do, he covered her mouth with his and breathed air into her lungs.

Nothing. He tried again. She stirred, and frantically he repeated the procedure until her eyelids fluttered and her body convulsed. Water spewed out her mouth and nose, and she gasped for a breath. Closing his eyes, he rocked in relief. "Sarah. Ah, love, I thought I'd lost you. God, if I'd lost you . . ."

He kissed her eyes, her nose, her mouth as she lay limply against him. "Morgan?" came the weak response.

"Yeah."

"We're alive?"

"Barely, but we made it."

Her lids flickered open. She gazed at him with red-rimmed eyes before she said, "I dreamed that I had died and you brought me back to life with a kiss."

"I think I read that in a fairy tale once."

She looked disappointed. "You didn't save my life?"

"Well . . . maybe a little."

Smiling faintly, she said, "My hero."

He wiped his bloody nose with his sleeve and laughed. "I've never been called that by anybody white."

"Your nose."

"I think it's broken."

"And your hand!"

"I *know* it's broken."

Seeing the splintered bone in his finger, she paled even more. "Morgan, you're in pain."

"Pain, my love, was believin' you were dead."

"Morgan, you're a romantic at heart."

"Nah. Water up my nose makes me stupid, is all." He looked toward the falls. "We'll have to wait here. If the others survived they'll be searchin' for us." When Sarah made no response, he looked at her again. She was sleeping.

He held her for a while longer, too exhausted to move, too drained by relief that he had managed to fish her out of the river and drag her to shore. She felt damn good in his arms. The past weeks of denying himself her nearness had been like death. And for what? She had wanted him; he recognized desire when he saw it in a woman's eyes. How easily he could have turned on the charm, taken advantage of her desperation. But it couldn't be that way with Sarah. He couldn't allow himself to be used by a woman he cared for, knowing she would be leaving him for another. He couldn't accept that rejection again. He'd taken it all of his life, since watching his mother spread her legs for men day and night, but always too weary or angry to notice her own son waiting in the background, wanting to be held, comforted, consoled. He would have done anything to make her love him—lie, cheat, steal. In fact, he had done so on many occasions, only to have her stare at him with emotionless eyes and turn away. She had used his love for her as surely as men had used her body, forcing him to beg for money, promising him a hug or kiss if he collected enough for their supper. He'd learned by example that sex could buy all the kisses and caresses one could ever desire.

Then came Sarah, and suddenly that kind of counterfeit love just wasn't good enough.

He moved her to a tree, where he sank down against it, cradling her in his arms. His body throbbed in a hundred places. He should do something about the finger, but that would mean putting Sarah down and he wasn't about to do that yet. He'd been yearning to hold her for too long.

He stroked her hair and tried not to imagine a future without her. He had gone through that only moments before, and the emptiness had been shattering. The grief had been consuming, like the passion he felt for her in the night. He wanted to kiss her and explain that he had never felt this way for a woman. But what use were all the words? He was tempted to give her what she wanted from him, though it had nothing to do with love. He would show her what sex was like when it was done for lust's sake and nothing more. Let her experience the hollow feeling that was left behind when the fire was quenched. Let her stare unseeing into the night and swallow back the loneliness and the sense of being used, because that was what she was going to feel living with Norman.

He lay her gently among the leaves and moved to the river, where he stared down at the murky image of himself, his bloodied nose, his broken hand, the wet black hair hanging in his eyes. Then he turned toward Sarah, watched as she slept. Squeezing his eyes shut, he said, "Hurry the hell up, Henry." *Save me from myself.*

THREE DAYS PASSED AND STILL THEY WERE ALONE. ALONE AND NOT alone. Two people existing in the same world, but having little to do with each other. Morgan had changed. Remote, surly, restless, he distanced himself from Sarah. He paced. He cursed the forest, and Henry, who he was certain must have died in the torrent or he would have located them by now. Once, when Sarah mentioned that she was hungry, he shifted his wild eyes to hers and snarled, "Get your food yourself. Who the hell do you think I am, one of your friggin' servants?"

Morgan frightened her. Occasionally she found him watching her from a distance, unblinking, craving, crafty. Then he noticed her staring at him and turned away where he sat by the water, his back to her, holding his wounded hand in his lap as if he were cradling a baby. Perhaps it was the pain that had turned him into this angry stranger—for surely the injury must be unbearable.

She had watched him set the splintered bone himself, body sweating, eyes glazed, teeth biting hard on a stick. His legs had given out from under him when it was done, and he had rolled, groaning, on the ground, whimpering in his throat, making her weep because she wanted to comfort him. But he sent her away with a pain-laced "Get the hell away from me."

He began to have nightmares, awakening her from intermittent sleep. His screams startled him from his dreams and he stumbled to the river and submerged his face in the water until he stopped shaking. Once or twice he tore his shirt off, and her eyes were drawn to the scars on his back, some cut deeply into the flesh, others barely visible thin white marks. The sight had frightened her as much as his mood swings, and the realization that she knew so little of him hit her with force. Merciful God, who had whipped him so horribly? Why? The thought of the pain he must have endured made her cry.

The nights were interminable without firelight. She longed to huddle close to Morgan, and once or twice he let her, only to shove her away after an hour and sit alone in the darkness. Despairing, she cried, "What have I done? Why are you so angry?"

"Shut up."

"I want to understand. You—you've changed, Morgan."

"I need a smoke. And a drink," came his shaky voice from the shadows. "Leave me alone if you know what's good for you."

So she did, hour after endless hour until morning crept like a specter through the leaves. She was hungry. They had not eaten in two days. Angrily, she marched to Morgan. "Give me your knife," she told him.

He laughed, an ugly sound. "So you can stab me in the back?"

"A tempting thought, but for now I want only to cut us some fruit if I can find it."

"Let's see you do that." He flung the knife at her feet. "Good luck," he added.

Frowning, she swept up the weapon and turned back to the forest, hesitating as she gazed at the trees. She forced her scraped and bruised limbs toward the floresta, realizing even as she immersed herself within its twisted and tangled vines that she had no idea where to begin searching for food. But she was hungry; for the first time she knew what true starvation felt like. It was a hollowness, not only of the stomach but of the entire body. It was a burning in her blood, a humming in her head.

"Sarah!" Morgan called out behind her.

She slashed at the vegetation, taking nefarious pleasure in rending it into tiny pieces. She stumbled blindly through the undergrowth, forgetting even her hunger in her quest to lash out in anger and frustration. She came to a bend in the river, and there, suspended over the water, she saw a papaya, so large and ripe it bent the limb on which it was growing. It bobbled invitingly, and the sunlight reflecting off the river turned the flesh the color of a sunset.

Her mouth watered as, dropping the knife, she waded into the river, remotely feeling the liquid warmth rise up her shins, her knees. The water stirred around her thighs as she reached for the fruit, closing her fingers around the mellow meat, feeling its tender flesh give beneath the pressure of her fingers and pour thick juice over her hand. She plucked it from its stem and, hearing Morgan stagger from the forest behind her, turned and laughed as she lifted the delicacy in her palm. "Morgan, I did it. Behold, a feast fit for a king . . . Morgan?"

His eyes dilated in terror, he stared at her. The smile faded from her lips as the paradise on which she balanced seemed to rise up around her in a succession of wildly singing birds that were more like a crashing of cymbals to her ears. The water undulated, closing like a vise around her hips and waist, and as she looked up in stupefaction, the browns and blacks and greens took the shape of a monster that reared out of the murky depths like a dragon. Its hypnotic eyes were all that she saw before it began to squeeze.

She screamed, only vaguely aware that Morgan was splashing through the water, tripping, throwing himself onto her, his face a mask of rage as he closed his hands around the constrictor's huge powerful head. He yanked it into the water, where it thrashed her away as if she were no more than Morgan's marmoset.

A moment passed before she realized she was free and that she was flailing at nothing. With her eyes and nose and mouth full of silt and water, she struggled up the bank, crying out as the water roiled with the life-and-death battle. Hysteria rose in her, and she screamed as the snake coiled its enormous body around Morgan and dragged him underwater. She covered her face in her hands and, rolling into a fetal curl, continued to scream as they surfaced. Morgan slashed with his knife into the body of the demon until the water churning over her legs was nothing but blood and the air was a cacophony of bestial sounds more horrible than any nightmare she could ever have imagined. And then . . .

There were bodies around her, brown bodies and hands and painted faces with glittering black eyes and gargoyled mouths and ears with lobes that fell all the way to their shoulders. "Save him!" she screamed in their faces, but her words became incoherent as she was lifted out of the water and carried toward the forest. She fought them, frantic to get back to Morgan as he stumbled from the water, his hand gripping the bloody knife, the dead monster slowly sinking into the muddy depths of the river.

She looked back and thought she saw him, but then she was certain that she must have imagined it. If only the leering faces around her were merely figments of her imagination instead of what she had feared most.

Savages. Cannibals.

Headhunters!

When she turned her head next, she did see Morgan, circled by the savages just as she was, looking battered and bruised from his battle with the boa. He seemed dazed, and when the Indians brought the two of them together, he stared at her as if she were a stranger.

"Morgan, thank God you're alive," she managed weakly.

Only then did he appear to realize their circumstances. Casting a look around him, he replied, "Yeah, but for how long?"

They were ushered through the forest, encouraged when they faltered, carried when they refused to go farther. When they reached the Indians' village it seemed like a metropolis, its conformity shocking to eyes that had seen nothing but the chaos of the jungle for the past weeks. There were curious, bare-breasted women holding babies on their hips. In the dirt around chonta palm huts dogs and boars rooted. Stunned and wondering what horrible fate awaited them, they looked into each other's eyes.

"Morgan! Sarah!"

Henry stood in the door of a chonta hut, a smile of relief illuminating his face. He ran to greet them.

THE JIVARO ACHUARA INDIANS BELIEVED THAT MORGAN WAS A GOD. Henry convinced them of it. His battling the much-feared and revered anaconda was proof of it, and "a stroke of bloody luck," as Henry had added under his breath.

Instead of shrinking their heads, the chief, Kukus, threw a celebration in their honor. Great bonfires were built. Kukus sat between Morgan and Sarah, with Kan close by so he could interpret for the chief, and honored them by bestowing upon them the coveted secrets of shrunken heads, or tsantsas, explaining that tsantsas imprison the spirit of a dead enemy warrior so that it cannot avenge the death. Then eight of Kukus's wives hurried to place bowls of mush and platters of food at their feet.

Kukus, handsomely autocratic, with his black hair cascading down his back and two tightly wrapped cords of hair hanging to his chest in front, gave a toothy smile and told them to feast.

"On what?" Morgan demanded, glancing toward his marmoset that was rolling in the dirt with several children. Relieved, he said to Henry, "I suppose it hasn't done you any harm."

"Far from it. Enjoy, Morgan. God knows, you and Sarah deserve it. You can't imagine what we've been through trying to find you. Once we discovered the falls, we thought for certain you both had perished."

"What about our supplies?"

"Sarah's trunk of clothes was lost, as were your whiskey and tobacco. Some of the ammunition went, but not all. There's enough if you still wish to continue . . . Do you wish to continue?"

He nodded, although his eyes had shifted to Sarah. Sitting in partial darkness near Kan, she leaned against a tree with her legs sprawled out before her. She breathed shallowly; she seemed weary. Her pale hair was coming loose from the braid that hung down her back, wispy strands clinging to her cheeks. Her eyes were huge, and looked very green in the firelight. He supposed she was still in shock. "We've come too far to back down now," he replied, speculating on the mound of food placed before them. Leaning toward Henry, he whispered, "Could that be some *body?*"

Henry howled in laughter. "Would it matter? Egads, Morgan, perhaps you're not so hungry as you look."

"Not hungry enough to eat someone's grandmother."

"The Achuara are not cannibals. Eat before you insult them."

The chief smiled and nodded, encouraging him to take the food. With some reluctance he reached for it, but found the bowl spirited from his wounded hand by a young woman whose breasts were firm and round as coconut shells, their nipples dark and prominent. Her eyes were wide and black as nightfall, her hair like a rich ink spray flowing over her shoulders. "She likes you," Henry murmured. "The chief will make you a gift of her tonight."

She flashed him a smile as she placed the bowl in his hands. He mentally calculated how long it had been since he'd had a woman. Then his gaze came back to Sarah, and he knew that such a thought was as irreverent as blasphemy before God.

Kan handed Sarah a bowl, announcing that the food was *pato no tucupi.* She wrinkled her nose, apparently not liking the look or smell of it. It was just like her to turn up her nose at something when she was dying of hunger.

Kan explained. "It is duck and greens."

"Only duck and greens? It smells vile." She nudged the bowl away, although she regarded it hungrily.

Sensing she wasn't going to eat unless he did, Morgan raised the bowl to his mouth and, using his fingers as a spoon, scooped the food onto his tongue, finding it not at all disagreeable. Only then did Sarah venture to try it.

"There is a legend," Henry began, "behind the *tucupi.* According to legend, the beautiful daughter of an Indian chief was hidden after death within the soft white pulp of the manioc root, which makes up the juices the duck and greens are cooked in."

Morgan frowned and swallowed. His mouth had grown numb; his facial muscles seemed frozen; he couldn't form a word with his lips without drooling like an idiot. A look told him Sarah was the same. Throwing the bowl to the ground, she covered her mouth with one hand and grabbed for the cup of *masato* with the other. As she attempted to gulp the fermented beverage, it ran out the corners of her mouth and dribbled down her chin. She and Morgan glared at Henry as he rolled backward in hilarity.

"Ooo shtufis muver foocher," Morgan yelled at the pygmy, who, leaping to his feet, danced through the laughing men and women.

"This is wonderful!" he called back. "Simply wonderful, Morgan. Why not try to enjoy it."

"Ooo've poozened oos!" he bellowed.

"I haven't poisoned you. You'll thank me tomorrow. As they say, eat, drink, and be merry; tomorrow we may die!"

Sarah was laughing, apparently unconcerned that more *masato* was pouring down the front of her shirt than down her throat. Morgan began to laugh then too, and the thought occurred to him that they were drunk. Whether the cause was the *masato,* or simply relief that they had survived the past nightmarish days, he couldn't tell. He felt good, and happy. The two people he cared most for in the world were at his side, and nothing else seemed to matter.

He fell back in the dirt, no longer feeling the heat or the pain of his bruised and broken body and spirit. He heard only Sarah's laughter, like a melody rising in the air, a serenade of songbirds, a chorus of angels. There was music, deep and throbbing in his head and chest, drumming like a heartbeat. The light emanating from the fires flowed like wax to the ceiling of trees, and as the women began their strange ballet around the flames, their skin reflected the light like onyx mirrors.

Their arms and hands flowed gracefully, each movement a story told, if he could only understand it. Then Sarah was among them, a bright star amid the night sky, hair shimmering with color as she spun, mimicking the women's movements. She glided toward the fire, her beauty flowering like a budding rose as she came into the glare of the flames, her gold hair shimmering, her dancing feline, her expression absorbed in the rise and fall of the drums. She had stripped herself of her shirt, and like the natives, danced bare-breasted in and out of the firelight. He had the vague idea of running to her and covering her beautiful breasts, but he couldn't move. Enchanted, he watched her—the flare of fire upon her white skin with the palest tint to her small nipples, the play of light upon her sublime face. She moved in front of him where he crouched on the ground, stretched her slender arms above her head. In a slow gesture she lifted herself up on her toes, raised one leg in an effortless arc, and pivoted, a breathtaking marionette controlled by invisible strings.

"Morgan." She laughed. "Come dance with me."

He stood, slowly, clumsily. Henry flashed in and out of his vision, also moving with the dancers. Morgan felt foolish. He felt eager. He felt drunk. He felt . . . absurdly happy and staggered by his desire for her.

"Isn't this wonderful?" she asked, her eyes bright, her mouth smiling. She caught his hand and pulled him into the light. "Dance with me, Morgan. We might never dance again after tonight." A flicker of fear passed over her face.

"Sarah." The word died in his throat as she pirouetted around him, brushing him with her skin, her hair, the perfume of her flesh. Oh, yes, he could smell her, just as he could smell the muskiness of the night, the fragrance of the flowers in the forest. The sounds had color, and the color, music. The Achuara's shaman, Nyashu, who watched them all from his hut, would have called it magic. Perhaps it *was* magic. Morgan was content to let it be so, for the moment. There had been so little magic in his life . . .

Her voice lilted to him. "Come dance with us, Morgan."

Enticing. Alluring. He felt intoxicated with lust. But that was nothing new. It had been a beast inside him the past days. Hell, since he'd set eyes on Sarah that first night in his house.

Her hands moved over him, tugging at his shirt and its buttons. "Take it off and dance with us," she pleaded huskily. "It's wonderful. I promise. It's like a fantasy, isn't it? Paradise found? Where we can feel happy and do what we please. Where no one can judge us, ridicule us."

"Sarah." He laughed, shoving away her hands. "You're drunk. You've been eating and drinking ayahuasca or coca leaves. Love, you don't know what you're doing."

"Don't I?" Her eyes twinkled up at him, first in amusement, then in acceptance as she smiled and pressed herself against him, running her hands up his chest to his face, her fingers teasing his lips. "I know exactly what I'm doing, Morgan," she said in a sultry voice. "What a great waste to die when you've never truly lived. I'm only sorry that it's taken me so long to realize what I've been missing."

She twirled away, leaving him to stand alone in the gyrating firelight, watching her every movement, his desire for her an ache that left him trembling. The Indian girl ran to him and forced a cup of liquid into his hands. He drank until the world blurred and his memories and cares crumbled away, until his body and mind and soul no longer ached.

And he danced, falling into the rhythm with the others, moving lithely in and out of the firelight and into the darkness, until he was humming and singing to himself.

Shadow dancers.
Shadow dancers.
Shadow dancers, all.

Chapter Thirteen

THEY REMAINED IN THE VILLAGE LONG ENOUGH TO MEND FROM their injuries, but the time eventually came when they knew they must leave. They had food and water, and numerous Achuara to escort them into the floresta. They traveled to the limits of the Achuara's boundaries, and although Morgan and Henry tried to coerce the Indians into guiding them to Japurá, they refused. The travelers were trespassing into the Xavante lands, beyond the Rio das Mortes, or the River of the Dead. The Xavante's hatred of the white man was well known among all tribes of Amazonia. The Spanish had failed at any attempt to buy their way into the warriors' trust. The savages had massacred what few missionaries had ventured into their territories. Even King kept a respectful distance, leaving their women and children alone during his raids for slaves.

Upon hearing Kukus speak of the terrors the Xavante inflicted on their victims, several of the Indians Morgan had hired in Georgetown refused to venture farther. Now two torturous weeks had passed since they had left the Achuara village, and even those Indians supplied by Wickham were having second thoughts. As the floresta grew darker, the traveling more difficult, the steamy heat worse than anything that they had experienced before, Morgan and Sarah and Henry wearily awoke each morning to discover one less Indian to carry their supplies. There was concern over whether the Indians were deserting, or meeting the same fate as those men they had discovered with their throats cut. But since they found no bodies, they chose to believe the men had decided against continuing the journey and, lured by their memories of compliant young women and ayahuasca back at the Achuara village, had returned to the friendly natives.

Their dwindling numbers, fatigue, and desperation forced them little by little to dispose of their supplies: clothes, blankets, hammocks. Next came their ammunition, the most burdensome but, in Morgan's opinion, the most important thing they'd brought. When Henry suggested they leave several crates, Morgan, at the end of his patience, snapped, "Don't be stupid. That ammunition is the only thing that's going to keep King from killing us."

"My good man, need I remind you to take a good look around? There are enough guns and bullets to supply an army. As of this morning, we only have fifteen of the thirty men we started with. At the rate we're going, we'll have fewer than that by the time we reach Japurá—if we reach it. By Jove, but I've come to regret ever having set foot in Brazil."

"It's a little late for that. Besides, you got us into this—"

Sarah had had enough. "Shut up!" she screamed. Tossing down her machete, flinging her helmet to the ground so her sweaty hair tumbled down her shoulders, she managed to ignore her fatigue long enough to march up to Morgan. "I'm sick of your petty arguments. I'm sick of your faces. I'm sick of this ordeal, and if I hadn't come this far I would order you to take us back to Georgetown."

"You think so?" Morgan shouted back.

"I know so, Mr. Kane."

He threw his head back and laughed. "That'd be the day. Hell, you wore a friggin' petticoat for the first half of this journey."

"Until I saved your stupid neck by tossing it to the alligators! And what did I get for the sacrifice? Not even a thank-you." She opened a bladder-sack of ayahuasca and proceeded to drink it as if it were water.

"I'd go easy on that if I were you," Morgan sneered.

"Go to hell."

"I'm already there," he retorted.

She drank again and narrowed her eyes. Once she might have trembled from the threat in Morgan's features. She wondered if it was the ayahuasca that made her return his fierce look so recklessly. Whatever, the thrill of standing so close to him, of feeling his presence flood her with exhilaration, made her feel wonderfully wicked, despite her tired state. "You know something, Mr. Kane? I used to be afraid of you, but I'm not anymore. Neither am I frightened of this bloody forest."

Glancing toward Henry, who watched with raised eyebrows, Morgan said, "Give the lady a pair of breeches and she grows herself some balls. I'm impressed. Maybe I should let her take us the rest of the way into Japurá, Longfellow. What d'ya think?"

"I think," she interrupted with a lift of her chin, "that I could do a damn sight better job of it than you." The Indians put their burdens aside and crowded around, their faces emotionless, eyes watchful. Morgan raised an eyebrow as she said, "First you tell us that we should reach Japurá in ten days. Ten days come and go. Two weeks. Three. And where are we? I think you don't know what the blazes you're doing."

Henry walked away. The Indians mumbled among themselves and shuffled restively as they awaited Morgan's response. Kan stood near, arms crossed over his chest as he looked into Morgan's eyes. Lowering his voice, Morgan said, "Watch what you say, Sarah, or—"

"Or you might find your authority usurped by a woman? How dreadful for your manhood."

They stood locked in silent combat while the air hummed with insect sounds and warbling birds. Morgan's sweat-drenched face was set like granite, his eyes a smoky fire. Sarah wanted to go up on her toes and press her mouth to his, for suddenly she realized she had intentionally antagonized him for no other reason than to provoke him into responding to her—be it in fury or passion. With chagrin she discovered that she was becoming desperate to experience either even though she knew he wanted no part of her as long as Norman stood between them.

She elbowed her way through the Indians and grabbed her machete and helmet in her blistered hands. No one moved, and she was forced to face Morgan again. "Well?" she demanded.

"Well, what?"

"What are you waiting for?"

"For you to make up your mind about who the hell is going to lead this sorry group."

"You, of course . . . that's what I'm paying you for."

Morgan ordered the Indians to take up their cargo. The natives moved slowly, talking among themselves, forcing Morgan to repeat his orders. Suddenly Sarah felt guilty. None of this was Morgan's doing. Had she listened to him in the first place, they would be safe and comfortable in Georgetown. Well, perhaps not comfortable. No doubt the mansion had been turned over to the new Governor. Perhaps her father's belongings had been auctioned . . .

"Sarah, have you taken your quinine?" Morgan asked.

Frowning, she took the medication and swallowed it. Her own quinine had been swept away in the river. However, Morgan had produced a supply from his belongings, explaining there was plenty to go around.

He hadn't shaved in several days. He was sweaty and dirty, his clothes tattered, hair falling to his shoulders. He looked like a savage himself. The rifle that hung over his shoulder by a strap added to the effect, as did the knife on his hip. Recalling those nights when she had danced uninhibited amid the Indians, she felt her face turn red. She thought him the savage, yet he had never taken advantage of her intoxicated state, no matter how she had tempted him, taunted him, using her apparent inebriation as an excuse. She had been terrified that he would sleep with one of the Indian women the chief had offered him, but he had wanted no part of them. Perhaps there was a God who listened to prayers in this godless place after all.

The first sign that they were not alone came, as always, in the silence of the animals, the cessation of bird calls. The rustling of leaves by the wind high above their heads sounded like an eerie clattering of dry bones in a graveyard. They had just risen from a sleep besieged by mosquitoes. Kan had shaken Morgan awake, and Morgan had punched Henry, and Henry, Sarah. They noted that their group had dwindled by another three, and it did not take long to discover why. The missing men were found not far from camp, headless.

Morgan moved to the crate of guns, falling to his knees as he threw back the lid and reached for the bullets, which he passed out among them, ordering them to fill their pockets and make certain the rifles were prepared to fire. Watching him struggle to stand, Henry asked, "Are you all right?"

"As well as can be expected, considering."

"They don't stand a chance against our guns," Henry said.

Morgan dropped to the ground and leaned against a tree, his eyes fixed on Sarah, the rifle thrown across his lap. "Come here," he said.

Knees shaking, she eased down beside him.

"This is it, Sunshine."

She nodded and studied his flushed face, disturbed by the fact that his normally sharp eyes seemed hazy as he regarded her from beneath heavy lids. "Morgan," she whispered. "Are you feeling all right?"

"A little tired. Achy. My hand hurts like hell."

"Would you like some ayahuasca?"

"Will you get up and dance for me again if I do?"

"If you promise to dance too."

"Don't think I have the energy. Sorry." He touched her face. "I should never have brought you here."

"I should never have asked you to."

He gazed over her shoulder at the forest, trying to focus his thoughts on some witty comeback, unable to do it. He was so tired. He had been since he and Sarah were swept over the falls. His senses were dulled; and his muscles ached. If the whole of Japurá Xavante swept upon them now, he might not give a damn; so long as it meant he could lie down and rest.

Sarah's cool hand touched his face. "Are you sure you're feeling well?"

"Well enough. I was just thinking about you and Norman and a house full of children."

"Not Norman. He doesn't like children."

"Do you?" he asked.

"Very much. I've always dreamed of having at least a dozen."

"They're God's gift to the world. That's what my mother used to tell me until . . ."

"Until?"

He shrugged. "Nothin'." He rolled the gun in his hands and shifted against the tree. "Sarah?" The words were dry. She leaned near him, so near he could easily have kissed her mouth.

"Yes?" she replied.

Above them a bird sang a tinkling, pianolike sonata.

The attack came as the little bird's song faded into silence. The dart whizzed through the air and passed through an Indian's temple. The second hit the tree next to Morgan's head. He threw himself against Sarah, forced her to the ground before rolling away and coming up on one knee, aimed the rifle into the wilderness, and pulled the trigger.

As Henry and Kan ducked behind trees, a cry rose from the others as the floresta began to move around them. What at first appeared to be bushes took the form of humans whose torsos were painted green and brown, and whose faces looked like masks of gaping skulls.

Nightmares.

Morgan looked down his rifle barrel and pulled the trigger, blinking against the sting of smoke and fire, watching the bodies crumble in front of him because they did not understand the power of the blasting beast that could rip their hearts to shreds with a single impact.

. . . and then the walls of the floresta faded to black. He was a child again, standing in his mother's doorway watching the drunken man stumble toward him, reach out, and cover his screaming mouth with his sweaty-smelling, salty-tasting fist.

He couldn't breathe! He couldn't breathe!

And the man was touching him. He kicked and screamed and the man's fist was crashing into his face and arms and back, forcing him to the floor on his hands and knees, pulling his hair and—oh, sweet Mary, Mother of God, the pain . . .

He just wasn't good enough anymore to be anyone's son. Immerse his body in God and cleanse his soul. He would heal.

Just don't leave me here forever. For the love of God, Mama, it wasn't my fault. Why did you desert me?

And then someone with gentle hands was smoothing his hair back from his brow and calling him *wonderful, beautiful friend.* A face hovered over him, its features almost angelic, in moments of emotion suffused with the kind of love that Morgan had waited all his life to experience. The eyes promising riches, the smile vowing love . . . if he would only . . .

"Morgan!"

He blinked and, lowering his rifle, looked at Henry.

"They seem to have retreated for the moment. Are you all right?"

He nodded and glanced toward Sarah. She was picking herself up off the ground and brushing off her clothes. Her face looked pinched and white. Her hands were trembling.

"You frightened us to death," Henry continued. "What the bloody blazes did you think you were doing standing out here firing like that? You looked as if you were asking someone to kill you." Henry paced the clearing, assessing the deaths and injuries, barking orders at the Indians, who were deliberating among themselves over whether they wanted to turn back while there was still time. "Time for what?" Henry yelled. "Where the blazes do you intend to go? They'll kill you!"

Kan ushered Sarah to a tree and forced her to crouch beside it. Squatting next to her, he began to reload their rifles while Henry continued to pace. "Morgan, how far do you suppose it is to King's plantation?"

"I don't know."

"But you must have some idea," Sarah joined in, her voice rising in exasperation.

Henry said, "The Xavante wouldn't dare cross into King's boundaries."

"What difference does it make?" Morgan tried to stand, swaying before catching hold of a tree for support. "We're either running from a devil or to one."

"But we stand a chance with King," Henry argued.

"Oh, yeah? What gives you that idea?"

"You must have a plan, Morgan. Surely you've given some thought to how you'll escape the bloody tyrant?" Henry came up beside him. "We're going to get through this. I promised you we would. I won't let him hurt you again. I'll kill him myself before I allow that. But you have to be willing to fight."

A shadow of a smile passed over Morgan's lips. "Damn, I could use a cigarette."

"So could I and I don't smoke."

"Thank God. Imagine how short you might've turned out if you had."

Henry laughed, and as he turned away, Morgan said, "Know why cannibals don't eat missionaries, Henry?"

"No, Morgan, but I have a feeling you're going to tell me."

"Not if you don't want me to."

"Will it make you feel better?"

"Probably."

"All right, then. Tell us."

"What was the question?" Sarah asked, sliding down the tree to the ground.

"Know why cannibals don't eat missionaries?" Morgan repeated, a smile spreading across his mouth. "Because you can't keep a good man down."

"Good grief." Henry groaned. "Morgan, you're disgusting."

SARAH HAD NEVER WANTED TO LIVE SO DESPERATELY AS SHE DID IN the hours that followed, as she crouched within her hiding place waiting for the savages to attack again. How could she have failed to see that the joy in living was not in wealth, but in the mere act of breathing, of witnessing the simple miracle of a hummingbird's wings fluttering as it hovered in space savoring the sweetness of an orchid's nectar. Joy was the sound of raindrops hitting the trees overhead, gathering upon the leaves, and running in tinkling torrents from limb to limb until they dripped to the ground like the beating of fairies' drums. Turning her face into the rain, she let it run over her cheeks and down the length of her hair, and wondered why she had never bothered to play in the rain before. It was a baptism of the heart.

The rain became a steady deluge as dusk crept in. Henry ordered Kan to raise the tent for Sarah, although she wasn't inclined to sleep in it. It was too confining and smothering. Besides, she felt safer with the others. She wanted to be prepared for the attack when it came.

"They won't attack while it's raining," Henry explained. "You have to understand heathens. They believe the sun and rain are gods. Even the earth is a god. They'll have a meeting to discuss the meaning of this rain, and if we're lucky, they'll take it as a sign to let us pass. Or they'll butcher us at sunrise. Who can figure them? Not me." He laughed that wild laugh that made Sarah smile, regardless of her fear.

The rain diminished, although the distant thunder and occasional flash of light above the trees told Morgan that soon another storm would advance upon them, deluging them once more. He sat on the gun crate, hat pulled down over his eyes, his shoulders hunched against the continuous raindrops. Except for him and a few nervous Indians standing guard around the camp, everyone was sleeping.

The drums had ceased their pounding during the storm, but with the break in the weather they started again, filling the night with an eerie rhythm that made his blood turn cold. A shiver ran through him as he stiffly left his perch. He tried to see the guards through the darkness, but it was impossible. The night was black as the pit, and there was no hope of building a fire. Feeling helpless, he kicked out at the pile of brush they had gathered.

That was when he heard Sarah weeping inside her tent. He moved to the shelter and nudged the flap open. He could just make out her figure crouched upon her sleeping mat, her hair like a sheet of moonbeams spilling over her shoulders to the mat. "Sarah?" he whispered.

Her face turned up to his. She moved quickly on her hands and knees to the opening and grabbed his hand, his arm, drawing him inside and herself against him, knocking his hat to the ground. Her arms closed around him and she held him, trembling. "The drums," she said. "Morgan, what does it mean?"

"I don't know."

"Will the Indians kill us at dawn? Is that it?"

He shook his head, unable to concentrate on anything but the feel of her against him. He lowered his rifle to the ground so he could slide his arms around her. Having pushed her away so many times in the past, he no longer had the willpower to do it.

"I'm afraid," she confessed. "I wanted so badly to be brave, but I'm so tired of being brave. Please don't be angry at me any longer. Please don't ridicule me for being afraid or being so foolish these last many weeks that I couldn't accept what I knew in my heart. I can't help being frightened. I don't want to die." She melted against him, and her shoulders shook. "I don't want to die," she repeated in a strained, broken voice.

He stroked her damp hair and traced the shell of her ear with one finger. "I won't let them have you, love. I promise you that."

She wept harder. "Oh, Morgan, I had such dreams. It isn't fair. There's so much to learn, to see, to experience. You don't understand."

"Yes, I do."

"How can you? You've done so much. Experienced so much. You're so . . . worldly." She wiped her nose on the collar of his shirt before looking up. "You can't know what it's like to face the prospect of never marrying, of never holding my own child in my arms."

"Don't you think men have those same dreams?"

"Do you?" She looked surprised.

"Of course."

Laying her head on his shoulder again, she sighed. "It seems a shame. I think we would have made our children wonderful parents. I have so much love to give and can't seem to find anyone who wants it."

He closed his eyes and held her tighter.

The rain was falling again as he settled on the floor of the tent beside her, rocking her in his embrace. Her warmth felt good, thawing the icy ache that had plagued him throughout the past few days. "Norman doesn't love me," came her soft, sad voice through the darkness. "Men of the aristocracy don't marry for love. They marry for convenience. And women marry for money and title. It all seems so ridiculous now. Why didn't I see that before? Well, it doesn't matter. I'm going to die and that's that. It just angers me that there is so much left unfinished. I never accomplished what I set out to do. I didn't save my father's reputation. He was such a great man."

They lapsed into silence as they sat together, Sarah in his lap, ear pressed against his heart, both listening to the drums fade under the renewed onslaught of falling rain. At last she said, "This is very nice, Morgan."

"Yes," he replied, "it is."

"I—I hope I die before you."

He smiled to himself.

"Aren't you going to ask why?" she pursued.

"Why?"

"I thought you had died once before and the pain was horrible. I shouldn't like to experience that again." She sat back. Her face looked young, a portrait of naïveté called Sunshine which embodied every fantasy he held sacred in his life. Youth. Kindness. Innocence.

"Morgan," her lips whispered. "Make love to me."

The words were so softly spoken he wondered if he had mistaken them for the wind, the rustle of rain in the trees, or the distant beating of the drums. Then her warm mouth, partially open, pressed against his throat in a kiss. "Please."

He groaned as the heat in his body magnified a hundred times. Her hands were moving over him slowly, fingertips exploring the curve of his shoulders, the curling hairs on the back of his neck, the moist skin behind his ear, the abrasive beard on his cheeks. "Make love to me," she repeated. "I have to know, Morgan. I want to know. It's one of the great mysteries in life, isn't it? It must be. It's the creation of life. The very beginning. It's not fair that I should die and never know the wonder of it with you."

She stared at him in such perfect stillness and anticipation that he did not know what to do. He felt shaken. Disbelieving. Cowardly, all of a sudden. He had wanted her with a desire that was staggering—but that had been a dream, a fantasy. The reality of actually holding her, loving her, felt too immense to take in.

As her hands began tugging at the buttons on her shirt, he reached out and stopped them. "Don't," he told her. "Please don't. I can't—"

"You don't want me, then," she said with an edge of pain.

"Ah, Christ, Sarah . . ."

"What are you afraid of?"

He caught her hands as they touched his face and pushed her away. She fell to her blanket and didn't move. Finally she rolled onto her side and stared into the darkness.

He could leave now and nothing more would be said. They could each wait out the remainder of the interminable night alone, and at dawn face their destiny alone, all due to his moronic pride that would not allow him to surrender himself, body and soul, to her unless she felt the same for him. What did it matter if she didn't love him? He knew what he felt. Love was in the giving, without thought of what one might receive in turn—or so he had always thought.

He lowered himself beside her, reached tentatively to draw the hair away from her face and over her shoulder. Only then did she roll onto her back. "Hold me. I'm so frightened, Morgan."

He lay down against her, her form so slight—like a frail bird beneath him. He was afraid of hurting her, of losing her, but mostly of never having loved her.

Her arms slipped about his neck, and his own about her waist, hands sliding under the tail of her shirt and against her warm skin. His fingers closed around her rib cage, which felt vulnerable beneath the strength of his hands. Her chest rose and fell raggedly at his touch.

He kissed her cheek, her chin, her throat, and nuzzled the tender skin over her collarbone. Her fingers tangled in his hair and twisted in his shirt. A gasp escaped her as he touched her nipple with his fingertips. "Oh, Morgan, kiss me."

She lifted her face to his, and he cradled it in his hand, tracing its contours before lowering his mouth onto hers and sliding his tongue into its sweet oblivion. The force of her response shocked him and made him forget that she knew little about the passion she aroused in him. He ground his hips against her, as if she needed proof of his need of her, and she whimpered.

He pulled away enough so that he was able to manage the buttons on her shirt. His fingers fumbled with them, and when he had managed the final one, he eased aside the clothing to expose her breasts to the light touch of his exploring, caressing fingertips, until the rose-tipped peaks were high and hard and she was moving restlessly beneath him and rolling her head from side to side, gasping his name and pulling at his shoulders with her hands. His lips descended to her throat in a hungry, urgent need to consume her, and he tried to recall a time when he had wanted a woman so desperately, yet ached so badly to take her gently to the stars.

"Slowly," he told her; then, pushing himself up, he went to work on removing her shoes, then unbuttoned her trousers, pulling them down her legs to reveal that she had no drawers on, only the stockings which she had fixed to her thighs with garters of embroidered flowers. There were tatters in the knees and on one of the ankles. Grinning, he tossed the trousers aside, but left the stockings in place. They were sexy as hell.

She turned her face away and shielded it with one hand, palm up, as if she were suddenly embarrassed. And when she tried to close her legs together, he caught them and drew them apart, bracing them open with his knees.

"Please," he heard her whisper. "Don't laugh at me. I'm too nervous. I might . . ."

"What?" he crooned. "What might you do, Sunshine? Scream for Kan? I wouldn't advise it. You might wake up a few Xavante if you do. We don't want that." He removed his shirt and cast it aside. "Not now. Too damn inconvenient. And besides, someone besides me might see that your stockings are tattered. Sarah . . ." He sought her cheek with an unsteady hand, cradled her throat, traced lacy patterns along the sensitive skin behind her ear. "You're beautiful," he told her. "And I've waited weeks for this." He flipped open the buttons of his breeches. "Long, excruciating weeks, Sarah, of wanting you."

He lay down upon her. She was sobbing quietly. Her heart beat against his chest, and her breathing was fast. He rolled off her slightly, but she responded by throwing her arms around him, and her legs. "Morgan, don't leave me."

"I won't."

"Hold me."

He drew her close and could feel her shaking against him. His lips brushed her temple and cheek before finding her mouth again. A surge of mindless excitement rushed through him as she pressed her body to his in response to his words and the arousing motions he was making on her flesh with his fingers. He shaped and lifted her breasts in his hand, prodding the nipples into erections. Hard shivers racked her body, and she gasped and held him nearer.

"Love," he murmured, letting his hand glide over her hip and down her silken inner thigh to the garter above her knee. "You're lovely. Perfect. Even more beautiful than I ever imagined. Why was I so stubborn? I should have taken you long ago."

Sarah's eyelids fluttered open and she stared through the dark at his face and eyes that regarded her with so much desire. An ecstasy of emotion flooded through her as he brushed her mouth in a tenuous kiss. "Oh, Morgan," she breathed, throwing her head back and allowing him to strew warm, moist kisses down her throat. His hands spanned her ribs and moved upward until curving sensually over her breasts, lightly at first, then roughly, making him groan and her sigh in her throat.

"My God, you're beautiful," he told her, his voice urgent. "Sarah, you don't know how badly I've wanted to hold you."

"Truly?" She caught his hair in her fingers and forced his head back. "Truly?" she whispered again. "And here I was thinking all that time that you couldn't abide me. Oh, Morgan, hold me and don't ever let me go. Let me live this final night of my life as if I'm loved and cherished. Pretend that you love me, if you must."

"I love you," he told her, and the words rang in the silence like haunting, musical bells. "I love you."

The tears rose and she couldn't stop them. They spilled through her lashes and slid down her face. The words were a sweet melody to her senses. All the while she had fantasized of the perfect life, the perfect love, and it had been there within her grasp for these past many days; she just hadn't seen it. Why had they waited so long? Why had they wasted so much precious time.

His hands brushed her like a hungry flame, searching, probing, while he kissed and tortured her and whispered soft phrases in her ears, until she was flushed and shaking with turbulent, mindless emotions.

Then his hands were between her thighs, stroking the silky skin and moving slowly up and up, and her heart and breath were stolen by the feel of his fingers teasing that burning, aching place of mystery, exploring her gently—so gently—sliding in and out and around, turning her wild and abandoned so that she was lifting her body to him and drawing it away, matching the rhythm of his fingers inside her. "Please, Morgan, please."

"Easy," came his quiet words, and this time he pushed deeper inside her, and there was an instant shock of pain that made her whimper. Then he began stroking her again, more gently, kissing her tenderly. Finally he whispered near her ear, "Sarah, are you certain? Once it's done there's no going back."

"I don't care," she told him. "I don't care."

"I don't want to hurt you."

He hesitated again, and she looked at him curiously. "You don't want me?"

"Lady, you have no idea . . ."

"Then why—"

"Sarah, I've never had a virgin."

"But—"

"I'm the *boto*. I'm supposed to seduce everything in skirts. Well, I do. Or did. But not if they're virgins. That can get you in trouble fast."

She smiled, happiness filling her heart. "Then this will be a first for us both, won't it?"

"You may regret it tomorrow."

"If there is a tomorrow for us, I'll worry about it then. Right now I want you to show me paradise. Make me a woman. Your woman, for tonight and . . ."

He hushed her with a kiss.

Her fingers twisted in his hair, her eyelids closing out the black night around them, her mind tuning out the vague beating of the drums and the light spattering of rain on the canvas roof. Tomorrow didn't matter— only now, and being held by a man who made her forget all reason, who could make her fly with a simple glance, and cry with an angry flash of his mesmerizing eyes. The happiness, the security, she had ached for were here in Morgan's arms.

Then he was moving against her, enveloping her body with his, pressing her down and her legs open even as he covered her face and throat and breasts with soft, tormenting kisses that made her moan with a need that was exquisitely painful and consuming.

Then his flesh was against her, smooth and hot and full—so full, persistently nudging at the apex of her legs. Foreign, frightening, he filled her gradually, stretching the tender skin until the sensation was like a burning, prodding ember. Seeking. Sliding. Insistent, the tip of him glided in and out of the entrance, but barely; and rising up on his knees, he lowered his head to momentarily watch the coming together of their joined bodies before looking up, into her eyes. They seemed to shimmer, those silver eyes; they seemed to say more than simple words ever could. Then he whispered, "Sarah," and drove himself into her.

It was a jolt of agony, and of ecstasy.

It was the blinding consummation of bodies and souls.

It was the coming together of spirits. Of hearts. Of dreams. Of fantasies.

She wept with the gladness, and as he began his movement against her, she clutched him in her arms and longed to sing out her joy. She felt like a bird given its freedom, soaring to a spiritual sun, blinded by its glory. And she knew it never, *never* could have been this way with Norman. This joy was too splendid. Too complete. Too perfect. There could never be another after tonight. *Ever!*

"Morgan. Morgan." The sound was an exaltation in the night, and she turned up her face to kiss him again.

His features were intense and beautiful. Oh, God, he was *so* beautiful, like a dark angel cast from some heaven into this virulent paradise of damnation. The very sight of him took her higher, and higher still until she was lost to thought, knowing only the sensation he was spinning and pumping inside her, grinding into her with every sleek, deep thrust of his hard body.

Her groans quickened as she moved her body against his, finding a strange thrill in the painful pleasure her motions seemed to bring him. She saw it in the clench of his jaw, the squeezing shut of his eyes, the flash of his teeth as he grimaced and moaned and gasped with the lovely torment. He whispered her name over and over, a litany of love to the night shadows.

Some deep, dark fire seemed to grow inside her, burning her, startling her, giving rise to a strange and frightening need that she couldn't comprehend, taking control of her breathing, spiraling into a tight blazing band that wound and wound with each strike of his body against that internal flame. Soft, panting animal sounds vibrated in her throat as she twisted against him. When the sobs poured from her throat, he covered her mouth with a kiss that only succeeded in taking her higher. She burst through the threshold, gasping and straining, and the world was a clash of bright lights and roaring sound, a glimpse of heaven amid the tumult.

And then the fall, like drifting on warm, peaceful air, and for an instant she wondered if she had died and touched God, so blissful was the peak of completion.

But now it was his turn. He gathered her to him, holding her close, his face buried in the hot curve of her throat and his body moving rapidly, powerfully, into and out of hers, and the swelling, straining length of him was like fire inside her, pounding and pounding until the passion was alive inside her again and she was pleading for surcease.

He took her there, rising to the apogee himself in that last instant, throwing back his dark head as his body stiffened and spilled deep inside

her. As he eased onto her, the sound of their hearts seemed to fill up the
quiet. But for the hush of rain against the roof and the vague beating of
the drums, there was nothing.

Sarah closed her eyes. "I knew it would be wonderful, and it was. Only
I didn't realize it would be so . . . glorious." She rolled her head and
watched Morgan as best she could. His face was buried in her hair; his
shoulders rose and fell heavily, raggedly. For a moment she imagined that
he was weeping, and timidly she touched her fingertips to the side of his
face. "Have I disappointed you?" she asked, distressed.

He shook his head.

"Displeased you? I'm sorry if I did. It was my first time after all,
and—"

"Hush," he mumbled. "Just hush and let me get control of myself."

She laid back her head and stared at the tent overhead. There came a
soft plop-plop of water nearby, and she wondered if the canvas ceiling
had started to leak.

Finally Morgan moved, sliding his body off and out of hers. He sat up
and reached for his shirt, but did not look at her before wiping his face
with the clothing. Then he cleared his throat. "It's hot. Isn't it?"

Sarah nodded and did her best to see his features through the shadows.
When he didn't say anything more, she held out her hand and wrapped it
lightly around his wrist. "I'd like you to stay with me for a while.
Please?"

He lay down beside her again. For one of the few times in his life, he
was lost for words. Oh, they were there, all right, poised on the tip of his
tongue as they always were when he'd finished with one of his lovers. But
the idea of saying one of those tired phrases to Sarah seemed a sacrilege.
It would somehow taint the moment, and the magic between them. Make
it something crude and ugly—as sordid as his past. She deserved something better . . .

Rolling into his arms, she rested her head on his shoulder while her
fingers drifted through the hair on his chest. "All right?" he asked after a
while.

She nodded.

"I was afraid of hurting you."

"You didn't. I enjoyed it very much. I'd like to do it again."

"Right now?"

She smiled.

"*Chere,* you're insatiable."

Her head came up and she watched him with those wide eyes that were
as naive as they had been an hour before. "I feel soulless without you,"

she said. "I feel as if someone has reached a hand inside me and pulled out my heart."

He laughed.

"I like it when you laugh," she told him. "It sounds so wonderfully masculine."

In the absence of light he could see nothing more than the dim outline of her face and the misty halo of her glorious hair. He buried his hands in it and, drawing her face down to his, said, "I want you again already."

"Then take me. Again. And again and . . . again."

He did, until they were panting and weak from exhaustion. When they finally fell together thoroughly spent, into each other's arms, neither moved nor spoke for a long time. Cradling Sarah next to his heart, savoring the piercing sweetness of her presence, Morgan kissed her temples. He felt . . . reborn. For once he felt as if his damned, useless life was worth living.

There were a great many things he wanted to say, but dared he? These feelings Sarah had awakened in him were new, so new, and therefore frightening. Throughout the past weeks he'd done his best to deny to himself just how much she had come to mean to him. He'd driven himself mad by reminding himself that while a woman like Sarah might find pleasure in his bed, she was meant for men like her fiancé—rich, educated, and refined. She would never stoop so low as to really fall in love with him, heart and soul. Or would she?

"I could stay here forever," came her voice in the darkness, making him smile despite his troubled thoughts.

"Careful what you wish for, Sunshine; it might come true."

"Would that be so bad?"

He lifted her chin and looked at her face, her enormous eyes, her smiling mouth. He smoothed her golden hair from her forehead, and where the words came from he couldn't guess, but they were said before he could stop them. "If I were to ask you to stay with me, would you? If I asked you not to return to England, but to remain here and marry me, would you do it?"

She did not move, but watched his face for a long, silent moment. Then, very slowly, she pulled away and sat up, turning her back to him.

He closed his eyes. Sarah looked around, her demeanor intense, something—fear or regret—haunting her face. She watched him as if she knew her refusal to respond to his proposal had hurt him deeply, and was sorry for it. Perhaps she was also frightened, uncertain what he would do if he was angered.

He *was* angered. Yet beneath all that pent, violent fury remained the one burning reality. He loved Sarah, and he would continue to love her long after she had returned to Norman and taken her place in the society she so desperately craved. He could not hate her for her need to live out her life in comfort, surrounded by all the security that money and position could buy. Christ, the past weeks he had battled his way to Japurá intending not only to avenge himself on Rodolfo King but also to rob the bastard of his gold, just so he could experience that sort of security himself . . . and perhaps buy the affections of someone who could lift him out of his hopelessness.

He reached for her, closed his fingers gently over her shoulder, and coaxed her down into his arms. He stroked her hair for long minutes, and at last she looked up at him, her eyes full of tears. "Morgan," she whispered. "I—"

He touched his finger to her lips. "I understand."

"But I don't. Oh, God, I'm so confused."

Her head, lying upon his chest, shook as she wept in the silence. He pressed his lips to her pale hair, smoothed it with his hand until he was certain she slept. Then from somewhere in the night came the sudden cracking of a tree limb, or perhaps it was simply the *curupira* weaving its mysterious magic over the hapless travelers. Sarah drowsily lifted her head and asked, "What was that noise?"

"Nothin'," he whispered, drawing her to him once again. Just the sound of his heart breaking . . .

Chapter Fourteen

THE FIRST THING HE NOTICED WHEN HE CRAWLED OUT OF THE TENT was the marmoset perched on the edge of a bowl, feasting on a goiaba. Then he noted that it was morning. The sun was pouring through a break in the trees and spilling over the campsite as if sent directly from God as some testament of His favor.

Morgan stumbled to his feet, doing his best to pull his shirt closed, not quite managing it. Not quite managing to button his breeches either as they fell open. He was forced to grab them before walking stiffly toward the staring monkey.

He felt like hell.

Then he saw Henry sitting on a fallen tree trunk, glaring at him with blazing black eyes and quivering white bones in his nose. Henry leapt from the tree and dashed across the clearing before Morgan could collect his scattered thoughts enough to speak, much less sidestep the fist Henry drove into his stomach. Morgan doubled over, had barely recovered before his head was snapped back with a splintering crack across his jaw that spilled him to the ground. Henry threw himself atop him then, as if he were mounting a horse, and proceeded to pummel Morgan's face and chest and stomach. Morgan did his best to shield himself, to little avail. His nose was bleeding profusely and the taste of blood was sickening.

"Blast your black heart!" Henry declared and before Morgan could blink his stupor away, Henry had jumped up, grabbed up a rifle, and leveled it at his face. "You bastard, I was under the mistaken assumption that you were more noble than to seduce an innocent like Sarah."

"I didn't—"

"Shut up, and for once in your miserable, worthless life, listen to what I have to say. Sarah's not a whore you can use when you're feeling like you need to take a poke at the world. You've ruined her; do you realize that?"

"Get that goddamn gun out of my face before I get mad. Or use it. Go on. Put me out of my misery so I won't bleed to death. Christ, I think you've broken my nose."

"Good! It serves you right! I'd like to break something else, and I just might before we're finished." Henry tossed the rifle to the ground and, doubling his fists, curled them up in front of his face. "Put 'em up. I mean it, Kane. I demand the right to call you out."

"Should I stand on my knees to make it fair?"

Sarah's voice interrupted them. "What's going on here?"

"I'm defending your honor," Henry proclaimed. "This black-hearted swine took advantage of you, Sarah, and I cannot abide it. Stand back, this could get ugly."

"Oh. Oh . . . my. But, Henry, it was I who took advantage of him," she confessed, her pale cheeks turning pink. Walking to the pygmy, she stopped and pressed a kiss to his cheek. More quietly, she said, "This is very embarrassing, but I invited him into my tent last night."

He looked unsettled.

"I hope you won't think unkindly of me," Sarah continued. "But I was frightened when I heard the drums."

"You might have called out to me," he stressed. "At least then he would not have had the opportunity to . . . well . . ."

"You're right, and I apologize. But what's done is done, and if I've offended you I'm extremely sorry."

"You? Offend?" Dropping his hands, he turned to face her. "Sarah, my dear, you could do nothing of the sort. *He* is the one who should suffer the consequences. *He* should have known better." He pointed to Morgan, who had by now managed to sit up, despite the ringing in his ears and the blood streaming from his nose.

Hair spilling wildly about her shoulders, shirt buttoned crookedly, Sarah looked away from Henry and around the camp. Morgan watched the realization turn her sleepy features into wide-eyed alertness as she cocked her head, listening for the drums. The jungle was silent. "Surprise," he drawled. "We're still alive."

"The Xavante?" she asked.

"Just as I'd hoped," Henry explained. "They've decided to leave us alone. But that's no guarantee they won't attack at some future hour."

She turned to Morgan, for the first time registering concern at his busted nose and mouth. That was short-lived, however, as she said to Henry, "We should get out of here as soon as we can, put as much distance as possible between ourselves and the Xavante. Where are the others? Why haven't they broken camp?"

"Kan is scouting the area, and I've sent out the other five in search of food and water."

"And the others?" She watched Henry's face expectantly.

"There are no others. They absconded during the night, with several of our rifles, I might add. I don't expect to see any of them again. I sent Kan and the rest out over two hours ago—"

"Kan would never desert me!" Sarah said.

"Yes, well, take my word for it, Sarah, you cannot always depend on those closest to you. When push comes to shove they are going to think about themselves first." Henry shot Morgan a glance before walking to the fire.

Sarah stood in a pool of sunlight and gazed toward the floresta. Comprehension had settled in. The morning was several hours old; she was alive.

Sarah did not look toward Morgan as he brushed past her and dropped to one knee near the fire. Yet in time her eyes were drawn to him, and her mind tumbled with the night's memories, bringing a rise of color to her face. She moved to the fire and knelt beside him, pretending to play with the marmoset while she gathered her courage to confront the problem. Morgan had managed to stop his nose from bleeding and was doing his best to button his blood-spattered shirt. She noted that his hands were shaking and his eyes were troubled. "Can I help?" she offered.

He did not say anything or acknowledge her presence. In every way he looked the brooding stranger he had been those many grueling days that they journeyed down the Amazon, hardly the man who had held her so passionately throughout the night—who had asked her to marry him. Hesitantly, she placed her hand on his arm. "Please don't be angry, Morgan."

He yanked his arm away and left her, swaying as if drunk, making Sarah frown and watch him guardedly. He moved toward Henry, who had begun to break down her tent. "Henry," he said, and his voice sounded dry. "We need to talk."

"I have nothing more to say to you, Morgan."

"The hell you don't. You don't beat a friend's face in, then walk away. I'm sorry if I've upset you, but—"

"Why don't I believe you? Could it be because I happen to know you haven't uttered one truthful word the entire time I've known you? I really don't think you know the difference between reality and illusion."

Standing, Sarah moved toward them. "What's this about?" Flinging the canvas to the ground, Henry stalked off to the far side of the clearing and began gathering up the cooking gear. Morgan stood where Henry had left him, shirt gaping open, hands on his hips. Kan appeared at that moment. Behind him hurried the five others. Breathing heavily, he announced, "We have seen the Xavante village and there is much excitement among them. They argue over whether they should attack again."

Sarah stepped forward. "Then we must leave as soon as possible."

"Stay out of this," Morgan snapped.

"But surely you can't mean to remain here any longer—"

"I said to shut up, Sarah." He rounded on her so viciously she stumbled back in surprise.

Henry leapt forward, placed himself between them, and glared up at Morgan. "Don't you dare vent your anger on her," he declared. "She's not the guilty one here."

"And just what the hell am I guilty of?" Morgan demanded. "I didn't rape her, you know. I didn't do anything more than any other man would have done if given the same chance."

The blood drained from her face as Sarah heard the words. She was shaken, not just over this breach of friendship, but over the ugliness of Morgan's tone.

"You took advantage of the situation!" Henry shouted.

Morgan watched Henry cross the clearing and begin to roll up the sleeping mats. His nose was throbbing, and his stomach where Henry had punched him felt as if it had been twisted into a knot. He felt like thin glass that might shatter from the least pressure.

And then he simply lost control. He vaguely realized he was moving toward Henry, reaching for him, jerking him around so forcefully his friend's feet left the ground. Lowering his voice to a harsh whisper, he said, "Maybe you need to use those bones in your nose to clean out your ears, *runt.* Sarah isn't the wounded party here. If anyone got hurt here, it was *me.* If anyone got used here, it was *me.* I care for her, Henry, in case you haven't noticed. I care a helluva lot, as a matter of fact, or I would've seduced her long ago. But I was the one taken this time. I asked her to marry me and she turned me down."

Henry stared up at him, his face emotionless but his eyes intense. "Morgan . . . are you in love with her?"

No response.

"By Jove," Henry whispered. "You are. Of course you are. Why didn't I see it sooner? My God, man, I'm sorry."

Morgan turned away, grabbed his knife and sheath off the ground, and proceeded to loop it around his hips and buckle it. "Let's get the hell out of here," he ordered.

ALL DAY LONG, MORGAN DROVE THEM RELENTLESSLY, SLASHING with the machete one moment, cursing the frightened natives the next. As one of the Indians fell to his knees, Sarah threw herself on Morgan and cried, "For the love of God, what do you think you're doing? You're killing these men!"

"I don't hear them complaining."

"Because you've frightened them to death." She hurried back to the suffering Indian and, along with Kan and Henry, helped him sit up. Kan hurried to cut a *cipo de aqua* and held it to the man's lips. Soaking the tail of her shirt with the liquid, Sarah mopped his face as he mumbled to her. "What is he saying?" she asked Kan.

Frowning, Kan shook his head and responded in the Indian's language. Again the trembling man spoke to Sarah, more urgently this time, and the others moved up around him, joining in on the conversation, their voices rising in volume. They glanced toward Morgan, who, leaning against a tree, regarded them all with a dispassion Sarah found more terrifying than his earlier fury.

Kan said, "They say this American is more of a devil than a *boto*. They say he is a dead spirit who is leading them to the place of no return." Kan looked at her, his eyes worried. "They believe Kane is no longer in his right mind. They say a fever is eating away his brain, that he no longer knows where he is going."

"But that's not true," she argued, both to Kan and to the round-eyed Indian who gaped at Morgan in dread. Turning to Morgan, she refused to acknowledge the odd brightness of his eyes, the flush of his skin, and demanded, "Tell them, why don't you? Tell them you know where we are."

He remained still and silent, his refusal to respond making the shrieks of birds and howlings of monkeys painfully unbearable. It was all she could do not to cover her ears and scream herself as the panic rose inside her. How many times during the past days had she questioned the reasons they had not yet reached King's domain? She moved toward Morgan, noting details that she had not noticed before. He'd lost weight. His eyes held a vacancy that had not been there even yesterday. "Tell them," she said. "Reassure them. Why don't you say something? Please."

His mouth curled in a smile. *"Chere . . .* I confess that I don't know what the hell I'm doing or where I'm going."

"But you said this was the way you escaped Japurá."

"Did I? Well, then, I lied . . . again. Tell them, Henry. You seemed so damn sanctimonious this morning, perhaps you would like to inform them all that they've been had. You see, *chere,* I don't know where we are because I didn't escape Japurá on foot. I hid in a supply boat until it reached Tefé, then jumped overboard when the captain discovered me pilfering food. I did make it overland for two days, evading King's henchmen who were intent on gunning me in the back. Then I ran into our Xavante friends and decided to take my chances in the river. That's when I found myself swept up in a bore tide and nearly drowned. Henry saved my worthless life."

"Oh, God," she said.

He leaned harder against the tree, wiping his forehead with his sleeve. "All that crap about *botos* was our pygmy friend's idea. It came about because just before he dragged me out of the water, he saw a pink dolphin. When he told the Indians in Georgetown about it, the rumor grew that I was blessed, magical; I was the long-awaited *boto.* They started searching me out, offering me food and other . . . pleasures. One thing led to another—you know how stories travel—"

Henry moved to his friend, his face pinched with remorse. "Morgan, I didn't mean the things I said this morning—"

"Shut up!" He yelled so loudly the Indians quelled and the animals' cacophony dwindled to an occasional staccato trill. "Shut up," he repeated, the sound made menacing by its sudden gentleness. "Shut up . . . just . . . shut up until I'm finished. I think the lady deserves the truth. After all, I was the bastard who took her innocence. She can go home to Norman and with a clear conscience confess on her wedding night that a black-hearted rake took advantage of a situation and ruined her. He'll forgive her for that. I'm sure he would forgive her for anything . . . if he's got any wits about him."

He sagged against the tree and slid down its trunk until he sat on his heels, one arm thrown over his knees, his hand gripping the machete and rolling it in his blistered fingers. "I'm very good at lying. A trait I was born with, it seems. Some children have a gift for painting, or singing, or even dancing. But God decided that deception would be my forte. I discovered this when I was six. You see, my mother was a prostitute. One night when she was out one of her regulars happened by and decided that I was better than nothing. He raped me twice, and after my mother found me and took me to the hospital and the doctors questioned her about my condition, she told me to lie or they would take me away from her and I would never see her again. So I did lie by telling them I couldn't remember anything. She took me home, and a week later I found myself stand-

ing on the orphanage steps watching her walk away, and she never—
never—looked back, no matter how loudly I screamed for her. So I figured . . . what the hell use was there in telling the truth?

"And then the widows and lonely wives started searching me out,
asking me to lie to them too, tell them pretty lies that made them feel
good and didn't hurt anyone. Occasionally they would lie back and say I
really meant something to them . . . until they met me on the street;
then they would look right through me as if I didn't exist—as if I had
never existed.

"And of course there was Randi . . . king of the frauds . . ."

Henry moved to Morgan and dropped to his knees. "Hush," Henry
beseeched him. "Morgan, I fear the Indians are right. You're ill. The
fever is making you delirious."

He didn't appear to hear. His eyes remained fixed on Sarah, who
watched him with tears running down her face. She turned and walked
away, and coming to a pile of brush, sat upon it, ignoring the scuttle of
lizards and God only knew what else that shimmied in the leaves beneath
her. She covered her face with her hands and tried to make sense of this
madness.

Dear God, how gullible she had been to believe all the fanciful tales of
heroes and *botos*. Oh, yes, she had believed even that, to some extent.
Morgan had been the epitome of every young, naive girl's dreams. Now
not only were her hopes of success shattered, so were her fantasies.

"Sarah." It was Henry, stooping beside her, placing a comforting hand
on her shoulder. "Sarah, Kan feels we should make camp here. It's up to
you."

"Why ask me?"

"Because . . ." His voice broke, making Sarah look up. "Morgan's
not . . . capable right now," he finished.

Some fear must have shown in her face; Henry rushed on. "He's not
himself. I should've realized he was ill. It's been coming on for days. It
may be some infection from the broken hand. I pray that's all it is, but we
won't know for sure for a few days."

Squeezing closed her eyes, she asked, "Is he rational?"

"He's very tired, Sarah."

"That doesn't answer my question, Henry. Is he cognizant enough to
know what he's saying and doing?"

"At this moment, I don't think so." He smiled and added, "But he
seemed fine last night, if that's what's worrying you."

She turned her face away, ashamed that he should guess the cause of
her disquietude. For the love of God, she had just been informed that

they were lost in the jungle, that the likelihood of their coming through this travesty was virtually nil. And all she could think of was whether or not Morgan had been in his right mind when he had held her in his arms and made her feel so wonderful, when he had asked her to marry him.

"Tell the others to make camp." She dried her eyes. "We all need to rest."

SHE LAY IN THE DARKNESS IN HER TENT, TOO EXHAUSTED AND HOT TO sleep. In desperation she had removed her clothes, but that only added to the misery. Insects crawled over her skin, forcing her to claw and swat and further curse her stupidity for coming here.

When she wasn't fending off bugs, she was crying for her father and the dispirited men huddled amid the trees, sleeping. Occasionally she cried for herself, for the death of her innocence and her dreams. But mostly she cried for Morgan. She'd been too stunned and upset earlier to fully comprehend all he had told her. But as she lay in the dark, the haunting words came back to her, the nightmares of a little boy who had been abused by a stranger and deserted by his mother. He had never had anyone, or anything, and here she'd been acting like a ninny all these weeks, desperate with the fear that she might find herself cast out of that damned, stupid London Society.

She felt like a fool. She felt brokenhearted for Morgan, and angered over his lies. She wanted to scream at him and hold him all at once.

Morgan came at her so suddenly she had little time to do more than gasp. When his hand clamped over her mouth, her heart seemed to hesitate in its beating. He whispered, "It's only me."

She closed her eyes as he settled his body next to hers. "They wouldn't let me near you. Did you tell them not to?"

She nodded. As his hand bit into her face, she whimpered.

"They're talking about turning back. We've come too far to turn back. We've sacrificed too much. But they won't listen to me anymore. They think I'm sick, or crazy. You've got to tell them no. They'll listen to you. I can find King's plantation. I know I can. We'll get your seeds, and . . . Why are you crying? Ah, Christ, I've disappointed you. I knew you would be if you learned the truth. But I tried to tell you. I tried a million times, but you wouldn't listen. You saw only what you wanted to see and heard what you wanted to hear."

She shoved his hand from her mouth. "You lied about everything!"

"Not everything."

She stared through the darkness at his face and felt the angry tears rise again. "You must think I'm little better than those women—"

He grabbed her and shook her. "I never thought that. Never!"

"All those things you said last night—"

"I meant them. I swear!"

She tried to roll away. He caught her and pinned her down.

"Get away from me!"

"Not until we've come to some understanding."

"The only understanding we're coming to is that I want you out of my tent."

"That wasn't how you felt last night."

"That was before I knew the truth about you."

"Which is? Sorry, sweetheart, but I'm the same man who crawled between your lovely legs last night."

"Never again!"

"You don't think so? I'm the man who touched you here." He drew his tongue across her breast, making her tremble. "And here." He slid his hand between her thighs, spreading her legs with his knees as he did so. Then he was releasing himself from his breeches and sliding his body into hers, making her gasp and lift her body in supplication and invitation, despite the fury that inflamed her as hotly as the passion he aroused in her. It was primitive. Mindless. Abandonment and surrender. Perhaps he was magic after all. For out of the desperation and disappointment there sprang a fountain of hope, and need, and a fulfillment that she had never known.

"Sarah, I'll be your hero. Just believe in me. Give me this chance to prove I'm worth something."

The words faded, and she felt too dazed to comprehend, too confused; her emotions and thoughts and body were in a turmoil that was as appealing as it was frightening.

"I'll get you your seeds, *chere,* and you and Norman can live happily ever after, if that's what you want . . ."

"Yes," she murmured, lifting her arms to pull him against her, burying her hands in his hair, then sliding them around his shoulders, holding him so close she could feel the tremor of emotion that passed through him.

She closed her eyes and let her body drift away, into the burning light.

Chapter Fifteen

MORGAN WAS GONE BY DAYLIGHT. HE DISAPPEARED WITHOUT TELL-ing anyone he was leaving. Twelve hours later Sarah and Henry sat outside her tent, dreading nightfall. "If he hasn't returned by dark, he's not coming back," she said. "Where could he have gone?"

"Regardless of what you think of him now, Sarah, he would never turn his back on his friends. Not like me. I should never have said those things yesterday morning." Sighing, Henry stood and paced. "I, more than anyone, should've understood him. Morgan's not a bad chap. He's just . . . confused sometimes. I'm as much at fault about those rumors and myths as he is. It all seemed a lark. Innocent fun. The natives needed to hold on to one of their last superstitions, and it gave Morgan an opportunity to enjoy respect, for a change. That's all he's ever wanted. Life has treated him rather badly. It seems no matter where he turns he meets strife, pain, heartache, and disappointment. I marvel at how his mind and soul can continue to stand up to such torment."

"It doesn't seem fair," Sarah said.

"It isn't fair. It makes me question God every day of my life. I suppose we are destined to face such obstacles; if we deal with them capably, without veering from what is right and true for us, then we will ultimately triumph. Still, that doesn't make watching my friend suffer any easier."

Sarah smiled. "You're a good friend, Henry."

"Am I? After my tantrum I'm not so sure. I confess that sometimes I have to remind myself just what it is that drives Morgan. Imagine never knowing who your father was, then being abandoned by your mother. Rob a child of a mother's love and what does he have left? Especially if he has already been stripped of his dignity and innocence by some animal like the one who assaulted him. How does a child deal with that? By building himself an imaginary world where he is able to feel a sense of importance and worth. The problem is, when you're fighting so hard to like yourself, it's difficult to take the time for anyone else. If you have never experienced compassion, how do you know how to show it? If love and kindness have been held back, how does one know how to be kind and love? We learn by example, and although I've done my best for Morgan the last year, I'm afraid I failed him yesterday. Now he's out there somewhere and he may be ill and needing me. If he would only come back, I would never—ever—raise my voice to him again."

At that moment Morgan walked into the camp.

Sarah leapt from her seat.

Henry turned on him and yelled, "You idiot! Where in the name of all Amazonia have you been? Morgan, have you any idea what we've been going through?"

"No." His familiar grin was droll and sarcastic.

Sarah stood to one side, allowing relief to flow through her, acknowledging its magnitude even as it left her weak and trembling, on the verge of tears. Although he appeared exhausted, there was a keenness in his eyes that she had not seen for days. His stance was strong and his step lithe as he moved across the clearing to her.

"Hello," he said softly, and the memories of their previous night together flooded her in a wave of heat that brought hot color to her cheeks. "I have something for you." He caught her hand and, turning it up, placed a withered pod in her palm.

Kan moved up beside her, appearing guarded. He had been furious at Morgan over his deceptions, and just as angry at himself for allowing his "Missy" to become involved in such a swindle. But as he reached out and protectively grabbed the pod from her hand, breaking it open with his fingers and spilling out the brownish-speckled seeds, he let out a grunt of surprise.

"What is it?" Sarah asked.

Kan stooped and retrieved the seeds. His eyes went back to Morgan's, and he said, _"Cau-uchu."_

"Cau . . . ?" Sarah repeated.

"Uchu," Morgan finished. "It means weeping wood." He smiled, and the act deepened the grooves of fatigue at each corner of his eyes. _"Chere,_ they are _Hevea brasiliensis_ rubber seeds."

The world seem to tip and sway. Grabbing hold of Morgan, she fell against him and, throwing back her head, searched his haggard face for the truth. "Oh, God, Morgan, you're not—"

"Lying? Not on your life, sweetheart. I told you I'd get you there and I have."

Henry joined them, as did the others. "What are you saying, Morgan? That you've found King's plantation?"

"We're standing smack in the middle of it. Those Xavante didn't decide not to kill us because they believed some rain god. It was because we were already within King's realms. They wouldn't have dared risk his anger."

Sarah let loose a scream of elation and threw herself into Morgan's arms, covering his face and throat with kisses and weeping in her excitement. "I knew you could do it. My darling Morgan, you don't know what this means. You've saved my life, you wonderful man!"

"I guess this means that you're not mad at me anymore?"

Grabbing his face, she kissed him on the mouth, then spun away and danced among the smiling natives. Grinning, Morgan looked askance at an amused Henry. "If this is what she does for three measly seeds, I'd like to see what she'd do if I brought back a pocketful."

Henry threw back his head in laughter.

THERE WAS DEFINITE CAUSE FOR CELEBRATION. THE INDIANS searched far and wide for game and returned with an anteater, which they skinned and roasted over the fire. Kan collected fruit, and Henry manioc. Long after they had feasted and sat about the fire, content and enjoying their sense of accomplishment, Kan took up his flute and filled the hot night air with the poignant, melodious songs of his people. He played until the hour grew late and most of the Indians retired to their pallets. Finally, only Morgan and Sarah and Henry remained.

Henry got to his feet, dusted off his seat and legs, and glanced awkwardly at his friends. "I suppose I'll call it an evening. You're probably wanting some time alone." Morgan frowned and Henry rushed on. "Not to worry. We'll talk later."

Morgan nodded.

"I'll bid you both a good night, then."

Without waiting for a response he faded into the darkness. In a moment his voice drifted to them as he fussed at one of the Indians for taking up too much room on his mat. "Bloody savage," came the words. "You'd think they were all raised in the jungle."

Sarah and Morgan laughed, then their laughter died as they watched the fire scatter a spray of embers over the ground. Sarah said, "What happens tomorrow, Morgan?"

Resting on one elbow, he chewed a blade of grass and shrugged. "The Indians will collect your seeds, then you'll go home."

"How can I thank you for what you've done for me?"

"I haven't done anything except spoil Norman's wedding night." He flashed her a smile that didn't reach his eyes.

She didn't say anything for a long while, giving Morgan the opportunity to watch her in silence. Her face was limned in firelight, her expression almost spiritual. Not for the first time, her frailty and vulnerability drove nails of guilt through him. Throughout the past day, when his mind was clear enough to allow him to think coherently, he'd tried to convince himself that he'd taken her virginity to spite her and her aristocratic fiancé. By convincing himself that she really didn't mean that much to him, he could accept the fact that it was Norman she loved, and Norman with whom she would live the rest of her life. But that was not the case. He had taken her in a moment of splendid madness.

When she turned her eyes on him, he felt shaken. Something seemed to change direction in him and threatened to weaken the tenuous resolve that had grown in him during his earlier absence.

"Will you come to bed with me?" she asked.

There was a terrible need to hold her, to melt his body into hers, to brand his memory into her mind, yet he shook his head. "No."

Silence. As if paralyzed, she stared into his eyes, her own bright with the same fierce desperation that had plagued him the past weeks. "I see," she said, fingers clasping and unclasping in her lap. "You won't make love to me unless I agree to marry you."

"No, *chere,* I simply don't intend to be used any longer—by anyone for any reason."

She turned her head away from him then. She felt lost and so confused. Yet she could not reach out and grasp the one certainty in her life— Morgan's love. While the awful things he'd revealed about himself before disappearing into the forest had filled her with compassion, they had frightened her too. He was so different from Norman and the world she knew . . . How could she promise to marry him? He wanted too much. Damn him, he wanted everything.

Sarah climbed to her feet and walked to her tent, pausing at the entrance to look back. Morgan continued to gaze into the fire, his hat cocked at an angle, the marmoset nestled in his shirt pocket. Its tiny, furry head rested against his heart. "Good night," she said.

"Good night, *chere,*" came the quiet reply.

THEY SPENT THE FOLLOWING DAY TRUDGING THROUGH THE *floresta* in search of the thousands of *Hevea* seeds her father had felt would be needed for a successful propagation. Hour after hour Sarah hacked at the wild undergrowth as she despaired over her dilemma. While the Indians shimmied up the *Hevea* trunks and shook the limbs so the seed pods rained to the ground, her eyes were on Morgan.

She ached for him. She understood the pain he'd been feeling the past weeks. He wanted her, not just her body but, more importantly, her soul. She had withheld that from him, and as she now suffered his withdrawal from her, she was swallowed by remorse. She could not find the remotest pleasure in their accomplishment, for it was that achievement that would take her back to Norman.

Staring down at the machete in her hand, Sarah almost laughed. Did she actually think she could return to London and step back into the role she had acted before? Playing the innocent sophisticate had been hard enough in the past. How in God's name was she to continue such a farce when everything about her had changed? Norman would never approve. But Morgan would. Morgan had continued to love her despite her tantrums, her depressions, her stumbles. He had desired her when she looked her worst. He had encouraged her instead of condemning her for her shortcomings.

Suddenly she knew she loved him despite his inscrutability and disreputableness, his rages and shortcomings. Indeed she loved him because of them. They made him vulnerable and honest and human and far from perfect—everything Norman wasn't.

She decided to tell Morgan her decision after supper. However, he took to his hammock without eating, and within minutes was fast asleep.

Sarah sat on the stump of a tree, picked at her roasted anteater, and gazed into the fire. Henry moved about the clearing, at last stopping to gaze toward the hammock where Morgan was resting.

"Something's wrong," Henry said. "I can't put my finger on it, but Morgan's not right somehow. He hasn't spoken a word to anyone all day. He hasn't eaten . . ." He shook his head. "I worry about him, Sarah."

She put aside her food and watched as the marmoset dashed to pluck a slice of fruit from the plate. "He asked me to marry him," she said.

"I know. You turned him down."

"But I didn't. I just needed time to consider—"

"Do you love him?"

"I love him," she replied. "Perhaps I didn't realize how much until he admitted his past, and his lies, and I discovered that I couldn't stay angry with him. To be honest, Henry, I haven't been so truthful with you either."

He stopped pacing.

"I didn't come here strictly for those damnable rubber seeds. I came here with the intention of facing King and forcing him to admit that he murdered my father."

"By Jove!" he cried. "Sarah, how in the name of Victoria did you intend to do that?"

"I don't know. I suppose I wasn't being rational. All I could think of was my father's ruined reputation and how it would affect me. I feel horrid about it, Henry. I feel responsible for this entire fiasco. You and Morgan risked your lives to bring me to Japurá, just so I could get these seeds and buy my way into a society that no longer holds any special meaning for me. I owe you an apology."

Henry sat beside her on the ground, his legs crossed, his face oddly chagrined. "As long as we are confessing, I suppose you should know the entire truth. In the beginning we had no intention of coming here for the rubber seeds. We only wanted your money to finance the trip to Japurá so that we, too, could take revenge on King . . . among other things."

Sarah stared at her friend's profile before saying, "That's why you kept attempting to desert me."

"Yes."

"I see . . ." She took a deep breath and released it as she watched the fire and shadows dance in the dark.

"Are you going to marry him?" Henry asked.

"I want to, but I'm afraid to. Does that make sense?"

"You're frightened of giving up your life in England."

"Yes."

"While in England, I had all the comforts money could buy, but I had no one to share them with. Not even a friend. It wasn't easy walking away from all that, but I did and I'm glad of it. Because now I have a friend who cares for me, not for what I am, but who I am. I imagine that loving someone, and being loved by someone, is much the same."

Sarah looked through the dark to where Morgan lay sleeping. "I think I'd like to leave Japurá tomorrow, Henry."

"And forget your plans to face King?"

"That no longer seems important." She glanced toward Morgan again. "Will he come with me, or do you imagine he will insist on facing King?"

"If he believed there was a future with you, I think he wouldn't risk confronting his old foe."

Sarah sighed and closed her weary eyes. Suddenly she felt very calm and sure, because she knew what she was going to do. What the future held she couldn't say, but she did know she'd be spending it with Morgan Kane.

* * *

DAWN. SARAH SAT STRAIGHT UP ON HER MAT AS THE AIR FILLED with a high-pitched wail of fury.

"Morga*nnnn!*"

She dragged on her clothes as quickly as possible, threw back the flap on the tent, and scrambled out on her hands and knees. Fists clenched at his sides, Henry stood in the center of the clearing, glaring at the Indians. "Don't stand there and tell me none of you saw him leave. Morga*nnnn!* Blast his hide. I should've known. I *should've* known!"

"What's happened?" she cried.

"He's gone."

"Gone where?" When Henry didn't answer, she stumbled to her feet and ran to him. "Gone where?" she demanded.

He shook his head and kicked out at the kettle of boiling water. She grabbed him and spun him around. "Where has Morgan gone?" she very nearly screamed.

He shoved a paper in her face, a note from Morgan. "To King, of course. Where else?"

MORGAN MOVED THROUGH THE TREES, STOPPING ONLY OCCASION-ally to search out the telltale scars grooving the smooth, light-colored bark of the rubber trees. He knew there was no chance of happening upon a *seringuero.* The rubber collector's day started at four in the morning, striking out through the darkness, a machete in one hand and a *machadinho*—a crude tapping hatchet—in the other. In a pack on his back he'd carry cups into which the thick white liquid would drain. A good *seringuero* on any other plantation could tap three hundred trees a day. Here, however, he would tap four hundred or be faced with the lash —a strap for every tree short of four hundred. This path was overgrown; therefore the trees were resting. The spiraling scars on the trunks were healing, but in a few weeks they would be ready to be drawn from again.

He walked along the pathway, his footfalls muted by the rotting vege-tation and the quiet scraping of brush across his shins. The curing huts were near. The stench of *urucuri* nuts burning, along with the stink of the heated rubber, brought about a familiar rise of nausea in the pit of his stomach.

Another half mile and he was forced to stop and rest. He was sweating profusely, and occasionally the tremors would rack him so hard he al-most lost his grip on his rifle. The pain was a throbbing fire inside every bone and muscle, but when it seemed to get so bad that he couldn't stand it, he would force his mind back to those months with King and recall the horror and pain that had been enough to turn him into an animal; then the present discomfort didn't seem so bad.

Strange how he could finally allow the memories back in. In truth, he invited them—as wretched as the recollections were. And relief came like a flood that poured through some door he had fought long to keep closed. Yet the dread was there too. And the fear. But the fever helped. It dulled reality. This seemed more like the dreams that had plagued his every night the past year. Only soon the nightmare would begin for real.

He came to a stream and followed its meandering path until the smoke from the curing huts became so strong he could hardly breathe. Judging by the sun, it was just after noon. Soon the *seringueros* would be hauling their cured rubber to the *matteiros*'s wagons, and once that was done the workers would return to their huts to rest through the hottest part of the day.

He waded through the water, refusing his body's need to submerge itself in the stream's cool, clear shallows. A small conical hut sat on a rise in a clearing whose remaining trees were dying due to the poisons in the air. Even before Morgan stepped to the door, he knew what he would find.

Still the blast of fetid heat set him back. He gasped for breath and better prepared himself for the inferno before moving in again. The emaciated figure of an old man stooped near the blazing fire, sweat pouring down his wrinkled cheeks. A cloud of smoke permeated the enclosure, and from the man's twisted hands a long pole protruded. He revolved it over and over a pit as the rubber coagulated on the end, forming a pillow-shaped loaf.

As he sensed Morgan's presence, he looked over his shoulder and blinked rapidly, doing his best to see through the smoke. His eyes widened briefly at the sight of his visitor, but when he appeared to hesitate in his routine, Morgan said, "Don't stop, Papa. The wagon will be here soon."

Stiffly, the old man swung the pole away from the smoke and tossed it down with the others near the door. Then the warning bell on the advancing wagon rang, and Morgan slipped out of the doorway and into the cluster of trees surrounding the hut.

From where he hid he could easily watch the advance of the lumbering wagon. He recognized its driver, Marcoi Chavez. Chavez had come to King's plantation the same time as Morgan, and for a while, during their long journey to Japurá, they had been friends. That friendship had ended, however, as soon as each man was assigned his respective job. Morgan was chosen to work inside the organization, as King's personal assistant, secretary, companion, and bodyguard. Chavez was sent out to work in the fields along with the other slaves. His resentment for Morgan had grown with each grueling task he was assigned. But Chavez was not like the naive and easily frightened Indians King rounded up from the floresta. He had brains and wits enough to realize what it took to get himself out of the rank and file of slave labor.

And that was cold-blooded, gut-wrenching cruelty. A taste for blood and perversion, and a delight in causing pain. But although he was recognized for such attributes, and rewarded for them, he soon realized that he was never going to be anything more than a *matteiro* in King's organization. He was never going to make it to *la casa blanca*.

He wasn't *pretty* enough to suit King's particular tastes.

So he took out his anger on the peons, and when Morgan found himself demoted to *matteiro,* making him even with Chavez, a bitter feud began between them. Not only was Chavez unsurpassingly brutal, but he held one hell of a grudge. He wasted little time in seeing to it that the news of Morgan's kindness to the *seringueros* was passed on to King, who believed the peons deserved little better than death for falling short of their daily quotas. When learning Morgan had overlooked such shortcomings, going so far as to lie on the tally sheets when recording the workers' production, King had called him to the house and demanded he list the workers who had not been producing to capacity. When he refused he had been handed over to Chavez for punishment.

Now, sinking back against the sweating wall of the curing hut, Morgan slid to the ground to wait out Chavez's visit. He prayed that the sadistic bastard wouldn't take to Chico with the whip. He didn't have the energy to stop him, and besides, he had to lie low until he decided what he was going to do about King. Even that seemed a monumental task for a mind burning with fever, and memories.

He tried to imagine what he might have done had Sarah agreed to marry him. No doubt about it, he would have called off this scheme to destroy King, concentrated on gathering up her precious seeds, and gotten out of Japurá as fast as he could. But she hadn't agreed. So he was right back where he'd started. With nothing to build his life on. Hopefully, Henry would realize the futility of attempting to follow him—he wouldn't risk Sarah's safety on such a foolish and pointless venture. Henry would wait for a few days, maybe a week, and when Morgan didn't show up he'd find a way to get Sarah back down the river.

Voices drifted to him, distorted by distance. They seemed to shimmer like the waves of heat radiating off the sweltering earth. Closing his eyes, he fought the urge to tumble back in time, yet as Chavez's voice rose, barking orders to the weary old man loading his stores into the wagon, the memory dragged Morgan down, and down, to the place where he had buried the pain and the twisted recollections of that day more than a year ago.

He was hauled from the house by several of King's men. He saw Chavez standing near the scaffold and for an instant he felt a huge relief that they were going to kill him outright as opposed to torturing him. Then Chavez uncoiled the whip. His legs seemed to freeze and he stumbled; his escorts were forced to grab him around the waist and carry him because he couldn't find the strength to walk.

The house bells were ringing. If he closed his eyes he could almost imagine that he was back at the orphanage on Sunday morning and the bells of the cathedral were calling in the flock for worship. Only these bells were ringing out to announce a break in the workers' routine, calling them in from their tasks for one purpose only.

There was a lesson to be taught.

Tight metal bands were locked about his wrists; then he was lifted up to the whipping block and the bands were attached to hooks that protruded from the frame overhead. His ankles were bound by ropes that were threaded to metal loops at the base of the scaffold. The clothes were cut from his body—every last stitch—and tossed away. He hung there, spread-eagled in midair, as the men, women, and children gathered around, their faces mirroring his own fear, every one of them recalling their own experiences with Chavez's whip.

Then Rodolfo was there, elegant in his splendid white suit, his breathtaking golden hair like a halo as he moved through the sunlight to stand before him. The patrao *watched him with those hypnotic blue eyes, like fire and ice, one moment burning, the next freezing—but always terrifying in their beauty and evil.*

"Morgan," he seemed to whisper. "My dear Morgan, you must know how this grieves me. To imagine your back opened this way breaks my heart. Spare us this torment. Confess who you're protecting and allow them to suffer for their own crimes."

He couldn't respond even if he wanted to. His throat was too dry and tight with fear.

"Morgan," King said. "Look about you. Do you see any of the people you're protecting stepping forward to spare you from this punishment? They knowingly took advantage of your generosity and now they would have you suffer in their place. That's because they aren't your friends, as you seem to think. Whereas I . . . I would save you from this if I could— if I thought you would, in turn, see our relationship in a different light."

He swept Morgan's hair back from his brow with cool, gentle fingers. "Let's put this misunderstanding behind us. We both know I don't really give a damn about this bunch of laggards. We'll forget all about them if you'll just agree to give me what I want . . . which is you. Your friendship, your loyalty, your soul. In turn, I'll make your every dream come true. All of them: wealth, respect, a sense of worth, a place to belong to forever and ever . . . and love. I love you. This ordeal grieves me more than you know."

Morgan looked directly into those deadly blue eyes and rasped, "Go to hell."

King's mouth stretched into a tight thin line across his face. "Very well." He spun on his heels and walked away, up the path to the casa. There he paused and, turning back, hesitated in the doorway. Morgan watched the wind whip his coat and lift his flowing hair about his shoulders, and for an instant he was tempted to call out—so tempted . . .

But he wouldn't. He had his pride. His dignity. His manhood, even if he had nothing else. He had fought all his life to retain some sense of worth despite the rejections and disappointments. He had begged only once in his life and that had been when his mother walked away, leaving him alone on the orphanage's steps, and he wouldn't do it again. Never again. Not even when the captain of the Mindoro *had strapped him to the mainmast and whipped him for insubordination. He had never wept or pleaded or begged for mercy, and he wouldn't start now. Not when he'd watched the others' faces as they wept for pity and an end to their torment, recognizing how the shattering of their self-worth had left them empty shells that walked and talked and looked like men, but inside were goddamned zombies.*

He wouldn't beg, by God, and he wouldn't give in to King's perverted demands. He'd rather die.

Then King was gone, swallowed by the formidable house, and Morgan was left staring at the doorway with fear closing in on his chest like a suffocating weight.

The first lash cut into his buttocks and the forked tip coiled around his thighs like a serpent, nipping dangerously close to his genitals, which drew in to his body in shock and pain. His body lurched and the metal clamps bit into his wrists as painfully as the whip. As the whip retreated, then snapped out again, and again, the agony mounted. The veins stood out on his forehead and throat in his effort not to scream. He wouldn't give Chavez that satisfaction. But the blows continued until the world was blazing red fire and his body had begun to tear at its bonds like a mindless animal caught in the jaws of a trap.

He'd begun fainting between the blows. Each strike that cut into his back pulled him briefly back to consciousness with a new surge of excruci-

ating agony. The pain rolled over him in crest after crest, pulling him out, dragging him in. Then they stopped and someone threw water over his face, forcing him awake. The yard was silent. The workers watched from their distance, sad-faced but closemouthed. King had been right. No one had dared to step forward and suffer for his own crimes.

He blinked and King came into focus, his electric blue eyes gazing up at Morgan. "You know what I want," he said. "If you agree, this will end, Morgan. No more pain."

Morgan hung in his bonds, strangling and choking in his blood. Somehow he managed to get up the strength to spit blood in King's face.

"Cut him down," came the words.

Then cruel hands were wrenching at his ravaged limbs, making him groan and wonder numbly if King had changed his mind after all, and—

He was being forced to his knees and hands, and someone dragged his head back because he was too weak to do it himself. Chavez was walking toward him.

"Morgan, I had wanted to save you from this," came King's words.

He groaned in his throat and tried to stand, to push the brutal hands away that were holding him down. The fear inside him was obliterating all else. Not that. Oh, God, not that. Anything but that . . .

Not rape. Please, God, please . . .

"You know what I want, Morgan. You can spare yourself this humiliation. You know what I want."

"Bastard!" He hissed it, sounding like some dying animal. It made him sick. He started to vomit and couldn't stop.

"You know what I want, Morgan."

"Go to hell!"

King turned on his heel and started back to the house, and Chavez was unbuttoning his pants and—

"Bastard!" he roared.

And King kept walking.

He tried to fight off the hands, but there wasn't strength and he kept slipping in his own blood and vomit. He tried to kick, but they were grabbing his legs and—

He threw back his head and screamed, "Yes! Yes, goddamn you, I'll do anything! Anything! Is that what you want to hear? Just have mercy . . . please. I—I beg you, not this. I'd rather die, Randi. Please, for the love of God, don't let him do this to me!"

When King returned there were tears rolling down his face. He slowly removed his suit coat and handed it to Chavez. Then, stepping up to Mor-

gan, he wrapped his arms gently around him, holding his weight against him as his starched, clean-smelling white shirt soaked up Morgan's sweat and blood, and he said to the others, "Get your goddamned hands off him or I'll kill you."

Chapter Sixteen

"SENHOR KANE, CAN YOU NOT HEAR ME? IT IS CHICO, SENHOR. CAN you not open your eyes?"

The pain in his head was vicious. The Indians had been right. Some fever was eating away his brain.

"Senhor Kane, please try to hear me. You have been unconscious for three days."

He forced open his eyes, wincing from the illumination of a candle somewhere close by. Gradually, the surroundings came into focus. He stared at the adobe ceiling and the walls where several long lizards scuttled with a flip of their tails toward the shadows. Then the old man's face and shoulders came into view. Behind him, an Indian woman gazed down at Morgan with worried eyes. Chico eased one hand under Morgan's head and, pressing a cup to his lips, said, "Drink, my friend. It is only a weak soup, but it will give you strength."

He tried to turn his face away, knowing that every morsel of food was treasured by the *seringueros,* to accept it would mean someone would do without.

"You must eat or you will die."

"Better me than you," he managed to respond.

"You have changed little," Chico said.

"In that case, you know I won't eat your food."

"It is the least I can do for you. I owe you my life. Now drink the soup and allow this guilt I have felt these many months to subside. There. Very good. The woman is a very bad cook, but it will fill your empty belly."

The soup was bitter, but he swallowed it without complaint. When he had finished Chico produced a cup of *masato,* which he pressed to Morgan's lips.

"This will dull the pain in your head."

Chico was right. Soon the discomfort had eased. The soup gave him strength. He was able to sit up and, leaning against the wall, study his surroundings, or what he could see of them in the semidarkness: an earthen floor, a few clay pots, several straw mats thrown into a corner. The smell of dirt permeated the air, and a moth fluttered in and out of the candlelight placed near his mat.

Chico Hinojosa was a *caboclo,* a man of Portuguese and Indian blood. King had hired him and his family five years ago while in Lima, Peru, promising that the old man, his wife, three sons, and a daughter would never know poverty again. Within a month of arriving at the plantation, he had watched his wife be beaten to death with clubs because she had failed to meet her quota of rubber for the day. And because one of his sons had tried to escape King by fleeing through the *floresta,* his daughter had been staked upon the ground, raped by no less than twenty men, and then doused in kerosene and set on fire.

"When I saw you standing there at the door," came Chico's voice, made raspy by the smoke he was forced to breathe every day, "I thought you were a spirit. They told us you were caught in Manáos and killed. Gilberto de Queiros waved before us a man's testicles and said they were yours."

Morgan grinned, then drank more of his *masato.* "There are probably a few husbands who would like to take credit for that, but I'm happy to say I still have mine."

Chico's mouth parted in a smile. "Why have you returned?"

"Revenge."

"No one takes revenge on King. It is like spitting in the eye of a devil and expecting that to destroy him."

"There are ways. But I'll need help."

At that moment the woman who had left the hovel earlier shuffled back through the door. Behind her came one of Chico's sons, Teobaldo. He regarded Morgan with hostility.

"Dios, Papa, what can you be thinking to hide him here?"

"Hello to you too, Teobaldo," Morgan said.

Ignoring Morgan's greeting, the young man demanded, "What is he doing here, Papa? If King learns he has returned and that you have taken him in, he will murder us all like he did my sister and mother and brother."

"Be quiet," Chico replied. "Our friend has been very ill."

"I can see that. Too bad he did not die. With any luck he will do so before *el patrao* learns you have helped him."

"I am too old and sick to fear *el patrao*," Chico argued. "If he killed me tomorrow I should be grateful."

Morgan smiled his thanks as he accepted another cup of *masato*. His eyes on Teobaldo, he said, "I'm moved by your gratitude. As I recall, you were one of the men I was trying to protect when I was tied up and whipped. Perhaps it's your own conscience biting at you that makes you so angry."

"Do not speak to me of conscience." He spit at Morgan's feet. "We all admired you. The young men respected you. When you were cast out of *la casa blanca* for refusing King's demands, we all thought you a saint, a hero. But then you turned on us all and went back to him. What happened, was your lover's rod not big enough to satisfy you? Is that why you finally ran away? Or perhaps you have an itch now and have returned because *el patrao* is the only one who can scratch it!"

In one motion Morgan left his mat. Throwing the cup aside, he grabbed Teobaldo's shirt with his fists and slammed him against the wall. "You bastard, if you weren't Chico's flesh and blood I might kill you."

"Do you deny the facts, senhor?"

"Yes, I deny them. I never let him touch me. Never!"

"You must have done something to enamor him to you. When you escaped he was like a wild man, taking out his vengeance on every man, woman, and child. Show him, Papa, what he did to you because he knew you were friends with the American. Show him!"

Looking back at Chico, Morgan relaxed his grip on Teobaldo as he said, "What the hell is he saying, Chico?"

"It is nothing, my friend—"

Pushing Morgan aside, Teobaldo grabbed his father and turned him around. He raised his shirt, exposing his lacerated flesh. "I would not call that nothing, would you, Kane? And that was only the beginning. There were women and children who were butchered, all because you had touched their lives in some way."

Closing his eyes, Morgan sank against the wall.

"Our wounds have barely healed, and now you come back. Why? Why could you not leave us in peace?"

"You call daily beatings and raping and being slowly starved to death peace?" he answered.

"If we follow his rules, meet his quotas, and show him respect, he leaves us alone."

"That's all right for strong young men like you, Teobaldo, but what about the weak, like your father? What happens when he can no longer meet his quotas? That day is not far off. Will you stand by and preach tolerance when King is dousing Chico in kerosene and setting him afire, or perhaps dismembering him and feeding his body to his own pet jaguars?"

"I suppose you have a better alternative," he sneered.

"Perhaps."

"I want no part of it. And neither does my father. You are death to these people, Kane. You are death to anyone you touch."

"And King's not? How long do you people intend to let men like King rob you of the very thing that could make you all a hundred times wealthier than King ever thought to become on rubber? Who the hell gave him the right to come here and take the land belonging to these Indians, and in the course of doing so rob them of their pride as well? When are you going to stand up and demand what is rightfully yours, Teobaldo? *You* should be pocketing the profits from this rubber, not King."

"King has an army on his side. Have you forgotten? No one gets in or out of this place without his knowing it."

Pushing away from the wall, Morgan said, "I did." He dropped to the mat again, clutching his ribs as the pain shot through him. Chico hurried to dip him another cup of *masato* while he wiped the sweat from his face with his sleeve. "The trick is to get inside. You gotta get to King himself."

"But that is not possible. He surrounds himself with guards, even when he sleeps. You know that."

"Yes." Morgan swallowed. "I know that."

"Then you know there is no way in unless we were all heavily armed and moving together as a combined force."

"Yes."

Morgan watched as Teobaldo paced about the house. Finally he stopped and raised his eyes to Morgan's once more. "You know it is against the rules for us to communicate in any way with those from other sections, unless by King's orders."

"The only way to do it would be under cover of darkness."

"But the risk of being caught . . ." Teobaldo shook his head. "It would mean certain death."

"Every day that you stay here you're risking certain death, amigo. Think about it. Any day King could walk in your door and point the finger at you for reasons as flimsy as not liking your looks, or because he's tossed a coin and you lose, or just because he's in the mood to see someone die. In hell's paradise, Teobaldo, there are no guarantees."

Teobaldo poured himself a cup of *masato* and took a drink. "Even if we could somehow gather forces against him, even if we could defeat him, what would be left for us?"

"Your freedom."

"Freedom. Yes, freedom. Freedom to do what? Return to Lima and walk the streets begging for handouts? Spending our days crouched in some squalid corner weaving baskets for merchants who pay us with bad milk or putrid bananas? And what about the Indians? Their tribes have been wiped out by interlopers like King who bring in their civilized diseases, or their whips. They have no families to return to."

"You remain here and continue what you're doing, Teobaldo. Only you'll do it without the fear of death looming at you from behind every tree. The people will pocket the profits, not King."

"Fancy words. You were always good with the big dreams, how you would someday be somebody. What are you now, Kane? Just a man twisted up with hate. A man intent on revenge. You had the perfect opportunity to begin again—you made it out, did you not? Yet here you are back, and you know and I know you will never leave here again. Never. For as soon as King discovers you, he will kill you."

Laying his head back against the wall, Morgan closed his eyes. "I am a dead man anyway. So what would it matter? You're right, of course. I made it out and discovered that the things I want most are beyond my reach." Imagining Sarah, he smiled, but then the smile faded as he looked at Teobaldo again.

"*Dios,*" Teobaldo whispered. "You sound like a man who has condemned himself to die."

"I am a man with nothing left to lose."

"They are the most dangerous kind, senhor. They rarely care who they take with them."

"If that were the case, I would have gone straight to King. But some good must come out of every battle, or what's the point in the fight? In your case, it means freedom and a chance to build a new life. For me it will be the realization that I have at last accomplished something, if not for myself, then for someone else."

"Which brings us back to where we started. What would we have but one vast floresta?"

"Everything the floresta has to offer: cacao, peach palms, Brazil nuts, coffee, and cassava, not to mention the rubber. In Japurá alone there are enough natural resources to make every man, woman, and child slaving for King very wealthy."

"You spout dreams, Americano. Do you not forget? You must have money to become a *patrao*. It takes many cruzeiros to employ good *matteiros* and *seringueros*. Then there are the ships to hire."

"What if I tell you there is a way for you to have the money that you need to begin your own plantation?"

Teobaldo regarded Morgan with skepticism. "I would say that the fever has eaten your brain. Look at us. We are poorer than those damn lizards on the wall."

"What if I tell you that you are standing on one of the richest gold mines in Brazil?"

"I would say you are loco."

"No," Chico joined in, "he is not loco." The old man, his legs crossed, sat on his mat and gazed into the candle flame as he said, "I have seen the many boats bring in more and more people to work, yet never have any of them been brought among us to collect rubber. I have watched rubber leave the plantation, yet King's wealth has grown far beyond what those shipments could have earned." With effort, he stood and walked to a corner of the room, dropped to his knees, and dug into the earth with his fingers. When he returned to the light, he held a nugget in his palm.

Breathless, Teobaldo snatched the rock from his father's hand. *"Dios,* Papa. Where did you get this?"

"From the stream. It washed into the cuff of my pants as I was bathing."

"And you said nothing of it? Why?"

"What good would it have done you?" Morgan demanded. "You said yourself there is no escape. And if you had even hinted to King, or anyone else, about the gold, he would have killed you where you stood. Your father is right about the boats. They're full of people he brings in to work the mines. He pushes them to the point of death, then orders them to dig their own graves and puts a gun to their heads and pulls the trigger. Then he brings in another boatful to replace them. Murdering them is the only guarantee that word of his find will not reach the outside. Were the government to learn of it, they would be crawling all over this place in a matter of days, and King's paradise would be no more."

"But where is this mine? And how does he get the gold out of Brazil without the officials learning of it?"

Smiling, Morgan said, "Rubber."

"Rubber?"

"La casa blanca is sitting on a vault that is as big as his entire house. When he gets ready to ship out his rubber loaves, he hollows every other loaf and fills it with ore. The loaves are then crated up and, when they

reach their destination, unloaded by a waiting party who sells the rubber and exchanges the gold for currency."

"And how did you learn of this if he's so cautious with his secret?"

"He . . . trusted me. At least for a while. He thought I would be impressed by the enormity of his find. He imagined that I would eventually get over my distaste for mayhem and murder, as do most of his associates when confronted with the possibility of sharing the fortune. Those who don't are executed."

"But he did not execute you."

"No."

Teobaldo squatted by his father and rolled the nugget in his hand. "Do you realize, Papa, that this rock could bring you more money than you would be paid in six months of working for that bastard King? This is a miracle."

"Not unless you can escape this place, Teobaldo," Morgan stated.

"I see your point. I take it you have a plan?"

"I'll do my part on the inside, but I'll need someone on the outside who can devise a way to get word to the *seringueros*—"

"A rebellion!"

"Yes. A rebellion. It will be army against army."

"But his army has guns."

"You know where his arsenals are kept. Use his own weapons against him. Make your own."

"That will take time."

"You don't have time. I don't have time. Once I'm inside . . ." Morgan shrugged. "King may, as you say, kill me on sight. I'll do my best to stall for time. What I need now is a man to lead the people, Teobaldo."

"I am that man, senhor."

"Then we begin tonight."

For the next week Morgan lay low, sleeping during the day in a shelter in the floresta, far enough from Chico's dwelling so that if he were discovered by one of King's men, there would be no proof that he had contacted the man. Long after nightfall, Teobaldo would search him out and relay the plans he'd set in motion regarding the rebellion.

"There is great enthusiasm among the people," Teobaldo told him on the fifth night. "But also, there is great fear. What if we fail?"

"You won't," Morgan told him.

"*We* . . . won't. You often forget to include yourself."

Lying on his mat of palm leaves and river grasses, Morgan gazed up through the dark at the canopy of trees as Teobaldo placed food on the ground that he had brought with him in a burlap sack. There was flat bread, fruit, and a runny white cheese that turned his stomach as he smelled it. There was also a pouch of tobacco and papers to roll it in. And matches.

"Every night that I come here, Kane, I see that you have grown weaker. You rarely eat the food I bring you. You are obviously ill. Why do you not allow us to treat you? Do you wish to die so badly?"

"Is that what you think?"

"Why else would a man refuse to eat? Refuse medicine that could cure him? And why would he willingly walk to the devil's door, knowing he will never walk back?"

"There could be a great many reasons, I think."

"Perhaps. But I wonder. Forgive my curiosity, but I have never known a man who has lost all will to live."

"Well, now you do."

"Has King done this to you?"

"I don't think so."

"A woman, perhaps?"

Silence.

"Ah," Teobaldo whispered. "She must have been extraordinary."

"Yes."

"You must have loved her very much."

"Yes."

"But she did not return your love?"

"She had lost her heart to someone before she met me."

"But tomorrow you could find another love."

"Perhaps, but she wouldn't be Sarah."

"A very pretty name."

"A very pretty lady." He looked at Teobaldo and asked, "Are the troops ready?"

Laughter. "I think you would have made an excellent general. Never let the memories of a pretty woman get in the way of the battle."

"There's no time to delay." He closed his eyes as the tremors rushed through him.

"What would you have me to do now?" Teobaldo asked. "We have never discussed the matter of your 'getting inside,' as you say. How will we know when to move?"

"I can't tell you when the exact moment will come. And there's no guarantee that my plan will work. King may kill me on sight. But instinct tells me he won't. Not right away." The effort to speak took most of his strength. He rested before continuing. "There should be a watchman

from each section posted close to the house each night. At some time
there will be two shots fired. That will be your signal to move."

"But King—"

"Will be dead."

"And you?"

"Dead also."

"Dios!"

"King's henchmen are a lot of damned zombies, and once he's gone
there will be a great deal of confusion before someone takes charge. Their
defenses will be down. That's when you strike. But for now . . ." Reaching out for Teobaldo's hand, he asked, "Will you help me to stand?"
When the young man had done so, he said, "Now take me to your
section, to the place where you'll go at daybreak to collect your rubber."

"But—"

"Not now. I'll tell you why when we get there."

An hour later Teobaldo helped Morgan sit down at the base of a rubber
tree. "Before you go," he told the boy, "roll me a few cigarettes with that
tobacco." When that was done, Teobaldo held a match to the cigarette as
Morgan inhaled, then released the smoke through his nose and mouth.
"Now get your butt home and get some rest. Go about your usual routine
of tapping the trees, and when you come upon me at daybreak, I'll tell
you what to do."

"But—"

"Everything must seem normal. It can't appear in any way as if this
meeting was set up, or King may become suspicious."

With some hesitation, Teobaldo agreed. Morgan watched as the young
man disappeared into the dark.

He smoked. And waited. He imagined that by now Henry and Sarah
had made great progress in fighting their way out of Japurá. Perhaps they
had even made it as far as the Achuara village, where he was certain the
natives could be convinced to escort the travelers as far as the Negro.
After that it would be clear sailing all the way to Coari, where Wickman
would be awaiting their return. Sarah and Wickman would have their
seeds. They could sail away to England . . . and live happily ever after.

And Henry?

He grinned. Maybe he would go back to Georgetown, and maybe he
wouldn't. Morgan wouldn't be surprised if his friend returned to Japurá
and tried to find out what had happened to him. By then, of course, the
danger would be over. King would be long dead and his tyranny nothing
but a fading nightmare.

He ground out his cigarette and, resting his head against the tree, closed his eyes and allowed his mind to relax. He was going to need all his strength during the next days. Mustn't let the fever, or his memories of Sarah, weaken him now.

Gradually, the whoops and cries of the night animals dwindled and became the quieter symphony of day birds. A light rain pattered on the treetops, rustling the leaves like a whisper and falling cool and sparingly on his face and shoulders. He dozed, until the sound of footsteps awakened him. He opened his eyes to see Teobaldo standing in the pathway, his hands poised upon the tree, his gaze locked on Morgan.

"Drop your things as if you've just happened upon me," Morgan told him. "Run like hell back to *la casa blanca* and tell King you've just discovered me. Quickly! Run, Teobaldo. Run!"

He looked down at the cup and *machadinho* lying on the ground, and settled back to wait again. A half hour passed before he pulled himself up by holding on to the tree. He dusted off his clothes as best as he could, ran a hand across his bearded face, and adjusted his hat over his eyes. He lit a cigarette, taking the smoke deep into his lungs, releasing it slowly through his lips. Then he began walking, doing his best to fight down the agony each movement brought him, battling just as hard to block out the image of Sarah that kept rising in his mind's eye.

There was still time to turn back. He knew these trails like the back of his hand. He could dissolve into the wilderness right now and King would not be able to find him.

If she had only agreed to marry me . . .

His foot caught on a root and he fell, facedown, on the ground. He struggled to push himself back up. When he was at last able to stand, he found himself surrounded by gun-bearing men who regarded him from beneath their hats with malice and murder.

Then King was there, materializing from the shadows like a beautiful pale specter, his shining gold hair that hung to his white-suited shoulders blowing in the breeze. His eyes burned with an incandescence. Had Morgan believed in God, or Satan, he might have thought that King was one or the other. Or perhaps he was both.

All his conceptions of heaven and hell were vanquished in that moment. There was no more guilt over his past, or dread of his future. Even his will to die seemed to vanish, as vaporous as the steam rising from the ground to swallow the trees. He saw his life as if he stood apart from it, fleeting images of one petty grievance after another streaking before him like moving pictures. All the lip service he had paid in his youth to Christ and God and the Holy Virgin, and to a long line of equally holy saints, seemed to make no difference as he considered his worthless existence, and the long road that had brought him to this moment.

Squaring his shoulders, he looked death in the face and smiled.

Chapter Seventeen

THE ACHE IN HIS ARMS WAS CRUCIFYING. HE FELT AS IF THEY HAD been lurched from their sockets. But some good had come from the pain; it had made him focus. Because of it, he could think sharply for the first time in days.

A door swung open behind him, and the guard sitting in a chair jumped to his feet.

"And how is our visitor this morning, Tatunca?" King asked.

"He seems very comfortable, *patrao.*" The dark-skinned man laughed and drove the butt of his rifle into Morgan's groin. The impact sent Morgan spinning on the end of his tether. The pain made him want to vomit.

Closing his hands around Morgan's bare waist, King stopped his twirling. He cupped his hand under Morgan's chin and raised his head so that he could gaze directly into his eyes. "Would you like me to cut you down from there, Morgan?"

"Yes," he gasped.

"Perhaps I will, but first you'll tell me why you've returned to paradise."

"You," he managed through his teeth.

Flashing him a smile, King said, "How very flattering. Yet you left me in the first place so . . . abruptly. I was given to think you liked neither my company nor my hospitality."

"I reconsidered."

"Did you?" His mouth curled in a manner that made him look boyish. "Why don't I believe you, Morgan? Especially since Gilberto and Diego had such a hellish time extending you my cordial invitation to return."

"They were trying to blow my brains out."

"Do you blame Gilberto? After all, you scarred him rather nastily on his face before you left us."

"It was me or him."

"Yes, I suppose it was." Moving away, King slid his hands into his pockets and regarded Morgan from a distance. "I was unhappy and angry when you left. I had so many plans for you. I wanted to share with you everything I had attained. I wanted that so badly, Morgan. Can you understand why I became so distraught that I wanted to hunt you down? Besides, you knew my secret. All of my secrets. I felt certain you would use them to destroy me."

"But I didn't."

"No. You didn't." The fury in his blue eyes diminished as he watched Morgan, his face full of emotions Morgan could only guess at. "Why?" King finally asked.

"Better not to burn bridges behind you, as they say."

King smiled and Morgan was stunned, as always, by the wrenching beauty of it. He tried squeezing his eyes shut, blotting the visage from his mind, doing his best to concentrate on the pain in his arms. He heard King move behind him, staring at his back. Fear rolled over inside him as memories tumbled through him. His body tensed. He felt as if he were being pulled apart, as if his feet, suspended just above the floor, had been tied with hundred-pound weights.

Something cool touched his back and he screamed and kicked, causing the ropes to whirl him around and around so that the barren room and King's face seemed to overlap and become mixed up with the pain biting into his wrists.

"Morgan." The word floated to him. "It was only my hand. See?"

Morgan opened his eyes, clenching his teeth against the humiliation that turned his face hot.

"Only my hand," King repeated. "Did you think Chavez had returned with his whip? Never mind. I'm sorry I startled you. I'll be careful from now on. I should have known you would be overly sensitive to someone moving up behind you."

"Are you going to cut me down?" he snapped, knowing the moment he said it that it was a mistake.

King's face turned cold, and he backed away. "I should watch my tone if I were you. I'm still angry with you, you know. I haven't forgiven you for anything, and I don't trust you. Why should I?" He spun on his boot heel and paced, hands thrust into the pockets of his breeches, his halo of curls spilling over his brow. Repeatedly he flung them back with a toss of his head so that they eventually framed his face in disarray. His features took on the mien of a man much older than his thirty years—the same age as Morgan. His mouth was petulant and his brow creased in thought. "I trusted you," he said. "Do you know what it means for a man like me to trust someone who then stabs him in the back? That's what you did when you left me. I thought we had something special. But then you disappointed me by disapproving of my methods. Surely you can understand why I cast you out of *la casa blanca*. And then you undermined my influence among my workers. Instead of whipping you, I could have killed you, you know. After that you promised you'd do anything to win back my favor and so I again took you into my house. I allowed you to heal your wounds in my bed while I patiently took another. I opened my heart and soul to you, Morgan. I confided things that I've never told anyone. You lied to me; you made me believe you had accepted the conditions of our relationship. It's thanks to me that you are alive now, and what did you do to show your appreciation? You ran away—the final insult."

Resting his head wearily against his arm, Morgan said, "I'm sorry."

"I'm supposed to forget that you broke my heart and jeopardized my entire organization just because you say you're sorry. As I recall, you said that when Chavez laid open your back. You said you would do anything—"

"I mean it this time."

"Give me one good reason why I should believe you."

"I tried to make it out there—"

"And of course you failed. You're a misfit, just like me. Born into this world by fornicating bitches who would rather spread their legs for a stranger than soothe their sons' feverish brows. They deserted us. Cast us from their lives more easily than they toss out their dirty sheets. Ironic, isn't it, that we both returned when we were older, and were both met with the same reaction? The difference is, I wasn't content with allowing my mother to turn away from me again. Not like you. I made her pay for all the times she forced me to crouch in some rank corner of some alleyway that smelled of human waste and rotting food and watch while she went about her so-called business of pleasuring men. Oh, she paid, all right. The ecstasy I got from holding her down and closing my hands around her beautiful throat is a feeling I won't soon forget."

His mouth curved in a smile. "Her dying words to me were not 'Forgive me' or 'I was wrong,' but 'Stinking little monster . . .'" He shrugged and walked to Morgan. "I must admit to feeling a certain distress as I looked down on her dead face. She was a very beautiful woman with her gold hair spread out over the pillow. She looked very young and almost kind. I couldn't help but wish that she had, at least once, looked at me with as much happiness as her death seemed to grant her. It occurred to me at that moment that death must bring with it a sort of absolution for the soul. A relief. But that makes sense, doesn't it? I mean, if it's true that our bodies are but vessels to carry our souls, and life is a sort of temporary stopping point before we go on to greater things, then it would stand to reason that joy should accompany the passing away of the flesh. And it also occurred to me, as I looked down on her dying smile, that I had not punished her at all. I had relieved her. I have to tell you, it was a bitter realization."

The strain of hanging by his arms was fast becoming a raw agony Morgan could not tolerate. The unsettling effect of King's words on his deteriorating sanity didn't help. But then that had always been the case where King was concerned. With his mind-twisting logic, he had managed to lure Morgan into his spell in the first place.

"Morgan, if I only thought that I could trust you . . ."

"You can. I swear it."

King was more than handsome when he smiled the way he was smiling now, allowing a trace of tenderness to touch the cold blue of his eyes. Had he, by some quirk of destiny, become a priest instead of an earthbound demon, he might easily have led the most unrighteous to the altar. As it was, he led them down a well-trod path of damnation with as little effort.

"If you returned solely for me," he said, "why did you creep across the floresta instead of boating up the river?"

"You know no one passes your guards on the river. They would have killed me at first sight."

"And do you think I won't?"

"Right now, Randi, I don't give a damn one way or the other."

He laughed. "Morgan, you were always shockingly honest, for the most part. That's why your betrayal stunned me so." He snapped his fingers. The door was flung open and Chavez entered. At his sides, on short leashes, were King's pet jaguars.

Morgan closed his eyes, unwilling to allow King to see the fear and pain he could no longer hide. He was shuddering. His teeth were chattering, and he couldn't stop them. Stepping closer, King said, "I want to believe you, Morgan. I really do. But I'll need time to reflect on the matter. You know I'm not a man who rushes into anything, especially when I've been hurt so badly once before."

He stood as still as a Greek statue, looking up into Morgan's eyes, his own unblinking, his hands in his pockets and his suit coat caught just behind his wrists. He might have been some dandy watching the passing of a parade during Mardi Gras, equally fascinated, exhilarated, and frightened by the pandemonium displayed before him. "I'm going to leave you alone for a while, Morgan. There are other bothersome matters I have to attend to, but I'll be back. Perhaps then I can come to some sort of decision where you're concerned."

He left the room, glancing at Chavez and the cats, who lingered just inside the door. Morgan fully expected Chavez to taunt him, perhaps bully him physically, yet he said nothing, just stared at Morgan with such malice he might well have been some harbinger of death that watched from a distance.

Then Chavez bent and released the growling cats. Morgan closed his hands as well as he could around the ropes that suspended him from the rafter overhead, knowing even as he attempted to pull himself up and away from the beasts that he was too weak. His fingers, wet with sweat and blood, could do little more than curl loosely around the ropes.

The door slammed and Chavez was gone. The jaguars, their black coats reflecting the fire that burned in the wall sconces, padded around Morgan, brushing his feet with their haunches, their occasional screams lurching him back from unconsciousness with heart-pounding frequency. He did his best not to recall the bloodcurdling cries of others who had been thrown to the hungry cats for punishment. Had the animals been fed recently, then chances were they wouldn't be looking for more meat. If not . . .

"God," he whispered in the silence.

HE AWOKE TO FEEL THE TOUCH OF GENTLE FINGERS ON HIS BROW. Then he told himself that he was dreaming again. He rolled his pounding head and called, "Sarah?"

"It's all right, Morgan. You're safe now in my bedroom. I've decided to forgive you."

The shock ran through him like a bolt of electricity. He opened his eyes and stared up at King.

"How do you feel?" Randi asked.

"Tired."

"You've slept off and on for thirty-six hours." He put his fingertips against Morgan's brow and frowned. "I fear you're ill. You've been running a fever. Haven't you taken your quinine?"

"I lost it."

"Morgan, didn't I teach you anything about the jungle? You simply do not go off without proper protection." He flashed Morgan a smile.

"Never mind. We'll have you right as rain before long. Tell me, do you feel like eating something solid? You've lived on nothing but broth the past days . . ."

Morgan did his best to recall how he had come to be here in King's bed and not still hanging from the rafters as food for King's jaguars. Had he dreamed it all? He tried to move his arms and the pain was like a knife blade in his back. He must have groaned aloud, for King, who had left the bed and was pouring whiskey into a glass, looked over his shoulder.

"Careful. You'll be sore for a while, but we can take care of that as well, just as soon as you're able to move about. There's a man I found in Singapore who can work wonders on sore muscles by simply massaging the right places. You'll think you've gone to heaven when he gets hold of you."

He brought Morgan the drink and helped him sit up, plumping the pillows behind his shoulders. Sitting on the bed, he leaned on one outstretched arm and regarded Morgan. He was wearing a loose shirt tucked into white deerskin breeches. Without either stock or cravat, the material fell away from his throat, exposing the fine gold hair on his chest. "By the time I returned to you, you had lost consciousness. I'm sorry I took so long, but you know how it is. There's the mine to deal with, not to mention the rubber. There seems to be an annoying sense of inertia these days among the *seringueros*. Then there were a few other problems, but I won't bore you with them now. Perhaps later, when you're stronger, we'll discuss the matter, like we used to, and you can get reacquainted with the business. As for now, do you feel strong enough to dress for dinner?" King didn't wait for an answer, just rolled off the bed and walked to the wardrobe. He threw open the door and pulled out a suit identical to the one he had been wearing a few days earlier.

"This should fit you perfectly. We're almost the same build, although you've lost weight since first coming to paradise. We'll get that back on you in no time. I've recently hired a new chef. Directly from Paris. By God, but his food is out of this world! You won't believe it. Dress quickly, won't you? I'll meet you in the dining room in half an hour. By the way, there's hot water and a razor. I know you'll want to shave. The bath has already been drawn. You know where it is." Hand on the doorknob, he paused and cast Morgan a last smile before exiting, leaving the room in quiet.

In an instant Morgan was swept back to the moment on the Belém docks when he had first come face-to-face with Rodolfo King. There had been a vibrancy about him that banished Morgan's usual caution when dealing with strangers. His handsomeness and friendly charm caused

people's heads to turn wherever he went. God, how he had admired
King. Even after he'd arrived here and seen the horrible, stomach-turning
truth about the man behind the fantasy King built for himself, he had
actually hoped he could change him. Indeed, it was as if two human
beings lived simultaneously inside King, one the epitome of good, the
other of evil.

The good, for a while, had given Morgan his first taste of friendship,
respect, happiness, and hope. The evil had brought all of it crashing down
inside him with a finality that was as deep and dark as an abyss. He'd
only begun to see the light again with Henry, and Sarah. But they were
gone. And he was here. All he had left was King.

HE DID NOT VENTURE FROM THE BED THAT NIGHT TO JOIN KING FOR
dinner, nor the next day, nor the next. Off and on he slept, vaguely aware
each time that King entered the room to check on his condition. He
awoke one morning to find an entire roomful of new clothes spread out
upon the furniture: breeches, suit coats, fine embroidered waistcoats, silk
shirts, leather boots, and an array of hats that could fill a storefront. Satin
cravats were tossed here and there, and fixed to them were stickpins of
diamonds, rubies, sapphires, or emeralds. No doubt they had all belonged
to King, but he was only too happy to shower them on Morgan, just as he
had done before. "Enjoy!" the *patrao* exclaimed with a flashing smile.
"There's more where those came from!"

And so the gifts continued to arrive throughout the days that Morgan
spent recuperating. There were cases of the world's best whiskey, tobaccos with the fine, thin papers of the Indies that were slightly spiced and
treated with the juices of hashish. And books. Stacks upon stacks of
them, with well-oiled leather spines and gilded pages, found their way to
his bed. Morgan would close his hands around them and turn them over
and over, relishing their texture and weight before opening the pages and
allowing his eyes to absorb the magic of the typeset words, and his mind
to feast on the images they painted on his imagination.

He had admitted his love of the written word to only one human being,
and that had been King. No. There had been the time before when, as a
child, he had confessed to the Mother Superior that he wanted some day
to be a great writer. She had laughed, kindly, if not condescendingly, and
replied that only the great minds of the world were competent enough to
successfully accomplish such an extraordinary feat.

"They are men with great insight, my dear Morgan. They are men of
great dreams and aspirations. They are well-educated. They are not angry

young men who hide behind garden sheds and smoke instead of going to Mass like they are supposed to."

"But I have a lot I'd like to say," he'd told her. "And no one wants to listen."

"Then say it in a confessional as you repent for your sins. I assure you, Father Joseph will listen."

So out of spite he had gone to confession that afternoon and as he stared at the curtained window at the priest's silhouette, he had begun to spin a tale so woven in fact and fiction. Relaying it as if he were the protagonist of the riveting story, Father Joseph had fallen off his stool in his apparent dismay and ordered Morgan to recite twenty Hail Marys in order to save his endangered soul. He had done so to please the doddering cleric, but Morgan had been filled with euphoria because—whether the father had wished to admit it or not—he had sat spellbound through the monologue.

At night, long after the lights had been doused, he had continued to lay in his bed, hands pillowing his head as he stared at the ceiling and visualized his words, scribed on the pages of a book, imagining that a hundred years from then there would be men and women who would read his work and be uplifted by his insight.

He had admitted this fantasy to King one night during that initial journey to Japurá, when they were ensconced in King's plush stateroom on his steamboat, and the chant of the engines and the churning of the paddle wheel had seemed no more annoying than some distant insect humming in the night. He'd lain half on and half off a settee, his long legs spread over the back and an arm of the delicate piece, while King had sat across from him, sprawled in his Jacobean chair—the very image of success that Morgan had envisioned all his life. Everything about Randi exuded prosperity. His features were flushed with laughter, his hair tousled, wild and windblown, and his eyes bright with exhilaration. Morgan himself had felt drunk with hope. The admission had suddenly poured from him, fantasies of writing books. "Of course I'll be poor and eccentric," he'd proclaimed. "I'll sit on park benches and feed the pigeons and watch the people parade by, and I'll study their idiosyncrasies and splash them across the page in vivid color and embellished reality."

"Why poor?" his friend had asked in amusement.

"Because writers are always poor until they're discovered and adored."

"They are usually dead before they are discovered and adored," he reminded him. He took a long drink of wine and added, "From what I've read, writers are always in the throes of depression."

Morgan replied, "Why is that, do you suppose?"

"Because they pour a lifetime of dreams into their work and watch as reality smashes it to smithereens. I think writing must be a little like self-flagellation, Morgan. Are you certain that's what you want?"

"Positive."

"Then here's to your success, my dear friend." He held up his glass of wine, and roared with laughter.

Then about a month after Morgan had come to Japurá, Randi had led him to a room in a portion of *la casa blanca* that he had never entered. There before him was his fantasy, complete in every meticulous detail: desk, chair, pen, ink, paper, and all around him, dressing the walls, volumes of glistening books.

He had covered his face with his hands and wept—not in joy but in outrage and disappointment. Already the nauseating and ugly truths about this *Paradise Found* had reared their dark, twisted heads. There would be a heavy price to pay for King's generosity. The sacrifice was his soul: the acceptance of Randi's sexual demands and a willingness to tolerate *el patrao's* cruelties. As he stood there, staring at the library full of books, he saw his fantasy curl and wither like pages in a flame.

"No," he'd stated in a dry voice, then turned from the room.

"Fine," came Randi's voice, vibrating with anger. "Go on and rot in obscurity, Morgan. No one will ever give a damn but you. No one will ever know you even existed when you're gone. Go on with your high ideals and warped sense of justice and disillusioned paradigms of righteousness. You make me sick. Did you think you could have it all without some sort of *sacrifice?*"

He'd walked to his room, dropped into a chair, and buried his head in his hands, looking up only when Randi came to the door and leaned against the frame, his hands thrust into his trouser pockets, his face and eyes sad as he regarded Morgan. "You're a monster," he'd said to King.

"I know."

"And even if I was inclined to submit to what you expect of me—which I'm *not*—I couldn't, just on the basis of your cruelty to these people."

"How very noble. And naive. Morgan, your innocence surprises me sometimes. There have been dictators since the beginning of time, men who had the power of life and death over the people. They controlled the actions and thoughts and speech of a populace who is more than eager to be ruled. Take Julius Caesar, and your own God-fearing Pope. Veer too far from *his* dictates and you'll find yourself damned and cast out of the church—all on his say-so. And what is God if not the supreme dictator?

Stumble on your road to His life everlasting and you find yourself flung out of heaven to burn for all eternity in hell."

"God does not maliciously torture and kill."

Randi threw his head back in laughter, and for a moment he looked so young and miserable Morgan almost forgot his anger and disgust, nearly left his chair to put his arm around his friend's shoulder.

Once he had regained his composure, Randi shook his head, spilling his hair over his shoulders. "My dear Morgan, you're a fool for all your ideals of goodness and evil. God neither tortures nor kills? Explain to me then why children such as ourselves must suffer the indignities of squalor and abuse. Why the poor hover in doorways, shivering and hungry, while the rest of the world wheels by in fine coaches, never once touched by the thick and filthy slush stagnating on the unpaved streets. Why people are stricken with the pox, or cancer, or rheumatism that twists their joints up until they scream out in pain." He shook his hand in Morgan's face before turning away and walking to a window where he stared out for a long while at his paradise.

Morgan took a deep breath and released it. "I don't profess to have any answers. But my conscience tells me that brutalizing these people isn't right. You can't make them all pay for your mother's indifference, or the world's apathy toward our plight when we were young. Somehow you must find a way to change the world for the better; end the victimization, don't add to it."

King had turned then, and the sunlight through the window made him seem unearthly. As always, Morgan had been struck with the uncanny beauty of him, envious and angered that his physiognomy could make him feel so shaken. What shook him even more was that King saw through him, right to the core of him, his countenance relaxing in a mocking half smile of understanding, his eyes appearing as if a light were flaring somewhere deep behind them.

"And tell me," he said quietly. "Were I to grant you one wish, dear Morgan, just one wish, what would that be? That I turn over a new leaf right now, suddenly put hedonism and murder behind me forever? Or that I give you your freedom so that you can return, without harm, to the real world?"

He had sat there, his hands clasped between his knees, painfully aware that he could say nothing, feeling the blood drain from his face. He knew which he would choose, and that knowledge tasted as bitter as bile.

King had walked gracefully across the room, one hand still buried in his pants pocket, the other he placed compassionately on Morgan's shoulder. "Sacrifice," was all he said, then he quit the room.

He had never—ever—wanted to die as badly as he did in that moment.

Chapter Eighteen

HE HAD COME VERY CLOSE TO DEATH ONCE OR TWICE IN HIS THIRTY years. But at no time had life seemed so expansive as it did at this very moment. So full of vibrancy. Of light and color and noise. As Morgan stood on the veranda, sipping cognac from a Waterford glass, he allowed his eyes to feast on the startling array of colors spread out before him, splashes of hibiscus pink and orchid purple capping greens of every shade imaginable. Mangoes, papayas, and bananas hung heavily from the limbs of the trees. The towering *Hevea brasiliensis* formed a cathedral ceiling of interlocking branches, the perches of wildly squawking birds—toucans, parrots, and the umbrella bird, whose colorful crest undulated with every breeze.

Odd how he had struggled so hard the past days to grow strong when he still intended to die. He had forced himself to eat the chef's meals, though for the most part he had secretly disposed of the medication King had supplied him for his fever. He didn't want to be completely well. He wanted to remain in a kind of stupor, or he might find himself questioning his decision to in effect, end his life.

He'd sensed that morning when he awoke that the time had come. He'd little choice. Since his health had appeared to stabilize and he had grown somewhat stronger, King had become impatient to get on with the "relationship." Morgan simply could not stall for time any longer. To do so would jeopardize the tenuous trust he had managed to build in King.

Earlier in the day he had ridden out with Randi to the mines, then over the plantation, listening abstractedly as the *patrao* explained the changes he had made in the collection and curing of the rubber. Then King had taken him to Chico's and Teobaldo's huts in order that Morgan could see that they were still alive and unharmed. It had been a fortuitous blunder on King's part because it had enabled Morgan to relay to Teobaldo, with a nod of his head, that tonight would be the night.

He had returned to *la casa blanca* and put his plan into action. He had searched out a revolver, which had been easy enough to find. King's house was fortified with enough guns to fight off the entire British army for a week. When Morgan first arrived at *la casa blanca,* Randi had explained to him that every dictator with any wits about him knows that there are always martyrs among the people who are willing to die for a cause; therefore, he surrounded himself with bodyguards at all times and kept a handgun within easy reach.

Morgan had found the one with which he intended to kill King and himself, a Colt .44-caliber revolver, in a secret niche beneath the library desk. It was now tucked under the back waistband of his trousers, hidden beneath his coat. It bit uncomfortably into his skin, a sharp reminder that, in minutes, his life would be over.

He finished his cognac and turned to find King leaning against the doorframe, his hands in his pockets. Morgan remained silent. King said, "The suit fits you perfectly, don't you think?"

He nodded and set his glass aside.

"That particular one was made in Italy. You know the Italians. They have a flair for fitting clothes. I think it's because of their immense appreciation of the human body. When they find one that is so . . . perfect, they tend to believe it should be revealed to its every advantage. I think we'll have all your suits made there. Would that please you?"

"Of course."

"Good." He smiled and, straightening, said, "Dinner will be ready in half an hour. I thought we'd relax first with a few drinks in the library. Come along, Morgan. Don't hang back, or I might begin to suspect that you're having second thoughts about tonight."

King laughed. Morgan didn't. He stepped from the veranda and moved down the hallway that ran the length of the house, enjoying the twilight shadows on his face, thinking that they had never felt so soothing. The idea came to mind that perhaps death would seem as gentle; perhaps he had feared it for nothing.

Reaching the end of the corridor, he turned right, and now the left wall of the hall was nothing but glass that looked out over the rolling green lawn to the river itself. The steamboat was docked there, and men were scurrying about its deck, scrubbing and polishing its already glistening floor, rushing to finish their chores before night descended. He rounded another corner and entered yet another corridor that overlooked a veranda surrounded by a low wall of brick and bromeliads. A man sat at a wrought-iron table, his hat pulled low over his eyes as he broke off a bit of banana and fed it to a marmoset.

Morgan stopped. Gilberto de Queiros looked up and his mouth stretched into a smile that twisted the scar on his cheek. Yet it was the monkey that held Morgan's attention. He was almost tempted to tap on the window, to try and catch the animal's attention just to see if it was *his* marmoset.

But of course it wasn't. It couldn't be. His was with Henry and Sarah now and . . . Besides, Amazonia was full of the animals, and monkeys especially frequented the compound for handouts.

"Something wrong?" came King's voice behind him.

"What's *he* doing here?" Morgan asked.

"Gilberto? He works for me, of course."

"How long has he been back?"

"Since long before you returned." He slapped a hand on Morgan's shoulder, making him flinch. "Don't worry," King said. "He won't bother you again. If he does I'll kill him. He knows that. Relax, Morgan. You're stiff as a brick."

He forced his eyes away from Gilberto and, refusing to glance at the marmoset again, continued to the library. He stopped just inside the doorway and waited as King brushed by him and headed for the decanters of liquor across the room. His eyes were drawn to the shadows, and as always, there sat a sleepy-looking sentinel, his broad-brimmed hat pulled down over his face. But Morgan knew that he didn't sleep at all. He would be the very quickest, the most alert and trustworthy, of King's employees. He would sacrifice his life to save his *patrao* from harm.

"Sit down," King said.

He did so, choosing one of a pair of Queen Anne chairs positioned in the center of the luxurious room. The high ceiling and wide walls made him feel small, and in a flash he recalled Henry standing before him in that pitiful hovel in Georgetown, his short arms flung wide as he described English houses with twenty-foot ceilings and dining rooms sixty feet long.

Henry, he thought. *Henry.*

If he could only see him again, he might actually tell him how much his friendship had meant this past year. And Sarah. Ah, God, if he could only hold her. But no. Best not to think about it. He'd made his decision and would live with it, die with it. Sarah was gone, returned to Norman. He'd refused to dwell on it. He couldn't start now . . .

"Morgan?"

He took a breath and glanced up, muttering his thanks as King handed him a drink.

"Are you feeling all right?" King asked.

"Well enough."

"You're looking a little pale."

"Sorry."

"No matter. Once you're stronger and able to ride about the compound, you'll get your color back." He sat in the chair opposite Morgan and crossed his legs. His hair rioted over his shoulders and lay upon his white suit like gilt. "You're understandably nervous. But don't be. You've made the right decision to come back to me. You'll realize that in time."

Morgan drank his whiskey even as he felt some emotion roll over inside him that wasn't fear at all, but a flash of the old gnawing anger. He welcomed it. Embraced it. It made him feel human; he hadn't felt it since that last night with Sarah.

Leaning forward, his elbows on his knees, King allowed a boyish smile to curve his mouth. "We'll pretend that the time before never happened. I was overeager and you were—well confused and uncertain. I reacted out of anger."

Morgan took a gulp of the liquor, closing his eyes as it hit his stomach. He wondered if it was the whiskey that made him light-headed, or the fever, or whether he was at last losing what little sanity he had managed to maintain since escaping Japurá those many months ago. He felt euphoric, like a soldier who had joined the war with the heroic intent of dying for his cause and now faced the final battle. His veins hummed with a sense of heightened anticipation.

"You do forgive me for my rashness . . . don't you, Morgan?"

Morgan's fingers tightened on his glass as he looked King in the eye and said, "You would have allowed them to rape me."

"Yes."

"You made me beg on my hands and knees like a broken animal. Do you realize how difficult it's been for me to recover from that? Every night that I tried to sleep and couldn't I've imagined myself killing you. Every time I experienced again the degradation, remembered the pain, and felt the loss of my dignity—or what little dignity I had before coming to this hellhole. You robbed me even of that, Randi."

There was silence that lasted half a dozen heartbeats. King left his chair and paced the length of the room, swirling his liquor with one hand, the other he slid into a pocket.

"Remember how we sat in this room before, when you first came to paradise, and I told you of all the places I had been, the plays I had seen, the boulevards I had explored?"

"Yes."

"You were like a child, Morgan. It gave me such joy to watch the curiosity and enthusiasm on your face. In you I saw myself, an image of me when I was hungry and naive, and eager to soak up the knowledge and energy the world had to offer. And so I educated you in those first nights. We sat right there in those chairs until the sun came up, discussing Rousseau, Voltaire, and Diderot. I was amazed at your ability to comprehend, and it breaks my heart that you were never given a proper education. You could have made a difference in this world, Morgan. You still could.

"We're survivors, you and I. Fighters. We've kicked and scratched our entire lives to get what we want from an apathetic world. Yes. I learned to take what I desire. And I wanted you, Morgan—your mind, your devotion, your exquisite body. I hoped that once you experienced the wonder of us, you would realize how right, and good, it could be. Yes, I was desperate. I thought that by breaking that damned, arrogant pride of yours, you would accept me at last, but I knew immediately afterward that I was wrong. Would it help if I admitted to you that I'm sorry? If I could take it all back, I would." He stopped pacing. "Look at me, Morgan."

Morgan placed his glass on the table at his side and looked up. It was a curious moment of intimacy that stretched taut between them, a powerful understanding that ripped the silence to pieces. King knew. Morgan saw the glimmering knowledge in his eyes. King knew why he had returned.

"Roberto," King called softly. The guard tilted his head and waited. "You are dismissed."

Roberto glided from the room, his huaraches making faint slapping noises on the floor. He closed the door behind him, leaving them alone.

Morgan left his chair. There was no air in his lungs, or in his throat. The gun pressed into his back like a dagger, and he wondered if he would be shaking too much to grab it when the time came. King put his drink aside and moved across the floor, stopping an arm's length from him. Finally he reached out, touching Morgan's hair with his fingertips, lifting the heavy black strands before letting them fall into place.

Now, Morgan thought. *Now!* Do it *now*. He could fire the bullet into King's head and by the time the guards rushed to his aid, he would have turned the gun on himself and . . . Holy Mary, Mother of God, why couldn't he *move?*

"I'm the only human being on the face of this earth who ever believed in you, Morgan."

His hand shook.

"I loved you."

He couldn't breathe.

"I love you."

"Bastard," he heard himself growl. He reached slowly and curled his sweating fingers around the grip of the gun—

"It won't work, Morgan. Dear Morgan, I know you too well, all your righteous ideals, your overblown convictions. I know you would never willingly surrender to me, voluntarily yield your manhood. It means too much to you, your dignity and self-worth."

Morgan gracefully, unwaveringly, raised the gun and pointed it straight at King's face.

And King smiled. "You won't kill me. If you did . . ."

The door opened behind King, and Sarah walked in. Behind her stood Henry.

". . . your friends would be horribly massacred, Morgan. Surely you don't want that."

He stared dumbly at Sarah and Henry while King peeled his fingers off the pistol grip.

"I suppose you'll want to be alone for a few minutes," King said. "I might add, Morgan, that the room has been stripped of anything that could be used as a weapon. You have no hope of escaping. You never did."

He left the room, closing the door behind him.

Perhaps it was the raging heat of the still twilight that pressed in on him as he stood there, unmoving, unable to take his eyes off Sarah. Or maybe it was his illness. Or defeat. Whatever, he felt as if it was grinding him into the leatherwood floor. He thought his spine might snap at any moment.

They continued to stand very still, their eyes locked on each other, her face a reflection of his own, white and drawn with shock. There was a tall case clock in the room, a monstrosity carved from the trunk of a colossal rosewood tree. The pendulum swung from side to side, each tick counting down the interminable minutes, crashing in the stillness. Finally he managed to put out one hand and clutch the back of the chair. His knuckles were white. Beads of sweat formed on his forehead. His head was hurting tremendously; to simply stand erect took a supreme effort.

Then Sarah was running toward him, her beautiful face a contrast of emotions: joy, fear, heartbreak. Oh, God, he had thought he'd never see it again. At once he was swept by blinding relief and happiness, then bitter futility. He managed to open his arms as she threw herself against him. He clutched her to him, hands buried in her glorious sunshine hair. His senses took in the clean smell of her, the wave after wave of emotion that ran through her as he pressed her trembling body against him.

"Why?" she wept. "Why did you leave me? How could you do it?"

He kissed her head, her brow, closing his eyes as he savored her nearness. "Sarah," was all he could manage.

She threw back her head and looked at him with outraged eyes. "I thought you cared for me. I thought you wanted to spend the rest of your life with me. You made a fool out of me. You didn't love me at all, did you? You used me only to come back here and sacrifice your life on revenge."

He stared blankly at her face. "Not love you? Is that what you think? Sarah, I'd rather die than live without you. I'd rather die than spend the rest of my life imagining you married to Norman and having his children." He gripped her to him again and buried his face in her hair. "I only want you to be happy. That's all I ever wanted."

He held her as the shock of seeing her again, of holding her, finally began to wear away and the reality of their situation began to enter his consciousness. Looking over her head at Henry, he said, "What happened? Why didn't you get her the hell out of here?"

"I honestly believed you would come back, Morgan, and when you didn't—"

"I trusted you to get her to Coari—"

"It wasn't Henry's fault," Sarah interrupted. "He tried to coerce me into leaving, but I refused. I wouldn't leave until I got what I came for."

"But you got your seeds—"

"It wasn't just the seeds . . . That man murdered my father in cold blood. I intended to force the confession from him and then . . . then . . . Henry made me take a hard look at reality and I discovered there was no point in sacrificing my future for revenge. It no longer seemed important. I had decided to take my seeds and go to Coari, but then you disappeared. I couldn't go back without you. Oh, Morgan, the thought of King killing you was more than I could bear. This is my fault. Had I not been so possessed by an idiotic need to face King and force him to admit that he murdered my father, you and Henry would never have returned here." She crumbled, and suddenly tears were streaming down her face. She collapsed against him, gripping him tightly, her face buried in his suit coat and shirt.

He held her until her sobbing had quieted, stroking her hair, luxuriating in the feel of it coiling around his fingers. At last she tilted her head and gazed up at him, her eyes wide and frightened, and once again he was conscious of a deep well of feeling within himself. But almost as quickly as she had fallen into his arms, she shoved him away, her features stormy as she paced in long strides around the room, her tumbling hair swinging and flying each time she turned. "Did you think I would simply leave you here? That I wouldn't suffer knowing that you had given yourself over to this monster? You must have a very low opinion of yourself if you believed your best friend and I would simply turn our backs on you and, thinking only of ourselves, crawl out of Japurá on our bellies. We love you, for God's sake."

"Yeah?" He tried to conjure up one of his droll and sarcastic grins, but he couldn't do it. He felt too damn tired, and sick, and concerned about her and Henry. Randi was wise to him now. Always had been. He should have known the bastard would be too perceptive to believe that Morgan would ever agree to give himself up to his demands.

"What now?" Henry asked.

Morgan walked to the desk, took up a cigar, and lit it with a match. "Where are Kan and the others?"

"Good question. When Sarah discovered you were gone, she took up a rifle and struck off through the jungle. Nothing I could say or do would stop her. Of course, I went with her. I ordered everyone else to stay put, thinking that if we were caught, at least Kan and the Indians would be free to get away."

Henry perched on the desk, hands on his knees as he watched Sarah pace. "It's been one hell of a long week, Morgan. We were found by several guards eight days ago. I must admit, had they not been so amused by us, they probably would have shot us on sight. But to find a blond beauty wandering the floresta accompanied by a short, squat pygmy with bones in his nose?"

Morgan grinned.

"Surprisingly, we haven't been treated too badly, aside from being locked up in a suite of rooms. We were never without food or drink. And he told us continually that although you were ill, you were recuperating nicely."

"Remind me to thank him."

"We aren't going to get out of here alive, are we, Morgan?"

"No. Not unless I can get my hands on a gun. If I could get two shots off, then there might be a chance. A slim one, I grant you, but—"

King reentered in that moment with guards at his sides. He still carried the gun, but his face was much less passive than it had been earlier. Morgan knew that look, and it didn't bode well for any of them.

"Sarah," Morgan called, and as Sarah hurried over to him, he took her arm and eased her behind him. He stepped in front of Henry as well, blocking King's view of them.

"How very noble," King said. "But useless. If I want them I'll take them, Morgan. You know that. But perhaps you can convince me to let them go . . . some way." His mouth curved in a smile, and lifting the gun, he cocked the hammer back and pointed it directly at Morgan. "Now move away from your friends so we can discuss this annoying problem."

Morgan crushed out his cigar and started to move aside. Sarah made a grab for his sleeve, but he jerked away. Then Henry slid from the desk and planted himself in front of him, his dark hands pushing him back. "Don't do it," he implored Morgan. "He'll kill us all, regardless."

"Shut up!" King shouted.

"Don't do it, Morgan. For God's sake, I'm the one who got you into this mess and—"

Morgan shoved him and he stumbled backward. Henry made one last effort to hold him back, physically pulling him down so he could whisper, "Two shots? Is that all you need?"

"Shut up!" King roared. Stepping forward, he closed his fist in Morgan's coat and dragged him away from Henry, jamming the barrel of his gun against Morgan's temple so forcefully that the pain momentarily obliterated the ache of fever.

"On your knees, Kane!" he ordered. Then there were hands on his shoulders, forcing him down. He struck out, and someone groaned. Suddenly the hands circled his throat, cutting off his air and bending him back until he thought his spine might break. His feet slid out from under him and he fell hard on the floor at King's feet.

Shouting voices and Sarah's screams washed over him, as nauseatingly painful as the rain of kicks and blows King's guards were landing on his back and stomach and face. Yet from somewhere he found the energy to fight, striking out with his fists and feet, spurred on by Sarah's cries and Henry's shouts.

Then from the corner of his eye he saw Henry move, and the world slowed, each second clipping by as if frozen in time; and suddenly he was no longer fighting for himself, but to stop the horrible nightmare before it could happen, knowing deep in his terrorized heart that he was too late.

He hurled the guard called Roberto to the floor, threw another man several feet through the air so he crashed against the clock. He clawed his way toward King, who was slowly pivoting on his heel and turning the gun toward Henry.

Henry, who was his friend. Henry, who had promised to take care of him no matter what. Henry . . .

"No*ooo!*" he yelled.

The gun exploded, and he was certain he saw the bullet streak with deadly accuracy. He was certain he heard the horrible thud of its impact, picking up his friend's body and flinging it weightlessly over the floor until it fell, twisted and broken with pain.

Piece by piece, the world seemed to crumble.

He crawled on his hands and knees, hearing nothing but the reverberations of the impact over and over. He saw nothing but the small hand lying lifeless, palm up on the polished floor.

Henry!

He felt afraid, so afraid. He didn't want to hurt or break him any more than he already was. He eased his arms around him and lifted him, cradling his head and shoulders in his lap, pressing his hand over the wound in Henry's chest to stanch the flow of blood.

As if from a distance Sarah's weeping came to him, and he thought he felt her hands on his face, his shoulders, doing her best to console him while her own heart shattered.

Henry opened his eyes.

"Don't move," Morgan told him, though his throat felt as if it would explode with the words.

"Good idea." Henry smiled weakly. "By Jove, Morgan, is that a tear in your eye?"

"Shut up, Henry. Just shut up."

"Morgan, I'm touched. I really am."

He closed his eyes and held him nearer, so near he could press his cheek against Henry's. "Please don't die," he whispered in his ear. "Please don't leave me here all alone."

"Alone? Poppycock, Morgan. You were never alone and you never will be. I'll always be with you, and there's Sarah. She loves you, Morgan. She had every intention of telling you that, but then you . . . were gone, and she . . . was very distraught." His eyes drifted closed.

Morgan gripped him tighter. "Henry!"

"I'm here, Morgan. Not to fear, old chap. Give me . . . give me your hand. There. That's a good friend. You never let me down. When the world looked at me as if I was an oddity, you were my friend. You treated me as if I was a human being, a man, and I . . . love you, Morgan. Did I ever tell you that?"

Morgan shook his head and, bending near him, said, "I love you, Henry."

He smiled. "I know. I always knew. But it's nice to . . . hear it at last."

"Please," Morgan pleaded, and this time Henry raised his hand and touched his friend's cheek.

"Morgan? Hold me, Morgan."

He held him tighter, so tight he could feel the final flurry of Henry's small heart against the palm of his hand.

Then he was gone.

Morgan held his lifeless body in his arms as gently as he might a child's, rocking, inconsolable. At some time he raised his head and saw Sarah on her knees beside him, her hands covering her mouth, face streaked with tears, shoulders shaking, and it seemed he could do nothing then but throw back his head and let loose the howl of pain and rage and grief that he had kept inside for a lifetime.

He eased Henry's body to the floor and slowly climbed to his feet. Sarah tried to stand, but she crumpled to her knees and made a frantic grab to stop him.

There was no noise but an intense roaring that he only vaguely recognized as the flow of blood through his head. The room was strangely out of focus . . . all but King. He stood in the center of it, his gun grasped in both hands, his eyes fixed on him—he looked frightened. Truly frightened. And Morgan realized with a sense of mindless pleasure that he must surely appear to be a madman.

"Stop!" King shouted, backing away.

Everyone seemed frozen, the guards poised but unwilling to move. King raised the gun in front of him, inch by inch, and aimed it square at Morgan's chest. "I'll kill you, Morgan, I swear to your Almighty God!"

Then Morgan was hurling himself onto King, driving him back, clutching the gun and shoving it upward, closing his own fingers over the trigger and pulling it. The blast rattled the walls and windows and ripped through the plaster on the ceiling, spraying them with debris. Somewhere there were shouts, glass shattering, rifles firing, people running.

They hit the floor and King groaned. Still they struggled for the gun, rolling over and over. It seemed forever before Morgan was at last able to wrench the pistol from his adversary's hands and twist it away. He stumbled to his feet and whirled on his heel, leveling the gun before him, aiming it at Roberto, who was nearly upon him.

He squeezed the trigger and Roberto fell.

Sarah screamed and he turned, aimed at the man who was grabbing her up by her hair, and fired again, splitting the man's head open.

The door burst open behind him and he crouched and spun, pulling up the muzzle of the gun at the last moment as he recognized Teobaldo, and behind him, Kan. "Get Sarah!" he shouted, then turned back for King, aiming the barrel between his eyes, feeling a new sense of rage as he contemplated pulling the trigger. "Bastard!" was all he could shout, over and over and over again. But though he did his best to force himself to fire, something stopped him.

"Kane!" Teobaldo shouted. "Come quickly! My men have taken the boat. It's the only way out!"

"You'll never make it," King said calmly, his voice muffled by the distant gunfire and shouts. "You're a dead man if you try to go down that river. You're a dead man, anyway, Morgan. Just like your little black friend there—"

Morgan kicked King in the head, fell to one knee, and shoved the gun barrel into his mouth.

"Morgan!" It was Sarah, struggling to rid herself of Kan's arms. "Morgan!"

"Right," he finally said. Removing the revolver from King's face, he grabbed him by his coat lapels and dragged him to his feet, turning him around, gripping the back of his collar and pressing the muzzle of the gun into the flesh at the base of his skull. "Walk," he ordered, and when his captive refused, he cocked the trigger and shouted, "Walk, you perverted son of a bitch, or I'll blow your brains out!"

King walked.

There was no point in leaving the house through the door. The long line of windows had been shattered, with fragments of glass strewn over the ground. They stepped gingerly onto the lawn, crunching the rubble underfoot. The heat of the evening hit them like a blast from a furnace. Across the lawn torches set the area on fire, appearing and disappearing in and out of the trees, adding to the unreality of the moment.

There came a sudden hail of bullets from somewhere close by, and a louder burst of yelling as slaves ransacked the house and outbuildings lining the river, dragging King's employees by their hair or clothes or feet to the platforms where these same men had roped and tied them to scaffolds and beat them with whips. Mobs of angry men, women, and children rushed upon them with clubs and machetes and *machadinhos,* and their screams of pain and horror filled the evening with terror.

They stumbled through the hibiscus bushes, despite the thorns that tore into their flesh, and when King tripped and fell to his knees, Morgan dragged him facedown through the brambles. He would have pulled him the entire way to the river had King not finally managed to secure his footing on his own and scramble up.

The steamboat was a great blaze of torchlight against the ink-black river. As Morgan shoved King toward the gang-plank, someone shouted overhead, and suddenly the rails were lined with gunbearing Indians whose sweating faces were lit by fire and the sweet, blessed taste of freedom at long last.

"Viva la revolución!" the cheer arose.

"Viva el Americano!

"Viva Morgan Kane!"

Chapter Nineteen

MORGAN FORCED KING TO THE BOW OF THE BOAT, SAT HIM ON A stool, and tied his ankles to its legs, then his hands behind his back. He surrounded him with torches so there was no possible way the guards remaining on the riverbanks would fail to see him. Then he pulled up another stool, sat upon it, and pointed the gun at King's head.

Sarah watched all this from the upper deck with Kan, who was doing his best to keep her standing when what she wanted was to collapse and cry her heart out. She barely heard him explain how he and the men had managed to make contact with the Indian slaves on the compound, learned of the impending uprising and waited impatiently for news of her and Henry's welfare. Then the exuberant cries of the insurgents rose in frantic jubilation; the cacophony was as frightening as the takeover had been. There were calls for vengeance against King and his men, talk of returning to the compound and murdering the employees who'd been left behind, and of course demands that Morgan turn King over to them so they could execute him.

Yet Morgan refused, never moving from his stool, his gun never wavering as he told the rebels that they needed King alive if they were going to get past the guards on the river. King's men would never attack if they believed their *patrao* would be endangered. Once the boat was safely beyond King's domain, the rebels could have him.

The night wore on, and the steamer moved ponderously downriver, piloted by a crew that had happily cast their lot with the anti-King forces. Occasionally they were approached by men in canoes who carried rifles. They fell back upon seeing King and shouted to the others hidden in the trees to let the boat pass. Eventually Morgan left his stool and began to pace, stopping to stare at King with such outrage that his body trembled visibly. Sarah positioned herself in the shadows near him and did her best to talk to him calmly, only to realize that he didn't appear to hear her. Weakened with fear and heartache, she sat down on the deck and tried her best to rid her mind of Henry's sacrifice, and her horror as she watched him throw himself at King in order to save Morgan.

Dear Henry, who had held her hand the past week when she had been terrified of being murdered by King, assuring her that once Morgan knew they were there, he would find some way to free them. He said he was certain Morgan must have some sort of plan to destroy King or he would never have taken up with the hated man. Henry, who never lost faith in anything. Now he was gone, and she must do what she could to continue to believe in Morgan, to help him believe in himself.

By the time sunlight filtered through the trees, the gun in Morgan's hand had begun to hang heavily at his side. He looked down at his coat, which was stained with Henry's blood, and groaning, he shed it, then threw it overboard. His shirt, too, was a grim reminder of his friend's death, and once noting it, he ripped it open down the front, spraying the deck with buttons. But he didn't remove it. It hung open, the tail of it half in and half out of his breeches, spotted with blood and dirt, ripped ragged by thorns and sticking to his skin by patches of sweat.

And he shook, freezing one minute, burning the next, so that he began looking to the water in desperation. But even as he glanced repeatedly toward its beckoning surface, he knew that it could never quench the fever of madness that seemed to be rising inside him so fiercely he could not think.

King sat on his stool, his curls fluttering in the wind as the boat cruised down the Japurá River. His blue eyes never left Morgan, nor did the knowing smile disappear from his mouth, even when the rebels on the upper decks chanted out their murderous rage toward him. At one point someone fired a rifle at him, purposefully missing him by inches; but still he didn't waiver, just squared his shoulders and laughed.

Sarah crouched in the shade, moving only when Kan brought her food or water, but eating and drinking little. Once she approached Morgan with a bowl of *feijoada* and a cup of water, yet he refused them both, looking at her as if he didn't know her. He was losing his grip on reality. That frightened her more than the threat of King's men, or even King himself.

"Morgan," she pleaded, "you need to rest. You need food and water. You can't continue like this."

He turned away and paced again. The hours dragged on. The heat intensified, shimmering off the deck in waves. They were being approached by fewer guards now, and there was talk among the men that soon they would pass out of King's domain and be safe at last. Others argued that they would never be safe, that even now those same guards who had not fired on the boat would be formulating a plan to rescue their *patrao*. Their numbers would be great and would represent a grave danger, should they decide to launch an offensive against the refugees.

"All the more reason why we should keep King alive," Teobaldo explained.

"Alive?" someone repeated. "Don't talk to us about sparing King's miserable life. Talk to the American."

So the murmurs started, whispers that Kane had gone crazy. Sarah refused to leave the bow of the steamer for fear of hearing them speak about Morgan that way, though in reality she was fighting her own doubts about his state of mind.

Sometime after noon, rain began to fall. Parched by the sun, her lips cracked by the heat, Sarah lay down on the deck and turned her face into the deluge. How cool it was, and delicious, running over her body in rivulets, drawing the heat from her aching muscles, soothing her blistered and bruised skin. Closing her eyes, she listened to the churning of the paddle wheel and the water slipping along the hull of the boat. For a blissful moment she tumbled back to those days when, perched between Henry and Morgan in the canoe, she had dozed in the twilight, enjoying their effortless slide through the darkening waters, thinking only of where they would camp for the night.

Lulled by the murmur of the engines, she slept, and when she awoke again the shadows had deepened. The river was no longer gold, but a rosy brown that reflected the patterns of overhanging trees and the wash of color from the cascading orchids that swayed from their limbs. Among the bright and muted hues something moved, a flock of parrots, spreading their long blue and red tails, flapping their emerald wings, and taking to the air in undulating waves of startling color and sound. A lone howler monkey cried out, and the haunting wail echoed through the jungle. Then a movement caught her eye, and she turned her head to find Morgan's marmoset crouched in a corner, peering at her through its ruff of gray-tipped fur. She held out her hand to it, but it refused to come.

"It was an accident, Morgan," came the words, barely discernible above the rhythm of the paddle wheel. "I think you know that I wouldn't have killed him had I known he meant so much to you. Had I wanted to kill him and that woman, I would have done so much earlier. But he sprang at me. It was reflex. You did the same when Roberto came at you. We do what we must to survive. We always have."

Morgan leaned against the railing. The gun hung in one hand at his side.

Fatigue showing around his eyes, King regarded him in silence before continuing. "You're sick, Morgan. You're going to die if you don't get treatment. What's going to happen to me if you die and leave me here with them? They'll kill me, and despite what you feel now, I don't think you want that. You don't want me dead."

"Yes, I do," he said in a hoarse voice. "I want that very much."

"Had you wanted me dead, you would have pulled the trigger when you had a chance, back at *la casa blanca.*"

Morgan pushed away from the railing and shuffled across the planking. The terrible ache in his head had encompassed his body. To move was an effort; to think was futile.

"You're failing, Morgan. How much longer can you go on? You've been stricken with malaria, you know. If you don't get treatment, it's going to kill you. The chills and fever will get worse, and the pain in your head will drive you out of your mind."

Morgan looked into King's eyes and sneered. "Shut up or I'll blow your stupid brains out."

"And who would be left for you, Morgan? Who else knows you like I do? Respects you? Loves you?"

Morgan lifted the gun, holding it with both hands, and the deck seemed to pitch and sway, causing him to stumble before righting himself. The revolver was too heavy. To raise it for more than a moment was a torment he couldn't endure.

"And what if you did kill me? What would it accomplish? Would it end the killing that's going on in the streets of New Orleans or London or Paris, or Georgetown for that matter? Even as we speak, someone's son lies dead in a gutter, a victim of neglect and starvation and abuse. I could have taken you out of the gutter. I was your only chance. Without me you have no hope of being anything but some whore's bastard. I took you in when she threw you out. Who else is going to take care of you like I can? Who else can make your dreams come true? Who else is going to make you worth something for the first time in your miserable life?"

Through the haze before his eyes Morgan saw the slight figure of a young woman move up to King, her legs encased in dingy breeches, her unbound hair reflecting the day's sunlight. She looked at King hard, then drew back her fist and struck him in the face, toppling him backward to the deck. Then she turned to Morgan, and he thought she was the most beautiful thing he had ever seen. As she stood before him, diminutive and lovely, somewhere in the back of his mind a memory turned over of a girl whose blue-green eyes could sparkle like the sun on Caribbean waters, whose hair was thick and soft and the color of a sunset. He could almost smell her lavender-scented white skin and taste its sweetness upon his tongue.

"Morgan? Morgan, please come with me and rest."

He raised one hand and touched her mouth with his fingertip. Smiling tiredly, he said, "Who are you?"

ANOTHER NIGHT. UNENDING. HORRIBLE. MORGAN CONTINUED TO stand guard over King, rambling incoherently and occasionally calling out for Henry, confused and frightened when his friend did not appear. Then there were problems with the engine and they were forced to shut it down while repairs were made.

They floated down the river, and although they had long since passed beyond King's boundaries, they doused the torches for fear that those who surely followed would realize they were in trouble and use the opportunity to attack. At last Sarah gave up her vigil with Morgan long enough to go inside, where she sat with Teobaldo, Chico, and Kan. Kan thought to lift her spirits by telling her that they had managed, with the help of the Indians, to get her seeds on board just after the siege of the boat. They were stored belowdeck with the crates of gold the men had succeeded in bringing on board. But even that did little to improve her state of mind.

The tense hours ticked by as the men worked to repair the engine. While a few rebel guards took their stations around the upper deck, most of the others bedded down for the night. Sarah returned to Morgan, who was sitting with his back against the wall, the gun lying to one side. But his eyes were still locked on King, who remained in total darkness.

Sarah eased herself to the floor beside Morgan. She could feel the heat from his body; his clothes were wet through, and his eyes were glassy with fever. *He's dying,* she thought. *Dear merciful God, don't let him die.*

"Miss St. James," came King's dry voice behind her. When she refused to acknowledge him, he went on. "You must do something to help him. I fear he's only barely conscious."

"I don't understand how this could have happened," she murmured, more to herself than to him.

"He told me he lost his quinine."

"So did I, but he gave me—" She closed her eyes. "No. Oh, no. He gave me his." She sank down beside him, her head near his shoulder. She wanted to wrap her arms around him, but King was right. Morgan wasn't aware that she was there. Closing her eyes, she whispered, "My darling Morgan, what are we going to do?"

She fought sleep as long as she could, but exhaustion pulled her down into a dark abyss. Minutes—or was it hours—later, she forced her eyes open, imagining that she heard whispers and movement in the darkness. She reached out for Morgan, touching his arm to find him fiercely hot and trembling. "Morgan?" she whispered. "Morgan!"

The whispers and scrapes grew louder. There were shadows moving over the rail, menacing figures wrapped in cloaks, hurrying toward King. Suddenly a guard yelled out from the upper deck and the night exploded in a terrifying uproar that made her throw up her hands to cover her ears. Gunshots boomed from overhead, shattering the wall near her head. Men screamed and running feet vibrated on the deck.

Suddenly Sarah realized what was happening. Somehow a group of King's guards had infiltrated the steamer under cover of night and made their way to the bow. She rolled into the shadows as more sheets blasted from the upper decks.

King, now freed from his bonds, stumbled to his feet, collapsing to his knees, he was helped back up by his companions, who did their best to protect him from the gunfire. Just then Morgan managed to get to his knees, swaying, dragging the gun from the floor but unable to raise it. Sarah grabbed for him, her desperate pleas drowned out by the gun blasts and yelling men.

"King!" he roared. "King, you bastard!"

Sarah screamed as the dark figure holding King threw back his cloak. It was Gilberto de Queiros! As he pointed his gun at Morgan, Sarah hurled herself against the American, shoving him down so that he hit the deck with a groan and a curse. She placed herself across him, and when King stumbled toward them, she pleaded, "Don't kill him. He's sick . . . If you have any compassion at all for another human being, you'll let him live. I beg you!"

King grabbed her and flung her away. In horror she watched as he twisted his hand in Morgan's hair, lifted his head from the floor, and bent his own face down. "My friend, you're a dead man, you and these ignorant revolutionaries who tried to destroy me. But we'll meet again, when we're both stronger. Then I'll have the great pleasure of looking into your eyes when I kill you." Then he kissed him on the mouth and leapt to his feet. As the bullets ricocheted off the floor near his heels, he spun away with his companions and disappeared over the rail, into the canoes that vanished like a mirage in the mist.

Morgan tried to rise, making it no further than his knees before Sarah caught him as he collapsed into her arms. She gripped him to her, rocking him in a desperate hold as she pressed her cheek to the top of his burning head. "It's over, my darling. Let him go; there's nothing more we can do."

She cradled his head against her shoulder, whispering of her regret, and her love—words and endearments she knew he could not hear. As his tears soaked her shirt, she clutched him more tightly, kissed his head, his brow, his temple, crying his name until his body stopped shaking and he leaned wearily, defeatedly, against her.

She eased him down to the planking deck, ignoring the voices of the rebels who were furious over losing King. Kan stooped beside her, placed his hand on her shoulder. "Missy?" came his gentle voice. "Is he—"

"No," she said. "He's not dead. But he's ill, Kan. Very, very ill. He may die if . . . Please." Her voice broke. "Help him."

She lay down beside Morgan, took him in her arms, holding him so that his head rested between her breasts; his arm closed around her and he drew her to him like a child might who was sick or frightened. He slept the sleep of deep exhaustion and high fever, and once or twice he wept in his dreams.

THERE WAS HEATED DEBATE AMONG THE SURVIVORS OVER WHETHER or not they should allow the boat to be docked long enough for Kan and the Indians who had trekked with Morgan and Sarah to search the floresta for cinchona, a tree bark that could cure him of his fever. "There's no time," a man named Jose stated as he faced Teobaldo angrily. "Thanks to Kane, King is free again. Had he allowed us to kill him right away, we would be safe now."

"It is thanks to Kane that you are free at all," Teobaldo responded. "Without King as hostage we would never have made it this far."

A caboclo with a scarred face stood up and shook his fist. "I say we go back and find King. Kill him before he has a chance to murder us!" A chorus of agreement followed, spurring the speaker on. "Otherwise he will hunt us down and slaughter us in our sleep."

"Kane is a dead man already. Even if he recovered from the fever, King will find him and kill him."

"Perhaps we should surrender the American to King now and—"

"Stop this!" Sarah shouted. "How can you say such a thing after he was ready to sacrifice his life for you? Not forty-eight hours ago you were cheering him as a hero. Now you're condemning him to death to save your own throats. You disgust me!" Grabbing her rifle, she fled the pilot-house.

Morgan's cabin was cramped and stifling, even with the porthole open as wide as it would go. The place stank of sweat and sickness. Kan stood at Morgan's bedside, sponging his flushed face and burning body with cool water while he chanted so quietly Sarah could hardly hear him from where she sat with the rifle across her knees.

"Is he going to die?" she asked repeatedly. There was a break in her voice she could no longer control, and as night descended, she sat in the darkness, unwilling to leave Morgan long enough to search out a lantern. His fever soared, then the chills set in and his body shook uncontrollably. He thrashed in delirium, screaming in pain, fighting Kan with the strength of five men until Kan, convinced that some demon had invaded his body, was forced to tie his arms and legs to the bunk and place a piece of wood between his teeth to keep him from biting off his tongue.

The night dragged on as Sarah fought sleep, afraid he would die if she closed her eyes. She endured Kan's chanting as long as she could and finally told him to get some rest since there was no hope of her sleeping. He refused, reminding her that jungle demons found their way into a man's mind that was weakened by fever. She assured him that she could deal with any demons and once again ordered him to leave. He did so with reluctance.

Lying on the bed as best she could, she held Morgan in her arms, her flesh burning where his body pressed against her; she stroked his head where it rested on her shoulder and spoke to him as if he could actually hear her. "I love you," she told him. "You're not alone. I love you, Morgan. I love you."

Finally, just before dawn, the tremors eased and she was able to release the bindings that held him to the bed. As she rubbed his wrists and ankles to restore the circulation, he lifted his head and looked at her. He seemed almost normal, though his eyes held a glazed expression that was as frightening as the fever that had fired them earlier.

His hands touched her face, and out of relief she smiled. But the smile froze as his fingers closed into her shirt and ripped it open so unexpectedly she barely had time to gasp before he buried his face in her breasts. Stunned, she grabbed his shoulders, her fingers sliding off his sweat-slick skin. He pressed her harder into the bunk, and she realized that he was delirious, and not rational as she had first thought.

She tried to shove him back while speaking his name as calmly as possible. He struck her hands away and slammed his forearm down over her face, driving it to one side. To speak was impossible. The pressure of his arm made her words come out like animal whimpers. He dragged her breeches down her legs, shoving them to her ankles, wedging apart her thighs with his knees so he was probing her with his body, in and out until he drove inside her, making her arm arch to him and away, first in shock, then pain, then—

"Is this rough enough?" came his words in her ear. "Does this get you going? The old boy won't give it to you like a real man, eh? Well, how do you like this? I'm gonna do it to you real good." His lips brushed her ear as he asked in a raspy voice, "Is this how you want it, bitch?"

Oh God, oh God, she thought frantically. *He doesn't know me. He doesn't know what he's doing!*

Then, as quickly as the hallucination started, it ended, and his body went slack on hers, and in hers, and he was unconscious again. She slid from beneath him, hit the floor on her hands and knees, weeping as she grabbed for her breeches and tried to drag them up her legs. She got them no higher than her knees, however, before she rolled onto her side and drew her legs up, buried her throbbing face in her palms, and began to sob. "Help us. For the love of God, someone help us!" she cried, beating her fist against the floor. A fog of hopelessness engulfed her. Her father was gone. Henry was gone. And now Morgan . . .

THE JARRING OF THE BOAT AGAINST SOMETHING SOLID AWOKE SARAH where she slept curled up in the corner of the cabin. She wearily opened her eyes. Her surroundings brightened gradually to a warm glow that gave life to the images and shapes around her. Then the boat's engine died; there was silence before the quiet gave way to the familiar sounds of the forest. Sarah rubbed her eyes and struggled to her feet while doing her best to assess Morgan's condition. Dear God, if he had died while she slept . . .

His head was turned from her. She moved closer, her hands clenched. There were flies on his face and neck, crawling over his chest and the hand that had slid from the bed and dangled, palm up, in the air. She swept her hand over his face, stirring the air so the flies rose in a buzzing swarm. Her heart throbbing in her temples, she touched his cheek and found it—

Warm!

He stirred and groaned, and she almost collapsed. Then the door was thrown open behind her and Kan entered. "What's happened?" Sarah asked.

"The men have agreed to give me two hours to locate the cinchona."

She swayed in relief. "Can you do it?"

"I will do my best, Missy, but even with the cinchona there is no guarantee he will survive, or that he will be the same man he was before.

While the cinchona will cure the fever, it cannot repair the brain if damage has been done. And it cannot cure the fever indefinitely. It will come and go for the rest of his life."

Sarah stroked Morgan's brow. "We'll worry about that in the years to come, Kan. Today we deal with saving his life. Now hurry. Two hours isn't long, and it might well mean his life."

She followed him to the deck, and prayed for his safe return as he and the other Indians disappeared into the floresta. Then the wait began. Minutes seemed like hours as she divided her time among pacing the deck searching the trees for some sign of Kan, rushing back to Morgan to check on his condition, and sitting in the galley with Teobaldo, alternately checking the time and feeding the hungry marmoset bananas.

Then the two hours were up, and when she stood on the deck gripping the rail, the men grew impatient and demanded that Teobaldo shove off before King and his henchmen caught up with them.

"But you can't!" she cried to Teobaldo.

"If we wait any longer we jeopardize our ability to escape King," a man said.

"Leave!" someone shouted, and a chorus joined in.

She ran to Morgan's cabin and retrieved her rifle, returning just as Teobaldo gave the order to start the engines.

"I'll shoot the first man who moves," she yelled.

The men's faces appeared stunned at first, then amused. Several laughed, but others looked grim and angry.

"We're not going to let a woman ruin our chances of escape!" announced the *caboclo* with the scarred face.

"I'm warning you, I'll shoot. If you think I'm afraid of killing you, you're mistaken."

"I am afraid of no woman!" the *caboclo* shouted, and as he moved toward her she turned her rifle on him and pulled the trigger. The shot echoed against the floresta walls, and the man fell to the deck, clutching his bloodied shoulder. The others backed away, their faces slack with surprise.

Kan and his companions burst from the forest in that moment, and though Sarah didn't show her obvious relief before the others, her body inwardly shook with it. It was all she could do to continue to hold the rifle up as Kan ran up the gangplank, waving his bag of cinchona for all to see. Only when he had disappeared belowdeck did she lower the rifle and follow him. Reaching the cabin behind Kan, she slammed the door and sank against it. "Oh, God, what have I become?" she said aloud. "I just shot a man and I'm glad I did it. I'm glad! I would shoot them all if it meant saving Morgan's life."

Stooping over Morgan and spilling his supply of cinchona onto the bed, Kan looked around and said, "I need boiling water."

"Boiling water." She nodded and turned back for the door.

WITHIN TWELVE HOURS THE CINCHONA HAD TAKEN EFFECT; MORgan's fever diminished. Sarah fell asleep after dinner and didn't wake again until the new day was several hours old.

"Mornin', Sunshine," came his voice, rousing her from her sleepy state.

Shoving her hair from her face, she blinked at Morgan, unable to believe her eyes. His mouth curled in that half smile that made her heart turn over. "Morgan? Morgan, is it really you?" He nodded and she squealed as she ran to him, throwing herself against him where he lay, propped up on the bed. With her face buried against his chest, she wept like a child.

"Shh," he whispered. *"Chere,* I'm gonna be all right."

"I'm sorry. I'm so very sorry about everything, about coercing you to come here—and about Henry!"

He held her as tightly as his weakened condition would allow and stroked her hair. "You didn't coerce me into anything, love. I'm my own man. I made up my own mind. I should've known Henry wouldn't leave Japurá without me."

Her eyes meeting his, she did her best to smile. "It's over, Morgan. Teobaldo says we're making good time and should reach Coari in another few days. Hopefully Sir Henry Wickham will be there waiting for us, and with his help we'll get out of Brazil and be in England in six weeks."

Resting his head back on the pillow, Morgan closed his eyes. After a moment he asked, "And what then, Sarah?" When she didn't reply, he gazed at her again. There was an abstracted look in her wide eyes, and he was seized by the realization that she was suddenly remembering all the reasons she had come to Japurá in the first place.

Rage boiled up inside him. He turned his face away and wished the fever had killed him. Nothing had changed. She was engaged to another, and now that she had her seeds, the marriage could go on as planned.

She got off the bed, and despite his resolve to ignore her and the fact that his heart was breaking again, he turned his head and watched her pace the floor, wringing her hands. Once, he had viewed her as a forlorn and grief-stricken child. Now she was a woman whose experiences all these many weeks had added an edge of defiance to the corners of her lips and the set of her jaw. When her eyes came back to his, he saw that their naïveté and innocence had been replaced with steely determination. Yet as she approached his bed, her face pale and her cheeks sunken, her hair a tangle of tawny curls, her resolution appeared to falter.

"Morgan." She took a breath. "You asked me to marry you . . ."

"And you turned me down."

"But I didn't. You caught me off guard and, well, there was a lot to consider. I am betrothed to Norman, you know. It's most likely that he's planned our wedding and—"

"Get to the point, *chere.*"

"I thought I was in love with Norman. I thought that what happened between you and me was only physical. When you asked me to marry you, I was forced to confront my feelings and . . ."

"And?"

She bit her lip and lowered her lashes. "Yes," she whispered.

"Yes, what?"

She frowned and, forced to meet his gaze again, said, "Yes. I will marry you if you still want me."

UPON REACHING TEFÉ THE NEXT DAY, NUMEROUS MEN CHOSE TO leave the vessel, taking with them their share of the gold, while others declined to set foot on land, claiming the farther they could travel downriver the more likely they were to escape King for good.

The boat set out for Coari just after dark. Morgan had grown strong enough to leave his bunk and take a chair on the deck, where he sat until well after midnight each night. Although he had recovered remarkably well, he was still thin, and his skin, once so dark from the sun, had taken on a gray pallor that made him look sicker than he was. His hair, which had grown dry and brittle with the fever, was becoming soft and lustrous again. Sarah ached to run her fingers through it. In truth, she found herself growing eager for a chance to hold him, to reassure him that she wanted to be his wife. But she understood his silence, and his need to be alone. Her own grief over losing Henry was almost more than she could bear; she could only image what Morgan must be feeling.

She awoke sometime after midnight to hear thunder rumbling. The stillness was eerie, and she was glad she had taken to sleeping in her shirt, which reached only to her knees. Unable to get back to sleep, she left her bunk and ventured to Morgan's cabin, to discover him gone. She found him on deck, sitting on the edge of his chair, his head in his hands and a cigarette burned down nearly to his knuckles, its ashes a tiny red torch in the black night. She watched him for some time as the darkness erupted in shimmering light and the wind whirled the smoke from his cigarette around his head. The first drops of rain hit her shoulders. She moved barefoot through the shadows and placed her hand against his hair. He looked up.

The rain came in that instant, a warm deluge that was driven onto them by the hot blast of wind that howled down the Amazon with a roar like the *Pororoca*. He reached for her, his wet hands roughly taking her arms and drawing her to him even as the white lightning rent the *floresta* with a crash and the pain inside him surfaced; his face twisted in despair and the tears came one last time, spilling down his cheeks.

Sarah gripped him close, burying her fingers in his hair turning her face up to the rain, and weeping for his loss—and her own relief that Morgan was spared. Then they were sinking to the floor and he was kissing her throat and face and mouth, his passion tasting of salty tears. She said nothing as his desperate hands dragged up her shirt and gripped her breasts less than gently, then slid between her legs, his fingers moving inside her before fumbling with the buttons on his breeches. As she opened her legs he mounted her, and she closed her legs high over his back, rising to meet his every fierce thrust while the rain beat into her eyes. Then his hands closed into the wet waves of her hair and forced her face around to his. He moved his lips down hard on hers, obliterating all reality.

Chapter Twenty

THEY ARRIVED IN COARI A FEW DAYS LATER. MORGAN WASTED LIT-tle time in collecting Sarah and the marmoset, and instructing Kan and Teobaldo that they could be located at the local hotel, a crude adobe with doorless cubicles connected by a common hallway down the middle of the building. Morgan rented a room for the night, and the proprietor awarded him with two mattresses and a length of material that they used to curtain off the doorway. It was even smaller than the cabin on the boat with dirt floors and walls. There was no window and the air was rank.

Morgan tossed the mattresses to the floor and reached into his pocket for a cigarette. "It ain't home, but it'll get us through the night. You stay here while I check around and see if I can find Wickham."

"I'd like to go with you," she told him.

"No chance, sweetheart. King's men could be here, and a woman like you won't blend in with the natives."

Smiling, she fell back on the mattress, spreading her hair like a fan. "Should I take that as a compliment?"

He tossed his match to the dirt and exhaled smoke through his lips. "What do you think?"

"I wonder sometimes. You seem to like my body well enough, but you don't say much about it."

"So I'm a man of few words."

"But a lot of action."

"You don't like it?"

"I like it very much. In fact, I would like it even more if you came down here and made passionate love to me right now."

"You're a hot one, aren't you, *chere?*"

"You made me that way. You'll have to live with the consequences."

"Later. I'll be back in a hour and then . . ."

"Then what?" When he didn't respond, she looked toward the door and found him gone.

Morgan milled about the streets, noting there were numerous whites drinking and whoring among the Indians, and that they sounded English. Which meant there was an English supply boat in dock.

A street of saloons ran near the piers. He began his search in the first he came to, wasting little time in ordering a bottle of cheap whiskey. As he drank, finding respite in the coolness of the dark room, he searched out an isolated Indian and made his way through the boisterous Englishmen and inebriated *seringueros* from bordering plantations. The Indian, swaying in his chair, looked up in surprise as Morgan poured him another glass of whiskey and set it before him. Then he kicked back a chair and dropped into it.

"Do you speak English?" he asked.

The Indian nodded and grabbed the glass, turning it up to his mouth and gulping it. Morgan refilled it. "I'm looking for an Englishman."

The Indian grunted and motioned toward the sailors.

"This man might have been here many weeks. His name is Wickham. Have you seen him?"

The Indian nodded and drank again.

"Can you tell me where he is?"

He shook his head, but before Morgan could pour him another drink, he fell facedown on the table and passed out.

For the next hours Morgan made his way through the noisy dens, at last finding a bartender who knew Wickham and explained that he came into the saloon early in the day, before the clientele became too rowdy. However, he didn't know where the Englishman stayed.

"Tell him when you see him that his old friend from Georgetown is at the Anaconda Hotel," Morgan instructed the swarthy-faced bartender.

On his way out, he tripped over a man who had fallen into the dirt and was too drunk to get up again. The man's hat had spilled on the ground. Picking it up, Morgan studied it critically, noting it was similar to the one he had left back at King's place. He tried it on, finding that it fit well enough. Leaving it in place, he walked off down the street.

He happened by the bazaar near the docks that was on the verge of closing for the night. Since the Indians were eager for one last sale, he managed to strike a few bargains, which included a knife much like the one he'd lost to King, a sheath in which to strap it to his hip, a pair of white breeches, and a vest made of snake hide. There were women's things as well, which he bought for Sarah. He paid for the purchases in gold, then headed for the public bath.

By the time he returned to the hotel, the hour had grown late. A number of sailors had made their way back to their accommodations, and by the sounds of their racket, they had brought with them the Indian women they had picked up in the saloons.

He was eager to see Sarah. He was proud of her. Damn proud. She had grown strong and resilient. That gave him some peace of mind. They were not out of danger yet—not with King stalking him. She might face the toughest challenge of all very soon, because there was no way he was going to leave this country with the threat of King looming over them. He wouldn't allow her to live in fear, as he had those months after first escaping Japurá. He would not permit King to stand in the way of her happiness. Besides, he was going to make King pay for killing Henry if it was the last thing he ever did.

He found Sarah pacing the room with her hands on her hips. At the sight of him, her countenance went from frantic to furious in the blink of an eye. "Damn you, Morgan, I've been out of my mind with worry! You said you'd be back in an hour; it's been nearly three."

"It turned out to be harder than I thought to find Wickham."

She paced again. "I've been terrified that something dreadful had happened, that perhaps King had found you and—"

"He didn't."

"But how was I to know? On top of that, these drunken heathens have been stumbling in and out of here until I was forced to take up my rifle and threaten to shoot them if they bothered me again."

Tossing the parcel into her arms, he grinned. "I don't blame them. They probably haven't seen a white woman in a long time. And they probably haven't *ever* seen a white woman who looks like you."

"Flattery will get you nowhere, sir."

"No?" He dug a cigarette from his pocket and slid it between his lips. "We'll see, *chere.* Now tell me what you think of your present."

She dropped to the mattress and unrolled the clothing: a white peasant blouse and a full, multicolored skirt. There were wooden combs and leather sandals with straps that would crisscross up her calves. When she looked up at him again, her eyes were bright and she was smiling. "They're beautiful."

"Thought you might be ready to get out of those breeches."

"Don't you like me in breeches? Don't I look enough like a lady to suit you?"

"*Chere,* you ain't no lady. Not anymore. But you are a woman, and those breeches make it damned inconvenient to get to you when I want you."

Her eyes narrowed. "Indeed."

"Yeah. So why don't you change now?"

"Now?"

"While I watch."

"Oh, you think so?"

"I know so."

She stood and began to remove her clothing, for the first time noticing that Morgan had changed as well. His pants and vest were new; he had bathed and shaved, and she thought she smelled bay rum, which he must have splashed on his face.

He seemed so tall, standing there in the doorway. The vest did little to cover his broad chest and his breeches were very snug, accentuating his maleness, which was growing ever more apparent as the seconds ticked by. He leaned against the wall, his hat cocked low over his left eye as he watched her through the stream of smoke rising from the cigarette. His thumbs were hooked over his waistband and his knife hugged his thigh, nearly to his knee.

"Get 'em off," he murmured.

Dropping her shirt to the floor, she said, "I really shouldn't. Not after you left me stewing in this stinking box for three hours with a bunch of randy sailors and a monkey that wouldn't stop somersaulting around the floor." Her breeches slid down her legs and she kicked them aside. Nude, she bent to retrieve the clothing, slipped the blouse over her head, then stepped into the skirt and tugged it up to her waist.

"The blouse comes off the shoulders," he pointed out.

It fell perfectly into place, baring her shoulders and the upper portion of her white breasts. The skirt hit her legs halfway between her knee and ankles. As she gave her head a shake, her hair tumbled in gold waves around her face. "What do you think?"

"You look like a whore."

"Well, that should suit you just fine."

"It damn sure does." He pushed away from the door and the curtain billowed behind him. He tossed the cigarette to the ground. When the marmoset made a mad dash up his leg, he grabbed it and gently tossed it toward the door and said, "Get lost."

It vanished under the curtain.

Backing to the wall, Sarah shook her head and lifted her chin. "I shouldn't let you touch me, not after the way you deserted me for three hours and—"

"Shut up."

He buried one hand in her hair and dragged her head back. His dark face lowered over hers as he said, "I'll take you when I want you, *chere*. Never forget that. And I want you now." He slammed his mouth onto hers with bruising force, making her whimper at first, then beat his chest, until she forgot about the anger and fear she had experienced during those hours he had left her alone, recalling only the maelstrom of desire he sparked within her. She kissed him back as forcefully, her hands knocking his hat aside and twisting into his black hair even as she pressed herself against him so closely she could feel the hard length of him straining within his breeches. He groaned, caught his breath as she ran her hand down the ridge of him and felt him grow even longer and thicker against her palm. And as he kissed her more deeply in response, turning his mouth first one way, then the other on hers, she adeptly flipped open the buttons of his trousers and released him into her hand.

His head fell back, spilling his black hair over his back as he groaned in his throat. She kissed his shoulders, his chest, inhaling the scent of his clean skin and bay rum, running her tongue over his hard nipples, nipping them with her teeth while her fingers ran lightly over the smooth, satin-and-steel length of him that turned hot and throbbing in her palm.

He gripped her shoulders and pushed her down to her knees, and as his fingers twisted into her hair he showed her a new kind of love she would never have imagined even in her most private dreams. A primitive love, and abandoned, making her wild and heady with the notion that at last she could control him with a flick and swirl of her tongue, with the pressure of her lips, making his hips writhe and his strong body tremble until he was praying softly, "Oh God, oh God, oh God."

Then he was picking her up, and with his fingers digging into the soft undersides of her thighs, he slammed her against the wall and drove himself into her, until she was mindless and clawing and throwing her head back and crying out with the force of her release.

SHE AWOKE IN THE MORNING TO DISCOVER THAT SHE WAS ALONE. Rolling on to her knees, wincing with soreness, she grabbed for her clothes and dragged them on. She would not remain confined in this room for another hour, much less another day.

She managed to remove most of the tangles from her hair with the combs Morgan had purchased for her the previous afternoon. She braided it into a thick, gold rope which she coiled around her head and secured with the combs. Then she put on the sandals, wrapping the straps around her legs.

The sun felt hellish on her bare shoulders as Sarah took to the street in search of Morgan. The hour was early enough that the sailors who had frequented the saloons the evening before were still sleeping it off in whatever hospice they had found for the night. There were mostly natives about now, many with baskets of fruit or vegetables or fish balanced atop their heads. A man herded goats down the middle of the road and the bells around their necks clanked discordantly, making her head ache.

She ran into Kan at the docks and he informed her that he had spoken to Morgan much earlier, when he had dropped by the boat to visit briefly with Teobaldo and Chico. Learning that Teobaldo and the others were anxious to set out from Coari as soon as possible, he'd made arrangements to have their portion of the cargo transferred from the hold to a storage building nearby. When that was done, the refugees had shoved off and were, by now, two hours out of Coari.

Sarah and Kan located Morgan and Wickham in a saloon at the far end of the village. The Englishman stood as she approached. Sarah noted his look of surprise as he quickly assessed her appearance. "My dear, you cannot know what a relief it is to see you," he told her. "I had almost given up hope."

"So had I." Smiling, she took the seat he offered and sat down, glancing at Morgan, who was slouched in his chair with his hat pulled low over his eyes. The marmoset was curled up on his shoulder, asleep. "I suppose Morgan's already informed you about the seeds," she said.

"Indeed, and as I was explaining to Mr. Kane, you couldn't have arrived at a more opportune time. There happens to be a boat stranded in dock without a cargo. I think it would take little to convince the captain to allow us and our freight aboard. It should be smooth sailing until we reach Belém, and customs."

"And how do you propose to get us through customs?" she asked.

"Quite simply, we hide the seeds in the stores of orchids we take aboard the *Amazonas.* We'll pass ourselves off as botanists who've collected a very rare specimen of orchid and are now returning to England."

"They are bound to search the crates."

"Possibly, but I happen to know there are a number of officials who will look the other way as long as their pockets are filled to their satisfaction. It will be a most delicate endeavor, but one I'm capable of handling, I think." He poured himself another drink. "I understand that there is a need for haste. In that case, I will get to work immediately. I think my Indians can have enough orchids collected within three days—"

"We don't have three days," Morgan told him.

"I see. Well, then, give me until tomorrow night at least. That will allow me to search out the *Amazonas*'s captain and gather whatever orchids we can. Once aboard, we will have plenty of time to hide the *Hevea* among the flowers before we reach Belém." Wickham quaffed his drink before pulling his watch from his pocket and checking it. "I'll be off. I'll contact you both to confirm the arrangements. Until then, keep out of sight. Once I've spoken with the captain, I'll let you know and you can move out of the hotel and into a cabin on the ship." Taking Sarah's hand, he smiled. "My dear, you cannot know what a relief it is to see that you're alive. I only regret that Mr. Longfellow met his demise in such a tragic way." Tipping his head toward Morgan, he finished, "Until later, Mr. Kane."

Sarah directed Kan to assist Wickham in any way he could, and as the servant left, she sank back into her chair and briefly closed her eyes. "Tomorrow night. A lot could happen before then."

"Once you're on board there's not much King can do," Morgan replied. "Besides, it's me he's after, not you."

Something in his tone made her uneasy, and sitting forward, her hands on the table, she gazed hard through the shadows, trying to see his eyes beneath the brim of his hat. "Once *we* are on board," she corrected.

His lips curled as he reached for his drink. "Didn't I say that?"

"No, you didn't, Morgan. I wouldn't like to think that you've some idiotic notion of deserting me again."

"Would I do that, *chere?*"

"I don't know."

"After last night, and all that's happened between us?"

Recalling the night of passionate lovemaking, Sarah felt her cheeks flush. "It wouldn't be the first time you've loved me and left me," she reminded him. "And don't change the subject. The fact is, there's a lot left undecided between us."

"Such as?"

"Such as, I agreed to marry you and you haven't given me your answer. Are you playing coy? Is that it?"

He flashed her a smile. "Coy? Me? *Chere,* in case you haven't noticed, I'm about as coy as a buck in rutting season."

"I have noticed. And you still haven't answered me."

"Have you forgotten that you already have a fiancé?"

Frowning, she looked away. "I've given that some thought . . ."

"And?"

"I'll figure something out before we reach London."

"What then? Do you set me up in your house, as your husband, and try to pass me off as a gentleman to your friends? I have as much in common with those people as Kan does with the Queen. Sorry, sweetheart, it won't work. If we marry, you make the choice between me and them. That means me and wherever I go."

Glaring at him, she said, "What you're saying is that if I want to marry you, I'll have to give up everything and go off to God knows where to do God knows what—"

"Exactly." Morgan slammed the glass onto the table, causing the monkey to jump up as if shot and leap to the floor. Standing and adjusting the hat over his eyes, he said, "That's that, then."

He left the saloon and stood in the blazing sun while lighting a cigarette and watching the people meander down the street. Hesitating in the doorway, Sarah watched him, taking in the way he stood, legs slightly spread, shoulders set at a reckless angle, as if he were challenging the world. He would never be happy in her rigid world. She understood, too, that he was battling his own emotional injuries—the loss of Henry, the fact that he had broken down several times in her arms; a man like Morgan would not easily recover from what he believed to be mental and physical weaknesses. He would erect that hard-as-steel wall around himself to prove that he was still a man. As if she could doubt it for a moment.

He tossed his match to the dirt and sauntered down the street, never looking back, although she knew that he knew that she stood there wanting him to. The marmoset, tail flicking, followed at his heels, rolling and tumbling and squeaking as it tried to get his attention. Sighing, Sarah fell in step behind them.

SHE COULDN'T FORGET MORGAN'S WORDS, OR SHAKE FREE OF THE feeling that he had sidestepped the issue of a commitment between them. The words *"It's me he's after, not you"* kept coming back to haunt her as all day she faced Morgan's disturbing silences and restless pacing up and down the hallway of the hotel. She refused to let him out of her sight, even when he ordered her to remain in their room while he walked to the nearest saloon to purchase a bottle of whiskey. She secretly followed him, dodging around corners and ducking behind water barrels. Then he disappeared into the saloon; at least she thought he did. She jumped when he walked up behind her and tapped her on the shoulder.

"What are you doing?" he asked. "I told you to stay at the hotel."

"I needed some air."

"Does that include spying on me?"

"I wasn't spying."

"You were spying. Now get your pretty little butt back to the hotel before I do something that will make your face turn red."

"Like what?" she demanded.

"Like throw you up against this wall and . . ."

The explicit explanation made her jaw drop. Without looking back, she hurried to the hotel and waited another fretful hour until he returned. Then she threw herself in his arms and held him tightly. "Please don't go away and leave me again."

Taking her head in his hands, he tipped up her face and searched her eyes. "What's wrong, love?"

"I'm frightened, Morgan. I'm afraid King will find you before we can leave this place. Before we can get out of Brazil."

"What makes you think he'll stop looking once we've escaped Brazil?"

"Then we'll keep running, forever if we must."

His lips turned up in a lazy smile. "What the hell kind of life would that be, *Chere?* When would we find time to settle down and have all those babies you want?"

"Then we'll never have babies. It doesn't matter, Morgan. I love you!"

"Do you?"

"How can you doubt it?"

"I don't." He closed his arms around her and kissed her so tenderly tears sprang to her eyes. Then he hugged her and whispered in her ear, "I love you too."

THE STORMS MOVED IN AROUND MIDNIGHT. THE THUNDER VIBRATED the ground on which Sarah tried to sleep, rousing her from her troubled dreams so that she tossed on the mattress.

"Sarah. Love, wake up."

Startled, she opened her eyes when Morgan touched her face. His fingers were wet, and as she struggled to sit up she brushed his drenched clothes and realized he had been out in the storm.

Stooping beside her, silhouetted by the dim light spilling through the doorway behind him, he said, "I've just spoken to Wickham. He's seen King's men in the village asking questions. He suspects King may be with them."

She clutched his arm. "Oh, God."

"Get your clothes on as quickly as possible. Wickham's waiting for us at the ship. He's made arrangements for us to board, and once there we'll be safe. The captain's called in his men and we're setting off at first light."

She nodded, and though her knees were weak, managed to drag on her clothes in the dark with Morgan's help. She didn't take time with the sandals, however, but swiftly tied them together and draped them over her shoulder as she followed Morgan down the corridor to the entrance of the hotel.

The rain was a solid wall of water falling from the sky. Standing on the threshold of the building, Morgan gazed out into the torrent and removed his knife from its sheath. Looking back at Sarah, he said, "Stay as close to the buildings as possible, and do something about your hair. All those blond curls will be like waving a flag in front of a bull." He plopped his hat on her head. "We'll duck down the alley and approach the docks through the jungle. That way, if anyone besides us happens to be out in this flood, the likelihood of our being seen won't be so great."

"Right," she said, and stepped toward the door. As he grabbed her, she looked around.

A fine mist covered his face, and his lashes were heavy with rain as he watched her eyes. More softly, he said, "Keep running no matter what. Run and don't stop until you see Wickham. Do you understand me, Sarah?"

She nodded.

"No matter what happens. No matter what you see or hear, you keep running. Promise me."

"I promise."

Flashing his lopsided smile, he kissed her mouth. "That's my girl. Are you ready?"

"No."

"Me neither." He turned her toward the door and shoved.

As bleak as the night was, there was an eerie, shimmering red glow to the sky caused by heat lightning, and suddenly Sarah understood Morgan's concern over their being spotted. As she dashed down the street, keeping close to the buildings, her shadow kept pace with her, dancing along the ground and walls, surrounding her in as many as three images as she reached the alley and ducked around the corner. The rain drummed on the roofs of the buildings, cascading from the eaves, drowning out the sounds of her footsteps and labored breathing.

The buildings backed up to the jungle, so slipping into its dark depths took little effort. The foliage and the crowding bamboo that grew near the creek they were forced to ford did nothing to lessen the deluge that pounded their heads and shoulders as they fought their way through the vegetation. At last they reached the docks. The piers appeared to be deserted. At the end of one wharf the hulk of the *Amazonas* could be easily detected. "Keep low," came Morgan's voice behind her. "Stay as close to the edge as possible. If there's trouble, jump for the water."

"But I can't swim," she reminded him.

A moment of hesitation passed before he said, "So you'll learn—fast."

They crept along the dock, slipping behind canvas-covered crates piled high, squatting behind overturned canoes, until at last they discovered Sir Henry and Kan standing beneath an umbrella at the end of the *Amazona*'s gangplank. The pair waved as they hurried on board the ship.

"By Jove, I was becoming frantic," Wickham declared, handing Sarah his umbrella. "Not ten minutes ago there were several men prowling the docks, and I thought for certain you would be found. Quickly, my dear. Get inside before you're drowned by this downpour."

Relieved, Sarah hurried with Kan through the corridor to a dimly lit room. Hesitating and throwing up her hand to partially cover her eyes, she blinked in the light. At last she managed to focus on several curious seamen, and finally on the captain himself.

"Miss St. James, what a great pleasure to meet you," he said in a thundering voice.

She almost wept as she accepted the man's proffered handshake. To actually hear a friendly English accent seemed too good to be true. She began trembling so hard in relief she was forced to sit in a chair the captain hurried to offer her.

Then Wickham joined them. Hugging herself, Sarah stared at the door behind him, anticipating Morgan's appearance. She couldn't wait to throw herself into the arms of the man she loved.

But there was no Morgan. Not after ten seconds, or twenty, or thirty. She got to her feet. "Where is he?" she demanded.

"My dear . . ." Wickham reached for her, his face concerned.

She batted his hands away and moved toward the door. He caught and held her.

"He'll be back," Wickham said. "He left something at the hotel and had to return."

"What? What could he have left? There wasn't anything. He's lying. He's gone back to face King. He never intended . . ." She took a breath. "I'm going back as well. I won't let him do this."

"You're going nowhere," Wickham responded with authority. "I promised him I would keep you here, and that's what I intend to do. By Jove, you're a headstrong young woman. Now sit in that chair and behave like the lady you are, or were before that bloody American coerced you into this fanatical escapade."

"The *bloody American* did no such thing," she responded hotly. "I am responsible for this escapade, and if anything happens to Morgan . . ."

Sinking into the chair, she closed her eyes. She choked and fell silent, then whispered, "Dear God, I simply wouldn't want to continue living."

The hours dragged by, and as the rain ceased and the dawn crept over the treetops, Sarah continued to pace. While the seamen rushed about the decks, preparing to shove off, she threw herself on the captain's mercy and pleaded for more time.

Sir Henry tried to reason with her. "Sarah, it's imperative that we get those seeds to England as quickly as possible. They are highly sensitive and even a day's delay in planting could mean disaster with the propagation."

She slapped his face. "How dare you measure a man's life as less important than those bloody seeds!"

Chagrined, he rubbed his cheek. "Miss St. James, we are not simply measuring one man's life here, but the future of an entire country— England!"

"England, sir, can go to hell!"

She ran from the cabin as the shudder of the starting engines made the vessel shift beneath her like some great cat stirring from sleep. That was when she heard the first gunshot. Running to the rail, she gripped it with both hands and peered through the dense steam rising from the river. There was nothing . . . then—

Morgan was running through the vapor, a flash of black hair and white breeches as he barreled his way down the pier toward the ship. "Run!" she screamed, knowing as she cried it that the steamer was inching away from the dock and he would be lucky to make it even if the gunman behind him didn't murder him first. She beat the rail with her fists, and with tears of fear and joy pouring from her eyes, she urged him on.

The shots rang out again and again, and through the fog Gilberto de Queiros appeared, slowing only as he raised his revolver and aimed at Morgan's back. Morgan stumbled and Sarah clutched her heart and prayed aloud. Then he was sprinting down the pier, and there were seamen crowding around her and yelling, "Jump! Jump!" and he did, stretching for the rail with his hands, barely catching it, almost losing it, before three sailors leapt forward, grabbed his wrists, and pulled him over.

He fell into her arms; they collapsed on the deck. Weeping his name and kissing his face and throat and chest, she demanded, "Where have you been? I was frantic, Morgan. Terrified!"

A moment passed before he could speak. "I had to go back. By the time I got ready to leave the hotel, there were several of King's men snooping about. I had to lie low until I thought they were gone, but they saw me and . . ." He took a deep breath and, upon releasing it, said, "Damn, I thought I wasn't going to make it."

Taking his face in her hands, she asked, "What was so important that you had to risk your life?"

His mouth curled as he rolled away and opened his vest. Huddled against his chest, the marmoset peered up at her with wide, unblinking eyes.

"I forgot my monkey."

Chapter Twenty-one

THEY STEAMED INTO BELÉM TWO WEEKS LATER. IT HAD BEEN A SOM-
ber fourteen days. Although the *Amazonas*'s crew had been more than
accommodating and Sarah and Morgan, and to a lesser extent Sir Henry,
shared a feeling of accomplishment there was no shaking the sobering
fact that King and his cohorts were still behind them. Their only hope
was that King had been unable to requisition a boat in Coari that would
be fast enough to keep stride with the *Amazonas*. But that wasn't likely,
as they'd notice several small freighters docked there. King was capable
of commandeering a boat if he was so inclined. And this time there would
be no Gilberto sent to do King's dirty work for him. The next foe Morgan
faced would be the *patrao* himself.

It was imperative that the *Amazonas* get through customs as soon as
possible. There could be no chance of King's confronting the cargo ship
at sea.

As Morgan and Sarah stood at the rail, watching the bustling Belém
port, Wickham joined them. "The captain tells me it'll be eight o'clock
tonight before we're up for inspection. That should give us time to put
our plan into action."

"Which is . . . ?" Sarah asked.

Offering Morgan a cigar, Wickham gazed out at the scattering of fishing boats. "We'll put on a banquet, with lavish food and all the champagne the port officials can drink. We'll be celebrating the find of a lifetime—the rarest orchids in the world. We'll ply them with drink until
they're so intoxicated they wouldn't know an orchid from an entire rubber tree." Raising an eyebrow at Sarah, he said, "You'll be a great asset, I
might add. I would imagine they don't often have an opportunity to sup
with a beautiful lady such as you. It'll mean getting rid of those distaste-

ful clothes, however, and dressing you in something more appropriate to
your station."

"I rather like these clothes," she said.

"No doubt, but they don't suit the occasion." Addressing Morgan, he
handed him a fistful of money. "See that Sarah gets the clothes she needs.
You should have little trouble finding ladies' apparel in Belém. In the
meantime I'll make the arrangements for the banquet. I've spoken with
the captain on the matter, and he intends to discuss the situation with his
cooks. I'll have the champagne brought on board as soon as possible.
Until then, the two of you stay out of trouble. Once we're through customs there will be no delaying or turning back. If you aren't aboard this
ship, you are out of luck. Do we understand, Mr. Kane?"

"Yeah," he replied. *"We* understand."

"Good. Then off with you. Be back no later than six o'clock." He
walked away.

Morgan made a rude gesture. "Bastard. He'll take the credit for this
when he's got those seeds tucked away at Kew Gardens."

"I don't care, if it means that I'll have my father's debts cleared," she
stated.

Leaning back against the rail and crossing his arms over his chest,
Morgan narrowed his eyes. "I might have thought that too, once. Now I
keep thinking of the sacrifices we made, and for what? What do *we* get
out of it?"

"The Queen's thanks?"

"Sorry, Sunshine, I ain't impressed." Tossing his cigar overboard, he
caught her arm and guided her toward the gangplank.

ALTHOUGH SHE HAD DREAMED THE PAST WEEKS OF RETURNING TO
civilization, Sarah was disconcerted to find that she was irritated by the
press of people around her. It was easy enough to spot the English amid
the Portuguese, and native South Americans. They were the only ones
wearing suits of English wool, frock coats of heavy material, top hats,
gloves, and twill shirts. The women fared little better in their burdensome
taffetas, velvets, silks, and bustles. All carried kerchiefs and mopped their
faces continually. Sarah and Morgan had ventured no farther than a third
of a mile into the city before she counted four ladies who, having
swooned from the heat, had been dragged into the shade by escorts who
were frantically waving fans in their faces in hopes of reviving them. With
chagrin she realized that, while she now found such clothing ridiculous in
such a clime, not so long ago she had been vain enough to dress in the
same manner.

They located a shop that sold ready-made clothing. The proprietress clucked her tongue at Sarah's attire, and when she learned she wore nothing beneath, the rotund woman nearly collapsed with the vapors. She would not be satisfied until she had wrapped Sarah in a corset, drawers, a chemise, and several petticoats, not to mention stockings.

While the shopkeeper bustled about the establishment, Morgan stood with his back to Sarah and watched the street while feeding the marmoset on his shoulder shelled nuts from his pocket. She wished with a passion that this night could be over. They were so close to freedom, yet so much could go wrong. Were the customs officials to discover the *Hevea* seeds, they could be hauled into prison. And there was King, who might have already arrived in Belém and be stalking Morgan at this very minute.

Sarah did her best to force back her panic. Every face had become a threat, every shadow suspect. But what frightened her most was the fact that Morgan, too, jumped at every sound or movement and continually looked over his shoulder. And there was something else. Something less tangible, but just as disturbing, that kept tapping her on the shoulder, filling her with a trepidation she could not shake.

Not once during the entire two-week voyage down the Amazon had Morgan said he loved her, and although their intimate moments together were impassioned and tender, he had stopped short of discussing their future, refusing to acknowledge her comments on marriage and babies and happily-ever-afters. She broached the matter as they were strolling in search of a gentlemen's clothier. "Morgan, we need to talk."

"So talk."

"Might we find a place to sit down first?"

He directed her to an open cafe, where he ordered her a *cafezinho* and himself a *cachaca.* He then tossed his hat onto the table, ran his hand through his hair so it lay loose and waving over his brow, and continued to feed the marmoset nuts as it perched atop the Panama and chattered.

Sarah frowned. "There are times when I think you care more for that monkey that you do me."

"Jealous, love?" He grinned.

"I'm jealous of anything or anyone who steals your attention from me."

"Chere, nothing could do that."

"So you say, but lately you've seemed preoccupied and not the least interested in discussing our future. That frightens me and makes me feel as if you don't want me in your life."

"Sorry." He dug in his pocket for a coin, which he paid to the waiter who brought their drinks. When the young man had gone, he reached for his liquor and sampled it before speaking. "I've never been in love before, Sarah. It's scary sometimes."

"Do you love me, Morgan?"

His eyes met hers. "Very much."

"Then marry me. Today. The captain could perform the ceremony and we could be husband and wife by tonight."

"What's the hurry?"

She shoved away her coffee. ".I'm afraid."

He quaffed the liquor and placed the glass on the table.

"I'm afraid that someone or something is going to take you away from me," she told him. "Swear to me you won't let that happen, Morgan."

Without responding, he stood, retrieved his hat from the table, and said, "Let's go."

They located a men's clothier and Morgan purchased his customary white suit. They were told the clothes would be delivered to the ship by six, then they made their way back to the docks. Try as she might, Sarah could not contain the unease that was growing within her at Morgan's unwillingness to discuss their future. Each time she brought up the subject, she was met with stony silence or a shrug that left her stewing in frustration. She was determined to confront him again when they were alone in his cabin. She was about to tell him so in no uncertain terms when they reached the pier where the *Amazonas* was docked. There were numerous, well-dressed men milling around the gangplank, and as she and Morgan approached, the group parted to reveal Sir Henry Wickham and . . .

She stopped, her mouth falling open, her breath leaving her in a rush. *Norman!*

Morgan walked on a ways before looking back. His eyes studied her, then followed her gaze into the distance. He knew. She saw it in the set of his shoulders, his jaw, the narrowing of his eyes as he regarded her resplendently dressed fiancé. He knew that the man with one thin eyebrow raised and his mouth curved in a disapproving smirk was Norman.

"Sarah!" Surrounded by his entourage of menservants, all shorter than his five-foot, eight-inch frame, Norman strode toward her, his narrow shoulders erect, his clothes fitted to him impeccably. The hot wind ruffled his thin blond hair, and by the look of his lean ruddy cheeks and the set of his narrow lips, word had already reached him of her escapade. Sarah turned her gaze on Morgan, feeling her knees wobble as she recognized the closed expression on his features. He hadn't even walked back to join her, but stood his ground, refusing to acknowledge either her or Norman who brushed by him as if he weren't there.

"Norman," she cried as he stopped in front of her, assessing her clothes and hair, and then fixing on her sandaled feet in unabashed horror. His eyes were much less blue and appealing than she remembered. "Wha-what are you doing here?" she asked.

His gaze came back to hers. "Is that any sort of greeting for the man to whom you are engaged?"

She closed her eyes as he gripped her arms, lifting her to her tiptoes to brush her cheek with a kiss. Setting her back, unsmiling, he said, "I came as soon as I received your letter. Surely you didn't think I would allow my fiancée to go through such an ordeal without me." He looked back at Morgan, who had begun to smoke a cigarette, but had yet to join them. "I've been in Belém two weeks. It was fortuitous that you returned when you did, as I was preparing to jaunt down that disgusting river in search of you."

Still in shock, with her eyes locked on Morgan, who had not so much as looked her way, she said, "Norman, you shouldn't have."

"Poppycock. You are my fiancée, are you not?"

She swallowed. It seemed as if the entire past months of her life flashed before her, every moment she'd spent with Morgan, every intimacy—

"Imagine my joy when I ran into Wickham. He informed me of your journey, and your success. I'm only sorry that I couldn't have been there with you." He looked at Morgan again, eyebrows lowered, cheek ticking with suppressed irritation. He suspected, Sarah knew. The mere fact that she had journeyed into the Amazon, in the company of men, without a chaperone, would be enough to send him into a state of apoplexy. Were she to confess that his suspicions of her and Morgan were correct, he would faint. She was considering doing just that when Morgan turned toward her at last, his eyes piercing as he moved past Norman and took her arm.

Norman's eyebrow shot up even more. "Here now, watch how you handle her. She is not some—" He shut his mouth as Morgan looked at him from behind his stream of cigarette smoke.

"Shut up," Morgan said. Then, turning Sarah away, he pulled her to one side.

"Morgan," she whispered. "I had no idea he would—"

"Be quiet and listen to me." He flicked his cigarette away, shooed the marmoset aside as it danced around his feet. "Keep your mouth closed about us for the time being, Sarah."

"But he already suspects—"

"*Chere,* there's no point in burning your bridges until they're crossed. Once we're safely through customs, then you can break the engagement, but for now, you may need him in your corner in case something goes wrong."

"But that will mean pretending I still care for him, Morgan, and . . . oh, God, I can't, not when you're so near and—"

"Then stay the hell away from me. Forget I'm alive." His voice angry, his eyes burning, he stepped away, shaking his head as she started after him, catching herself and stopping as he added in a loud voice, "I'm nothin' to you, right?"

She stared at him in shock.

"You used me, right? You got your goddamn seeds and your hoity-toity boyfriend and now I'm no longer good enough!"

"See here!" Norman shouted, jumping toward them. "You can't speak to her that way."

"Yeah," Morgan drawled, "I forgot. She's a lady."

He turned and walked off down the pier and up the gang-plank. Sarah watched him go, uncertain whether she should laugh or cry, but sure that something was going to happen soon . . . something dreadful.

THE CLOTHES WERE DELIVERED BY SIX, AND HAVING BATHED AND styled her hair, Sarah began to dress, refusing to don the corset and tossing aside the petticoats. The long-sleeved dress would be uncomfortable enough, she decided, with its high collar that made her neck itch and its snug-fitting bodice that made her sweat.

She had avoided Norman as much as possible, though he had grilled her for the better part of an hour about her journey down the Amazon, the subject turning too frequently to Morgan as he slyly tried to ascertain their relationship. She refused to be drawn in by the manipulation, not so much to protect her own reputation, but to avoid any possibility of conflict between the men. She didn't care any longer what Norman thought of her, but Morgan had been through too much strife, both mental and physical, to have to face more now. Dear God, just let them get through customs without calamity . . . Tomorrow she would inform Norman that she was marrying Morgan.

At last she finished dressing. She wondered if Morgan, in the cabin next to hers, had grown as nervous as she. Though she was to meet Norman on deck, she could not pass up the opportunity to see Morgan. This might be the last time they would share each other's company in privacy for a while. She had to assure him that nothing had changed between them, that she had every intention of breaking her engagement to Norman.

She knocked on his door. When he didn't respond, she entered the cabin to find him sitting in a chair, staring at a shaft of light spilling through the porthole. But for his suit coat, he was dressed. He held a burning cigarette between two fingers, its cylinder of ashes evidence that he had not smoked in several minutes. The marmoset lay curled on his knee. "Morgan?"

He didn't move.

Sarah eased the door closed and leaned against it. "Morgan?" she repeated, and this time he turned his eyes up to hers. "Are you all right?"

He took a breath and nodded, then left his chair. The monkey, having leapt to the floor, rubbed its eyes and waited as Morgan opened a pouch of Brazil nuts and emptied them on a table. "Brazils are his favorite," he said, and pouring a cup of water, he added, "He won't eat unless he has something to drink. Damn picky little nuisance." The marmoset had scurried up the table leg and was turning the treat in its tiny black hands. Bending nearer, Morgan whispered, "Give us a kiss good-bye, Nuisance."

The marmoset pecked him on the cheek, making Morgan laugh and Sarah smile. Then he reached for his coat and said, "Ready to shine, Sunshine?"

UPON ARRIVING ON DECK, THEY WERE IMMEDIATELY MET BY NORman and Sir Henry, both of whom were exquisitely dressed. "Smashing!" Wickham declared when greeting Sarah. "My dear, you'll turn these men's heads in an instant. Now tell me what you think of my preparations."

Sarah did her best to ignore the looks that passed between Norman and Morgan. It wasn't easy. The air was fraught with tension, and as Norman placed himself between her and Morgan, she began to feel nauseous. Forcing herself to look away, she noted the linen-covered tables set out beneath brightly striped awnings; smartly dressed sailors were hurrying to place chafing dishes and crystal glassware. "Very impressive," she told Wickham. "I only hope this works."

"We'll dock in an hour, by which time it'll appear as if we are all having a grand celebration. We'll ask them to join us, of course. The champagne will flow freely and—"

"We get the point," Morgan interrupted. "In short, we get them drunk on their asses so they don't give a damn that we're smuggling Brazil's lifeblood out from under their noses."

"Crassly put, Kane, but I would say that sums it up. Sarah, I will point out the customs official on whom you will concentrate your efforts. Smile very prettily, and charm him, of course."

"Anything else you want her to do while she's at it?" Morgan drawled. "Like hike up her skirts if he starts snooping around?"

Norman's shoulders snapped back at that, but it was at Sarah whom he glowered.

"I hardly think that will be necessary," Norman replied.

"But you're not discounting the possibility."

Stepping between the two, Sarah frowned and motioned toward the collection of men gathering on the docks as the *Amazonas* eased into port. "This is hardly the time to debate the issue. We are supposed to be celebrating, after all."

"Well put," Wickham said. "And so we shall. May I have the honor of introducing you to the gentlemen, Miss St. James? Would you mind, Sheffield?"

"Certainly not," he replied.

Glancing toward Morgan, she took Sir Henry's arm.

BY NIGHTFALL THE DECK OF THE *Amazonas* WAS PACKED WITH seamen and customs officials standing shoulder to shoulder as they toasted the "botanist's" good fortune. As Wickham had predicted, by the time the fourth case of champagne was opened, there appeared to be little interest in the priceless cargo.

After what seemed like hours of smiling her way through introductions, proficiently sidestepping the officials' inebriated attempts at seduction and Norman's disapproving stares, Sara managed to slip away from the crowd long enough to catch her breath and clear her mind of the champagne's effects. Nightfall had brought little relief from the heat. Clouds had converged on Belém by midafternoon, yet brought no rain. No wind blew, and by dusk one could easily detect mist rising from the river. Sarah continually bathed her face and throat with her hankie, but the effort was useless. Her clothes were wet and her hair had begun to hang limply down her back.

Her concern, however, had little to do with personal comfort. For the past hour she had frantically searched for Morgan, to no avail. Since their conversation that afternoon at the cafe, and Norman's untimely appearance, she had been unable to shake the sense of panic that had gripped her each time she let Morgan out of her sight. The last time she had seen him had been from a distance, but she'd noted that his face was grim and that there were patches of fatigue beneath his eyes as dark as bruises. With a derisive gleam in his eye, he'd regarded the official who was leering at her, then placed his glass of champagne aside and walked away.

She found him at the stern, his elbows on the deck rails as he gazed out at the twinkling lights of a nearing ship. As always, the sight of him arrested her for a fraction of a moment. It seemed so long ago that she had watched with fury and envy from the bushes as he held and kissed another woman, and she easily recalled the unsettling desires he had caused within her. Even now, after all they had shared, she felt the same way. The heady, dizzying sensations that he awoke in her had become as emotional as they were physical. He was a part of her, body and soul.

Flickering oil lamps hung along the rail and cast a patchwork of light and shadows on the deck. As Sarah moved up beside him, she followed his gaze over the river. She slid her arm under his and looked up at his face, illuminated by the pale newly risen moon. "We're going to make it," she said confidently. "I know it. Wickham was right. They are so caught in their cups they couldn't care less what sort of cargo is in that hold."

He flicked the butt of his burning cigarette so the ashes snowed down on the star-studded water, then he turned to face her. "I've been thinking of Henry," he told her. "Sometimes I get the feeling that he's standing there behind me, urging me on. Other times there's this yawning emptiness, as if someone's reached into my chest and ripped out my heart, and I think I'm gonna die from the pain. Other times . . ." He shook his head and looked out again at the dilapidated freighter that was maneuvering up to the wharf. He took a deep breath. "Other times I honest to God think that he's not dead. I keep thinking, what if I left him there and he was still alive? Maybe I was mistaken and his heart hadn't stopped beating after all. I find myself watching the faces of the people, expecting to hear him laugh or call my name or . . . something.

"And when I think of him being dead, I realize that life has gone on, hasn't it? If I died tomorrow, the world wouldn't end. You'd go back to England with Norman and take your place in society. You'd think of me sometimes, and you might even imagine what it would have been like if we had married and had children." Smiling, he took up her hand and kissed it gently. "I love you, Sarah. I love you so much it hurts."

"And I love you," she assured him.

He leaned again on the rail, and the distant lights reflected in his eyes. "It seems that all my life I've been searching for the right words to say how I feel, spending too much time thinking and too little talking. All the things I should have said to people who mean something to me come back to me, and I realize that I failed miserably at the relationships that really counted." He closed his eyes. "Henry died for me, because he loved me. You sacrifice for those you love, in whatever way you can."

Turning to Sarah, he took her in his arms and kissed her passionately, then tenderly, then held her against him for a very long time, until a burst of laughter from a group of men nearby made him step away and say in his more typical way, "Yeah, well, we'd better get back before Norman and Wickham come looking for us." Still, he lingered another moment, and there was something in his face and in the less-than-gentle way he squeezed her hand that filled her with a fear she could not comprehend. But before she could speak of it, he had propelled her back across the deck to the revelers, who were by now in high spirits and as eager as before to share her company.

Swept up in their frivolity, she found herself separated from Morgan. She caught glimpses of him as he stood alone, his hands in his pockets and his eyes on her . . . so tall, so broad-shouldered, so handsome. Her shining knight, her hero. *I love you too!* she wanted to scream, for suddenly she felt smothered by some sense of impending doom that hung in the air as palpably as the steam hovering over the docks.

That's ridiculous, she told herself. Insane. As she looked around the laughing men, then at Norman, whose sharp eyes continually trailed back to hers, she tried to convince herself that there was nothing amiss. Everything was going exactly as Wickham had predicted, and within the hour they would be sailing out of Belém's port on their way to England. Then she could face Norman and break their engagement, and . . .

"Where is Morgan?" she asked aloud to no one in particular. She pushed her way around a portly man with a drooping mustache, causing him to spill his drink down the front of his suit. With some relief, she spotted Morgan standing again at the deck rails, leaning forward in an attempt to better view the freighter that had by now dropped its gangplank and was unloading seamen who were looking toward the *Amazonas* curiously.

"Miss St. James?"

She turned to find Antonio Pepino, the Officer of Customs, smiling drunkenly at her. "Would you care to see my Customs House?" he asked. "It would give me great pleasure to show it to you and your distinguished friends, Sir Henry and Sheffield."

Wickham, who stood nearby, nodded and smiled. "Good idea, sir, and while we are about our inspection, the captain's men can begin to clear the deck for our departure."

"Come along, my dear," Pepino said.

Herded off the vessel with Pepino, Wickham, and Norman, she was ushered toward the two-story brick building at the end of the dock. Sarah looked back repeatedly for Morgan but was unable to find him among the seamen and officials who were disembarking from both the *Amazonas* and the smaller freighter that had docked earlier. The crews merged; there was cajoling and guffawing, a burst of rowdy singing.

"Come along, my dear," the customs official said again. "You needn't trouble yourself with these men. They are only seamen from the *Rose*. They've a load of bananas from Coari which they'll be unloading at dawn."

"Coari?" she said, her heart skipping a beat. She strained harder to make out the faces, but they were all turned away and . . .

"Over there we have a ship from Spain," Pepino went on. "She'll be unloading Castile soap, wines, figs, and lemons. That ship there is from Africa, and those crates are packed with ivory and myrrh, and these here with cinnamon, cloves, and pepper from the Spice Islands."

She forced a tight smile. "How very interesting."

She thought she caught a glimpse of Morgan moving down the gangplank but the shadows were dancing too erratically, and the lights from the piers and the boats obscured her sight. Then she was entering the stuffy, low-ceilinged Customs House. The collector was introducing her to the deputy collector and a team of weighers and measurers; then the surveyor, who explained he was the only authorized official allowed to measure the alcoholic content of liquid cargoes. And on and on until she lost track of the minutes and the faces and the names.

The choking sense of fear pressed in on her until she was forced to excuse herself and slip into a much less crowded room so that she could catch her breath. She closed her eyes and thanked God as Wickham's voice came to her.

"I do beg your pardon, gentlemen, but the captain has informed me that he is about to set off."

"What a shame," someone cried. "And I had not got the chance to speak with the young lady."

"Perhaps on our next expedition."

"Of course."

"Now we really must rush or he is liable to sail without us."

Sarah hurried from the room and, smiling her appreciation at the inebriated officials, took her place between Norman and Sir Wickham, allowing them to usher her out the door.

"Don't look back," Wickham said under his breath. "The bloody bastards are so inebriated they cannot see straight."

They hit the pier at a fast walk, weaving around the straggling seamen, ignoring those who whistled and shouted at Sarah, stepping over one or two drunkards who had not been able to make it back to their ships before passing out. As they reached the gangplank, the captain, standing on the quarterdeck, shouted, "Prepare to cast off!" and the engines roared to life and the seamen hustled to their positions. Sarah scanned the deck, and suddenly she froze, partially turning back toward the pier as she said:

"Where's Morgan?"

"I'm certain he's about somewhere—" Wickham began.

"I'm not boarding until I see him."

"But I assure you—"

"Morgan!"

"Sarah," Norman said, his irritation apparent.

"Where is Morgan?" Grabbing up her skirts, she moved back toward the dock.

"Sarah," Norman said, "I demand that you come to your senses this instant."

Wickham agreed. "We must leave immediately. We cannot take the risk of remaining—"

"I'm going nowhere until I see him, I tell you!"

And then she did see him, and her heart froze. He stood beneath a gas lamp at the end of the pier; he wasn't alone.

Sarah briefly closed her eyes before running back down the plank, shoving Wickham aside as he attempted to grab her, vaguely hearing his cries for the captain's help as she struck out down the pier, toward Morgan and . . .

King. Dear God, it was King! There was no mistaking that flowing blond hair or the stance that so resembled Morgan's. In a flash it all came to her. Somehow Morgan had known, or sensed, that time had run out; he had virtually told her good-bye; he had tried to prepare her without frightening her. At last he had given up, or given in, refusing to run, to cower, to jeopardize her safe return to England. He had made up his mind long ago that he would never leave Brazil again. That was why he'd withdrawn from her in the past weeks and would never respond to her talk about marriage.

"Morgan, no!" she screamed.

Then the two men were struggling, and there was a gun; she saw it reflect the orange light from the lamp overhead as Morgan did his best to turn it away from him. For a moment he seemed to have the upper hand as he drove King backward, slamming him into a stack of crates that wobbled precariously under the impact. Their feet were scuffling on the wood pier, and as she neared she could hear their grunts and curses. Then King was yelling like a madman, and the gun disappeared between them, and—

The explosion ripped apart the night.

Sarah stumbled, jarred by fear and shock. Then time stood still as she waited, waited—the groan of pain sounding like a roar so loud to her heightened senses that she covered her ears with her hands.

The blood. So much blood spreading over Morgan's back.

She covered her eyes, her mouth, unwilling to accept what she saw but horrifyingly transfixed, her mind grasping for some logical explanation without accepting the truth.

Then he was falling back, drifting toward the pier.

And King was left standing, his long legs spread, his gold hair blowing in a sudden gust of wind, his flushed, sweating face contorted in anger, yet mirroring the same horror and pain her own features must have shown. The gun dropped from his hand, and he fell back, looking at Sarah in surprise as she screamed Morgan's name.

Somewhere behind her, men were shouting. Their running feet seemed to shake the entire wharf. King turned and fled into the darkness. A gun fired, but he kept running. Another shot, and another from the seamen of the *Amazonas,* and for an instant it seemed that King must be an illusion, some unearthly being who could not be stopped or wounded by mortal weapons. Then a young seaman dropped to one knee, aimed his rifle, and fired.

King spun, grabbing his side, but stumbled on. The seaman shot again. The impact stopped King in his tracks; he appeared to balance for a moment at the edge of the pier. Then he toppled into the water below.

Morgan lay on his back, his shirt and coat front covered in blood.

Sarah dropped to her knees, unable to breathe, feeling the overwhelming grief rake her throat. She wept his name, and when he opened his eyes and looked up at her, she almost collapsed.

Gently, so gently, she lifted his head and shoulders and held him in her lap. She touched his face, his hair, his lips.

He smiled and spoke weakly. "We almost made it, Sunshine."

"Don't talk. We'll get a doctor. You're going to be fine, my darling. It's over now. All over. They shot King and . . ." He closed his eyes and she gripped him tighter.

"Be happy," he whispered.

"Morgan." She wept, and kissed his mouth. As Norman and Sir Henry ran up to them, she pleaded, "Get a doctor. Someone please get a doctor."

Wickham bent to one knee and briefly examined the wound in Morgan's abdomen. His face paled. "My dear, I fear there's nothing we can do. I urge you to come along now. The police are coming. If the *Amazo-*

nas is delayed, we are certain to be found out. Come along, I beseech you!"

She shook her head, and as Norman reached to pull her away, she turned her tear-streaked face up to his and said flatly, "I'm not leaving him."

"Sarah, be sensible."

She shook her head.

"We cannot allow you to stay," came Wickham's words.

"You cannot force me to go. I won't. I won't, I tell you! My place is here, with the man I love, whom I intend to marry—"

Norman's face turned rigid. "He's dying, Sarah."

"No!" She buried her face against Morgan's chest and cried. "Oh, God, no. He's not. He's not dying, and I won't leave him!"

Morgan's hand touched her cheek, and she raised her face above his, doing her best to smile encouragement. His eyes were hard and gray, and there was no hint of the tenderness with which he had looked at her in the past weeks. "I want you to get the hell away from me and let me . . . die in peace. Go home with Norman, and don't think for a minute that I would ever have followed you there . . . or married you." Closing his eyes, he turned his face away and, gritting his teeth, gripped her dress in his bloodied fingers and shoved her away. "I don't . . . love you. I used you. Now get the hell away from me so I can die with some sort of dignity."

"You don't mean that, Morgan. You don't!"

A sudden spasm of pain washed over his features, and for an instant his eyes came back to hers, and his fingers made a desperate grab for her hand. "Sarah," he called softly.

Then he was still, and his eyes closed.

"Missy," came Kan's voice, and numbly, she looked up as he elbowed his way around Norman and Wickham.

"Help him," she said quietly.

Kan took her in his powerful arms and pulled her away, though she shook her head and fought him as he forced her to stand. Wickham bent over Morgan's body. Then, turning swiftly back to her, his eyes sorrowful, his lips pressed in a grim line, he said, "I'm sorry. He's dead."

The black sky and sea seemed to open up and drag her down, and somewhere she heard a woman screaming.

Chapter Twenty-two

Three Months Later, August 1876,
London, England

NORMAN STOOD AT THE DOUBLE WINDOW, HIS HANDS HELD LOOSELY at his back as he contemplated Sarah where she sat beneath a tree, feeding nuts to her filthy, flea-ridden monkey. He looked over at his mother. "I suppose I should speak to her."

"I highly recommend it," she replied. "You are due at Lord Pimberton's at half past. Shall I see you there, dear?"

"If you would be so gracious, Mama."

Lady Sheffield offered her plump cheek to her son for a kiss, then moved to the door. "And, dear, do try to convince her to leave those savages at home. While our friends have been highly understanding, I fear their tolerance is near an end."

"I'll do my best, Mama. You know how they are about her. They won't let her out of their sight for a moment." He waited until his mother had gone before joining Sarah in the garden. "Sarah, have you forgotten that we're dining with Lord Pimberton tonight?"

Sarah scratched Nuisance beneath his chin before looking up at Norman. "I haven't forgotten," she replied.

"But you haven't dressed."

"Yes, I have."

"But you cannot go to Pimberton's in breeches."

"Why not?"

"It isn't done." The bushes rattled and a savage peered at him from behind the foliage. "By gad," Norman whispered. "He has a spear."

"It's not a spear. It's a blowpipe. He can hit a bird at fifty yards with an arrow from it."

"What's he doing in there?"

"I'm not certain. Would you care to ask him?"

"Good God, no." Pulling a wrought-iron chair next to hers, Norman sat down. "I'll be very frank with you, Sarah. Since our return to England your behavior has left a great deal to be desired. I've been patient—"

"And very understanding," she added.

"Very."

"I can't think of anyone who would be so understanding about his fiancée falling in love with another man and giving herself to him the way I did to Morgan."

Norman sat back in his chair and arched one eyebrow. His right eye began to twitch. "Nor can I," he stated flatly.

"Doesn't it bother you at all that I'm no longer a virgin?"

"Keep your voice down, Sarah."

"They don't care that I'm not a virgin." She pointed to Kan, who was shimmying down a tree. He swung from a limb, then dropped to the ground and dusted off his hands. "They believed that Morgan was the *boto,* you see, so it was a great honor for me to be taken as his lover."

"Indeed." Norman drummed his fingers on the chair arm. "I had hoped that you could somehow get over this . . . infatuation with that American so we could discuss our future."

"It wasn't an infatuation, Norman. I loved Morgan very much. I still do. I simply can't understand why you wish to go through with the marriage on those terms."

"Because I love you."

"Rubbish." She stroked the marmoset's head. "I'm not so naive any longer, Norman. I suspect you've some reason for wanting so desperately to marry me that you'd ignore my behavior. I would respect you more if you'd simply confess what it is. Perhaps then we can come to some sort of enlightened understanding." She looked at him without smiling.

He reached for her hand and the marmoset bared its teeth and hissed. Kan took a stance beside Sarah and crossed his arms. As three short, skinny Indians with blowpipes came and stood behind him, Norman sat back in his chair. "Very well; you want the truth. In order to get in on this scheme of your father's, I was forced to liquidate a great deal of capital. My family knew nothing about it, but they will soon enough if Sir Joseph Hooker does not manage to propagate those damned seeds at Kew Gardens. Those seeds were my only hope of building a life away from my family—bloody bunch of meddling vultures that they are. With our marriage and the success of this venture, the two of us could control the greatest rubber empire in the world."

The marmoset jumped from Sarah's lap and scurried to the brick wall surrounding the garden, shimmied up the vines clinging to the brick, and disappeared over the top. Frowning, Sarah left her chair, thrashed her way through the undergrowth, and pulled herself to the top of the wall by the woody ropes. The monkey was running toward the town house whose property backed up to hers. "Damn monkey," she said. "Nuisance, come back here!"

"Sarah," came Norman's voice behind her. "Have you heard a blasted word I've said?"

"Of course." A light came on in an upstairs window, and Sarah's eyebrows went up in surprise. Looking over her shoulder, she asked, "Were you aware that someone has moved into the Sunderland place?"

"By gad," Norman said, "now you're spying on your neighbors. Isn't it enough that you traipse around London looking and acting like some jungle savage? Must you also peep into windows?"

"Nuisance!" she called as the marmoset dashed toward the house, disappearing around a corner. Huffing, she threw her leg over the wall, causing Norman to gasp and curse under his breath. She dropped to the ground on the opposite side, brushed off her breeches, and strolled toward the house, hands in her pockets as she assessed the overgrown garden. When she'd moved into the St. James town house on her arrival in London, she'd learned that no one had lived next door since old Sunderland had died three years before with no heir. Obviously, the courts had at last sold the house. The new owners wouldn't be pleased to find themselves startled by a monkey, as one of Sarah's neighbors had been just after she and Norman had returned to London. The lady had suffered severely with the vapors when she'd found the marmoset sitting on the foot of her bed in the middle of the night.

"Sarah!" Norman called. "Sarah, for the love of . . ."

She looked back to discover that Kan and the others had scaled the wall, and with blowpipes in their hands, were trailing behind her. The sight, though humorous in these surroundings, reminded her of the many days these men had so faithfully followed her into the Amazon. Only one thing was missing: Morgan.

Fresh pain hit her with a force, and as tears rose to blind her, she blinked and did her best to focus on her purpose: the retrieval of her pet.

She followed the marmoset to the front of the house just in time to see it scamper through the front doorway, but as she opened her mouth to shout out, the door slammed. Frowning, she marched up the steps and banged on the door. No reply. She knocked again. Still nothing. "Hello!" she called. "Whoever you are, you have my monkey and I want him back!"

Kan and the Indians took up positions at the foot of the steps, staring back at the pedestrians as they paused outside the gates and gaped at them in horror. Traffic snared in the streets as drivers stopped their coaches. Two policemen ambled to the gates and peered at them from beneath their helmets.

"Would there by anything wrong, Miss St. James?" one of them asked.

She was somewhat bemused that they knew her, though she wasn't surprised. What other female would be walking the streets in khaki breeches, escorted by savages, and chasing a marmoset? Already the onlookers were mumbling, raising their eyebrows and looking down their noses at her. By the time she arrived at the Pimbertons' for dinner, word would have reached them of her latest escapade. Turning her back to her audience, she banged again on the door. "Give me my bloody monkey!" she yelled, and the ruckus from the streets intensified.

Norman appeared, elbowing his way through the crowd, face red, jaw set as he strode down the walk and up the steps, taking her by the arm and forcing her away from the door. "Excuse us," he told the bystanders. "Please pardon us. She's still upset, you see, over the death of her father. Grief has made her irrational . . ."

"Loony," someone said. "Nuts."

Norman walked her home, into the town house, where he slapped aside the palm and fern leaves that brushed his face, then bumped his head on a rattan cage filled with squawking blue parrots. He forced her to sit in a chair while he paced. "I'm not certain I can continue to tolerate this behavior," he said. "You are becoming a laughingstock among our friends—"

"Your friends," she corrected him.

He sighed in exasperation. "I've done my best to stop the rumors of your smoking cigars—"

"But I like cigars. I enjoy the flavor and the effect of the tobacco very much. It gives me something to do with my hands when I'm sitting in the garden and thinking about . . ."

"What? Or should I ask, whom? No, don't tell me. I know already. That bloody American. It can't be helped, I suppose, considering your sordid relationship, but I must insist that you cease this ridiculous behavior. My God, the servants tell me that at night you dance nude from the waist up while those savages beat drums and play flutes."

"What I do in the privacy of my home is no one's business, Norman. That includes you. I have not agreed to marry you, you know." She left her chair, walked to a box of cigars on a table, and lit one. "And something else. I am no longer the innocent, naive ninny you proposed to. You will not talk down to me ever again, not if you hope to see this merger—note I did not say marriage—come off between us. You need me, Sheffield. I don't need you. Therefore . . ." She smoked and smiled. "You'd better be very nice to me, or you'll spend the rest of your life under your mother's thumb."

He stared at her with his eyes bulging.

Sarah turned and plucked the Panama off the hat rack and plopped it on her head, cocking it to one side. "I do believe we have a dinner party to attend, my lord. Shall we go?"

SARAH STOOD AT THE BOWED WINDOW OF LORD PIMBERTON'S PLUSH town house in Mayfair and gazed out at the street, seeing not so much the traffic and people as she did the reflection of those standing behind her, their heads together and their brows knitted in disapproval as they regarded her. Since her return to London she had grown accustomed to their whispers and gasps, their averted glances and uplifted eyebrows. She couldn't fault them. In their world a breeches-clad and booted female with her hair falling wildly about her face and shoulders was unacceptable, although they had done a respectable job of forgiving her, considering the tragic circumstances of her last months in South America. Rumor had it that she'd been kidnapped by a tribe of heathens and dragged down the Amazon until she was saved by Sir Henry Wickham and returned to civilization.

That, of course, was Norman's story. As everyone could see, the episode had caused her severe trauma, but in time she was certain to be her old self again. Of course, she knew she would never be the Sarah St. James who had worked so hard to conform to Norman's social circle, to be the kind of sophisticated woman he would find worthy enough to marry. That prim and proper, sheltered and naive young lady no longer existed. She had faced destitution, danger, death, and heartbreak—so much heartbreak. She'd lost her father, her friend, her lover . . .

She watched her reflection in the glass and saw the tears rise to her weary eyes. Odd how often the memories still came, especially at night, when she would grip her pillow against her as if she expected it to reach out to her with long, strong arms and hold her, to stroke her hair, to kiss her and call her *"Chere."* She would wake up weeping and so empty and hurting for Morgan she thought she might die. Dear God, how hard she had tried to forget, only to find herself building a fantasy world of jungles and animals, even going so far as to smoke those disgusting cigars, pretending she liked them when, in truth, they made her want to throw up. She was rebelling, of course, but it was also her way of holding on to every detail that had been Morgan. She couldn't forget. Not yet, no matter what Norman believed would be for the best. She wasn't prepared to give up Morgan. She suspected she never would be.

Sighing, she blotted her eyes and turned back to the guests. Almost immediately she was approached by Lady Carleton, a buxom woman of forty who, though her mouth was smiling, was regarding her with less-than-enthusiastic approval. "My dear Sarah," she began, "Lord Sheffield tells us that you are still greatly grieved by your father's passing, not to mention your horrible ordeal at the hands of those savages. I cannot imagine why you surround yourself with such reminders after all you endured." She looked pointedly at Kan and the others, who were lined up against the wall wearing formal black coats, no shirts beneath—and loincloths that hung to just above their naked knees. Lady Carleton stared at them through her quizzing glass before it slid through her fingers and dangled on a ribbon between her voluptuous breasts. She cleared her throat and pursed her lips in obvious distress before addressing Sarah again. "Have you heard that Lord Hawthorn recently met a gentleman from Brazil?"

Her mind was slow to comprehend what the woman had said, which was often the case of late. No matter how she tried to concentrate, her thoughts were always wandering, until at times she felt quite insane. As she stared at the woman, her words at last echoing against some spark of awareness in her muddled mind, Sarah felt a sharp pain of consternation turn over inside her.

"I beg your pardon?" she said.

"A very wealthy man," Lady Carleton explained. "In the rubber business, I believe. He is here looking into investments, or so he says. Lord Hawthorn found him rather odd."

Sarah took hold of a chair-back. "What was his name?" she asked in a dry voice.

Lady Carleton looked at her with raised eyebrows and then, taking up her quizzing glass, peered at Sarah closely. "My dear, you look absolutely dreadful. Dreadful! Perhaps I shouldn't have brought up the subject of Brazil. Oh, my, I do apologize. Of course the matter would distress you. Perhaps I should get Lord Sheffield. Yes, yes. I'll do that immediately."

Something of Sarah's feelings must have shown in her face, because she looked up to find Kan standing beside her, his watchful eyes regarding her with concern. "I don't feel very well," she told him. "Will you take me home?"

He nodded, took her arm, and ushered her out the door without a thought to bidding her hosts, or Norman, a proper farewell. As the coach

rolled away, Sarah gazed out the window and watched the familiar land-
marks go by. How dreary they all seemed, cloaked as they were with the
continual rainfall. Oh, if she could only turn her face into the sun's
glorious warmth, perhaps this brittle coldness in her chest might thaw at
last. Then again, perhaps it wouldn't. Odd how she once believed that
anything and everything was possible. Since losing Morgan, she had lost
all hope and faith in herself and her future. When Morgan died in her
arms, so did her dreams die in her heart.

Lady Carleton's words came back to her as she looked out at the empty
streets and housefronts.

*"Have you heard that Lord Hawthorn recently met a man from Brazil?
A very wealthy man. In the rubber business, I believe. He is here looking
into investments, or so he says. Lord Hawthorn found him rather odd."*

Sarah closed her eyes, refusing to acknowledge the fear that had
plagued her night after night in her dreams—visions of Rodolfo King
walking toward her down the pier, his white suit covered in blood from a
wound in his side, a gun in his hand, the barrel still smoking, and behind
him, lying sprawled and bloody and broken beneath the lamplight . . .
Morgan.

Of course King was not alive. She had seen him shot; watched as he
tumbled over the edge of the pier to the water below. And even if he were
alive, he wouldn't bother to follow her to England . . . Why should he?
Unless he wanted revenge . . .

THE RUMORS REACHED SARAH AGAIN OF A STRANGER FROM BRAZIL,
and while she might have done her best to ignore them, this time the
reference was more shocking: the stranger had asked about her.

She was drinking tea at the residence of Norman's cousin, Lady Rees,
when another guest said, "I was approached yesterday by a gentleman
who said he was from Brazil. He asked me if I was familiar with Sarah St.
James, and of course I told him I was."

Gripping her cup and saucer unsteadily, Sarah replied, "Did he,
perchance, tell you his name?"

The woman's mouth pursed in concentration. "Yes, I believe he did.
What was it now? Oh, dear, it seems to have slipped my mind."

Sarah calmly took a sip of her tea. "Could you describe him, do you
think?"

"Tall. Yes, he seemed very tall, and sinister, if you ask me. But then
that's the way of his type, I suppose. Living among those savages and all,
one could hardly remain refined in those circumstances. Still and all, he

was an odd chap. Peculiar. He spoke briefly of his plantation in . . . let me see . . ."

Wetting her lips with her tongue, Sarah said, "Japurá?"

"Why, yes!" the lady exclaimed. "That's exactly it. Japurá! He wore white. All white. I commented on his suit and he said that women and men wore white in Brazil because it was much cooler in the equatorial sun than dark colors."

Realizing that the teacup and saucer had begun to rattle, Sarah put them on the table. Taking a deep breath, she forced herself to ask, "Did you by chance tell him where I live?"

"He already knew. He seemed to know a great deal about you."

"I . . . see."

"My dear, is something wrong? Sarah?"

She had exited the house before realizing that she had failed to bid her hosts a proper good-bye. The fresh air did little to clear her mind of its tumult, and she had walked halfway back to her own house before remembering that she had taken the coach to Norman's cousin's. Then, as she stood there, hearing the traffic hum around her, she realized that the man from Japurá might be watching her at that very moment.

It couldn't be King. King was dead. But she hadn't seen King die. Not really. She'd seen him shot, but . . .

She hurried to her town house and locked the door behind her. The servants, as always, moved quietly about the rooms, not one of them daring to approach their obviously addled employer unless forced to do so. Hiding within the lair of palm fronds and dumbcane leaves, she cuddled the marmoset in her lap and tried to reason with herself that Rodolfo King could not possibly have followed her from Brazil. He was dead. She had watched him die. No, she reminded herself. She had seen him shot.

THE NEXT DAY SHE SPOKE TO NORMAN. HE SCOFFED. "BALDERDASH. We both saw King fall."

"But we didn't see him die, not like . . . Morgan. Who's to say that King was dead when he fell toward the water?"

"Be reasonable," Norman said. Regarding himself in a mirror on the wall, he straightened his cravat and eyed his hair critically before turning to face her. "Why would King bother to travel six thousand miles to take revenge on you?"

"For the same reason he wanted to kill Morgan. I know about his cruelties and his gold."

"I'm certain all of South America is aware of that by now, considering that the men who overthrew him are free. No, it was your American paramour he wanted to kill, and he killed him. That is the end of the matter."

"Then who is strolling about London in a white suit, proclaiming he is from Brazil and that he knows me? And why?"

Norman shrugged as he pulled out his watch to check the time. "Perhaps he is one of the rebels who escaped King."

Sarah blinked as the realization hit her. "Or possibly it's one of King's men. Gilberto de Queiros. Dear God, it could be!"

Shaking his head, Norman turned for the door. "You're becoming overly suspicious, Sarah."

"Norman, you don't know the sort of man King was. You can't appreciate—"

"I can appreciate that you're becoming overwrought over nothing." Stopping at the door, he looked back at her with one eyebrow raised and his mouth curled in a smirk. "If you're so frightened of these . . . ghosts, my dear, you might consider marrying me. I can offer you all the security you could wish for."

Coming out of her chair, Sarah eyed Norman severely. "You wouldn't have anything to do with these rumors, would you?"

"Me? Why on earth for?"

"To try and frighten me into going through with the marriage."

"Hmm." He opened the front door. "An appealing idea. Sorry to say I hadn't thought of it. Ah, well. I suspect you'll come around eventually . . . when you realize you've ruined any chance of ever marrying into a halfway respectable family. Good night, Sarah."

Sarah stared at the door as Norman closed it behind him, her anger mounting though she tried her best to check it. Unable to do so, she stormed to the threshold, threw open the door, and ran down the steps into the night as Norman's coach pulled away from the house, shouting, "It'll be a cold day in the Amazon before I marry you, Sheffield!"

The clop of the horses' hooves and the jangle of the reins echoed back to her. Angrily, she turned toward the house in time to see the marmoset scamper out the door and around the corner. Cursing, she ran after him, knowing she would never catch him before he made it to the Sunderland house. She followed him, regardless, aggravated enough with Norman to take out her irritation on the unsociable neighbors who had been refusing to acknowledge her calls and demands that they stop luring away her monkey. Of late, Nuisance was spending more time at the Sunderland place than he was at home, and she was growing miffed.

She marched up to the door and beat on it with her fist, causing it to creak open on its own. Nudging it further ajar, she peered down the dimly lit hall and called, "Hello!"

Nothing. She bit her lip, took a cautious step over the threshold, noting that the floor was covered with dust. A quick look in the parlor to her right, and she found the room empty of furnishings. Stunned, she moved on her tiptoes to the other rooms; all were empty and dusty.

How could that be? For the past week she had seen lights shining from the windows at night; there was a sconce burning in the foyer, someone was allowing her marmoset in and . . .

She shivered as a wind blew along the hallway. Standing at the foot of the winding staircase, she looked up through the dark, feeling her heart thump in her throat. This wasn't possible. Someone must live here. She'd seen the lights. She'd witnessed her monkey coming and going . . .

She climbed the stairs, halting briefly as the old wood groaned underfoot, though by the time she reached the upper floor her knees were shaking badly. She paused long enough to allow her eyes to adjust to the dark, and discovered a thin stream of light spilling from beneath a closed door at the end of the corridor. Common sense told her to leave the house that moment—this situation was wrong, all wrong—yet she moved toward the door, some perverse sense of curiosity and rebellion driving her on until she stood with her ear pressed against it in an attempt to hear what was going on inside the chamber.

There was no sound. She closed her hand around the doorknob and turned it, easing the door open as she did so, squinting to see through the slit of light that poured into her face from the room. There seemed to be nothing, no furnishings. She opened the door farther. The floor was bare, but there was a chair before the curtainless window, and beside it a table with a burning lamp. Nothing else. No one.

She walked to the window and gazed out on her house.

Her bedroom could be easily seen through the leaves of the trees. A shiver crept up her spine as she turned to look about the stark quarters. Some hint of a smell hung in the air; she couldn't place it, though it was disturbingly familiar.

Her gaze flew back to the door as the sound of footsteps crashed against her ears. Fear swallowed her as images of Rodolfo King rose before her mind's eye. The footsteps were nearing, advancing up the steps at a slow pace, hesitating when the stairs creaked with the climber's weight, continuing down the corridor toward the room. Sarah glanced toward the closed window. Nailed shut. Heart hammering, fear making her dizzy and frantic, she searched the room for some place to hide. But there was no place—and the door was being pushed open now, and she could do nothing but gape and try to force back the scream that was clawing up her throat and—

The policeman stepped into the room and regarded her in amazement. "Miss St. James? What are you doing here?"

She clutched the chair and managed to say, "My monkey."

"I beg your pardon?"

"I'm looking for my monkey."

"Here?"

"He's here . . . somewhere." She glared at the constable harder and asked, "Why are you here?"

"I was on patrol and noticed the front door was open."

"Who lives here?"

"I haven't the slightest."

"But someone does live here."

He regarded the room before replying. "I wouldn't know."

"But this light was burning and there's the chair . . ." She moved to him until they stood toe to toe and she was staring up into his eyes. "Whoever is staying here is spying on me, officer."

One eyebrow drew up.

"You can see my bedroom from this window. Have a look. Whoever it is, he is watching me." He smiled, and Sarah frowned. "You think I'm daft . . . don't you?" He didn't respond, so, leaving him where he stood, she strode down the stairs and traversed down the corridor to the kitchen, determined to find her marmoset and get out of there as soon as possible. She found Nuisance perched on a cabinet, his little jaws working to chew whatever food he was holding in his hands. She had swept him up, ignoring his agitated chattering, before she stopped, turned slowly back to the table to stare down at the mound of nuts the monkey had been eating. Not just any nuts, she realized, and picking one up, she stared at it and whispered, "Brazil nuts."

DAYS PASSED, AND RUMORS CONTINUED TO REACH SARAH OF THE man from Brazil. Her fears grew when she learned from someone that the gentleman in question was "tall and blond, with an icy demeanor." The next day another acquaintance declared, "Blond? Poppycock! He was dark and wicked as the devil. When I asked him his name, he only smiled and replied, 'It's not important.' "

While no lights had shown from the Sunderland place since Sarah had made her discovery, more and more she felt as if she were being watched. She no longer discussed the matter with Norman. He thought her insane;

and besides, he would only use her disquietude as a weapon against her, to try and frighten her into marrying him as soon as possible.

She met briefly with Sir Joseph Hooker and Sir Henry Wickham and warned them of the possibility that King was in London, but obviously word had already reached them of her unbalanced mental state; they only smiled, patted her hand, and assured her that once the seeds had been successfully propagated, the stress of her circumstances would be relieved and she would begin to feel better.

One evening she was pacing her parlor while Kan played his flute and her servants watched with trepidation from behind the forest of tropical foliage. She turned to the Indians, who were reclining on the floor polishing their blowpipes, and announced, "I have a mission for you."

They put their weapons aside and looked at her expectantly.

"I'd like you to find out who the man from Brazil is."

Kan, placing his flute across his lap, regarded her with his ever-present patience and said, "He is the *boto.*"

Had he smacked her across the face, she would not have reeled so in anger and shock. "Kan!" she cried. "How could you do this to me? You know how I've grieved for Morgan, yet—"

"The *boto,*" another repeated; then they all nodded their dark heads.

"Morgan is dead."

"The *boto* cannot die."

Covering her face with her hands, forcing down her despair, Sarah did her best not to burst into tears. "Stop. Please don't go on. How can I make you understand that there is no such thing—person—as that bloody *boto?* Morgan was a man, and he died in my arms."

Kan picked up his flute and played a tune so haunting it brought goose bumps to Sarah's flesh. Hands clenched, eyes burning with tears, she stated more emphatically, "He's dead. Do you hear me? He's—"

The music stopped, and Kan said, "Is he?"

"Yes!"

"By whose word?"

"Wickham's . . ." Turning away, she stared at the parrots, who cocked their royal blue heads at her and fluffed their feathers. "I won't believe it. I can't. Morgan would not play this cat-and-mouse game. Why should he? If Morgan were alive he would storm up to my door and take me away from this wretched place." Burying her hands in her hair, she closed her eyes tight. "I'm mad. Insane. I've lost my mind totally because I want to believe you. Dear God, the hope has been alive inside me since the moment I found the marmoset eating Brazil nuts at Sunderland's; I just didn't want to acknowledge it." Spinning around to Kan, she cried,

"Only Morgan knew the monkey favored Brazil nuts!" Dropping to her knees, she glared into Kan's dark, calm eyes. "But Wickham told me Morgan was dead."

"Perhaps," he replied, "he lied."

"Yes. Yes!" She gasped. "Of course. He didn't want me to remain with Morgan. He wanted me to go back to Norman. *Bastards!* They made me believe Morgan was dead so they could get me on board the *Amazonas* before the police arrived. There's only one way to know for certain, Kan. We have to see Wickham."

SHE ARRIVED AT SIR HENRY'S TOWN HOUSE AN HOUR LATER. HE greeted her in a dinner jacket, since he was entertaining friends. He showed her to his office, closing the door behind him as he watched her pace the room. "You seem upset," he told her.

"Really?" Sarah glanced at her image in a mirror; it reflected wild hair, glassy eyes, cheeks sunken from the past weeks of sorrow. Gazing at herself, she said, "Morgan is alive . . . isn't he?"

"I beg your pardon?"

She turned to face him. "You lied when you told me he was dead."

"My dear, you are obviously overwrought. Allow me to send for Lord Sheffield—"

"Lord Sheffield can go to hell. Lord Sheffield is not my keeper and he never will be. I've come here for the truth and I shan't leave until I hear it."

"And what might that be?"

"Morgan was left alive on that dock. Wounded horribly, near death, but alive. You lied to me when you said he was dead."

Wickham's smile was sad. "Sarah, the man was dead. Surely you cannot think me so cruel as to purposefully break your heart."

She glared at him, feeling the tears rise again, choking off her breath, making her tremble.

"I'm sorry if that grieves you," he said, then added more gently, "We realize how deeply you cared for him—"

"Loved—love him. I love him."

Wickham lowered his eyes. "This happens occasionally, my dear. When one loses someone they . . . love and don't have the opportunity to witness the actual burial, they experience difficulty in accepting the demise. Such is your case, I'm sorry to say."

The tears spilled down her cheeks. Chin quivering, she managed in a choked voice, "Can you stand there and swear, beyond any shadow of a doubt, that Morgan is dead?"

He shook his head. "Sarah, for the love of God, what good can come from holding on to such—"

"Can you?" she screamed, causing his gaze to fly back to hers. "Well? Answer me, damn you!"

"There was a wound I could put my fist through—"

"Can you!"

". . . no."

The world reeled, and falling against a chair, Sarah clutched at it in desperation. Wickham rushed to help, but she shook her head. "Don't you dare touch me." Eyes flashing, she stared at him. "You have allowed me to grieve inconsolably the last months—"

"You cannot think that he could have survived such an injury."

"There's someone in London who says he's from Brazil, and that he knows me."

"I would believe it to be King before I could accept that it was the American. Besides, if this man were Morgan Kane, why would he not have approached you before now?"

"I don't know. I simply . . . don't know."

Chapter Twenty-three

Two weeks passed, and there were no further sightings of the man in white. The first week Sarah made herself as accessible as possible, straying from her town house to walk the parks, even venturing to the Thames, where she sat on the banks and watched the water . . . for what? Some mythical *boto* to materialize from the river?

There was no doubt about it now, she was quite insane. She had accepted the fact, even relished it to some extent. At last all invitations had stopped arriving. Acquaintances pretended to look the other way when she met them on the street. She rarely saw Norman, which didn't break her heart; but it did leave her with a nervousness in her stomach she was loath to acknowledge. The days and nights grew long, with only the Indians and her monkey to keep her company. She took to sitting in the garden throughout the day, daydreaming or napping, watching the foliage on the trees begin to yellow as the first hint of an early autumn moved in.

She had dozed while enjoying a rare afternoon of sunshine when she awoke suddenly, jolted by some sound or movement close by. She raised her head, expecting to find one of the Indians or the marmoset. There was nothing.

A servant stepped from the back doorway at that moment, an envelope in hand. "This was just delivered, Miss Sarah," the woman told her.

Still groggy, Sarah tore into it and pulled out the note.

Miss St. James, it is imperative that I see you. Meet me at the Kew Gardens nursery, near the Palm House, this evening at half-past nine. Come alone.

Respectfully, J. Hooker.

Sarah wondered why the Director of the Gardens wished to see her so late in the evening, then reminded herself that the issue of the seeds was not one to be discussed publicly until the propagation had been successful and the young plants were on their way to Ceylon. Perhaps something had gone wrong. The thought made her frown. So many had sacrificed for those seeds; Norman's future depended on them, as did her own to a lesser extent. Since her return to London, the only thing that diverted her at all from Morgan was the fantasies she'd had of traveling to Ceylon and starting her own plantation. Were that dream to be snatched from her now . . .

She arrived at the gardens a half hour early. Her driver was stopped briefly at the main gate; after being shown Sir Joseph's letter, the guard waved the coach through, locking the gate behind.

The sky was growing dark as she left the coach and moved down the walk, enjoying the heady fragrance of flowers and the song of birds in the nearby trees. Then she entered the nursery, or "the pit," as Hooker and Wickham referred to it. The wet heat and heavy smell of humus took her breath away, reminding her of the rain forest. The tinted, yellowish-green glass overhead blocked out what little light remained of the day, and only the lamps burning at intervals along the sunken room illuminated the interior. Dim as it was, a moment passed before she realized that the thousands of sprouts peeping up through the moist soil were the *Heveas*.

Easing down the steps into the pit, Sarah wandered along the walkway, studying the tender plants as best she could, looking up occasionally in search of Sir Joseph, vaguely noting the passage of time as she thrilled over the successful propagation of the plants. At last she realized that nine-thirty had come and gone, and still the director had not appeared. She left the pit, mopping her face with her sleeve, shivering as the night breeze brushed her face.

She returned to her coach to discover her driver absent. Odd. She looked about the gardens, the beds of flowers all colorless in the night. Perhaps Hooker had become tied up with business, she thought, and taking a cautious look around, she moved down the walk toward the director's office, passing the Cottage Garden and Succulent House on her way, reaching the administrative building only to discover it dark and locked.

A shiver of apprehension crawled up her spine as she turned and looked out over the gardens. How serene the manicured beds and shrubs appeared in the moonlight, yet there was something sinister in the shadows spilling over the ground from the occasional tree or fountain or statue. The marble likeness of a dancing cherub, its face turned up to the sky, reflected the celestial glow with an eeriness that made her skin crawl. Then she realized: it was the silence, the stillness, as ominous as it had been deep in the Amazon.

Doing her best to breathe evenly, she moved back toward the coach, chastising herself for her ridiculous fears. Norman was right. She was extremely overwrought. Sir Joseph had obviously been detained, and . . .

Where was her driver? "Maynard?" she called. "Maynard!"

She hurried down the flagstone path toward the Palm House, a shimmering iron-and-glass structure with a high, domed ceiling. Perhaps Hooker had meant that he would meet her there, where many Amazonian plants thrived in the tropical atmosphere. There were lights burning inside. No doubt Maynard had ventured there, believing she would be occupied for some time with Hooker.

She stopped. To her left, a pond's glassy surface reflected the moon and the Chinese guardian lions erected on its opposite edge. On her right, Japanese cherry trees cast shadows across her way. This is ridiculous, she told herself. She had battled across thousands of miles into the Amazon, had faced cannibals, headhunters, man-eating animals, and she couldn't get up the courage to walk in the dark by herself.

Sarah.

It was a whisper, so lightly brushing her ear she thought she had imagined it. Then it came again—softly—chilling her, making her heart slam and her nerves tingle. She turned, eyes aching from the strain of searching the shadows, ears burning from the silence, flesh crawling with the sensation of cold fear as an image materialized from the darkness, an image dressed in a white suit, a Panama cocked low over the left eye.

She backed toward the Palm House, her mind refusing to accept what her eyes saw. Morgan. Morgan. Oh, God, it was Morgan! The man who had followed her, had asked after her, had watched her from the Sunderland place—it had been Morgan all along. Dear God, he wasn't dead!

Then he removed his hat and his gold hair spilled over his shoulders. Flashing his white smile, he said, "Hello, Sarah."

She whirled and ran, too terrified to scream, her only thought to reach the Palm House, where there were lights—

She flung open the door and stumbled into the floresta. The humidity made her gasp. The sudden ruckus from the blackbirds and sparrows that inhabited the monstrous building made her cry out. She fled through the towering palm, banana, coffee, and coco trees, tripping over offshoots of the giant bamboo and tumbling facedown into the moist earth. Lying as still as possible, she listened hard, and heard the door open and close. On her hands and knees, she crawled through the low-growing cycads, finding herself stabbed by the fiercely spiny leaves of the ferox. Curling up beneath the giant fronds of an *Angiopteris* fern, she listened for King's footsteps.

"It's very ironic, and apropos, that we should find ourselves face-to-face at last in these environs," came his voice. "There really is no way you can escape me, Sarah. There's no reason why you should try. My war is not with you. I have no intention of hurting you, but I do need you. We have one thing in common, you see. Morgan."

Sarah stifled a sob.

"I suspect that Morgan is alive."

Don't listen to him. He's mad. He'll do or say anything—

"I was fished out of the river by my men, and as I recuperated in Belém I learned that Morgan survived his injury."

He's lying!

"He was in Belém Hospital for four weeks, then he disappeared. Where else would he go but here? To you. So I came to London and found you. I've been watching you, waiting for Morgan to make his move. But then I realized: Morgan knows me too well. When the officials were unable to find my body, Morgan suspected I was still alive. He probably figured that I would be behind him wherever he went, so he decided, upon arriving in London, to keep his distance from you. Naturally, he wouldn't risk endangering you in any way, not until I was taken care of. So it seems Morgan and I have come to an impasse, Sarah. The only way to lure him out into the open is to threaten the very thing he loves most, his only reason for living. You."

Don't believe him, she told herself. *He'll say anything, do anything to get what he wants. Rodolfo King is evil and demented and—*

"Sarah, it'll do no good to run. Even if you escaped and went to the authorities, no one would believe you. They all think you're insane. All of London is whispering about it."

She slid on her stomach through the mossy compost where the South American *Equisetum gigateum* fern spread its luxuriant leaves over the ground and towered ten feet above her. Glancing up through the fronds, she watched the blackbirds fly through the draping, flame-colored orchids and bromeliads, and for an instant she was swept back to those months when the world was hot and green and—

She screamed as King came at her through the bushes, and jumping to her feet, she ran, slapping away the foliage that clawed at her face and hair while the birds' excited trills escalated to a shrieking cacophony.

Bursting through the overgrowth of ferns, she tumbled into the pool of water that was blanketed with giant Amazon water lilies. She thrashed amid the fleshy leaves and white flowers before dragging herself out on the opposite side, gasping, her eyes searching for some sign of King. She finally managed to climb to her feet and backed toward the exit. If she could get out of the enclosure she might stand a chance. She could easily lose herself on the grounds.

He moved up behind her so swiftly she had little time to react. He was pressing something over her face. The horrible stench momentarily burned her nose and mouth and brain. Then blackness swallowed her.

THE ROCKING MOTION OF A COACH AWAKENED HER. CONFUSED AT first, she rubbed her aching head and did her best to recall what had happened. The dim glow of the coach lantern hurt her eyes. She closed them; then King's voice jolted her to complete awareness.

"You're awake," he said, and threw a newspaper into her lap.

She glanced at the headlines, searched the columns until her attention caught on the lower corner and the cryptic message there that brought a rise of hope she tried to ignore.

M.K.
I have Sarah.
I'll see you at St. Paul's Cathedral.
Tonight.
Randi

Throwing the *Times* aside, she declared, "I don't believe you. Morgan is dead."

"We'll know soon enough."

The coach stopped. As King shoved open the door, allowing the misty night wind to swirl around them, he turned his cold blue eyes on her and smiled. "Be warned, Miss St. James. If you make one unnecessary sound, I'll kill you without a moment's hesitation."

"You're going to kill me regardless."

"Not so." He took hold of her arm and forced her to the street. "I don't have any reason to kill you."

"What reason did you have for murdering my father?"

"He was a threat to my empire, but now my empire is gone, and the man—my supposed friend—who brought it down is out there, walking London's streets, and I'm going to kill him." As she struggled to wrench her arm from his hand, his grip became fierce. "Lovely lady," he said through his teeth, "don't test my patience. Just because I have no intention of killing you doesn't mean I won't change my mind."

He forced her down the dark walk toward the cathedral, whose great towers were shrouded in fog. King followed, nudging her on when she faltered. The wind whipped her hair as she mounted the steps toward the monstrous, intricately carved doors. London stretched out around her, windows shining like ten thousand stars in the night, winking through the haze. A shiver ran through her as she paused and gazed down the empty streets. King stood beside her, leaning against one of the dozen fluted pilasters that lined the facade. He regarded her with a smile.

"You're very beautiful. I can understand why Morgan fell in love with you. You remind me of my mother. You look very much like her. She, of course, was a slut and a bitch. I killed her, which was no great loss, believe me. I did the world a favor by getting rid of her. She was a parasite. A disease. I have no patience with people who don't work to their potential, who feed off other's sweat and toil and expect to prosper. Morgan and I had to fight for everything we attained."

"Morgan is dead," she said. "You killed him."

He looked at her, his pale hair blowing. "Ye of little faith," came his soft voice. "Of course, I thought so too at first. My God, you can't know of the grief I experienced the moment I pulled that trigger. It was an accident, you know. I didn't mean to shoot him, but there was the struggle . . . I only meant to frighten him into coming back to me. Then, as I was recuperating from my injuries, the realization came to me, just as it did on the night I killed my mother, that he didn't love me and he never would. It's the rejection; I can't stomach it, Sarah. It's a wretched weakness, I confess, and I detest myself for it. I should be stronger; alas, I'm not . . . I suspect he'll be here soon."

"You're insane."

"No, I'm not. That's what makes me so dangerous, you see."

Occasionally a coach rolled by. A pedestrian or two appeared, then disappeared through the darkness. Teeth chattering with cold, heart hammering with fear, Sarah watched the streets in hopes that a policeman would happen by.

King took her arm and they moved into the church, closing the heavy door silently behind them. Their footsteps rang out as they hurried across the marble-floored entry, walking swiftly over the slab of black marble that marked the crypt of Christopher Wren. All around them the soaring glass portraits of Christs and angels stared down at them, their kind, serene faces glowing with ethereal light, their white hands extended, offering salvation. At last Sarah and King moved out of the nave into the transept, whose domed roof rose hundreds of feet above them. The ornate room was known as the Whispering Gallery; its acoustics allowed a person to whisper at one point along the wall and be heard with absolute clarity a hundred feet away. It was true. She could easily hear King's every breath and . . . something else . . . some living sound, or presence, that brought a rise of fear and expectation crawling up her back as she stared down the unlit corridors branching off the room.

That was when she saw Morgan.

She closed her eyes, refusing to believe it. He was dead. Dead! That he was walking toward her through the dark, dressed in his white suit, was proof that she was as crazy as King.

"Ah," King said. "He's here."

Knees shaking, she looked at Morgan again as he passed beneath a wall sconce and stopped not ten feet from her, his hands in his pockets, his hat cocked low over his eyes. His lips smiled, and he said, "Hello, *chere.*"

She sank against the wall. King caught her, laughing as he righted her. His eyes and smile appeared kind when he said, "Go to him if you want. I'll not stop you."

She stared at King, speechless, too shocked to move or contemplate the reasons for his indulgence, too numb to accept Morgan's appearance as anything but some trick of her imagination.

"Sarah," Morgan said. "Come here."

"No." She shook her head, tears burning her eyes, and cried, "I don't believe it!"

"I'm very much alive, *chere.* I rented the Sunderland place and watched you the last weeks."

She moved to him, cautious, her thoughts fragmenting while she struggled to retain her sanity. Dear God, if she reached for him and found he was an illusion—

Then he was reaching for her, pulling her against the very real and firm wall of his chest. His presence swallowed her, as always, wrapped around her, and brought her senses to a straining peak. Burying her face in his coat, she wept and clutched him as hard as she possibly could, absorbing his scent, feasting on the rhythm of his heart against her ear.

He brushed her hair from her brow, cradled her head in his hands, and turned her face up to his. He kissed her tear-streaked cheeks. "Sarah, love, I've missed you."

Her shoulders shook. "Why? Why did you let me go on thinking you were dead? Didn't you know how horribly I've grieved?"

"I suspected King would be watching you, waiting for me to approach you."

"But we could've gone to the authorities—"

"I wasn't prepared to take you away from Norman unless I was certain that you weren't happy."

"I love you, Morgan. I wanted to spend the rest of my life with you. How could you think that I would return to London and meekly marry Norman with no thought of what we'd shared?" Searching his face, noting the creases of fatigue about his eyes, the pain that had deeply etched the lines around his mouth, she wept again.

"This is all very heartwarming," King said behind her. "But we really should get on with business."

"Which is?" Morgan asked.

His hands in his pockets, King shrugged. "A life for a life. I let Sarah go if you come peaceably with me."

"No!" Sarah swung around to face him.

"Shut up," Morgan ordered, then, taking her arm, turned her around and shoved her away. "Walk out of here and don't look back."

"No."

His voice angrier, Morgan repeated his demand.

"I refuse. I stood on that damned dock and watched you sacrifice yourself once before, and I won't do it again!"

Grabbing her face in his hands, he bent his head near hers and whispered harshly, "I stand a better chance of survivin' if I ain't got you underfoot, lady. Now get the hell out of my hair; for once in your life, do what I tell you."

He pushed her again, and this time, caught between her need to scream at him and kiss him, she stumbled into the dark.

She glanced back once and saw both men standing face-to-face, as they had that night on the dock. All the horrible memories came rushing back, flashes of King and Morgan fighting, then the horrible roar of the gun exploding. For a moment she covered her ears, certain she had heard it again, and she had—dear merciful God, they were struggling for the gun; it was falling to the floor and Morgan was kicking it away, into the distant shadows.

"Run!" she cried.

Morgan shoved King with all his strength, knocking him to the floor; then he spun and ran for Sarah. They had covered no more than a few yards before he was forced to slow, then stop. Bent at the waist, his hands twisted into his clothes, he groaned and gasped for breath. "Go on," he told her. "I can't go any further. I'm still too weak."

She looked around and did her best to get her bearings. Wrapping her arm around Morgan's waist, she walked him more slowly through the cavernous room doing her best to keep to the shadows, listening for King's approach, which miraculously didn't come. Sarah eased Morgan into the first pew she came to and went down on her knees to better see his face. "You're alive," she said. "Oh, how I have fantasized about this moment. I am almost too frightened to believe it. Perhaps it's only another dream—"

"No dream." He touched her face, traced her mouth with his fingers. "Still love me?"

"Can you doubt it?"

"No." He shook his head. "I've watched you grieve for me. I wanted to reach out to you so many times, Sarah, but I was afraid that Randi would do exactly what he did."

"We could have gone to the authorities—"

"And what? He's committed no crime here." Morgan closed his eyes and drew Sarah close, wrapped her in his arms.

A door opened and closed.

Sarah pulled away and took hold of his arm. "I can't," he told her. "I hurt too much, *chere*. Besides, I won't run again. I decided to end it for good in Belém. It was damn bad luck that he got the upper hand."

"I won't allow you to remain here just waiting for him to kill you." Taking his face in her hands, she looked him in his eyes—those wonderful eyes. Even now they made her tremble. "If you think I intend to lose you again after all I've suffered, you're dead wrong, Kane."

He grinned. "You're crazy."

"So they say. Would you have me any other way?" Smiling, she helped him stand, just as King's voice called out:

"Morgan, I'll allow the girl to leave, but you and I have unfinished business. You can run the rest of your life, but I'm going to find you. My patience is growing short, Morgan. You know I grow weary of these adolescent games."

Morgan moved away so suddenly she could do little but follow, catching a glimpse of King as he struck out after them. They passed the choir stalls with their exquisitely carved woods and elegant wrought-iron grilles and gates, and continued on through the cathedral. As they burst out of the nave, a priest stood riveted in the shadows, a look of shocked disbelief on his features. Morgan made for the entrance, and the clergyman called, "I've just locked those doors!"

Morgan tore open a side door, and with Sarah behind him, took the steep curving stairs two at a time, driving himself on despite the pain. King's voice floated up through the dark. "Stupid, Morgan. Very stupid.

Where the hell will you go from there? Do you think your God will reach
down and pluck you from harm's way?"

They reached the platform where the colossal bells hung silhouetted in
the night. As King's footsteps drummed up the stairs beneath them,
Morgan grabbed Sarah, and stepped through the open portico onto the
bell-tower ledge, where he shoved her against the wall before disappearing again.

The wind whipped her hair and burned her face as she stared out over
the city hundreds of feet below. Snatches of voices came to her, first
King's, then Morgan's. She did her best to concentrate on the words, but
the wind cast them away before she could understand. Far below her, she
saw the priest run from the church and into the street. Closing her eyes,
Sarah prayed harder than she had ever prayed in her life, took a deep
breath, and swung back for the tower, jumping into the chamber just in
time to see Morgan and King fighting for the gun King clutched in his
hand.

She searched for something to use as a weapon. There was nothing.

The men struggled, grunting, feet shuffling. Morgan slammed King's
hand against the wall in an attempt to dislodge the gun.

The shriek of whistles sounded, and as Sarah looked down at the street,
she saw the police converge on the church. "Hurry!" she cried. Then
there were footsteps booming up the bell tower . . .

"You won't kill me, Morgan."

Sarah turned and wept in relief to find Morgan with the gun and King
standing in front of a stained-glass window depicting the Archangel Mi-
chael casting Lucifer from heaven.

"You couldn't kill me in cold blood," King said. "You wouldn't be able
to live with the guilt."

"Shut up," Morgan said. "I've waited nearly two years to do this."

"Then why haven't you pulled the trigger? I'll tell you why. Because
you know deep in your heart that you're no different from me. I just took
advantage of opportunity, while you let it pass you by."

Sarah moved close, her eyes on Morgan's pained, sweating features.
"The police are coming," she told him as quietly as possible.

"If you're afraid he's going to murder me," King said, "don't be. He
doesn't have the guts to pull that trigger. Do you, friend? After all, I'm
the only human being who ever thought you were worth—"

Midnight, and the bells pealed out the hour, causing Sarah to scream
and cover her ears just as the police stormed into the tower, their shouts
drowned by the earsplitting knell. Yet Morgan stood his ground, gun
pointed directly at King as the patrao said again, "You can't kill me,

Morgan." But she couldn't hear anything except the screaming bells. Then King was smiling, throwing back his beautiful blond head in laughter before he spun and leapt for the window, crashing through the multicolored glass where Lucifer writhed amid the paradise he had destroyed, cast down by a righteous sword.

The bells fell silent. The police swarmed around them, easing the gun from Morgan's hand and speaking to Sarah, although she could not hear them. Her gaze was locked on Morgan, unbelieving as an officer snapped cuffs on his wrists and turned him back toward the door. Morgan's eyes came back to hers, and he smiled.

BY MORNING THE PAPERS WERE EMBLAZONED WITH EVERY SHOCKING detail of King's death. The headlines shouted speculation as to the cause of his demise. Had Morgan shot him? Even Sarah didn't know, Morgan was silent, remaining in his cell, refusing to see Sarah throughout the night. The police who had witnessed King's fall had been strangely divided in their reconstruction of the events. A few swore they saw or heard the gun go off, and were certain that it was the impact of the bullet that had hurled King through the window. Others attested that what they saw was a man who had seemed to laugh in the face of death; who had foolishly believed he could somehow defy God. Hours into the new day, the coroner found no evidence of a bullet wound in King's body, declaring that the fall to the street had killed him. At last Morgan was released from Scotland Yard.

SARAH AND MORGAN WERE MARRIED THREE DAYS LATER, A QUIET ceremony in the registrar's office with only Kan and the Indians in attendance. The marmoset ran up the official's leg, causing him to grow apoplectic. He refused to continue the ceremony until Morgan tucked the chattering monkey into his pocket and made him stay there by bribing him with Brazil nuts.

It was late by the time they returned to the town house, dismissed the servants, and settled amid the clutter of potted palms and ferns and bamboo. The parrots squawked and whistled as Morgan uncorked a bottle of champagne and poured them each a glass. Settling on the settee beside Sarah, he touched his glass to hers. "To my beautiful wife."

She smiled and took his glass, put it on the table along with hers. "I can think of better things to do on my wedding night than drink champagne."

"Yeah?"

"Yeah." She tugged at the buttons on his shirt and breeches, sliding her fingers beneath his clothes, her fingertips brushing the bandages still binding his waist. Burying her face against his chest, Sarah inhaled his scent, touched the tip of her tongue to his flesh, and reveled in the taste.

"Sarah." He laughed. "Easy does it, *chere,* I'm not certain I'm up to this yet—"

On her knees, she straddled him. Hair spilling over her shoulders and onto his chest, eyes flashing like turquoise fire, she twisted her fingers in his thick mane. "I'll take you when I want you, Kane. Never forget that. And I want you now."

She kissed his mouth, and vaguely she felt his fingers unbutton her shirt, then slide beneath the fabric to caress her breasts gently, then urgently, his thumbs massaging the peaks that were swollen and aching with desire. Then he was lifting her up and she was arching her back, offering the nipples to his lips and tongue, which took them, wet and soft and hot, teasing the sensitive centers until she thought she might weep with pleasure.

His arms wrapped around her, and he stood, then slowly lowered her to the floor, the fern and palm fronds sweeping aside as he pressed her into the rug and removed her clothes with little effort, then his own. He came into her swiftly, but she was ready and eager. And as the sound of Kan's flute and the Indians' drums filled in the night air outside the house, Morgan buried his face in her hair and whispered, "Love me, Sarah."

She did, with abandon, closing her eyes and letting her mind drift back to the hot, steamy days and nights when they had watched each other from a distance, longing for the other as they had never longed for anyone else.

It was paradise all over again, a tumultuous fulfillment, thunder and lightning, and the sweet celebration of the love that would last them a thousand lifetimes.

"I love you," she whispered.

"I love you," he whispered.

And upon the wall their shadows moved together and danced to the seductive rhythm of the drums.

Epilogue

RAIN HAD BRIEFLY SENT THE CREW AND PASSENGERS OF THE *Bark Witch* scurrying for cover, but the clouds soon parted, revealing a clear azure sky and a rainbow that rose from the sea behind them and ended far upon the horizon in a splash of shimmering colors. Morgan stood at the taffrail, feeding the marmoset a ripe papaya as he watched Sarah turn her face into the sun, glorying in its heat, exalting in the roaring of the sea and the singing of the wind in the riggings. She leaned far over the railing until the spray covered her face in a mist; then she threw back her head in laughter, turned her flashing eyes his way, and cried, "It's wonderful, isn't it? We're free, Morgan. I can hardly believe it!"

He smiled in response but didn't join her, not yet. He was enjoying the vision of her too much to spoil the moment.

"Promise me something," she yelled.

"Anything!"

"That we never, ever go back to England. That we never live any place where the sun doesn't shine twenty-four hours a day!"

He laughed. Finally joining her at the rail, he asked, "Are you happy?"

"Deliriously happy. I'll be even happier when those are in the ground." She glanced toward the numerous crates spread out over the deck, the lids removed allowing the hot sun to warm the rich earth in which the tender green shoots of the *Hevea* were thriving.

He took her in his arms. "Of course, there's no guarantee that we'll succeed," he reminded her. "No one has ever successfully propagated rubber trees outside Brazil."

"Morgan," she said, "I have all the faith in the world in you. There's simply nothing we can't accomplish together. We'll establish the greatest rubber empire the world has ever known!"

"There's the risk that the natives won't accept us."

"We'll simply tell them that you're the *boto.* You're magic. You can do *anything!*"

He could not find the words to tell her how happy she made him, so he drew her close and kissed her long and lovingly. He felt shaken as she kissed him back and gripped him tightly, as if the sunshine of her beauty and faith could banish the nightmare years of loneliness and pain and confusion. And they had. The past was gone, obliterated by the radiance of her emotions as she turned her face up to his. In her eyes was mirrored every dream he had ever imagined, and something he had craved all his life: love and a hope that gleamed as hot and bright as the sun.

Somewhere near the bow of the *Bark Witch* the Indians had begun to sing and beat upon their drums. The lilting sound of Kan's flute shimmied through the air, as crystal clear as bird song. Smiling, Morgan lowered his head and lightly brushed his wife's eyes and cheeks and mouth with kisses, pressing harder upon her lips until they parted and he entered her in a motion that was at once gentle and passionate and consuming.

Above them all the sails snapped and billowed in the wind as the *Bark Witch* carried them toward their future, and a blazing Malayan sun.

AUTHOR'S NOTE

Rodolfo King is fictional, but his character was based on rubber barons who actually lived in South America during the latter part of the 1800s and early 1900s. And while Morgan and Sarah's attempts to smuggle the *Hevea* seeds from Brazil are fictional also, the story is based loosely on fact. By the end of the nineteenth century, Brazil was awash in decadence and far wealthier than any other country, with all its riches derived from rubber—a monopoly that crippled other civilized countries. The arrival of the twentieth century saw an escalation of slavery and an abuse of Amazonian Indians that shocked the entire world. However, thanks to those brave men who smuggled the *Hevea* out of Brazil, the situation changed radically. Accounts differ as to who those men were, but by 1910 the seeds had been successfully propagated on English rubber plantations in Malaysia and Ceylon. By 1920 the prosperous Brazilian rubber trade had fallen off completely. To this day, it is practically non-existent.